MR. DALE AND THE DIVORCÉE

THE BRAZEN BEAUTIES

SOPHIE BARNES

MR. DALE AND THE DIVORCÉE

The Brazen Beauties

Copyright © 2021 by Sophie Barnes

This is a work of fiction. Names, characters, places and incidents are either the product of the author's imagination or are used fictitiously, and any resemblance to actual persons, living or dead, business establishments, events or locales is entirely coincidental.

Cover Design by The Killion Group, Inc.

ALSO BY SOPHIE BARNES

Novels

The Brazen Beauties

Mr. Dale and The Divorcée

Diamonds in the Rough

The Dishonored Viscount

Her Scottish Scoundrel

The Formidable Earl

The Forgotten Duke

The Infamous Duchess

The Illegitimate Duke

The Duke of Her Desire

A Most Unlikely Duke

The Crawfords

Her Seafaring Scoundrel

More Than a Rogue

No Ordinary Duke

Secrets at Thorncliff Manor

Christmas at Thorncliff Manor

His Scandalous Kiss

The Earl's Complete Surrender

Lady Sarah's Sinful Desires

At The Kingsborough Ball

The Danger in Tempting an Earl

The Scandal in Kissing an Heir

The Trouble with Being a Duke

The Summersbys

The Secret Life of Lady Lucinda

There's Something About Lady Mary

Lady Alexandra's Excellent Adventure

Standalone Titles

The Girl Who Stepped Into The Past

How Miss Rutherford Got Her Groove Back

Novellas

The Townsbridges

An Unexpected Temptation

A Duke for Miss Townsbridge

Falling for Mr. Townsbridge

Lady Abigail's Perfect Match

When Love Leads To Scandal

Once Upon a Townsbridge Story

The Honorable Scoundrels

The Duke Who Came To Town

The Earl Who Loved Her

The Governess Who Captured His Heart

Standalone Titles

The Secrets of Colchester Hall

Miss Compton's Christmas Romance

Mistletoe Magic (from Five Golden Rings: A Christmas Collection)

FOREWORD

Although Divorce was extremely rare during the Regency period, it wasn't unheard of. However, there were different levels of divorce depending on how far one was willing to go and what one could afford. For the majority, obtaining a *divortium a mensa et thoro* (separation from bed and board) from the ecclesiastical court might have been enough. This process ended the husband's financial obligation toward his wife and permitted the couple to live apart, though neither was allowed to remarry.

In order for such a thing to be possible, two additional steps had to be taken. First, the husband had to win a criminal conversation suit (also known as a crim. con) in which the wife was accused of adultery and charges were brought against her lover in civil court. Since a wife was considered her husband's property, she was not permitted to testify on her own behalf and the case itself was tried as a form of trespass or property damage.

The final step in severing all ties with his wife, was for the husband to bring a Private Act (or Bill) of Divorcement before Parliament, resulting in a *divorce a vinculo matrimonii* (divorce from the chains of marriage), which allowed both parties to remarry.

"This process cost hundreds to thousands of pounds and took months to years. Once proven, a *vinculo matrimonii* could make children illegitimate, and husbands could end mothers' custody of and access to children. Husbands could keep their ex-wives' money, just doling out alimony. From 1800-1857 Parliament granted 200 such divorces, four of which women had instigated." - The Law and the Lady: Consent and Marriage in Nineteenth-Century British Literature by Heather Lea Nelson, Purdue University.

Interestingly, Jane Austen herself was acquainted with a divorcé. In 1807 she wrote to her sister, Cassandra, gently criticizing a certain Sir Edward James Foote for only wanting to choose the plainest name for the child his wife, Mary, had recently given birth to. Mary Foote (née Patton) was Edward's second wife following his divorce from Nina Herries.

CHAPTER ONE

London, 1818

I t was horribly hard for Wilhelmina Hewitt to find the words she needed to start this discussion. But after all her husband, George, had done for her, she felt it her duty now to help him as best she could. Even if the subject she wished to broach would probably shock him.

"Would you like a brandy?" he offered, the gentle sound of his voice conveying the warmth and consideration he'd always shown her.

Her resolve – the complete lack of nervousness she experienced in spite of her decision – surprised Wilhelmina. Instead of panic, an extraordinary sense of calm overcame her. She knew she was making the right choice, no matter how much it was destined to upend her life.

She considered her husband with deliberate practicality. The man she'd married twenty years earlier when she'd been eighteen and pregnant reclined in the armchair opposite hers, his gaze expectant. Their fathers had been like brothers. They'd attended the same schools, had fought side by side in the American War of Independence, and had later perished together at sea.

Wilhelmina and George had both been ten years old when news of their fathers' deaths had arrived. With their properties less than one mile apart, they'd quickly found solace in each other. As one would expect, the incident had deepened the bond they'd already shared since birth. So when Wilhelmina faced the greatest ordeal of her life eight years later, George hadn't hesitated for a second. Having recently been denied the woman he loved, he'd insisted he'd never want to wed another. So he'd chosen to protect Wilhelmina instead. George had, she acknowledged, sacrificed more for her than what was fair. It was time she returned the favor.

Deciding to be direct, she cleared her throat. "I think we ought to get a divorce."

George's eyes widened. He stared at her as if she were mad. "I beg your pardon?"

Wilhelmina took a deep breath. "How long have you and Fiona been seeing each other?"

His gaze slid away from hers as his cheeks grew ruddy. "You know the answer to that."

"By my estimation it's almost exactly two years. Two years of pretending Fiona is my dearest friend – that it is me she comes to see thrice a week, not you." The lovely widow, ten years George's junior, had caught his attention one evening at Almack's. The two had struck up a conversation, which had led to a dance. When subsequent run-ins with Fiona had increased George's interest in her, Wilhelmina had decided to step in and help the pair. By covering for them, she'd allowed them to conduct their affair in private and without scrutiny.

It was, she realized, an unconventional arrangement. But then again, her entire marriage was far from ordinary. The one and only attempt she and George had made to consummate their union turned out to be a spectacular failure. Bedding each other had been impossible due to their being like brother and sister and, Wilhelmina admitted, due to her own aversion for the act itself. So she'd happily encouraged George to pursue such relationships elsewhere in the years since.

"I'm sorry. I did not realize you were opposed to our meetings. You never—"

"George." Wilhelmina gave her husband a reassuring smile. "I believe you've misunderstood my reason for suggesting a divorce. It is not because I'm offended or upset by the relationship you and Fiona enjoy, but rather because I believe you have fallen in love with her and she with you."

He sat utterly motionless for a moment, then finally nodded. They'd always been frank with each other. "You're correct, but divorce is not the answer, Mina. It would be public and messy. Our reputations would be destroyed in the process – yours especially."

Bolstering herself against the truth of his words, she shrugged one shoulder. "I'll manage."

"No." He shook his head. "I won't have that on my conscience."

She stood and went to crouch before him. Her hand clasped his. A pair of dark brown eyes filled with concern met hers. "You gave up on love for me once – on starting a family of your own. Please, allow me to return the enormous favor you did me when you decided to save me from ruin and Cynthia from illegitimacy."

"Ah, but I did marry for love, Mina."

"I know, but not in the way you should have."

"If you think I have regrets, you're wrong. I'd make the same decision again in a heartbeat."

"Because you're the best man there is, George. And as such, you deserve every happiness in the world. You deserve to have a life with Fiona just as she deserves to have a life with you." She carefully released his hand, then stood and crossed to the sideboard where she proceeded to fill two glasses with brandy. Returning, she handed him his drink and took a sip of her own.

A frown appeared on George's brow. "You've no idea how hard it would be to break up our marriage completely. We're not just speaking of legal separation, Mina, which in and of itself is enough to see one shunned from Society. What you're suggesting would require parliamentary involvement with three readings of the divorcement bill before the Lords. Witnesses to your adulterous behavior would have to give evidence."

"I've thought about that. Obviously, the simplest thing to do would be to pay a few men for the trouble."

He gaped at her, then took a sip of his drink. "No. I appreciate the offer, but we'll do no such thing."

"George. I really—"

"It's absolutely out of the question."

"You're certain I can't persuade you?"

He gave her a steady look. "Quite."

"All right," Mina agreed after a moment's hesitation. She knew when George was beyond budging. "But this arrangement with Fiona is untenable. It's just a matter of time before someone catches on to the fact that the two of you are lovers, and when they do, she will suffer the most. So if you refuse a divorce, you should at the very least consider moving out of Town. Find a small village somewhere so you can carry on with each other discreetly."

"And leave you here by yourself? Would that not raise a few eyebrows?"

"Not if you come back from time to time and visit. Plenty of husbands travel for work."

"My work, as you well know, is here in London."

"It doesn't have to be." As the designer and manufacturer of fine furniture, George had made a name for himself amid the upper class. Having a Hewitt sofa was all the rage. So much so they'd both been admitted into upper class circles and counted Viscount and Viscountess Pennington among their dearest friends.

"You already have employees who are trained to handle new orders along with the shop on a regular basis. Whether you sit in your study here and create new designs or you do so a hundred miles away would make little difference, would it not?"

"I suppose not."

"Especially if you were to set up a home near Croft, which in my mind would make your life simpler since that's where the carpenters are."

For the first time since this conversation had begun, George allowed a hint of humor to tug at his lips. "You've put a frightening amount of thought into this. If I didn't know any better, I'd think you were eager to be rid of me."

"Not at all," she told him in earnest. "I merely desire to see you happy."

He seemed to mull this over a moment. "I'll think on it. Right now, there's still Cynthia's upcoming wedding to consider. Moving ahead with any drastic changes should probably wait until she has spoken her vows. I'd hate to give Mr. Petersen or his parents a reason to call things off."

"Agreed."

George finally smiled. "Good. That's settled then. Care for a game of cards?"

Wilhelmina located the deck and returned to her seat. She knew George was being protective. It was in his nature. But she hated feeling like she was becoming a hindrance to him, a burden keeping him from the life he deserved.

Of course, altering his perspective only required a change in circumstance. This was apparent when he came to speak with Wilhelmina six months later. In the sort of bleak tone one might use when there'd been a death in the family, he announced that he'd gotten Fiona with child.

"I'm sorry," he muttered. Slumped in the same chair he'd used for their previous conversation on the matter, he clasped his head between his hands. No man had ever looked more defeated or miserable. It broke Wilhelmina's heart. The joy George would surely have felt over the pregnancy was being overshadowed by the complication of his marriage to her.

Now, faced with a choice between the scandal of divorce or bringing an illegitimate child into the world, she knew his hand had been forced by fate. As such, the only thing she could think to do was offer comfort and reassurance as he'd so often done for her. "It's all right. I will survive this, George. We all will."

"I've spoken about it at length with Fiona. She asked me to convey her gratitude. What you are willing to do is—"

"The correct thing."

"Mina…" His voice was thick with feeling.

"Moving forward, we'll need a plan," she told him matter-of-factly before she too succumbed to emotion. "Right now, only the three of us know the true nature of this marriage or that you and I share a bond stronger than what most married couples enjoy. If we are to succeed in dissolving our marriage completely, we'll need to put up a good façade. The fewer people we confide in, the better."

"I've considered this too," George said. "I think we need to tell Cynthia and her husband, Henry, what to expect. I also think it would benefit you if one or two of our closest friends, like the Penningtons, were brought into our confidence. This way, you won't be completely alone afterward."

"Maybe," she agreed. "From what I gather, you and I shan't be permitted to see each other once the divorce has been settled."

"Not that we'd have much opportunity to." When she gave him a puzzled look he explained, "Although getting through this may take a long time, Fiona and I intend to leave England as soon as it's over since staying here and facing the aftermath could be difficult for our child."

Wilhelmina's stomach clenched at the idea of George moving overseas. He'd always been there and while she was happy to help him marry Fiona, she instantly knew his absence from England would lead to an unwelcome emptiness in her heart. For his sake, she forced herself to maintain her composure.

"Where will you go?"

"Massachusetts has a well-established logging industry, but it's my understanding that the area surrounding the Great Lakes shows promise. It's reputed to be an especially stunning part of North America. Most importantly, it's far away."

It certainly was. Wilhelmina forced a smile and tried

not to panic. This was for the best. George would be with the woman he loved and start a family. With Cynthia already settled a few months earlier, her future had been secured. As for Wilhelmina herself, she'd weather the storm as best as she could, most likely by focusing all her energy on the property she owned near Renwick. George had helped her purchase the small farm nearly five years ago. After a serious bout of influenza, he'd insisted on making sure she'd have a property in her own name in case he died. She'd not been there often, but having it did reassure her.

"You do realize your child will likely be born out of wedlock," Wilhelmina said. She hated bringing this up, but decided it was best to face the facts, no matter how unappealing. "From what I gather, the proceedings we intend to undertake could last a couple of years."

George's gaze finally sharpened. "I'm aware, but once it's done, my son or daughter shall have my name."

Wilhelmina nodded. "With this in mind, let's get to work on ruining my reputation."

James Sebastian Dale was not partial to large social gatherings. He much preferred spending his evenings at home, alone, and in the company of a good book. But with his son, Michael, home on leave from university, it was James's fatherly duty to make sure Michael improved upon his social skills. He'd need them when the time came for him to pick out a wife.

So with this roundabout way of ensuring the continuation of his family name in mind, James had arrived at the Pennington ball, offered Michael a couple of pointers, and encouraged him to ask a young lady to dance. Standing on the sidelines, he watched his son with pride. The boy cut a dashing figure in his evening attire and, James noted with satisfaction, his dance partner wasn't the only woman who looked to be admiring him.

"I'm glad you were able to join us this evening," James's host, long-time friend, and former client, Viscount Pennington, murmured as he came to stand next to James. Heralding from an affluent family, James had attended both Eton and Cambridge, and was thus well-acquainted with numerous peers. "One doesn't often have the pleasure of your company."

"As you know, I'm married to my work, though I will admit it is good to get out on occasion."

"You deserve to be revered," Pennington said. "Not only for your legal mind, but for your dedication. I dare say most men in your position would rather choose a life of leisure."

James snorted. His father was one of the wealthiest landowners in England so James had no need for employment. He could afford to do nothing, but what would be the point of that? "Such an existence would bore me. I find I relish the challenge of a good case, never mind the satisfaction of delivering an indisputable argument in court."

"To be sure, I cannot complain. Had it not been for

you I fear Mr. Hardwick would have gotten away with murder after his cotton mill burned to the ground. I'm glad he was held to account for his negligence."

"Agreed."

Pennington had risked his own reputation by making his dealings with Hardwick publically known, but as the primary investor, he'd felt responsible for the women who lost their lives due to negligence.

"Does Michael intend to become a barrister too?"

James returned his gaze to the dance floor and located Michael. "He's more timid in nature than I and would rather avoid public speaking. As such, he is studying to become a solicitor instead."

"I wish I would have followed your example with regard to my own children's education. It would do them good to work for a living, if only temporarily."

"They're still young enough for you to encourage them to do so." A glimpse of shimmering gold caught the corner of James's eye.

He shifted his gaze and tried to locate it while Pennington proceeded to argue his point. Another hint of gold flashed in response to the bright glow from hundreds of candles placed in the overhead chandelier. James stared at the dance floor. An unfamiliar sense of expectation gripped his stomach as the dancers swirled about, repositioning themselves, until...

Every cell in his body tightened. His mouth went dry and his heart beat with increased force. Because there, smiling at the man with whom she partnered, was the loveliest creature he'd ever laid eyes on. Elegant and stunningly beautiful with her blonde curls framing her heart-shaped face, eyes sparkling with merriment, and a teasing smile curving her full-bodied lips, the lady James beheld stole his breath.

Of course, she was probably some man's wife – the sort of woman he had no business ogling. But how could he not when her body alone, clad in shimmering silk, was so perfectly curved and proportioned. He swallowed, fisted his hands by his sides, and tried to add as much indifference to his tone as possible when he asked Pennington, "Who's the woman in gold? I don't believe I recognize her."

"That would be Mrs. Hewitt. Her husband is Mr. George Hewitt, the furniture manufacturer."

Disappointment raced through James's veins and settled in his gut. "I see," he muttered.

"Ah! It seems the dance is ending." Pennington gave James a nudge. "Come on, Dale. I'll introduce you."

"I really don't think," James began, his frown deepening when Pennington walked away and left him no choice but to follow. The viscount was clearly oblivious to the reason behind his interest and did not realize an introduction would be useless given the lady's attachment.

Muttering a curse, he cast a hasty glance in his son's direction, noted he was now happily engaged in conversation with a couple of young men his age, and went in pursuit. Having affairs with married women wasn't his style, so what was the point in meeting the woman?

"Mrs. Hewitt," Pennington said, drawing her attention as he approached. "Allow me to introduce you to Mr. Dale, the finest barrister of my acquaintance. Mr. Dale, I present to you Mrs. George Hewitt."

Hands clasped behind his back, James executed a short bow while holding the lady's gaze. In spite of schooling his features, he doubted he managed to hide his admiration. This close, she was even lovelier than she'd been at a distance. There were finer details he'd missed before, like the length of her sooty lashes, the charming laugh-lines at the edge of her eyes, which were, he saw now, not simply blue but a merging of sky and ocean.

His heart kicked into a faster rhythm as muscles flexed and strained in an effort to hold himself steady. She wasn't for him, but damn if he wouldn't allow himself a moment to simply reflect on her beauty.

"A pleasure," he murmured.

"Likewise." Her voice was soft and slightly melodic. The edge of her mouth curved to form a partial smile, and James was lost – lost in the momentary triumph of being the subject of her appreciation.

He reminded himself for the umpteenth time that this was a married woman. They would never share more than a brief conversation. But while they did, he would drink in every second, absorb every nuance, and tuck them all away in a private corner of his mind.

"Mrs. Hewitt hails from Cornwall," Pennington said. "She and her husband both grew up there within one mile of each other."

"How lovely," James said, and immediately wanted to kick himself for the bland remark. The problem was he had no desire to speak of her husband or think on the fact that theirs was a love match nurtured since childhood. He'd once imagined himself caught up in such a union. His wife had certainly been most convincing in her feigned affection for him, until they'd spoken their vows.

He tamped down that memory. Clara had been duplicitous and more than ready to jump into other men's beds in an effort to, as she'd put it, cure her unhappiness.

"He and I moved to London three years ago," Mrs. Hewitt explained while James tried to figure out who *he* was. Ah yes, her husband. "We wanted our daughter, Cynthia, to have a proper coming out, you see, and since neither Mr. Hewitt nor I have any other relations here in Town with whom Cynthia could visit, we relocated."

"Your daughter is most fortunate to have such considerate parents," James said. He added a smile and instantly felt his heart soar in response to the blush creeping into Mrs. Hewitt's cheeks.

Careful now, you old dog. Don't let yourself get carried away.

"She married Mr. and Mrs. Clive Petersen's son, Henry, a little over six months ago. We're both extremely happy on her behalf."

"A fine match indeed," Pennington said. "Mr.

Petersen's success within the shipping industry does demand a great deal of respect."

James nodded. "My felicitations to you and your family, Mrs. Hewitt."

She met his gaze, the warmth he found there holding him captive. "Thank you, Mr. Dale."

Pennington cleared his throat. "I'd hoped to introduce Mr. Dale to your husband, Mrs. Hewitt, but I fear it will have to wait. Apparently, the set I'm meant to dance with my wife is about to begin." He gave her a studious look. "Would you excuse me?"

His tone struck James as slightly odd. It was almost as though he worried he'd made a mistake when he'd chosen to introduce her to James.

If she noticed, she showed no sign of it. "Of course."

Pennington awarded her with a soft smile. "It's always a pleasure to see you, Mrs. Hewitt." Straightening, he offered James a more thoughtful look, which again struck James as odd. "I trust we'll have a chance to talk more later. If not, I hope it won't be one more year before our paths cross again."

"I'll try to make more of an effort to stay in touch," James promised.

The viscount gave him a solid slap on the back and went to collect his wife, leaving James alone with the delectable Mrs. Hewitt. Or as alone as a man could be with a woman while still surrounded by dozens of people. He glanced toward the dance floor where a quadrille was starting up. How long had it been since he'd last enjoyed such activity? He honestly couldn't recall.

For a fleeting second he contemplated inviting Mrs. Hewitt to partner with him for the next set, then dismissed the notion since it would probably be inappropriate in light of the heated effect she was having on him. And yet, he desperately wanted her touch, if only in the most innocent manner allowed. So he offered his arm. "Would you care to take a turn of the room with me?"

Pleasure filled every aspect of her expression. "I'd be delighted to, Mr. Dale. Especially if we can head toward the refreshment table since dancing has left me quite parched."

"But of course. I find I could do with a cool drink myself."

Her lips quirked as if she struggled to keep vast amounts of humor at bay. Those dazzling blue eyes of hers sparkled. And then she placed her hand on his forearm and it was as if James's world burst open and pleasure poured in. He was wearing a jacket for God's sake, cut from superfine wool. Beneath that, he had on a fine linen shirt. Yet Mrs. Hewitt's touch singed him all the way to the bone, in spite of her gloves.

He sucked in a breath and tried to dismiss the potent effect she had on him. This was madness. He'd never responded to any woman with such electrifying force before, not even Clara. *It's purely physical*, he reminded himself. After all, he barely knew the woman. But devil take it, he wanted to. Desperately.

He cleared his throat and steered her along the edge of the ballroom at a slow pace, determined to savor each second he'd be permitted to spend in her company.

Equally determined not to get carried away on a dangerous dream, he said, "Perhaps we can locate your husband. Pennington says he's a furniture manufacturer?"

"Yes. He's rather sought after, so if you're in the market for a new dining room set, you may have to wait a while." Amusement and something akin to pride lit up her eyes.

"You must have married at a young age, Mrs. Hewitt, to have a daughter who's already found a husband," James told her before he could gauge the wisdom of his words. Ordinarily, he was a man who paid close attention to what he said. His profession demanded he do so. And complimenting a married woman on her looks was probably not good form. In fact, he doubted her husband would approve. Yet James could not seem to stop himself from wanting to make Mrs. Hewitt aware of how attractive he found her. So he'd made an attempt to do so in the most subtle way he knew.

Now that the words were out, however, he realized it sounded as though he was trying to judge her age. Which was something he ought not have any interest in learning.

Idiot.

But rather than cut him a critical gaze, the lady smiled. "You flatter me, Mr. Dale."

Did he? It warmed his heart that she thought so.

"Indeed," she added, "I was but eighteen years old when my daughter was born."

Which meant she was in her mid to late thirties. "I never would have guessed. I'm sure every bachelor here will be disappointed to learn that you're not one of the debutantes."

What the hell was he doing?

A delightful flush colored her cheeks. "If I may be equally bold, I'm certain the young ladies looking to marry will fix their eyes upon you, Mr. Dale. Unless you're already wed?"

Good God. She was openly flirting with him *and* fishing for information about his matrimonial status. The awareness of her interest and possible shared attraction caused fiery sparks to prick at his skin. A warning bell sounded inside his brain. The path he was on was hazardous to be sure, and it was high time he stepped off it. Before he did something stupid like lure her into a private corner somewhere and kiss her senseless.

The very idea...

He shook his head and forced his mind back to her question. Was he married? "Not any longer. My wife died quite unexpectedly eight years ago."

"Oh." Mrs. Hewitt's eyes dimmed. "I'm so sorry."

James was too, though only for Michael's sake. In spite of Clara's unfaithfulness she'd been a doting mother, and Michael had suffered tremendously from the loss.

"It was especially hard on my son." He knew she had a daughter so it only seemed fair to give her similar information about himself.

"And is this son of yours also in attendance this evening?"

"He is."

"Then you must also have married at a young age, Mr. Dale, for I swear you do not look a day over five and thirty."

Her teasing manner – the infectious gaiety with which she spoke – ignited his blood like nothing else. For the first time in more than twenty years, he experienced pure desire. It wasn't something he thought he'd ever know again after the wretched pain and humiliation Clara had caused him. He'd thought himself closed off from physical want and need forever. Until this very moment, when he found himself trying to think up ways in which he might see Mrs. Hewitt again.

Which wouldn't do at all.

This had to stop.

And it would.

As soon as they reached the refreshment table.

Only three more yards to go. Give or take.

He dreaded each and every one. "I was one and twenty when I married. A year later, Michael was born."

They were finally at their destination. Was it just his imagination, or did Mrs. Hewitt give his arm a gentle squeeze before she removed her hand?

Before he had a chance to properly savor the gesture, his closest friends, Grayson Grier and Colin West, made their presence known. James introduced them both to Mrs. Hewitt, then turned to fill a glass of lemonade for her while Grayson's and Colin's curious gazes burned into the nape of his neck. There would be questions to answer later. For now, he ignored his friends as best he could and handed Mrs. Hewitt her glass. Her fingers brushed his, ever so briefly, but it was enough for every cell in his body to feel as though it exploded with pleasure.

Lord help him.

Unable to tear his gaze from her, he watched as she set the edge of her glass to her mouth and drank. A sheen of moisture remained on her lips afterward, and a wicked desire to lick it away with his tongue over-whelmed him. He gritted his teeth and tore his gaze away, only to find his friends watching him with unabashed amusement.

Damn.

"Are the three of you longtime friends?" Mrs. Hewitt inquired when no one else spoke.

"We met at Eton and went on to study at Cambridge together, but it was the army that forged a truly unbreakable bond among us," Grayson said.

"War does have a curious way of bringing men closer together," Colin added in a somber tone.

"I know what you mean," Mrs. Hewitt said in a way that suggested she'd suffered great loss once. James hoped she'd expand on the matter so he could learn more about her. Instead she asked. "Which battle did you engage in?"

"The Battle of Aboukir," James said. "Under the command of General Abercromby."

Their commander had been killed in action, but it was the death of their friend, Richard Hughes, that had made a truly lasting impact on them all. In merely the blink of an eye, their quartet had been reduced to a trio. James shuddered in response to the memory, which remained as clear as ever in spite of all the years that had passed.

"Aboukir is close to Alexandria, is it not?" Mrs. Hewitt asked. She took another sip of her drink. James did his best to refrain from looking at her this time.

"It is," Grayson confirmed.

"And if memory serves, General Menou was in charge of the French army," Mrs. Hewitt added.

"Your knowledge on this matter is remarkable," Colin said.

James was equally impressed since few of the women he'd known made any attempt at keeping abreast of current affairs, never mind ones taking place in other parts of the world.

"What can I say?" The lady shrugged. "I like reading the daily papers."

"And I like knowing I have the most well-informed wife there is," a man slightly shorter than James but of similar build declared as he sidled up next to Mrs. Hewitt. Handsome, with dark blonde hair and piercing green eyes, he awoke an ugly sensation in James – a gnarly feeling he did not like in the least. Jealousy, quick and forceful, drove its way through him.

"Gentlemen," Mrs. Hewitt said, "my husband, Mr. George Hewitt."

This good-looking specimen of masculinity, encased in what appeared to be a trim body, was the man Mrs. Hewitt would go home with. And just like that, James was assailed with the most alarming desire to bury his fist in Mr. Hewitt's face.

Bloody hell. He needed to get himself away from the pair of them immediately.

CHAPTER TWO

Wilhelmina did not have to look at Mr. Dale to know he kept his gaze upon her during the rest of the introductions. She could feel the heat of it all the way to her toes. Blood still raced through her veins on account of the innocent contact they'd shared while they strolled. Never before had she been so drawn to a man. And if his flirtatious manner was anything to go by, he'd been drawn to her too.

Not that she would ever have acted upon the attraction. For although she'd encouraged George to enjoy a variety of lovers throughout the years and he'd supported her doing the same, Wilhelmina had never wanted to start an affair. Mostly because she'd feared the repercussion if she were ever found out. As a married woman, taking lovers was not as socially acceptable as it was for the husband, so she'd worried over the harm it might cause to Cynthia.

But there was another deterrent – the one she'd never confided in anyone, not even in George – and that was her absolute repugnance for copulation itself. Her one and only experience had been far from pleasant. It was not something she ever wished to repeat.

Still, she could not deny the physical response Mr. Dale had managed to coax from her body - a body she'd thought incapable of experiencing desire. She met his gaze, so intense it weakened her knees and forced her to clasp hold of George's arm. What a shame it was that Mr. Dale's interest in her would soon be forgotten. But with the divorce plan already in motion, it wouldn't be long before Mr. Dale wanted nothing to do with her. Which was likely for the best.

"Tell me, Mr. Dale," George said in a manner that instantly put Wilhelmina on edge. A shiver stole through her. "What were you and my wife discussing before I arrived?"

Mr. Dale straightened. "My friends and I were relating our wartime experiences to her."

"I wasn't referring to that," George murmured, "but rather to the turn you took together about the room. Your attention was fixed upon her with great interest."

"It would have been impolite of me not to pay close attention to what she was saying."

George chuckled. He drew Wilhelmina closer to his side. "Do you think me a fool, Mr. Dale?"

"Of course not." Deep lines appeared on Mr. Dale's brow. His jaw hardened.

"George," Wilhelmina hissed as she realized his

intention. Before coming here tonight, they had agreed that having her flirt with a couple of rakish scoundrels would lend credibility to George's accusations and witness reports later, but they'd never talked about using respectable gentlemen for their scheme. Indeed, they'd gone to great lengths to hire fake paramours like Mr. Randolph, with whom she'd danced. To help seal her fate the Pennington's, the only friends of George and Wilhelmina's acquaintance in whom they'd chosen to place their trust, had set the stage for her downfall.

Good grief, what had she been thinking to allow herself to keep Mr. Dale's company? She'd known what was underfoot and yet she'd agreed to take a turn of the room with him anyway. Because she'd been charmed and because, for once in her life, she'd wanted to feel the passion she knew could exist between a man and a woman. So she'd stolen a moment for herself and as a result, George must have drawn the wrong conclusion. He probably thought she'd encouraged a scoundrel for the sake of the ploy, when nothing could be further from the truth. Heaven's, she had to stop George before he said something truly disastrous like—

"Then don't pretend you have no interest in my wife when it was plain for all to see."

Wilhelmina gasped.

"Mr. Hewitt," Mr. Grier clipped, "Mr. Dale is a gentleman through and through and you, sir, are dangerously close to insulting his good name."

Wilhelmina sensed a brief hesitation in George. She tugged on his arm, desperate to draw him away. Her heart knocked hard against her breast. This wasn't the plan. Mr. Dale did not deserve to be accused of wrongful behavior. Yet rather than offer the apology she had hoped for, George leaned toward Mr. Dale and smoothly asked, "Do you covet her, by any chance?"

"Good God," Mr. West sputtered while hot embarrassment swept through Wilhelmina.

Mr. Dale glared at George. "No."

George grinned and took a step back. "Just as well. Considering everything else I have learned this evening, I doubt she would find the time to fit you in between the rest of her lovers. Isn't that right, my dear?"

He gripped her upper arm and yanked her closer. Wilhelmina yelped and then George was dragging her off. Mortified, she tripped after her husband who was marching her straight toward the exit. Before they reached it, however, Mr. Randolph gave chase.

As previously instructed, the fellow challenged George in a performance worthy of the Theatre Royal. "She may be your wife, Mr. Hewitt, but you have no right to treat her so roughly."

George spun toward Mr. Randolph, released Wilhelmina while pulling his arm back, and promptly delivered a blow so hard it sent Mr. Randolph sprawling. Gasps and shocked utterances resounded in the ballroom. The music ceased playing.

"On the contrary, sir," George sneered, "I have every right."

"Mina," Mr. Randolph chocked with high drama

while two other gentlemen helped him rise. "Come with me, my love. I'll keep you safe, you know I will."

"As will I," said another one of the men Wilhelmina and George had hired. Mr. Clarence was his name.

Not too far behind them stood Mr. Dale, his dark gaze resting upon Wilhelmina with utter contempt. Her heart shriveled in response to his hard censure, but the truth was, they'd only just met. She owed him nothing. The same could not be said of the man who'd been the husband she'd needed as well as the father her daughter required. So she turned her gaze away from Mr. Dale and surrendered herself to the part she would play for George's sake – so he could have the happily ever after he deserved – and prayed her path would never cross Mr. Dale's again.

Still, she could not stop from addressing George's actions later that evening when they'd left the Pennington residence and were headed for home. She'd had no chance to say good bye to Cynthia before departing, and hoped she and her husband would be all right. Society could be cruel and with every gossiper's tongue now wagging, life would not be easy for anyone connected to Wilhelmina or George.

"You should have left Mr. Dale alone," she said while the hackney they'd hired bounced along the cobbled street. "He didn't deserve to be so rudely insulted."

George frowned. "You knew the plan, Mina. If you didn't want to risk me going after him, then why on earth did you flirt with him as you did?"

She slumped against the squabs. Instead of the

victory she'd expected to feel at the end of the evening, the only sensations she experienced were defeat, loss, and guilt. "Because I got caught up in the moment. I... I genuinely liked him."

"Bloody hell."

She heard the misery in her own laugh while doing her best to hold back the tears. "That sums it up rather nicely."

"Mina, I'm so sorry."

"Well, it's not as though I would have been able to pursue a relationship with him anyway," she muttered. "And he would have discovered the so-called truth about me eventually, I suppose. I just..."

George put his arm around her and pulled her against his side, offering comfort as always. "Don't fret. Once we've put this debacle behind us you can start over wherever you wish. I'll make certain of it."

George intended to sell his furniture business and split the funds between them as soon as their divorce was final. Wilhelmina wasn't the least bit comfortable with this decision. After all, George and Fiona would need the funds to start over in America. Wilhelmina would have to fight George on this issue, she reckoned – the man was often too kind for his own good.

"Of course," she said, attempting to keep an optimistic façade for George's sake.

"Hopefully when all of this is behind us, you'll meet a man with whom you'll know both love and passion," George continued. He dropped a kiss on the top of her head. "You deserve that, Mina, more than anyone else I've ever known."

She appreciated the sentiment but doubted his wish would ever come true. Because once they got their divorce, she would be ruined beyond repair, and no man would want to shackle himself to that.

CHAPTER THREE

I t was Friday, March 21, 1820, nineteen years to the day since Richard Hughes had been felled in battle. Joined by Colin and Grayson as had become tradition, James sat in a quiet corner of White's and drank to the memory of his friend.

"He would have been four and forty years old by now, had he lived," Colin muttered morosely. The scar he'd received during the war puckered his right cheek.

James took another long sip of his drink and savored the bite. The memory of the carnage he'd witnessed still haunted him to this day. Limbs had been blasted to smithereens by friendly fire and enemy cannons alike. It had been worse than hell, both bloody and gory, but at least Richard hadn't been one of the wretched souls forced to writhe in the desert sand while he suffered. His death had been swift. One shot, and he'd been gone, like a flame snuffed out in an instant.

"Do you suppose he would have married?" Grayson asked.

James scoffed. "Only a fool would tie himself to a woman for any duration of time. You're lucky you managed to avoid the parson's mousetrap, Grayson. And at least you realized your mistake quick enough to get an annulment, Colin. I wish I'd been as wise."

"You wouldn't have Michael then," Grayson pointed out.

"But you could have divorced your wife once you realized what she was up to," Colin said, "as Mr. Hewitt is doing."

James clutched his glass and clenched his jaw. It had been two years since he'd let himself get swept away by impossible notions of shared desire with a woman he'd known he could not have. He would never have done more than flirt with her once he found out she was married, but that hadn't stopped him from enjoying their brief interaction.

To learn she was just as deceitful as Clara – that she would have welcomed a proposition from him – had twisted his opinion of her completely. Worst of all, it had filled him with an uncanny amount of rage, jealousy, and self-loathing, knowing she'd taken numerous lovers and that he would not be among them.

He'd always prided himself on being an excellent judge of character, but he'd been wrong about Clara, and he'd been wrong about Mrs. Hewitt too. His miscal-culation where she was concerned was so unbelievably drastic it drew him to the courtroom in an effort to comprehend his error. For two years he'd followed those damned divorce proceedings, searching for some shred of the wonderful person he'd thought her to be.

In her place, he'd found a silent hauteur he did not recognize, denying him all attempts at justifying his initial opinion. And so, as the case progressed and he learned more about her misdeeds, his hatred for her increased alongside his own self-loathing.

To think he'd been so blindly snared by false charm yet again made him feel like the veriest fool.

"Divorce is a nasty business," James told his friends grimly. "No one who values their privacy or their repu-tation would ever embark on such a thing. Unless the person they wished to be rid of was utterly abhorrent."

"The papers did outline all of the lady's affairs," Grayson said. "I suppose Mr. Hewitt felt his wife made a laughingstock of him and decided to seek revenge."

James couldn't blame the man. He knew damn well what it felt like to learn the one person you thought you could trust was a traitor, a liar, and a cheat, with no regard for the vows spoken in church.

Poor bastard.

He'd seen the hard glare in Mr. Hewitt's eyes during the trial and watched his wife's unrepentant expression while her lovers described their affairs in sordid detail.

Christ, how he loathed her.

It wasn't just the adultery either, but also the deep disappointment he'd experienced as her true character came to light. Heaven help him, he'd *liked* her! If she'd not been taken, he would have encouraged additional meetings between them. And would have gotten himself unhappily trapped with yet another vile woman.

James winced and took a deep swallow from his glass. "The world could benefit greatly from men like Mr. Hewitt who are brave enough to face the repercussions in order to teach their wife a lesson."

"It would certainly make a woman think twice about straying if the road to divorce were an easier one," Colin said. "After all, they stand to lose a great deal more than we men."

This was true. As humiliating as the proceedings might be for both parties, a man could win back his place in Society over time. The same could not be said of the woman, who would lose her right to her children, have the funds previously at her disposal reduced to a paltry sum just large enough for her to scrape by on, and be shunned forever.

"Let's speak of something else," James suggested. He was weary of contemplating Mrs. Hewitt and her husband, of the picture all the statements made against her had painted. "How is your ward, Juliana, faring, Grayson?"

"The last report I received informed me that her French is improving," Grayson said without making eye contact.

"And?" Colin pressed when Grayson said nothing more.

Grayson frowned, took a deep breath, and slowly allowed his gaze to meet James's. "She sacked her governess."

Shocked laughter exploded from James and Colin simultaneously, forcing them both to choke on their drinks. Coughing fits followed while Grayson proceeded to glare at them. When James eventually managed to catch his breath, he said, "Please don't tell me you gave her permission to do so?"

"Of course not," Grayson said, his voice filled with undeniable annoyance. "There's a good chance she did it to get my attention and force me back to Sutton Hall. I'll have to give her a lecture and hire another governess. Damned nuisance."

Sobering, James asked, "When did you see her last?"

Grayson knit his brow and stared into his glass, appearing to mull that over. "It was before Christmas, so…four months ago, perhaps a bit more."

Colin gave a low whistle, which earned him a glower.

"Forgive me if I'm overstepping," James said, "but that does seem unusually negligent of you."

Grayson sighed. "Juliana is meant to have her coming out next year. Her governess had a plan which involved an endless amount of lessons in etiquette, conversational skills, dancing, and so on. I believed I'd get in the way, so I chose to stay in Town a bit longer than usual."

James studied his friend for a moment before deciding to be completely frank. "You are all she has left, Grayson, and she is a child, stuck in a great big manor with only servants for company. I believe she'll be happy to see you."

"I've no idea what to say to a sixteen-year-old girl," Grayson grumbled. "It was easier when she was younger and I could bring her a doll or buy her a pony. Now she's at that awkward stage between child and woman. It's perplexing."

Which was no doubt the real reason Grayson had stayed away, because he wasn't sure how to deal with Juliana any longer. The balance in their relationship would have shifted as she grew older, and she would most likely be less inclined to heed him. Michael had gone through a similar phase, arguing with James at every available turn and refusing to follow James's advice for the sole purpose of being contrary. James was glad those days were over and did not envy Grayson having to endure it now, least of all with a girl.

"I'm sure her interests aren't much different from those held by women." Colin saluted his friend with his glass. "The latest fashion and London gossip ought to make excellent topics."

"As you are the only one among us who has zero experience with children, I'm not sure you should be the first to offer advice," James said. He shifted his gaze to Grayson. "Do not share any gossip with her. Most of it will be unsuitable for her young ears, and the rest will just make her stupid. Instead, I would suggest you try and get to know the young woman she's growing into. Find out what her new interests are and cater to those."

"I'll think on it," Grayson muttered.

"You're not entirely correct," Colin said.

"About what?" James asked.

Colin raised an arrogant brow. "I do have some experience with children. Isabella Bankroft has two."

James groaned. Isabella Bankroft was Colin's latest mistress. "I'm not sure that signifies, unless you've actually met them."

"I can't say I have, but she speaks of them a great deal."

"That doesn't count," James and Grayson told him at the same time. Both men chuckled while Colin merely shrugged.

"Will you break things off with her when you return to Woodstone Park?" Grayson asked. Colin, being the enterprising landowner he was, had promised his steward he would be back next week to help oversee the planting of this year's crops.

"Why?" Colin asked with a sly smirk. "You interested?"

"God no," Grayson said. "I've enough to worry about right now."

"Have you heard the latest news?" someone across the room asked in a loud voice, distracting James from the conversation.

He instinctively turned to see who had spoken. A young man, whom James immediately recognized as the Earl of Everton, addressed a group of men who sat around a nearby table playing cards. Among them, James spied the Duke of Cloverfield, one of Viscount Rockburn's youngest sons whose name James could not recall, and two others with whom he was not acquainted.

Since it was rude to stare, James returned his attention to his own friends. It was getting late in the day and he still had work left to do at home. The case he currently worked on was due for review with his client in the morning. He prepared to take his leave, but Everton's next words stopped him.

"She's free, my dear fellows. The divorce is final."

There could be no doubt as to whom he referred.

"Is that so?" Cloverfield drawled with alarming amounts of interest dripping from each word he uttered. He sounded much like a fox licking his chops while approaching a wounded rabbit. "Considering all she's been through, I'm sure Mrs. Hewitt would welcome the comfort I'm willing to give her."

James shuddered and noted the concern on both his friends' faces. They did not like the tone with which these young men spoke either. Even if the woman to whom they referred was something of a harlot.

"She goes by Mrs. Lawson now," Everton said.

"How come?" someone who wasn't Cloverfield asked.

"Lawson must be her maiden name," Everton said in a pensive manner. "As a divorced woman, she may have chosen to revert to it."

"It will certainly avoid the embarrassment of having

two Mrs. Hewitts later on, should Mr. Hewitt choose to re-marry," Cloverfield said with a chuckle.

"I'm sure the poor man wants to distance himself from his cuckolding wife as much as possible," Everton added.

"I propose a bet," one of the other men said with gusto. "Twenty pounds to the first man who secures her as his mistress."

James gripped his armrest with one hand and squeezed his glass between the fingers of his other. A pause followed, and then someone else remarked, "Is she not a bit old for such sport?"

Even Colin, who chased skirts with the best of them, edged forward in his seat, his posture tense.

"There are many benefits to bedding a more mature woman." James did not need to look in order to know it was Cloverfield who spoke, his voice dripping with predatory delight. "For one thing, she will have a wealth of experience, and for another, she will be less likely to get herself with child, which means—"

"One would be free to enjoy her without the need of French letters," Everton said.

"Exactly so," Cloverfield said while heat began to gather at the base of James's skull. "With Mrs. Lawson's situation taken into account, I daresay she can even be convinced to engage in more salacious acts than most, as long as she thinks you can help her regain her social standing. Considering her beauty and that gorgeously curved figure of hers, bedding her would certainly not be a hardship for me. I propose one hundred pounds to the man who becomes her next lover."

Disgusted by the casual disregard for common decency this group of young men conveyed, it took every ounce of restraint James possessed not to leap to Mrs. Lawson's defense and deliver a scolding. Jaw tight, he looked at his friends whose expressions were grim. Both gave their heads a swift shake to warn him off. He had to refrain. The woman whose name was now being bandied so loosely about had fallen from grace. It wasn't his place to protect her and if he tried, he would most surely regret it.

Indeed, the only way to associate with Mrs. Lawson from now on and not have one's own reputation tarnished by association was by turning her into the very creature Cloverfield had just described – a woman so desperate she would do anything for a small handout.

Unwilling to hear more of such plans, James downed the remainder of his drink and stood. "Forgive me, but I must be off. Perhaps we can meet for dinner before you leave Town?"

They agreed on a day, time, and location before James strode away. He cast one final look of repulsion at Cloverfield and his companions before he escaped to the cool evening air outside. It was a good twenty minute walk to his townhouse on Portman Square. Most members of the upper class would take a carriage, especially at this hour when it was starting to get dark. James, however, preferred the exercise. Lord knew he got little enough as it was with most of his days spent at his desk poring over legal documents and compiling defense strategies for court battles.

As much as he loved his work, he missed being more physically active. Of course he had a morning routine he repeated each day in an effort to stay somewhat fit. It included various stretches, rapid squats, and the lifting of bags filled with grain. But it would be nice if he had more time to ride even though a trot through Hyde Park could not be compared with a gallop across the craggy hills and valleys of his ancestral land.

James rounded a corner. The glow from a newly lit gas lamp cast a halo upon the pavement. Further on, James spotted the lamplighter himself. The young lad raised his long stick, pushing back darkness with wondrous illumination.

There was something to be savored in the progress one experienced in Town, yet there was no denying the craving he had developed in recent weeks for clean country air and vast expanses of green. With spring already banging at the door, the Clarington House gardens would soon be filled with bright displays of daffodils, hyacinths, and tulips, for those were his mother's favorite flowers and she'd personally seen to it that thousands of bulbs were planted.

Perhaps he'd go for a visit once his current case was over. He'd invite Michael to come along with him, though he would probably be loath to leave Town with the Season just now beginning. But it would do them both good to spend some quality time together and for

Michael to reconnect with his grandparents. It had been too long since they'd all been beneath the same roof. Plus, it would be damn good to get away from any gossip pertaining to the newly minted Mrs. Lawson. Escaping her would be difficult here in London where news travelled faster than the wind. And he really, *really*, did not wish to think of her any longer.

He entered Portman Square and proceeded toward the black door leading into number five. Collecting his key from his pocket, he undid the lock and stepped inside, happy to be home in familiar surroundings. This was his sanctuary – a place of his own design – furnished exactly to his liking.

In keeping with James's preference for minimalism, it housed only five people: James; Michael; Atkins, the butler; Mrs. Dunkley, the cook; and Miss. Tabitha Harris, the maid. A housekeeper seemed as unnecessary as a valet, secretary, and company of footmen, so James chose to manage without.

"Is my son at home?" James asked Atkins when the older man came to greet his master.

"In the parlor, sir." Atkins took James's hat and gloves, set them aside on the hallway table – a Hewitt edition, James noted with unhappiness – and helped James out of his greatcoat.

James thanked his butler and entered the parlor. It was his least favorite room in the house - the only one still decorated according to Clara's taste with all the fripperies she'd brought with her into the marriage or purchased later cluttering every surface. Escaping the memory of her was impossible in here, but he'd left the room intact for Michael's sake.

His son, whose hair was the same dark shade of brown as his own, reclined at a slightly crooked angle in one of the pale blue silk upholstered armchairs. His long legs were stretched out before him, crossed at the ankles. At three and twenty, he was just starting to fill out in the shoulders, but it would probably take another couple of years before he completely lost the gangly look he'd had in adolescence. Between his hands was today's copy of *The Mayfair Chronicle*.

He looked up at the sound of his father's arrival, set the paper aside, and rushed to his feet. "Good evening."

James considered his son, who appeared more stiff than usual. Echoing his salutation, James crossed to the sideboard. "Drink?"

"Yes." Michael cleared his throat. "Thank you."

"Everything all right?" James asked with a frown while deliberately keeping his voice as casual as possible.

"Quite." The word had barely been spoken before he said, "I trust you had a nice evening with West and Grier?"

"I did. They send their regards." James handed Michael a glass of brandy. Ordinarily, his son preferred port, but since it took time to develop a taste for the stronger drink, James made sure he tried it from time to time. Considering how tense he looked tonight, James also believed he might actually need it. "How was dinner?"

"Good." Michael returned to his seat. "Cook made roast beef with oven-roasted potatoes and green beans, which as you know is my favorite. I believe she tried to make up for my having to dine alone."

"Sorry about that." James took a sip of his drink and lowered himself to the edge of the sofa adjacent to where Michael sat. "Why didn't you meet up with friends if you wanted some company?"

Michael set his glass to his lips and drank. James's mouth twitched with humor when Michael quietly winced. He was making an effort to like the brandy, but it would be a while yet before he acquired a taste for it.

"I didn't. Want the company, that is. Not tonight at any rate." Michael twisted his glass between his hands, not meeting James's gaze. "I needed to think. About how to broach an important issue with you."

James sat back. He was slightly stunned by this admission. "You and I have always been open and honest with one another. I've always done my best to listen and offer unbiased advice. And you're a sensible man, Michael. I doubt there is anything you could say to appall me, so don't worry, just spit it out."

Michael tapped his fingers against his glass. He slanted a look in James's direction and opened his mouth as if intending to speak. Instead, he just stared at his father, who grew increasingly anxious by the second. Michael closed his mouth, swallowed, then took a deep breath, and finally managed to get out the necessary words. "I think I'm in love. That is, I don't think I am, I know I am. But I fear you will not approve of the lady."

Ah. A delicate subject indeed.

James leaned back and settled into his seat. For a moment there, he'd feared the boy had taken up gambling and lost a wager, or gotten himself challenged to a duel. God forbid. Instead, all the innocent man had done was loose his heart to a woman. Well, it had to happen sooner or later.

"Like I said, you're a sensible man, Michael. Whoever she is, she must be respectable."

"She's a widow," Michael informed him, neatly skirting the issue of her reputation.

James decided to leave that point alone for the moment. He took another sip of his drink. "I take no issue with her being a widow, though there might be a few raised eyebrows if you started associating with her prior to her husband's death."

"If you're asking me whether I had an affair with a married woman, the answer is no, I did not."

The indignation in Michael's eyes could not be denied. James was sorry for it, but he breathed a sigh of relief all the same. "Forgive me, but I had to ask since it would explain your concern with how I'd respond."

Michael huffed a breath. "We met for the first time two years ago. She'd just gotten married, however, so I knew I ought to forget her."

"But you couldn't?" Lord help him, James knew exactly what that was like, to be haunted by a woman one could not have. To this day, dreams of holding Mrs.

Lawson in his arms still plagued him, causing him to wake in a sweaty, lust-filled state of anger that ruined his day whenever it happened. If only he could scrub his brain clean of her.

"I was enamored with her right away, though only in the most superficial of ways since one cannot love a person deeply without getting to know them properly."

"And you feel you have done so now? Gotten to know her?"

"I've met her for numerous walks in the park, on the less travelled paths where we wouldn't be prone to curious gazes." Michael suddenly smiled. "She and I can talk for hours about the most mundane of things without either of us getting bored."

"These walks of yours," James said while allowing his lips to curve with humor, "did they perchance take place during all of those errands you've run in recent weeks?" Each trip Michael had taken to the post office and the bank had taken hours. He'd also started seeing his friends a great deal more than usual, though James now wondered if he'd been gazing into this widow's eyes instead of playing whist.

"Forgive me. I did not want to make a big thing of it until I knew for certain where I stood."

"And where exactly is that, Michael?" James cautiously asked. The nervousness he'd experienced earlier bloomed to life once more.

"I've asked her to marry me and she has accepted. I'd like to have your blessing."

Slowly, James set his glass on the low table in front

of the sofa and propped his elbows on his thighs. He clasped his hands together and took a moment to adjust his mind to the shocking news his son had just delivered. There had been no word of warning, no indication Michael had formed an attachment. He'd done so in secret, behind James's back.

James raised his gaze to Michael's and forced himself to remain as calm and composed as he could while feeling as though the rug had been swept out from under his feet. "She must be a very special woman indeed to have captured your heart."

"Oh yes. She is the most wonderful person in all the world."

"And does this wonderful person have a name, or do you intend to leave me guessing?"

The air seemed to stretch tight between them. Michael's gaze flickered. He suddenly got up and crossed to the fireplace. An unbearable length of silence passed while he stood there, staring into the dancing flames. A log snapped in the grate.

"Mrs. Cynthia Petersen." Michael spoke to the fire, his back toward James.

"Hmm…" The name was oddly familiar, though it felt like an age since he'd heard it last. He searched his brain, rummaging through every meeting he'd had in recent years, every social gathering he had attended, each trial, and…

A memory stirred. He knit his brow in concentration. Every muscle and tendon strained. And then the lady to whom the name belonged became clear. He gritted his teeth and muttered a curse.

"She is Mr. Hewitt's daughter, is she not?" he asked, just to be certain, deliberately avoiding all mention of *her*.

"Yes."

One simple word. It dug its unrepentant claws into him and cackled with glee.

James took a deep breath and regarded his son. Although they'd occasionally had their differences, their disagreements had been brief. They'd never fallen out for long. But James feared that was about to change, because this time, Michael's heart was involved. He was in love, and there was no way in hell James could allow him to marry the woman he pined for. The lady's mother had wrecked any chance of that with her wanton behavior.

Pained by the knowledge that he was about to cause his son heartache, James stood and went to stand beside Michael. His hand settled heavily on Michael's shoulder. The lad turned and met James's gaze with anxious hope in his youthful eyes.

Hating himself for what he was forced to do and despising Mrs. Lawson for turning him into a villain, James crushed his son's dream with two words. "I'm sorry."

CHAPTER FOUR

What a hellish day. Swiping away her tears, Wilhelmina dropped into one of the dusty rose armchairs that stood in her parlor. She'd said her goodbyes to George and Fiona two nights ago under the cover of darkness. They'd sailed for New York yesterday. Today she'd gone to the bank to collect the funds she would need for the coming week, only to discover her account had been frozen.

"What do you mean?" she'd asked the clerk.

"Apparently the courts are conducting some sort of investigation." The clerk had retrieved a very official-looking letter which he'd handed to her. "It has to do with your…circumstances."

Clearly. The court wanted to make sure the funds she had were hers to keep and that she did not owe money to her former husband. She and George thought they'd avoided such an outcome by ensuring her independence before the trial began nearly two years ago. Apparently, they had been wrong and she would now have to find other means by which to get by.

The realization hammered away at her already frail composure. George, her dearest friend and constant companion, was gone. She had no clue how to pay her expenses, and three of her acquaintances had crossed the street to avoid her as she walked home.

She'd barely managed to hold it together while she removed her bonnet and pelisse. Both items were hastily tossed onto the hallway table before Wilhelmina fled to the parlor so Betsy Faircloth, her maid of all work, would not see the state she was in. Heavens, she still wore her gloves.

Wilhelmina tugged at the butter-soft kidskin leather while heaving great gulps of air into her lungs. She'd not cried like this since her mother died. Her throat ached from it and her chest felt as though it were weighed down by lead.

Reaching into her skirt pocket, she retrieved a handkerchief and did her best to blot the tears. A good cry for the purpose of working through her emotions was one thing. Wallowing was quite another when there were chores to be done, money to be found, and bills to be paid. She could not afford to feel sorry for herself for more than five minutes. Least of all when Cynthia needed her to be strong for both their sakes.

A weary sigh crept through her. Her poor daughter, widowed at only one and twenty years of age. With a shake of her head, Wilhelmina stood and went to ring for some tea. Henry Petersen had been a reckless fool. He'd also been incredibly unlucky to have his curricle's wheel snap off in the midst of a race. A fault in the wood had been to blame. Cynthia's husband had broken his neck on impact a year and a half after the wedding.

"Here we are, ma'am," Betsy said when she brought a tray some twenty minutes later.

"Thank you, Betsy."

The tray was placed on a nearby table. Betsy picked up the teapot and started to pour. A knock at the front door caused her to pause. She glanced at Wilhelmina, then set the teapot aside. "I'll just see who that is, shall I?"

Moments later, Cynthia burst into the parlor. Her cheeks were flushed and her eyes had an anxious look about them. She panted for breath as if she'd run all the way from her home in Berkley Square. "He said no. Oh God, Mama, can you believe it? The man is a monster."

Wilhelmina blinked. She had no clue as to what her daughter might be referring. Clearly, she had been rendered insensible due to distress, which was no state at all to be in when trying to offer an explanation.

"I thought we agreed you would not come here," Wilhelmina said as she rose to greet her. "It will not do your reputation an ounce of good."

"Neither will staying away," Cynthia complained. She placed a loving kiss on her mother's cheek and plopped down on the sofa where she buried her face in her hands. "I am done for, Mama."

"I am sorry," Wilhelmina said with a sigh. She gestured for Betsy to bring one more cup. "It will pass, but it will do so quicker if you sever your ties with me completely for the next few weeks. The trial is still very fresh in everyone's minds."

Betsy returned with a cup and saucer and promptly departed once more so mother and daughter could speak in private. Wilhelmina prepared both cups and handed one to Cynthia whose misery was written all over her pretty face. "I wouldn't have cared if the whole world loathed me as long as Michael and I were together, but now I shan't even have him."

Cynthia took a deep breath and expelled it. Apparently this had something to do with a man, and while Wilhelmina desired nothing more than for her daughter to fall in love again and remarry, finding a man who accepted who her mother was might not be easy. "My pet, I don't know who this Michael is, but he must be rather dear to you if you're using his Christian name. That said, if he has cut ties with you because of your connection to me, then—"

"It is not him, Mama. It is his father." Cynthia's eyes swam with heartfelt emotion as she gazed back at Wilhelmina. "Michael proposed and I accepted, but Mr. Dale has denied us his blessing. Worse, he has forbidden Michael from seeing me."

Wilhelmina's hands jerked. The teacup she held clinked sharply against her saucer. It was a good thing she was sitting down or she might have crumpled beneath the weight of those words and the name of the man who now barred her daughter from happiness. He'd been at her trial – a dark imposing figure of righteousness glaring at her from the back of the courtroom. His hatred for her had been palpable, as had his reason for being in attendance. He'd wanted to witness her total destruction.

Her heart pounded hard against her breast as she recognized what she would have to do for her daughter. Setting her cup and saucer aside with a clatter, she clasped her hands in her lap to stop them from trembling. When she'd met Mr. Dale at the Pennington ball, he'd struck her as a serious and sensible person. He was a barrister after all, the sort of man for whom logical reasoning ought to have merit, so if she could just make her case on Cynthia's behalf, surely he'd listen.

"I had no idea you'd formed an attachment," she began. "If Michael has proposed and you have accepted, I presume you've known him a while."

"He and I were actually introduced to each other at the Pennington ball two years ago. We danced, shortly before you and George staged the instigating moment of your separation. I'd recently married Henry though and was deeply in love with him, so nothing came of my meeting Michael besides a bit of fun conversation. Then, after Henry died and I felt as though I was stuck in a hole I couldn't crawl out of, I crossed paths with Michael again. It was on the street – a fleeting encounter. He was on his way to the Old Bailey to meet his father while I had an appointment with Henry's solicitor, Mr. Rendell. The will had been read the previous week and I wished to seek his advice on a few legalities."

"George could have helped you with that, I'm sure."

"He was rather busy at the time with legal issues of his own."

Wilhelmina closed her eyes briefly. Three trials were necessary in order to acquire the sort of divorce they'd wanted – the kind where entering into another marriage afterward would be possible. The first, *divortium a mensa et thoro,* resulted in separation from bed and board, the next involved a criminal conviction placed against her, and finally, a Private Act of Divorcement had to be brought before Parliament to fully dissolve the marriage. She and George had been in the middle of their *divortium a mensa et thoro* when Henry died. Consequently, Cynthia was forced to suffer her grief and all the potential problems the death of a spouse incurred mostly alone.

Reminding the public of her connection to Cynthia and George could have harmed not only herself but Henry's family as well.

"I'm sorry," Wilhelmina whispered as fresh tears welled in her eyes. "I'm so terribly sorry for what George and I put you through."

"Don't be." Cynthia gave Wilhelmina a watery smile. "It wasn't supposed to turn out this way and it's not your fault that it did. I was meant to have Henry to lean on. His death was so unexpected."

"And you were forced to endure his loss while George and I made a spectacle of our marriage."

"George deserves to be with the woman he loves and to make sure the children he and Fiona have are legitimate. It was right of you to help him as you did."

"I never would have done it at the expense of your happiness." Wilhelmina shook her head. With Henry dead and Mr. Dale refusing to let his son wed her daughter because of her, the repercussion of the divorce was turning out to be truly formidable.

"Then it is a good thing you were unable to predict the future."

"How can you say that when you are now being denied the man you love?"

Cynthia placed her hand over Wilhelmina's. "Because it doesn't change how much I admire you for giving up your own social standing for George – for being willing to face persecution from your peers in the name of a cause you believe in. Mama, you are without a doubt the bravest woman I have ever known."

Undone by her daughter's words, Wilhelmina swiped away the dampness from her eyes. "I do not feel very brave at the moment. Indeed, I was in the process of putting myself back together again when you arrived."

"Why? What happened?" Concern puckered Cynthia's brow.

Unwilling to add to her worries, Wilhelmina shook her head. "I just need a little time to adjust, that is all. It is difficult, accepting George's absence. Even if he and I have kept our distance from one another since the first trial began, I knew he wasn't far. It is strange knowing he's presently moving farther and farther away with each moment. But I refuse to sit here feeling sorry for myself. It's not in my nature."

Cynthia gave her hands a squeeze before removing her own. She straightened her spine and angled her head. "No. It's not."

"So." Wilhelmina squared her shoulders and picked up her teacup. Cynthia needed her, and this gave her something concrete to focus her energy on besides her own problems and frayed emotions. She sipped her tea and regarded her daughter. "I shall call on Mr. Dale and see if I can change his mind."

Exhausted after a difficult trial in which his client's claim to the land he'd recently purchased was being contested, James plodded up the steps to his front door and entered his home. God, it would be good to relax in the quiet of his study while savoring the silence he was allowed to enjoy within these walls. All the shouting and protesting he'd encountered in court had brought on a headache, so he looked forward to reclining in his favorite chair while a cool compress soothed the pain.

"Good afternoon, sir," Atkins said. The butler held out his hand and took James's hat and gloves.

"Good afternoon," James replied. "Is my son at home?"

"Indeed he is not."

James's heart sank. He'd hoped to speak with

Michael, to try and repair the rift between them. Ever since James had denied him his blessing to wed Mrs. Petersen, however, Michael had avoided him. He sighed as he pulled off his greatcoat.

"However," Atkins said, "there is a lady waiting to see you in the parlor."

James frowned. This was most unusual and irregular, not to mention highly unwelcome news. "You know my office hours, Atkins. Why didn't you ask her to come back tomorrow morning between eight and ten?"

"I did, but she insisted. When she mentioned the need to discuss a personal matter with you and said it pertained to your son, I thought it might be best for you to decide whether or not to turn her away." Atkins met James's regard with a stiff mien. "Her name is Mrs. Lawson."

Tension gripped every sinew in James's body. A shiver of anticipation clutched at his nerves. "Christ."

"My sentiment exactly."

James raised an eyebrow at his butler who didn't so much as bat an eyelash. "Admitting her was a mistake, Atkins, though I daresay I can appreciate your reasoning. Please tell her to leave now. I want that woman out of my house right away."

"Very good, sir."

"Once she's gone," James added, "please have a cool compress delivered to my study, would you?"

The butler inclined his head and James strolled off. He sought out the sanctuary he had been craving for most of the day and dropped into the deep leather armchair behind his desk. Leaning back into a slouch, he stretched out his legs, crossing them at the ankles. Heaven have mercy. The woman who'd reignited desire for him with little more than her presence was currently in his parlor being dismissed by his butler. He could hear Atkins's voice through the wall, followed by a softer, more muted tone.

He clenched his jaw as anger started to brew at the base of his skull. How dare she come and disturb his peace? How dare she risk his and Michael's reputations with her presence? It was bad enough that the parlor was filled with the memory of Clara. Now it would also be stained by *her*.

"Damn you."

He thrust his hand over his eyes and watched the colorful sparks that danced behind his lids. The parlor door opened and closed. Footsteps sounded. James went utterly still in the ensuing silence. He held his breath and waited. Was she gone?

A knock on the study door ricocheted through James's brain. "Enter!"

"I've brought the compress, sir." Atkins's dry voice scraped the air.

James parted his fingers and peered at his butler. "And Mrs. Lawson?"

Atkins paused for a second before he confessed, "Refuses to budge."

"Refuses to budge?"

"Indeed." Stepping forward, Atkins handed the compress to James on a silver salver. James took it and laid it across his brow. Ah. Much better. "I fear the only way to make her leave is to carry her from the house. If you agree, I'll call a few Runners to help."

"No." James straightened with a jolt and immediately winced in response to the knives being thrust through his skull. He squeezed his eyes shut for a second, then took a deep breath and told his butler, "We don't want anyone else to know she is here. So just let her be. I'll have supper in a couple of hours. If we're lucky, Mrs. Lawson will let herself out at some point once she tires of waiting."

Much to James's irritation, she did not. He sat at his dining room table alone, gnashing his teeth. With Michael's noticeable absence and Mrs. Lawson still in the parlor, he could not even be allowed to enjoy his meal. And it was all *her* fault. If she'd upheld her marriage vows to her husband, James could have given Michael his blessing. His son would be overjoyed at present and there would have been no disharmony between them. Instead, Michael now suffered and James had become the villain. It wasn't to be borne!

He regarded Atkins who'd come to inform him of his visitor's continued presence in the parlor. Tossing his napkin aside, he made his decision. "I'll see her."

The slightest shift in the aging butler's eyebrows conveyed his relief. Atkins apparently was glad his master had chosen to get involved. His authority would be harder for Mrs. Lawson to argue.

James stood. He was beyond ready to get the persistent woman out of his home. It was damned rude and inconsiderate of her to dig in her heels and refuse to leave. Didn't she realize she put poor Atkins in an awkward position?

Scowling, he made his way to the parlor. Of course she didn't. Mrs. Lawson was a selfish shrew with no consideration for others.

He thrust the parlor door open, abusing the hinges. The door slammed against the wall with such violent force it seemed the room shook.

A startled gasp drew his attention to his unwelcome guest. She sat, bolt upright, in the simplest chair the room offered. *His* chair.

"Madam," James growled while doing his best not to lose himself in the ocean-blue depths of her gaze or ponder the perfect full lower lip of her mouth. "My butler asked you to leave three hours ago. In case you need reminding, that is the exit." He pointed in the direction of the front door.

"Thank you, Mr. Dale, but I wished to speak with you." The melodious softness with which she spoke was like an elixir to his senses.

James balled his hands into fists and stared her down. "Any person with an ounce of common sense would have taken a butler's dismissal as a clear indication that I do not wish to speak with him. But since you clearly lack all semblance of courtesy and respect, allow me to be equally rude and to say that you, Madam, aren't welcome here. Now get out."

Those gorgeous eyes of hers narrowed. Brackets appeared at the corners of her mouth. She rose, not like some dainty debutante, but like an experienced, head-strong woman refusing to cower. Straightening herself, she raised her chin. "Not until you've heard me out."

James might not like her. He might not even believe her worthy of his notice, but he was man enough to admit she deserved his respect, if only for her boldness.

He crossed his arms. "Say your piece then, if you must, and leave."

She swallowed, betraying some small amount of apprehension. The edge of James's mouth twitched. So, she was not as composed as she let on. Perhaps she was even nervous?

He permitted himself to study her more closely. Unlike the first time he'd met her, beneath the glow of chandeliers, she no longer sparkled. Gone was the merriment from her eyes, which were now cradled by deep blotches of grey. No humor existed about her mouth, which remained a slash of severity on her face.

Only two years had passed since he'd been this close to her, and while she was still a striking woman, James was shocked by how wrecked she looked. It hadn't occurred to him when he'd seen her in court. She'd been at one end of the room, he at the other. All he'd noted was the resolve in her expression. It had been hard and unyielding. But that too was gone now, replaced by a sort of exhausted determination, like that of an injured animal refusing to go down without a fight.

"My daughter wishes to marry your son," Mrs. Lawson said with the stiffness one might ascribe to an over-starched governess. "Your son has proposed and she has accepted. The only hindrance to their future happiness is you."

James disagreed, but refrained from saying so. "You hope to change my mind?"

"Cynthia has endured a great deal of late, so I'd like to try and give her what she wants."

"Perhaps you should have thought of that before—" He stopped himself and muttered a curse. It would not do for him to be reduced to the sort of man who insulted women, no matter who they were or what they'd done. He was better than that, damn it. But God help him if Mrs. Lawson did not drive him to the brink of insanity with her mixture of enticing beauty and disgraceful conduct. She was like a poisoned slice of delectable cake he longed to devour, even though he knew a single bite would kill him.

He took a deep breath and tightened the reins on his anger. "Forgive me, Mrs. Lawson, but Michael fancies himself in love and as such, he will be inclined to act rashly. It is my duty as his father to protect him from doing something he'll later regret."

"Like marrying the daughter of a woman who openly cuckolded her husband?" Her voice increased in strength with every word she spoke. Eyes blazing, she continued to tear herself down with unforgiving force. "A harlot whose lovers outnumber the stars in the sky? A creature so vile she ought to be spat upon in the street?"

The harsh self-deprecation sliced him to the bone.

He did not like the manner in which she described herself. But it was the truth, wasn't it? Still, that last part burned the tips of his ears. "Surely that has not happened?"

"I am prepared to suffer the repercussions of my actions," she said, "but my daughter is innocent of any wrongdoing. She does not deserve to be punished for my misdeeds."

James stared at her. She'd not answered his question directly, but she'd said enough to indicate that she had indeed become the target of disturbing attacks. Disgust aimed at those who would treat a woman – any woman – thus, curdled his stomach. And yet, he was not in any position to aid her. "I'm sorry for your daughter, but her connection to you cannot be dismissed, and I fear my son's career will be hampered if he's related to you through marriage."

She held his gaze for a long drawn out moment before releasing him from the spell those blue eyes placed on him. Pain etched lines upon her brow, revealing her anguish as she spun to face the thick velvet curtains obscuring the windows. "I wonder what it must be like for men like you, so far above reproach they cannot sympathize with those who stumble."

"You dare to mock me in my own home?"

Her shoulders slumped and her head fell slightly forward, offering him a view of pale skin that stretched between the edge of her spencer and her bonnet. James's fingertips burned with the yearning to reach out and touch it. His chest ached with the strength it required for him to remain where he was.

"No, I am merely reminding myself of how foolish I was to come here and plead my daughter's case to a man whose profession demands him to uphold the law with unfailing precision." She turned toward him once more. Resignation had swept all animation from her face, leaving being a dull facade devoid of life. "Everything is black and white to you – good or bad with no shades of grey in between. You have seen my husband accuse me in public. You watched me be condemned in three consecutive trials. So your opinion of me is now set in stone. You've dismissed the personal bias a lesser man might have allowed on the basis of his encounter with me. Or is it that encounter which makes you hate me more?"

"I cannot deny the disappointment I experienced when your true nature came to light."

A sad smile crept over her lips. "Perhaps I should have begun this meeting by offering my apologies. Please allow me to do so now, Mr. Dale. I ought to have known my husband would jump to conclusions when he saw the two of us having a close *tête-à-tête*. I'm sorry for the insult you suffered because of it, and while I doubt this will help, I thought you should know that I genuinely enjoyed our conversation that evening."

"As did I, Mrs. Lawson."

She stared at him a moment longer and as she did, her eyes filled with a sharp emotion he couldn't quite place. It was gone again in an instant, secured behind

the battlements she'd put in place with strategic efficiency. "Thank you for your time, Mr. Dale. I'm sorry
to have ruined your evening."

He almost laughed. It wasn't just one evening she'd
trampled upon. It was every second of every waking
hour since the moment he'd met her. And several nights
in between. He clenched his jaw and managed a nod.
She curtseyed, and then she was gone, leaving him
alone in a room he despised.

CHAPTER FIVE

A rare day of sunshine and warmth allowed Cynthia to take a stroll in the Pennington garden with Michael. Her mother had arranged the meeting and though she could not be present herself, she'd convinced the viscount to invite Michael for a drink and the viscountess to invite Cynthia for tea. The older couple presently sat on a nearby bench, serving as chaperones.

"We could elope to Gretna Greene," Michael suggested while Cynthia stopped to admire a lovely collection of pink peonies.

Their sweet perfume was among her favorites. "I would prefer to avoid such drastic measures if at all possible."

"As would I," Michael agreed, "but Papa is being impossible."

Cynthia bit her lip. She wanted to tell Michael

everything, including the secret she herself harbored, but to do so she'd have to betray her mother and risk Michael's rejection. The prospect terrified her, but at least Mr. Dale's lack of support gave her additional time to gather her courage.

She loved Michael to distraction and wished to marry him more than anything in the world, despite the obstacles in their path and the guilt she felt over not being totally honest. "Your father is a barrister and you a solicitor. Perhaps if you try presenting your case with logical arguments for support, he would be more obliging?"

Michael clasped her hand and gave it a squeeze. "As much as I hate confrontation, I do believe you may be correct."

As they continued their stroll in silence, Cynthia tried to think of a way in which to broach the issue that tugged at her conscience. Her stomach turned itself inside out at the prospect of facing her greatest fear.

She could begin with, "I've something important to tell you…"

Or maybe, "Michael, you ought to know…"

But starting was the easy part. It was what came after that seemed so impossible for her to say.

Before she was ready, they'd circled the entire garden, returning to the Penningtons. She'd lost her chance, it seemed, and would have to find another. Hopefully sooner rather than later.

∾

Exhaustion was becoming a state of normalcy for Wilhelmina. Each day she went to the bank, only to receive the same answer. Her account was still inaccessible to her. She'd spent money she could not afford to squander on a solicitor who'd petitioned the court on her behalf. The effort had been in vain and now she was worse off than before with fewer savings at the ready and bills piling up around her ears.

Although it was now mid-May, today had been damp and chilly. She shivered and drew her shawl tighter around her shoulders. Rolling her neck, she stretched the aching muscles there, then dipped her quill in the ink-well once more and continued to write. Numbness had gradually conquered her heart and soul, which made the task of selling her London home so much simpler. After all, this was where she, George, and Cynthia had lived. Happiness had existed between these walls. She could still see George standing by the sideboard just over there, pouring himself a drink before he came to sit in his chair – the very same one she now filled. A sigh quivered against her breast. Sentimentality was a useless emotion. She'd already sold the pianoforte and the dining room furniture.

The nib of her quill scratched the paper on which she wrote. *A sizeable house on a quiet street offers a rural feel with all the amenities of the City.* She bit her lip and considered the phrasing. A knock on the door offered a welcome distraction.

Betsy entered. "I beg your pardon for the disturbance, but there's a gentleman here to see you. Says his name is Mr. Dale."

Wilhelmina stared at Betsy while her comment sank in. It had been two months since she'd quit his house, intent on helping Cynthia and Michael one way or another. Accordingly, she had defied his wishes and he was most likely here to pummel her for it with verbal abuse. Still, she had no intention of giving him the satisfaction without some recompense. Not after he'd kept her waiting for him for three hours.

"Tell him I'm busy. If he desires to wait, he is welcome to do so."

"Very good." Betsy paused on her way out the door. "Should I offer him refreshment?"

Wilhelmina had never been the vindictive sort, but the ease with which Mr. Dale had judged her and the fact that he was prepared to punish Cynthia for simply being her daughter did not make her charitable. "No."

The door closed and Wilhelmina returned to her work. She finished writing her advertisement, then checked her ledgers. The money she'd made on the furniture she'd been able to sell would soon be gone. London was not a cheap place to live, but at least she had the farm. She'd go there as soon as she'd settled the last of her business here – the moment the house had been sold and the last of her bills paid off.

She glanced at the clock. It was almost exactly three hours since Mr. Dale had arrived. Time to go and see if he was still here. Pushing back her chair, she stood and stretched her back, then blew hot air into the palms of her hands in a futile attempt to chase off the chill in her bones. Hugging herself, she exited the study and approached the parlor. She paused for a moment to gather her wits, took a deep breath, and entered.

A critical gaze met hers. "Mrs. Lawson. I trust this is how you enact your revenge?"

"If you refer to making you wait for as long as you made me do, then I will admit I may have chosen to give you a taste of your own medicine. That being said, I was not enjoying a pleasant read or having a feast while you sat here. In truth, I was extremely busy."

"So I gather," he clipped, those dark eyes of his piercing every layer of fabric and skin. "In fact, it has come to my attention that you have been setting up clandestine meetings between my son and your daughter – aiding them in their continued romance even though you know I'm against it."

"You are correct." She would not deny her interference or insult him by lying. As much as his condemnation irked, he had good reason to feel as he did. After all, he did not know the truth, and while she had considered confiding it in him for Cynthia's sake, she'd swiftly abandoned such a course.

Mr. Dale was a barrister. He fought to uphold the law with integrity. Revealing she and George had not only perjured themselves but paid other people to do so as well would not improve Mr. Dale's opinion of her. In fact, she feared it might land her in prison while undoing everything she and George had worked so hard to accomplish. And then where would they be if the courts decided to render the divorce invalid on the basis of fraud? Would George be found guilty of bigamy? He might have gone to America, but that didn't make him immune from criminal charges.

So rather than say anything more, she waited for Mr. Dale to respond.

He glanced at the fireplace. "Do you not care for warmth, Mrs. Lawson?"

The change in conversation made her brain trip. She swiftly recovered and shrugged. "It will be summer soon enough, Mr. Dale. I see no reason to light a fire until we are well into October."

"Hmm…" He shoved his hands in his pockets and swung his gaze back to hers.

She took a sharp breath. The intensity of his regard weakened her knees. He truly was a handsome man, even when he looked like he might like to strangle her. A pity they'd lost the chance to be more to each other. Her heart fluttered on that lamentable notion. Even now as he stood there looking at her as though she were a perpetual thorn in his side – an unpleasant problem he could not escape – she felt a magnetic pull.

Pointless, to be sure, since no one had ever loathed her more than he did.

As if to prove this, he told her in a crisp tone, "Stop meddling, Mrs. Lawson. Keep your daughter away from my son or so help me God, I'll destroy her reputation quicker than you can hop into another man's bed."

Wilhelmina gasped. The threat was a blow she had not been expecting, the insult a smarting reminder of what he believed her capable. She gritted her teeth and glared at him, hating him even though he had every right to speak as he did. He was a father and he was doing what he believed was in his son's best interest, but did he really have to resort to such brutal cruelty?

"Fine." She had worse problems to deal with right now, like how to put food in her belly and pay Betsy's salary until she managed to sell off more things. Sadly, Cynthia would have to accept the consequences of the divorce and sever ties with Michael. "I'll speak with my daughter. You may rest assured she will be apprised of the risk she'd be taking if she were to thwart you."

"Thank you."

She scoffed. "It's not as though I have any choice."

"Nevertheless."

When he did not move to leave, she raised her chin and set her hands to her waist. "If that is all, I would like for you to depart so I can return to my work."

She bit off a, "*Sir*," for good measure.

Something dangerous flashed in his eyes. He hardened his features and stiffened his posture while she fought the urge to admire the chiseled edge of his jaw, the perfect line of his aquiline nose, his firm lower lip, and those deep, dark, coffee-colored eyes that threatened to be her undoing. He might be well over forty, but he was still a striking man. There was power in the breadth of those shoulders and strength in his overall stance. Unwittingly, she wondered what it might be like to be held in Mr. Dale's arms. Not that she'd ever know.

Removing his hands from his pockets, he bowed.

"I'm sorry to have disturbed you. Good day, Mrs. Lawson."

He strode past her without further comment and left the house and her heart as dismal as they'd been before his arrival.

Damn that woman.

Nearly three weeks had passed since he'd last seen her, and yet she remained at the front of his mind.

With yet another curse, James forced his attention to the legal brief he was meant to deliver the following day – something to do with a widower who sought legal guardianship over his new wife's children. Apparently the father of said children protested, even though he'd sired them out of wedlock. It was the sort of messy case that ought to hold his interest, and yet his thoughts kept drifting back to Mrs. Lawson and her dreary home.

He was fairly certain she skirted the truth regarding her reason for not lighting a fire. Out of pride perhaps? Certainly, having the purse stretched too thin was not the sort of thing one wished to confide in a stranger. Not that they were strangers, per se, but they definitely weren't friends.

The sound of the front door opening and closing caught his attention. Michael was home. James glanced at the clock. It was nearly five in the afternoon. In another hour or two his son would depart for the evening, avoiding his company as had become his habit. For the most part, James had allowed him the space he required to work through his feelings. He'd kept his distance. But perhaps it was time to try and mend the breach. They'd always been close, after all.

James stood, crossed to the door, and opened it. He arrived in the hallway just as his son started up the stairs. "Michael. A word, if you will?"

There was a noticeable pause. Only Atkins moved about, hanging up Michael's greatcoat and organizing his hat and gloves. The steady ticks from the longcase clock seemed louder than usual.

A heavy sigh sounded and then Michael stepped off the bottom step and approached his father. "Ten minutes. Then I need to get ready."

James nodded his agreement, ushered Michael into his study, and followed him into the room. The door closed. "Care for a drink?"

"No thank you."

James crossed to the sideboard and poured himself a brandy. "Please have a seat."

Michael glanced at one of the two chairs facing James's from across his wide desk. He hesitated, making his reluctance to settle in for a longer discussion known. Another sigh, and he sat. James took a sip of his drink, returned to his own seat, and faced the resentment in Michael's eyes.

"I don't like what's happened between us," James began. "We used to be close."

"And then you betrayed me."

The unexpected charge caused James to flinch. "How?"

"I came to you in good faith, certain you would at the very least try and help me find a way in which to marry the woman I love. Instead you imposed your will, denied me my happiness, and have since threatened to ruin her reputation. Frankly, it is a miracle I am speaking to you at all right now."

This was, James had to admit, a fair point. Had his father acted similarly, he'd have been furious too. Although...

"You cannot deny that a union between you and Mrs. Petersen would be problematic." When Michael merely glared at him, James added, "Her mother is the most scandalous woman in England. It would be absurd to suppose that becoming related to her through marriage wouldn't have dire effects on you or your career."

"Naturally, I have considered this, but I had hoped you, as my father and the most competent legal head in existence, would try and help me find a solution. Instead, you seem more concerned with your own grudge against Mrs. Lawson and how my marrying her daughter may affect you."

James's mouth dropped open. He'd never heard his son speak to him thus, with such conviction and force of emotion. Perhaps he should have become a barrister after all, for indeed, it was rare to see a man convey his point with more precision. Lord help him, he'd never been prouder, even if he were the one receiving a dressing down.

He gathered himself and tried not to smile. This was a serious matter. "It is true that I am no fan of Mrs. Lawson or her behavior. She treated her husband abominably and in so doing, she revealed herself to be a person of low moral standing – the sort of woman who is not to be trusted. Naturally, I am concerned by how your marrying her daughter would affect me. To have no apprehension would not only be ignorant but foolish. But it is my duty toward you and your future that forces me to do what I must to prevent the match."

"You've always taught me not to rely too heavily on any argument with a flaw in its foundation, yet you are doing exactly that." When James angled his head in question, Michael said, "You assume I will heed you because of the bond we have shared since my birth, because I have always respected your authority. But what if there is a stronger force at play than the duty I feel toward you? What if my love for Mrs. Petersen won't just go away because you say it must?"

"Michael, you are but four and twenty years of age with a lifetime ahead of you."

"Already two years older than you were when I was born."

Damn.

James set his glass to his lips and took a deep swallow while eyeing his son. "I'll never regret fathering you. How could I when you are the best thing that ever happened to me? But I did believe myself in love with your mother. And since I was certain she loved me in return, I rushed into marriage with a woman who—"

He cut himself off abruptly. James had never disparaged Clara to Michael, and he wasn't about to start now for the sake of trying to win an argument.

"The point is," he went on, "you don't really know what love is at your age or at any age really until you have struggled through hardship with that person and seen each other at your weakest. All you have done with Mrs. Petersen, however, is go for walks, sip tea, and dance. So while you may enjoy her company and while you may claim to share similar interests, it isn't love. More likely, it is lust, Michael, and that is something you can cure with another woman. It certainly isn't enough to warrant marriage."

Michael leaned forward. His posture was rigid, his eyes flashing with tightly contained anger. "Don't make the error of diminishing the bond she and I have just because you've never known such powerful love yourself, Papa."

"Michael. I loved your mother with all my heart."

"Until you realized she didn't love you. Frankly, it would not surprise me if you were jaded by your experience, but I will be damned if you let it influence me." Michael winced and shook his head. He eased back into his seat and relaxed his posture. "Forgive me. I did not mean to insult you. I'm just so saddened and perplexed by the situation I find myself in."

"I'm not offended by your outburst. You're being

honest with me and I respect that, Michael. Indeed, I welcome it since it's much preferred to the silence you have been dealing me in recent weeks."

Michael sighed. He closed his eyes briefly, then met James's gaze once more. "I've met Mrs. Lawson, you know. She does not strike me as the viper you and the papers describe her to be. In fact, I rather like her, and considering the lovely daughter she has raised, I cannot help but wonder if perhaps the husband made up his allegations so he could simply be rid of her."

"Anything's possible I suppose. But if he wasn't trying to defend his honor, then what would be his motive?" When Michael merely shrugged, James said, "Don't forget the Pennington ball. You and I were both there. We witnessed the accusation Mr. Hewitt made against his wife and saw two of her lovers rush to her defense. In public. And that is without considering the trial or the fact that the lady herself has made no attempt at denying her guilt."

"I suppose," Michael muttered. "I just can't shake the feeling that something is off about this whole thing."

"It wouldn't be strange for you to look for hope in every possible corner, but I fear that when it comes to your marrying Mrs. Petersen, there is none. Not unless you are prepared to walk away from your career and risk social ruin. Your life as you know it would in effect be over."

Noting the indecision in Michael's eyes, James added, "I think it might be good for us to get away from Town for a bit and spend some time in the country. I've been feeling a need for a change of scenery and fresh air myself lately. What do you say? We'll visit my parents for a week or two and once we return, the world will surely look brighter."

Michael didn't appear the least bit convinced. It was clear he did not wish to leave London or, more precisely, the woman who resided here. But he must have realized that moping about would do him no good either. Eventually he shrugged. "All right."

Pleased with the headway they'd made, James told Michael to go and start packing. In the meantime he'd finish up his brief. Once he'd delivered it in the morning, they could be off.

"I cannot bear this anymore," Cynthia lamented while she and Wilhelmina shared a pot of tea.

Wilhelmina glanced up from her mending. A tear on the hem of a day dress needed fixing after the garment had snagged on a nail or splinter during her most recent outing. She'd gone to see her solicitor about finalizing the sale of her house. The property had been purchased by a young couple who'd recently arrived from Manchester, so Wilhelmina would have to move out soon. As difficult as it would be to part with the place, Wilhelmina was relieved, for she sorely needed the money.

"I trust you're speaking of Michael?"

Cynthia sighed as if she carried the weight of the

world on her delicate shoulders. "He was at Almack's the other evening. I went with some friends who'd convinced me I ought to get out more. It was awful, seeing him across the room and not being able to approach out of fear for what his father might do if he found out we'd spoken. So I had to suffer watching him dance with other women. He didn't look happy, which only made it more intolerable."

"I'm sorry." Wilhelmina desperately wanted to fix the situation for her daughter and make her every dream come true. She was her mother. It was her duty to see to her happiness, but she was at a loss. Mr. Dale had been very clear and Wilhelmina dared not thwart him more than she already had.

A thought struck. She set her mending aside and clasped her hands together in her lap. "I'll be departing for Renwick on Thursday. Why don't you come with me? Get away for a bit and clear your head? You can help me muck out the stables, milk the cows, and feed the pigs."

Cynthia actually laughed. "You must be joking." When Wilhelmina merely smiled, Cynthia said, "What happened to the caretaker and his wife?"

"They're still there, but I don't intend to let them toil away while I do nothing. Besides, I rather think it would do us both a world of good to exorcise all the pent up aggravation roiling around inside us through hard physical work."

"Do you know," Cynthia said as she straightened herself in her seat. "I believe you may be correct.

London has not been good to me since Henry's death. The brief joy I knew with Michael has been snuffed out completely, lowering my spirits and making me dread every day."

"So we are in agreement then?" Wilhelmina asked. "You'll come with me to Renwick?"

"Indeed I shall, Mama. More than that, I shall enjoy every moment of it."

Wilhelmina grinned. For the first time in months – years even – she felt as though there was light upon the horizon.

CHAPTER SIX

I t took James and Michael three days to reach their destination by mail coach, during which they spoke little to each other. After being crammed together with other passengers heading north, James didn't mind the two mile walk they had to take once the coachman dropped them off on the main road. He wasn't sure Michael felt the same. His mood had not improved since leaving London. If anything, Michael seemed more forlorn than ever. And he clearly wasn't ready to forgive James for disapproving of Mrs. Petersen. Even though any sensible person could figure out it would be a calamitous match, Michael was hell-bent on blaming James for not being able to marry her.

James sighed. Hopefully Michael's temper would ease in response to the fresh air and sunshine. It was early summer, and the day was pleasant and bright. Colorful wildflowers crowded each side of the country lane that would take them to Clarington House. Already, James could see the wide stone edifice peeking out from behind a cluster of trees in the distance. Extensive fields of green swept toward the horizon on either side, a mile in each direction before the tenant lands began.

With his leather satchel flung over one shoulder and a carpet bag in each hand, James quickened his pace. He was suddenly eager for a glass of cool lemonade on the terrace with a few of Cook's tasty sandwiches to go with it. Behind him, his son huffed a breath. He sounded disgruntled. James grinned. The young man detested walking, but it was good for him to use his legs and to recognize the value of having a carriage take him wherever he needed to go.

"We're almost there," James encouraged. "Come on."

"I don't understand why we could not hire a private coach," Michael grumbled. "It's not like we can't afford it."

"True, but then we would have been denied that riveting conversation about the difference between silk and satin." James threw his son a grin.

Michael rolled his eyes. "Those women made my ears bleed."

"Really? I see no evidence of that." Another eye-roll was followed by silence. James told himself Michael just needed time. He'd soon recover whatever heartache he suffered. The lad was still young. A brief separation from Mrs. Petersen, followed by an introduction to other more suitable ladies, would do the trick.

Satisfied with this plan to cure Michael of his problematic infatuation, James started along the final stretch of road, lined by elm trees. Planted centuries ago, they seemed to bow in greeting, their lustrous canopies shading the travelers from the afternoon sun.

"My feet hurt," Michael complained.

"Don't worry," James told him brightly, "you'll be able to rest them soon."

They reached the front door of Clarington House ten minutes later with Michael insisting he'd gotten a blister.

"You can discard your boots and soak your feet once we've greeted your grandmamma and grandpapa," James said. He grabbed the knocker and gave the door three loud raps before trying the handle. The door swung open with ease, granting them entrance before the butler managed to arrive.

"Mr. James and Michael Dale," the servant exclaimed as he hastened toward them a moment later. Robert Warren had replaced the previous butler three years earlier and was roughly the same age as James. He was also less stiff than his predecessor and lighter of foot. "Welcome to Clarington House. Mr. and Mrs. Dale will be overjoyed to see you both, I'm sure."

"Thank you, Warren," James said. He and Michael had set their bags on the floor and were now in the process of shucking their outerwear garments. Warren stepped in to help while a pair of able footmen collected the luggage. "I apologize for arriving unannounced."

"No need," Warren said with a bit more butlerish flair than he'd initially shown. "The maids will have your rooms ready within the hour. Until then I recommend you join your parents for refreshments."

"Might I request a pitcher of lemonade?" James asked.

Warren smirked. "It is waiting for you on the terrace as we speak. I'll have some extra glasses brought out right away."

The butler strode off and James turned to Michael. "Shall we?"

Michael shrugged as if indifferent, but James had not missed the eager look in his eyes at the mention of lemonade. He stifled a grin and led the way through. Had he been as prone to emotional contrariness when he was that age? James shook his head and entered the drawing room at the opposite end of which a pair of French doors were flung open to let in the fresh countryside air. He crossed to them and stepped out onto the uneven paving stones he'd helped his father lay nearly thirty years earlier. They matched the grey façade of the building while lending a rustic feel to the place. Complemented by the perennials his mother had planted, the space provided a peaceful retreat.

James's mother, who sat facing the house, spotted him first. "Good heavens, James. Is that you?"

His father turned in his seat. "My God. And it looks like you've brought Michael with you."

They both stood, allowing James to embrace them with all his might. His parents had never been frugal in their show of affection, neither between each other nor toward their children, and while that might not be the norm among upper-class families, James was grateful for it. He'd never doubted his parents' love for each other or for him.

"It's so good to see you again," Mama said as her eyes began to shimmer. She hugged Michael next.

"And your visit could not have come at a better time," Papa said. He dropped back into his chair with a heavy exhale. Discomfort strained his features. "I hurt my back a couple of days ago helping the Hendersons un-clog the drainage canal from their pond. Otherwise, there's a good chance their farmland will flood the next time it rains."

"Won't their plants be big enough by now to survive it?" Michael asked.

"Lord, no," Papa said. "The Hendersons have a good deal of newly planted brussels sprouts which won't be ready for harvest until October. But that aside, if too much water gathers, the roots of the established crop like peppers, eggplant, and celery will likely rot."

"I'll ride out and offer my help tomorrow," James said.

A maid arrived with the two extra glasses. James and Michael sat and drank the refreshing liquid as soon as James's mother was done serving them. A plate with those tasty sandwiches James had dreamt of during his walk was passed around and a comfortable conversation ensued until the readiness of their rooms was announced.

"I'll freshen up and see to my blister," Michael said. He smiled at his grandparents. "Thank you for the warm welcome."

"It's a few years since you were last here so if there's anything you need, don't hesitate to ask," Mama said.

"The horses are at your disposal, should you feel like a ride," Papa added.

"Thank you," Michael repeated. He pushed back his chair and stood. "I'll probably take a short nap. What time is dinner?"

"Seven o'clock," James said at the same exact time as his parents. They all chuckled and Michael strolled off.

A pause followed and then Papa said, "You usually write before showing up, and while we certainly don't mind a surprise visit from any of our children, I cannot help but wonder about the reason for it. Besides your simply missing us, that is."

James smiled in response to his father's attempt at humor, and then he related the issue regarding Mrs. Petersen and her mother. "Naturally, a union between them would be impossible," he said once he'd finished.

"It shouldn't be," Mama said with a frown. "Mrs. Petersen should not be made to suffer for something her mother has done. It's completely unreasonable."

"I do not disagree," James said, "but it is how the world works, and I just don't want Michael to throw his life away on some fleeting fancy the way…"

Papa raised an eyebrow. "Just because you had a bad experience with a woman, doesn't mean Michael will. The fact that Mrs. Petersen's mother has loose morals doesn't mean Mrs. Petersen herself won't take her vows seriously."

"Of course not," James agreed, "but if Michael marries her he'll be related to Mrs. Lawson and as such I fear doors will be closed to him rather than opened. Papa, I want Michael to have the chance to shine. But how can he do so if he pursues a marriage that's bound to put his own values and integrity into question?"

"He does have one advantage," Mama pointed out.

"Which is?" James asked.

"The same as yours," she said. "Michael does not need to work. If he truly loves this woman, he could give up his career for her and settle down to a comfortable life in the country."

"And do what?" James asked, aghast at the notion of his son becoming the sort of entitled man he despised. London was full of them – men who sat about doing nothing all day while funds were delivered to them on a silver platter. They had no appreciation for the things they had, they just wanted more: a bigger house, fancier clothes, a faster carriage.

"He could help me," Papa said. "This thing with my back reminds me I'm not as sprightly as I once was. And as much as I appreciate your stepping up while you're here, you'll eventually go back to London. But Michael could stay."

James shook his head. "He spent four years getting his education, so I want him to try and use it. This thing with Mrs. Petersen will pass, you'll see. As for solving your problem, Papa, I'm sure we can ask one of the grooms or footmen to step in when needed. If not, I'll help you hire someone who can do so before I leave."

Papa frowned, but rather than argue, he nodded, for which James was grateful.

"When's the last time you came here?" Cynthia asked with a cough. She, Betsy, and Wilhelmina had arrived at the modest farm no more than half an hour ago and had instantly opened all the cottage's windows to air out the musty smell from each room. Dust swirled about them as they pulled protective sheets off the furniture in the parlor. Even though Wilhelmina had hired the Wilkinses, an elderly couple, as caretakers, she'd told them they only needed to tend to the animals. And so they had.

"April?" Wilhelmina told her daughter.

"That's not so very long ago," Cynthia said. "I wonder why it's so filthy."

Wilhelmina drew her finger along the edge of the mantelpiece. It came away with a thick layer of fine grey powder. "When I said April, I meant last year."

"Ah." Cynthia bundled a sheet and went outside to give it a good shake.

Wilhelmina addressed Betsy. "Can you please put some water to boil for some tea? I think we can all do with a cup."

"Aye." Betsy bobbed a quick curtsey and left.

"Are you able to manage the rest of the rooms down

here while I see to the upstairs?" Wilhelmina asked Cynthia when she came back inside.

"Of course."

Grateful for a daughter who wasn't afraid of a bit of hard work, Wilhelmina left her to shake out and fold the sheets in the downstairs rooms so they could get started on dusting and sweeping. Since the house wasn't lived in, Wilhelmina had seen no reason to hire additional servants. On the rare occasion when she'd come for a visit, she'd brought Betsy with her to help cook and clean. If necessary, she'd ask the Wilkinses for additional help, which they seemed happy to give in exchange for a few extra coins.

She climbed the creaky stairs and gave each bedroom a swift once over. Disheartened by the smell that clung to the bedclothes, the mildew she found in the linen cabinet, and the leak she spied up under the ceiling where wallpaper bubbled, Wilhelmina feared it would be past midnight before they retired. First, they would have to roll up their sleeves and wash everything – a grueling chore she did not look forward to in the least.

When James woke the day after his arrival at Clarington House, he got up, dressed with the efficiency of a man who'd managed without a valet for years, and went down to breakfast. Dinner last night had been pleasant enough even though it was clear

Michael hadn't let go of his grudge. Today, James would make a proper effort to mend the breach between them. He'd start by inviting Michael to join him when he went to visit the Hendersons later.

But when he entered the dining room and greeted his parents, he learned his son had already eaten and gone out.

"He took me up on the offer regarding the horses," Papa said while James took a seat across from Mama. "Claimed it would be nice to go for a gallop without having to worry about knocking over pedestrians."

"Can't blame him," James said. He poured himself a cup of coffee and reached for a slice of toast. "Riding is much more enjoyable out here in the open countryside. There's more room for it. Did Michael say when he'd be back?"

"I'm afraid not."

"Hmm… I had intended to have him join me today." James piled some eggs and bacon onto his plate and started to eat. "Helping the Hendersons would have taken his mind off Mrs. Petersen. It would have provided us with a common goal which I'd hoped might help fix our differences."

Mama sighed. "He needs time to accept your reasoning, James. You can't deny him the love of his life and expect him not to be angry or hurt. But I'm sure he'll come around eventually. Just give him some time and let him work through this at his own pace."

"He's not in love with her," James grumbled. He spooned a portion of eggs, bacon, and toast into his mouth and chewed. "He may think he is, but he's wrong."

"As wrong as you were when you claimed you would die if Clara refused your hand in marriage?" Papa inquired.

"Exactly. Which is why it is up to me to make sure he doesn't make a similar error in judgment."

"We tried to protect you too," Mama reminded him. "But you did as you wanted anyway."

"Yes. I recall." James sipped his coffee. His parents had warned him that Clara did not seem as smitten with him as he was with her. They'd claimed she wanted a marriage of convenience while he believed he was getting a love match. He'd ignored them, insisted they knew nothing of how she felt about him. Stupid young fool. How blind he'd been. "Michael isn't as headstrong, thank God. He's also got a surprising amount of common sense for someone so young. So as long as Mrs. Petersen isn't nearby, infecting him with infatuation and lust, I dare say he'll see reason soon."

"I'm sure you're right, dear."

James frowned. His mother did not sound the least bit convinced and when he looked at Papa, James saw he was doing his best to force back a smile. Clearly neither believed Michael's feelings for Mrs. Petersen could be banished with the ease James described. Well, he'd show them. Michael had little experience with women. Of course he would fall for the first one who returned his interest.

"Say, are there any dances scheduled at the assembly

hall anytime soon?" He stuffed more food into his mouth and glanced at his parents.

"I believe the next one will be in three weeks," Mama said.

James sighed and finished the remainder of his meal. So much for introducing Michael to some of the local gentry. A practical country girl would have cured him of Mrs. Petersen's hold. Ah well. Back to the idea of physical exercise and fresh air it was. He downed the remainder of his coffee and stood. "I'll see you both later."

"Good luck with the digging," Papa called after him.

James raised one hand to acknowledge the comment while striding from the room. He collected his hat and gloves and put on his greatcoat. Warren handed him the luncheon he'd ordered from the kitchen the previous evening. It would prevent him wasting precious time by having to come back at midday.

Once ready, James left the main house and went to the stables. As always, his father kept an enviable selection of horses. James picked the same one he'd used the last time he'd come for a visit – a golden Arabian stallion named Jupiter. After the saddle and bridle had been secured by the head groom, James swung himself onto Jupiter's back and left for the Hendersons.

Seven hours later, he felt as though he'd taken a beating from a champion bare-knuckle bruiser. Everything hurt. Muscles he'd not used in months screamed in response to each move he made. A reminder he might need to exercise more on a regular basis. Sitting at his desk all day was not good for his constitution. It didn't feel like shoveling dirt was either, but he knew from experience he would feel better in a few days if he kept up the work.

"I'll be back again tomorrow," he promised Mr. Henderson when he prepared to head back to Clarington House. "If my son comes with me I reckon we'll finish the job in less than five days."

"Thank ye, Mr. Dale." Mr. Henderson extended his freshly washed hand and James shook it.

They were both grubby from head to toe, but at least Mrs. Henderson had been able to give them clean water and soap. Still, James longed for a hot bath and a change of clothes. With the promise of such fine luxury no more than a hard ten minute ride away, he took his leave and started across the fields, which was faster than taking the roads.

At just after five in the afternoon, the daylight was starting to fade into more muted tones. The sun dipped low against the sky, spreading a flare of magical light across the rippling hills. Taken by it, James drew his mount to a halt for a moment and let himself savor the beauty. A gentle breeze cooled his face while a flock of siskins chased each other across the sky. He recognized them by their yellow plumage.

Inhaling deeply, he nudged Jupiter into an easy gait. This was Suffolk. No court case waited for him in the morning. He had no reason to rush besides his own desire for cleanliness. But that could wait. Of greater importance was taking time to stop and look – to truly admire the beauty of his surroundings – and to appreciate just how privileged he was to be able to come here.

Perhaps burying himself in work was the wrong approach. He'd done it as a means to escape the memories of the war and of Clara, but maybe there ought to be more of a balance. Maybe he should pay more attention to Michael – figure out who he was besides being his son, and offer more guidance.

James blew out a breath. Was he to blame for this business with Mrs. Petersen? He'd taken Michael to the Pennington ball, but since the scandal, he'd stayed away from social functions. Michael had been left to the company of friends he'd known from university, and whoever else he'd met with when he wasn't at home. And without James really being aware of what his son got up to, it had been nearly impossible to guide him. Certainly not with regard to romance. In fact, the more James thought on it, the more he decided he'd done his son a terrible disservice. He should have taken him out more and made sure he recognized what sort of woman would make a good match.

After all, his closest female role model had been his mother.

Christ.

James shook his head. It was time for him to pull himself together. He needed to push his work aside and give his son the attention he obviously needed.

A feminine laugh, bubbling with mirth, intruded upon his thoughts.

Instinctively, James swung Jupiter toward it and frowned. It was probably one of the farm girls who lived nearby since the nearest gentry were a good five miles in the opposite direction. And if she was frolicking about with a local lad, it was none of James's business. She'd laughed, after all, not screamed or shouted for help.

He prepared to resume his homeward trek when a body popped out from between the tall grass. James's heart jolted. He'd recognize Michael anywhere, even at a distance of roughly twenty yards. And if he'd decided to work through his frustration by taking advantage of one of his father's tenants, James would give the boy a thrashing the likes of which he'd never experienced before.

Increasingly incensed, he started toward his son. Michael hadn't seen him yet. He was too busy tucking his shirt into his trousers. Another person stood and James nearly fell from his horse. Good God. It couldn't be. And yet, there was no mistaking the identity of the woman who tried to put herself back in order. Mrs. Petersen, the very woman James had tried to remove his son from by coming all the way here, smoothed her rumpled skirts and pulled her bodice back into a more acceptable position.

Rage, hot and swift, tore up James's back and heated his neck until it burned. "What the hell is going on?"

Michael turned, eyes wide with surprise, shock, and horror while Mrs. Petersen clutched her discarded spencer against her like a shield. Good. They deserved to be scared.

Jaw clamped so hard his teeth hurt, James dismounted, grabbed the reins, and stalked toward them. He glared at Michael, then at Mrs. Petersen, and back at Michael. "Well?"

"I came upon her by chance when I was returning home from my ride," Michael said. He was doing his best to keep his chin up and his eyes fixed on James.

A twinge of pride shoved its way past James's defenses. He steeled himself against it. "And so you chose to ignore my dictate in favor of a good tup, is that it?"

Michael's cheeks flushed, but he did not avert his gaze even as Mrs. Petersen gasped. Instead he raised his chin higher. "I love her, Papa."

"Then you're a damned fool, Michael." James leaned forward and stared into Michael's brown eyes with penetrating force. "The fact that she would spread her legs for you in a field for all the world to see makes her no better than her whore of a mother."

The blow Michael dealt to his cheek caught James off guard. He knew he'd been unacceptably crass, especially with Mrs. Petersen there to overhear, but he'd not expected Michael to punch him. If his stunned expression was any indication, Michael shared James's surprise. Not that the punch was undeserved. James just hadn't thought his son capable of resorting to violence. Once again, he'd underestimated him.

"Where are you staying, Mrs. Petersen?" James

inquired while rubbing his cheek. He'd address Michael's rebellious streak later. And then he'd have to teach him how to deliver a proper punch – the sort that would knock a man off his feet.

"A mile from here," she said, her voice quivering. "With my mother."

James snorted. Of course Mrs. Lawson had a part in all this. James gave his attention back to Michael. "Take Jupiter back to the house. Wash up and get yourself ready for dinner. I'll escort Mrs. Petersen home."

"But—"

"If it's a fight you want, Michael, I should warn you that my blows are a hell of a lot harder than yours."

"I don't trust you to be alone with her," Michael said, not budging one inch, "so, I shall be escorting her home as well."

Michael's point was valid. Considering how Mrs. Petersen clutched Michael's arm now, the woman was clearly terrified of him. And rightly so, James had to admit, although he would never lay his hands on her. But he supposed words could be hurtful too, and frankly, he wasn't sure he trusted himself not to insult her further. He was simply too livid.

"Fine. We'll all go. Mrs. Petersen, please lead the way."

∾

Shame burned Michael to the core as he trudged across the field. Gripping his horse's reins, he pulled the beast along, thankful for the shield it provided between himself and his father.

Lord, he couldn't believe he'd actually struck him, but neither could he fathom the vehemence with which his father had spoken. The words had blinded him with rage and in a split second, he'd lost all sense of reason.

Heart pounding, he ground his teeth together while Cynthia gripped his arm, her forceful hold indicative of her need for support and assurance. Well, Michael decided. He'd not deny her. Not after this last altercation.

"When I offered marriage," he whispered, "you accepted. Do you stand by that decision?"

"Of course, Michael. I love you. But—"

"Then we must find a way through this," he continued, keeping his voice so low his father would not be able to hear. "We've not much time to agree on a plan. Just promise me you will meet me tomorrow at dawn. Exactly where Papa just happened upon us. And bring a travelling bag."

"Michael..." She spoke his name with distress, which only made him wish he could whisk her away from all of this right now – save her from having to witness the upcoming quarrel between his father and her mother. "There are things you need to know. Additional facts I must share with you before we speak our vows."

He met her gaze as they approached her cottage. "Besides the details pertaining to the divorce?"

Troubled eyes met his. "Yes."

It was still hard for him to fathom what she'd revealed to him today, though it certainly helped improve his opinion of Mrs. Lawson by leaps and bounds. And since he did not believe it possible for Cynthia to tell him something more shocking, he chose to reassure her by saying, "As long as you and I love each other, then that's all that matters. The rest will sort itself out. Just promise me you'll be there tomorrow."

"I promise," she said at the same exact moment as they reached their destination.

CHAPTER SEVEN

Wilhelmina wiped her hands on her apron and tucked a few stray strands of hair behind her ear. Exhaustion pulled at every muscle. Milking cows and mucking out stalls was hard, laborious work and although the Wilkinses did their part, they did not move with the sort of speed or efficiency Wilhelmina desired. In fact, it felt like they were prepared to get by with the bare minimum. Not that Wilhelmina blamed them since both were at least twenty years older than she. Still, she was glad the pigs and chickens were able to tend to themselves. All they required was food.

She entered the kitchen on throbbing feet and stretched her back. The clock on the counter made her frown. It was nearing five o'clock. Cynthia should have been back from Renwick by now so Betsy could start on dinner, but there was no sign of any food being prepared. She glanced at a chair and sighed. She dearly wanted to sit and rest, but that would clearly have to wait.

Rubbing the back of her neck to try and undo the tension there, she plodded toward the front of the house and soon located Betsy. The maid was returning a carpet she'd taken outside for a beating. The musty smell that hung in the air yesterday had been replaced by crisp freshness thanks to the thorough cleaning the room had undergone since their arrival. It was two in the morning before the sheets they'd laundered had finished drying so they could make their beds. By six, they'd been up again, so it really wasn't a wonder if they were exhausted.

"Has Cynthia not returned yet?" Wilhelmina asked the maid.

"I haven't seen her." Betsy straightened and rolled her shoulders.

"It's been three hours since she set out." Concern began taking root. Wilhelmina had been so busy she'd not noticed the time until she'd returned to the house. "She should have been back by now."

"Maybe she got distracted by some of the shops?"

"Maybe, although it does seem unlikely when she knows we need the supplies she was sent to buy. The trip should not have taken more than two hours at most."

"I'm sure she'll be back soon."

Wilhelmina nodded. "I'll check the road for her. Can you make some tea in the meantime? If dinner is to be delayed, a hot soothing drink will be in order."

"Of course."

"Thank you, Betsy." Wilhelmina went to the front door and pulled it open. The late afternoon sun spread a warm glow upon her surroundings, sharpening the colors. Thankfully there were still a few hours left of daylight.

Wilhelmina walked toward the garden gate and scanned the road. It was empty, save for a couple of birds pecking after insects. Increasingly worried, she dragged her gaze across the rest of the landscape, until she spotted three people crossing a field. Wilhelmina raised her hand to shield her eyes and breathed a sigh of relief when she recognized Cynthia. But she immediately stiffened the moment she realized who her daughter was with. Good heavens. What on earth were Mr. Dale and his son doing here?

Steeling herself for the difficult conversation she feared she would have to engage in, she opened the gate and stepped through it. But as the group drew nearer and the expression on each of their faces became more evident, Wilhelmina gave up imagining she could simply exchange a few awkward words with Mr. Dale and his son. Indeed, Mr. Dale himself looked more furious than she'd ever seen him. His son appeared almost equally cross while Cynthia herself looked slightly terrified.

Wilhelmina squared her shoulders. Clearly an altercation was brewing and if Mr. Dale had upset her daughter, then he would have *her* to deal with. She clenched her jaw, stiffened her spine, and balled her hands into fists at her sides. Raising her chin, she was prepared to stand her ground by the time the first angry words hit her.

"I believe I told you to keep your daughter away from my son," Mr. Dale thundered. "Yet here she is once more, leading him astray."

"Papa," Michael warned.

Mr. Dale ignored him as he drew to a halt before Wilhelmina and pinned her with his dark gaze. Rage burned there with such forceful fierceness she had to fight the urge not to retreat.

"Again you seek to lay the blame at our door," Wilhelmina clipped. "In case you're unaware, however, the chance of a young woman forcing a man to submit to her lustful ways is far more unlikely than the reverse."

"Mama," Cynthia groaned.

"Your suggestion is not only vulgar but outrageous," Mr. Dale seethed, "though it certainly is in keeping with your reputation."

Wilhelmina glared at him. "You go too far, sir."

"Really, madam. Am I to believe the two of you did not follow us to these parts?"

"Indeed we did not, Mr. Dale."

"Considering your previous efforts to help them meet in secret," Mr. Dale said with cutting force, "I'd not put it past you."

Wilhelmina's heart began beating faster. The man was in effect declaring her a meddlesome liar. "Well, you are mistaken, Mr. Dale. This is our home now, so if you happen to be visiting friends or relations in the area, our coming across one another is merely a coincidence. Though not a very happy one, I can assure you."

He snorted. "I don't believe in coincidences like this, happy or not. What's far more likely is that you learned my family seat is at Clarington House and then set out to acquire a piece of property in the area. All so your daughter and my son would have some means by which to keep on seeing each other."

Outraged, Wilhelmina leaned toward him, so close she could see flecks of gold in those brown eyes of his. "What you propose is preposterous, sir."

"And yet, it is exactly the sort of thing I believe you capable of," Mr. Dale seethed. "In light of the fact that I do not want my son anywhere near your daughter, I was not thrilled to discover the two of them having a tryst in a field."

Wilhelmina's gaze darted to Cynthia's. Irritation pooled in the pit of her belly as soon as she saw the guilt there, but if Mr. Dale imagined she'd chastise her daughter with him bearing witness, he would be disappointed. "I trust you purchased what I asked for?"

Cynthia nodded. "Yes, Mama."

"Then go inside the house and give the supplies to Betsy so she can get started on dinner. You can help her peel the carrots."

"Michael, I—"

"Go," Wilhelmina snapped, forcing Cynthia into the house before Mr. Dale exploded – as he appeared on the verge of doing. She stared the irate man down.

"Just so you know, I purchased this property five years ago, long before I ever met you, Mr. Dale, and I can assure you that learning of your proximity to it, for however long you plan to be in the area, is most unwelcome. However, considering your presence, I promise to keep a vigilant eye on my daughter from now on. Perhaps you should do the same with regard to your son."

"Oh indeed. He will be on the first coach back to London in the morning."

"What?"

Clearly this was news to Michael who looked like he was ready to spit nails.

"Provided, that is, Mrs. Petersen has no intention of giving chase," Mr. Dale said, ignoring his son.

"Oh, I can assure you she will do no such thing," Wilhelmina hissed. "In fact, I shall do all I can to save her from being related to you in any capacity whatsoever."

Mr. Dale held Wilhelmina's gaze for a long, steady moment before he eventually nodded. "I wish I could say it has been a pleasure. Good day, Mrs. Lawson."

Wilhelmina silently cursed him while watching him walk away. How could she ever have enjoyed his company when he was without a doubt the most awful man she'd ever met? It baffled her mind. Although, to be fair, he did have cause to be angry if what he'd told her was true.

Returning inside, she sought out Cynthia, who was in the process of peeling potatoes while Betsy chopped some carrots. Tight-faced with glistening eyes, Cynthia clearly did her best to stop from weeping.

Willing herself to stay strong, Wilhelmina asked Betsy if she could give them a private moment. As soon as the maid was gone, she addressed her daughter in a firm voice. "Is Mr. Dale correct? Did he find you having a tryst with his son in a field?"

Cynthia's lower lip quivered, but she forced herself to meet Wilhelmina's gaze. "I was returning from town when I ran into Michael. He was out for a ride and I could scarcely credit him being here of all places. I was overjoyed to see him, Mama. He offered to escort me home but we both wanted more than a fleeting conversation we knew would end as quickly as it had begun."

"While I can appreciate your wish to spend time with the man you love when given the chance, you knew Betsy and I waited for you. She and I have pushed ourselves to exhaustion all day, and yet you thought it all right to lie about in a field with a man you're supposed to be staying away from?"

"I'm sorry, Mama."

Wilhelmina sighed. "As am I. This business with Michael cannot be easy for you, but his father is adamant in his wishes and considering what he believes to be true, he's not entirely wrong to be angry."

"I disagree."

"Of course you do."

"Mama, even if you were guilty of adultery, your actions should not deny Michael and me our happiness."

"Perhaps not, but they do, and I am sorry for that, Cynthia. However, I will always be viewed as the scandalous divorcée, and if Michael marries you, I will become his mother-in-law. The connection will invariably influence his position within Society. Believing otherwise would be naïve."

Cynthia returned her attention to the potatoes, and for a moment Wilhelmina just watched her peel them in silence. She could sense her daughter's thoughts bursting to break free, until she finally asked, "Is it not possible for you to confide the truth in his father?"

Wilhelmina dropped onto a vacant stool and heaved a deep breath. "He is a barrister, Cynthia. A man of the law. If he learned the truth it might make everything worse. Especially given his clear dislike of me. I'd not put it past him to have me arrested if he found reason to do so."

"Then there is no hope."

"None that I can see."

Cynthia brushed aside the tears that suddenly started to fall and pressed her lips together. Unhappy with the pain she'd caused her, Wilhelmina wished she could hug her, but the fact was she desperately needed a bath. Grime from a full day of working outdoors with animals caked her gown. She'd not even had a chance to wash her hands yet.

So rather than wrap her arms around her daughter in a tight embrace, Wilhelmina crossed to where she sat and dropped a kiss to the top of her head. "You've loved and lost once before, my dearest. You will survive this."

A choked sob rose from Cynthia's throat. She did not argue, but the anguish she put on display cut Wilhelmina's heart in two. Giving up Michael would in some ways be harder than having to go on after Henry's death. While Cynthia hadn't confided too much about her new romance, Wilhelmina believed Michael had helped her overcome heartache. Knowing he lived but that she would not have a life by his side had to be the cruelest blow imaginable to Cynthia.

Deciding to give her some space, Wilhelmina called Betsy back to the kitchen, then climbed the stairs. She had no energy left to ready the bath she so dearly wanted and would therefore have to settle for using the washbasin in her bedchamber. A change of clothes was also in order.

Wilhelmina entered her room and shut the door. Leaning against it, she glanced at the cheval glass in the opposite corner and gasped. Her hand flew to her mouth and then, whether because of fatigue or the torment stretching her nerves to the limit, she laughed.

Brown dirt was smeared across her right cheek. Tangled strands of hair, having escaped their pins, stuck out from her head at odd angles. The apron she wore, which had been white that morning, was now a deep shade of grey. Mud clung to the hem of her gown while other brown splotches stained the front of her skirt.

She'd never looked more frightful in her life and since she was having the worst luck ever in recent weeks, it made perfect sense that this was how Mr. Dale had seen her.

How utterly fitting.

"I am not going back to London tomorrow," Michael informed James as they returned to Clarington House together. "And I don't regret what happened between Mrs. Petersen and me. We love each other, Papa."

"First, you *will* go back to London, even if I have to pack you into the carriage myself," James said, gripping the reins so hard his hands hurt.

Tension pulled at every muscle, not least on account of Mrs. Lawson's most recent appearance. He did not want to view her as a hardworking individual or the sort of woman who didn't think herself above common chores. Because that was the sort of person he could respect, like, and possibly even admire. To even suppose Mrs. Lawson shared the same values as he with regard to making oneself useful was dangerous indeed. But the state she'd been in had clearly suggested she herself had engaged in hard labor. She'd not just sat about sipping her tea while others did the chores for her. And damn him if her wholesome appearance had not made him want her with every fiber of his being. Which had only increased his anger.

"Second," James said while doing his best to rid his mind of Mrs. Lawson's appeal, "we've discussed your so-called love for Mrs. Petersen before. And if what happened today tells me anything, it's that your heart is the last thing you're using to make decisions."

"Your implication insults what she and I share," Michael growled.

"Believe me," James said. "I know what I speak of."

They continued in silence for a short while before Michael quietly told him, "I'm sorry you were unhappily married. That can't have been easy."

It hadn't been. He and Clara were so very young. She'd thought she could change him though – convince him to give up his plan to work for a living in favor of claiming a yearly allowance. He'd believed she would gradually develop an appreciation for his way of life once she tried it. Neither had been willing to compromise anything for the other, and eventually she had found comfort in other men's beds while he gave himself to his work. Still, discovering her betrayal had been a blow. One he never wished to endure again.

"It blessed my life with you," James said. "What I feel for you, this constant terror whenever you're out of my sight, the concern for your wellbeing, the knowledge that I would give my life for yours in a heartbeat, that's deep and unwavering love."

"What you've just described is exactly how I feel about Cynthia. She is my world, Papa."

James sighed. His son was clearly infatuated with the woman and would not change his mind except through experience. Hopefully, by sending Michael back to London and making sure he acquired a job, his feelings would change. Eventually, other women would come along and he would forget the lovely young widow.

So after returning to Clarington House and taking a much needed bath, James penned a letter of recommendation for Michael. He handed it to him after supper along with ten pounds intended to keep him properly clothed and fed until James was able to join him.

"I'll head back to Town as soon as I've finished helping the Hendersons," James told Michael when he handed him the letter after dinner. "Shouldn't be more than a week. Two at most."

"What if other tenants require help later?" Michael asked. "I saw Grandfather wince a few times while we sat at the table. His back is clearly paining him."

"My intention is to hire a capable man before I leave – someone who can ride out in his stead."

"I think that's an excellent idea." Michael tucked the letter of recommendation inside his jacket pocket. He forced a smile. "It's been quite a day and tomorrow does not promise any improvement, so if you don't mind, I'll retire."

James glanced at the clock. "It's not even nine yet. I thought we might join my parents for tea in the parlor."

"You go ahead. I still need to pack."

Dissatisfied with the recent turn of events which seemed to have deepened the rift between them rather than mend it, James asked, "Do you hate me?"

"Absolutely."

The grim response hung in the air long after Michael was gone. Heavy-hearted, James went to find his parents. Hopefully they'd have some words of wisdom to make him feel better.

Cynthia's heart beat frantically as she waited for Michael to join her. There was an awful mixture of wrongness and rightness to what she was doing. She was a grown woman for heaven's sake. She'd been married, had lived through the pain of losing her husband, of seeing his still body stretched out lifeless before her. She'd helped arrange his burial, all the while acutely aware the accident might not have happened if they hadn't argued before the race.

Henry had loved her and yet she'd never forget the way he'd looked at her prior to climbing up into his curricle, as though she were the most useless creature he'd ever laid eyes on. To have Michael look at her thus was more than she could bear.

Yet bear it she must since anything less would be wrong. Already, she'd delayed too long.

Yesterday, when they'd lain side by side in the grass, watching the clouds drift by overhead, and he'd said he'd stand by her forever regardless of what her mother had done or his father's attempt to tear them apart, the truth about the divorce finally spilled from Cynthia's lips along with every detail pertaining to her existence.

"Mr. Hewitt was her friend," she explained when she turned her head to one side and saw Michael gaped at her in dismay. "He married her in order to save me from illegitimacy and now she's returning the favor. So his child won't suffer that fate."

"But that means..." He'd pushed up onto one elbow and stared down at her with sudden intensity. "First of all, no woman should ever endure what your mother went through, but beyond that I need you to know that I do not care if you're illegitimate. Indeed, we ought to tell Papa as I'm sure he'll—"

"No." Cynthia held his gaze with unwavering fierceness. "Mama swore me to secrecy and I am breaking her trust by confiding in you. To tell your father would be the utmost betrayal so you have to promise me, Michael. Promise you will not utter a word of what I've just told you to anyone else."

He did not even blink. "Of course. You have my word."

She breathed a sigh of relief and welcomed the loving caresses that followed even though a small voice at the back of her mind compelled her to tell him the rest. Except doing so was delayed by his kisses, by the beautiful lovemaking they'd engaged in after, and then by Mr. Dales unexpected arrival and all this had led to.

So Cynthia had determined to share the rest of her troubles with Michael the following day. Even as she'd penned a note to her mother and packed her things, she'd decided she wouldn't allow him to whisk her away until he was fully aware of what he was getting into.

But when he came to meet her in the meadow as planned, the words she so desperately needed to speak failed her. Perhaps it was due to the magical pre-dawn glow, or how handsome he appeared as he rode toward her while leading another horse by the reins.

No. It was because she lacked the courage required to risk everything she held dear.

And then he was on the ground, pulling her into his arms. A kiss followed and whatever remained of her resolve flitted away completely.

Tomorrow she'd make her confession, she thought, as he helped her mount the mare he'd brought her.

Or maybe the day after that.

Everything ached when Wilhelmina woke. Wielding a shovel the day before had clearly left a mark on some previously unused muscles. She groaned in response to the soreness gripping her back as she sat. Her neck felt stiff and when she turned her head to the right, a twinge of pain shot through her. Conscious of having made some sort of movement with which her body did not agree, she rolled her head from side to side a few times, then stretched her arms up into the air and yawned.

Daylight glowed along the edges of the curtain. She glanced at the clock and immediately cursed. It was past eight. There were chores to be done. It was time to rise and get on with the day as quickly as possible.

She swung her legs over the side of the bed and stood. Ten minutes later, thanks to the serviceable clothes she'd elected to bring with her, she was dressed in a plain lilac day dress. Her hair was swept up in a simple knot at the nape of her neck. A quick breakfast accompanied by a cup of tea would have to suffice. Water had to be hauled for the animals, who also required feeding. Afterward the cows would need to be milked, eggs gathered, and dung cleared out of each stall and pen.

Wilhelmina could only hope the Wilkinses and Betsy hadn't been up for too long. She did not want to be the sort of mistress who lazed about all day while others did the work, even if she paid them. To her relief, hot tea waited for her in the kitchen, but the freshly baked bread on the counter suggested Betsy had been up for a while. Wilhelmina cut herself a slice, filled a cup with tea, and perched herself on a stool.

"Good morning," Betsy said when she swept into the kitchen five minutes later. Her arms were filled with leafy greens. "Turns out Mrs. Wilkins has quite the knack for growing cabbage. Thought I'd use a couple to make a hearty stew."

"Sounds wonderful." Wilhelmina took a bite of bread and chewed. "Do you know if Cynthia's up yet?"

"I haven't seen her today, so probably not."

Wilhelmina nodded and sipped her tea. Cynthia had been miserable yesterday. She'd retired early, but that didn't mean she'd slept. Accustomed to the effect a bleak mood could have on the mind, Wilhelmina feared she'd probably lain awake until the early hours of the morning. And since she would not be eager to rise and face the day, Wilhelmina was reluctant to wake her.

But when Cynthia still hadn't risen an hour and a half later, Wilhelmina decided to check on her. Taking a slice of fresh bread along with a cup of tea, she climbed the stairs and approached her daughter's bedchamber. The floorboards creaked beneath her feet with every step she took.

Balancing the plate of bread and the cup of tea in one hand, Wilhelmina did her best to ease the door open as quietly as possible. She stepped inside Cynthia's room and turned toward the bed. Air rushed from her lungs and she nearly dropped the items she held as her brain tried to come to terms with what her eyes saw.

The bed was neatly made with no hint of having been slept in. Shaking, Wilhelmina set the plate and teacup aside on the dresser and quickly opened the drawers. All were empty.

"No." The hoarse word felt as though it was ripped from her throat. She shook her head and crossed to the wardrobe. Disbelief clasped her shoulders and pulled on her nerves while incredulity pricked at her skin. This could not be. Cynthia would not do this – she wouldn't just leave.

Yet her carpet bag was gone along with most of her clothes.

Clasping a hand to her mouth, Wilhelmina turned, eyes searching for some piece of evidence that would disprove what she knew to be true. Her gaze settled upon a folded sheet of paper propped against the mirror that stood on the vanity table. Wilhelmina approached on wary feet. Her fingers trembled as she picked up the letter, and her insides tied themselves into knots as she read.

Dearest Mama,

When Michael and I met yesterday, we agreed our futures were ours to determine. While we both know you and his father wish us the best, neither of you has the right to come between us. Not when we are both of age and legally able to make our own decisions.

The last thing I want is for you to worry, and so you should know that he and I are bound for Gretna Greene. Hopefully you will welcome us once we return, for I very much fear Michael's father will not.

Until we meet again, I remain your loving daughter,

Cynthia.

Wilhelmina read the letter three more times in order to fully comprehend what it said. Her daughter had fallen in love and in so doing, she had snuck off like a thief in the night, without a word. Clutching the letter, Wilhelmina tried to breathe, to make some sense out of what she was feeling. Logically, she ought to be angry and disappointed, and yet a peculiar blend of relief and concern were taking hold.

On one hand she wanted her daughter to marry the man she loved, even if Wilhelmina ended up paying the price. On the other, she feared what Mr. Dale would do once he learned of the elopement. She also worried Cynthia and Michael hadn't thought their plan through.

They were young and eager to pursue their own fairy-tale, but would they be prepared for the ramifications?

Mr. Dale's blunt opposition to the union Cynthia and Michael wanted might aggravate Wilhelmina. She might even have helped them meet in secret while in London. But that didn't mean she was delusional. As a fallen woman, her connection to them would make life difficult, and she very much feared they weren't aware of how much.

One thing was certain, and that was that if Mr. Dale went in pursuit and caught up to them, there would be hell to pay. He'd threatened to ruin Cynthia once before. This time Wilhelmina feared he'd follow through out of spite. Which meant she had to be there in order to offer her daughter protection. Michael might manage to do so to some degree, but she wasn't confident he could withstand the full extent of his father's wrath. And Cynthia would be the one to suffer the consequence.

Mind made up, Wilhelmina went to her room and tossed a few items of clothing into her travelling bag. She was tempted to walk into town and catch the next northbound coach without determining whether or not Mr. Dale was aware of what had transpired. But, she reminded herself, if the positions were reversed, she'd be even more furious once she discovered the information had been kept from her. Also, his carriage would probably travel faster.

So as reluctant as she was to visit Clarington House, she returned downstairs and announced her departure to Betsy. She and the Wilkinses would have to manage as best as they could until Wilhelmina returned.

"Are you sure you don't want me to come with you?" Betsy asked.

"Thank you, Betsy, but knowing you're keeping an eye on things here will ease my mind."

Betsy nodded and gave Wilhelmina an impromptu hug. "Bring her home safe."

Wilhelmina assured her she would, upon which she left the house and walked toward the gate at the end of the garden path. She undid the latch and pulled the gate open, only to stop and stare as a gleaming black carriage drew to a halt before her.

The door swung open and Mr. Dale, dressed in a grey frock coat, brown breeches, and newly buffed boots, leapt onto the road. He straightened and swung his dark gaze toward her, then gave her a full head to toe perusal before asking, "Where the devil do you think you're going?"

Indignation prompted her hackles to rise. "To find you."

He glared at her with clear distrust. "Do you know what has happened?" When she nodded, he said, "They took two of my father's best horses. I thought it my duty to inform you."

"You're going after them?"

"Of course. Michael has made a monumental error in judgment – one that could ruin his life."

Determined not to rile him by getting into an argument, Wilhelmina raised her chin. "I'd like to come with you."

"Absolutely not."

She squared her shoulders and took a step forward. "She is my daughter and while you may not believe a woman like me can be capable of love or concern, I can assure you that my daughter's well-being is my highest priority. So please, take me with you."

"Do you honestly think our spending time together in a closed carriage for hours on end would be wise?"

Probably not, Wilhelmina thought, but the alternative – walking into Renwick and choosing a slower mode of transportation—was less desirable. "I promise I won't say a word. If you tire of me, you may toss me out along the way."

He tilted his head. "You truly do think the worst of me, don't you?"

"It's no less than what you think of me," she countered.

Pinching the bridge of his nose between his fingers, he closed his eyes briefly and finally shook his head. "God help me but I'm bound to regret this." With apprehension in his eyes, Mr. Dale sighed and gestured toward the carriage. "Get in."

When Wilhelmina hesitated, he took a deep breath and appeared to reach for a secret supply of good manners and patience. With a grimace, he offered his hand to assist her and said, "Please, Mrs. Lawson. Time is of the essence."

CHAPTER EIGHT

J ames was fairly certain he must have lost his damn mind somewhere between Clarington House and Mrs. Lawson's cottage. His intention to chase after Michael had not included bringing the infamous divorcée with him. But when he'd seen her standing by her garden gate holding her oversized travel bag, he'd not had the heart to make her walk into town and wait for the next available coach. Not when they shared the same destination.

So here he was, sitting across from a woman he couldn't get out of his head no matter how shameful he found her actions. She was like two different people: the beguiling beauty he'd met beneath the glow of the Pennington ballroom's chandeliers, and the selfish sinner cavorting behind her husband's back. It was hard for him to consolidate the two people, so vastly different in temperament and moral standing. And yet, he'd seen a third side to her as well in recent weeks. The homemaker ready to push up her sleeves and get to work was so unexpected, he wasn't sure how to make her fit in with the rest.

While he had been giving his full attention to the view since they'd set off, he now dared a glance in her direction. Thankfully, her gaze was turned toward the opposite window in an obvious attempt to avoid looking his way. Satisfied she would not catch him studying her, James accepted the opportunity he had been given to do precisely that.

He allowed his gaze to assess her profile, to commit the shade of the dark blond curls protruding from beneath her fawn-colored bonnet to memory. Bouncing slightly in response to the carriage's movement, they seemed to caress her high cheekbones. Long, coal-black eyelashes matched the hue of her neat eyebrows. Her nose was gently curved – a delicate feature that seemed to serve as a contrast to the fullness of her mouth. Tinted a deep rose color, her lips reminded him of the cherry blossoms that bloomed in the London parks each spring. His gut tightened. He'd not been wrong to be dazzled by her when they'd first met, for although she had to be nearing her fortieth year, Mrs. Lawson could easily outshine any young debutante with her appearance, no matter the soft creases marring the corners of her eyes.

His gaze traced the delicate column of her neck, her straight shoulders and rigid back. Then lower toward the soft folds of her skirts. Her hands, clad in black leather gloves, were tightly clasped in her lap. James frowned as his gaze wandered back up, over the fullness of her breasts. His fingers instinctively flexed, alerting him to a primal response he had no business having. With a silent curse, he tore his gaze away from that part of her body, only to find himself pinned by her ocean blue gaze.

Embarrassed to have been caught, James struggled for something to say. An apology was the least he could offer, but somehow he could not bring himself to say the words. Perhaps because doing so would prove his guilt? So he cleared his throat instead and said, "You look lovely today, Mrs. Lawson. Better than when I last saw you."

James cringed. If she chose, Mrs. Lawson could easily misconstrue his comment as a veiled insult, which wasn't at all how he'd intended it.

To his relief, she smiled – not in the wide and joyful way she'd done when they'd first met, but enough to suggest she had no desire to quarrel. One eyebrow rose as if in challenge. "I could say the same of you, Mr. Dale."

He supposed that was true. "I was returning home from one of my father's tenants when I happened upon our children in that field."

Her expression dimmed at the mention. "I'd like to apologize on my daughter's behalf. When you came to see me in London, you made your disapproval of her relationship with your son quite clear. It's the reason I brought her with me when I left, because I believed a change of scenery might do her good. It never occurred to me we would happen upon you here in Suffolk of all places."

James wanted to believe her, he just wasn't sure he could. Women like her, like Clara, were not to be trusted. Still, it would be hard to travel with her for several days if he questioned everything she said. So he decided to give her the benefit of the doubt while taking her words with a grain of salt.

"I chose to visit my parents for similar reasons," he said. "Noting Michael's despondence after I told him I wouldn't approve of him marrying your daughter, I thought some time away from Town might help."

"Instead we unwittingly brought them together."

"And gave them reason to run away." James shook his head. "I'd like to blame you for that, but I fear doing so would be rather unfair."

"Oh?"

He'd no intention of making her privy to his recent struggles with Michael, so he simply shrugged one shoulder and said, "Our children fancy themselves in love and as such, they are prepared to disregard the consequences of their actions."

She frowned. "You refer to the familial connection your son would have to me if he and Cynthia were to marry."

"Michael is a bright young man with a promising future ahead of him," James told her plainly. "I'd hate for him to squander it on a momentary bit of passion."

Mrs. Lawson's jaw tightened while her breaths grew

slightly harder. Obviously, she was fighting to keep her mouth shut and her opinions to herself. For some bizarre reason he could not comprehend, James wanted to hear her thoughts, even if they were contrary to his own and would lead to anger.

Leaning forward, he held her gaze, which had now turned steely grey. "What?"

"Nothing," she muttered, and promptly turned her attention back to the window.

"Say it." When she still refused to speak, he decided to add a bit of levity to his voice as he told her, "I promise I'll not toss you out of the carriage."

She gave a soft snort and swung her gaze back to his. "Have you tried to consider this situation from your son's point of view and without your dislike of me clouding your judgment?"

He tilted his head. "How do you mean?"

"If Michael…" She must have noted his disapproval, for she instantly said, "Forgive me, but may I call him Michael?"

James wasn't too comfortable with it, but he supposed it would make their conversation easier. After a brief moment's thought, he nodded. "Go ahead."

"Well, if he truly loves Cynthia, would it not be better for you to try and help him find a way to be with her rather than throwing obstacles in his path?"

Disgruntled by her critical suggestiveness, James crossed his arms and leaned back against the squabs. "Michael may think himself in love but he is still young and his acquaintance with your daughter is too brief for him to be prone to such deep emotion. This is nothing more than a brief infatuation and as such, it would be a travesty if it led to marriage."

"You're certain of this?"

"Quite."

"I hope so." She gave him a most intense look. "Because if you're wrong, trying to force them apart could ruin your relationship with him forever."

"What would you know of such things?" James asked, his anger toward her rising once more on account of the worry he'd felt since learning of Michael's elopement.

"Enough to tell you that young love can be stronger than you think and that trying to quash it can wreck more than one life."

He stared at her. She spoke as if from experience, and to James's shock, he envied the man to whom she'd given her heart. Rattled by the jealous spike he'd felt in response to her words, he asked, "Is that why you did it?"

She did not pretend to misunderstand his meaning. "My marriage was one of convenience, Mr. Dale. That is all I will say on the matter."

When she closed her eyes to block him out, James knit his brow and gave his attention back to the view. Her contradiction of character perplexed him. Something about the facts he'd been given during her divorce hearings did not square with the woman who'd entertained him in a chilly parlor or faced him while covered in dirt. He could not put his finger on where the misalignment was, but it was there – he could sense it – and he would not be satisfied until he found it.

He was not her friend and he did not want her advice. In spite of Wilhelmina's initial sense that Mr. Dale might desire to strike up a conversation for no other purpose than to pass the time, this notion had swiftly crumbled the moment he'd asked her to explain her unfaithfulness. What he wanted was to pry, possibly even to accuse, and if she were to stop him from learning the truth, she'd do well to avoid the subject entirely.

So she watched the fields slide by as they raced after Cynthia and Michael while doing her best not to let the monotony bore her. She thought of George and Fiona who would be trying to figure out where exactly to settle by now and wondered if she would ever see either of them again. Probably not.

The depressing thought caused her eyes to sting. Thus far, she'd been too busy to sit and think – to allow the full weight of her sacrifice to weigh on her heart. Now, with nothing to do besides ponder the events that had led her to this very moment, her mind became overcrowded with memories of her childhood, of how she and George used to swim in the village pond with all the other children, how they'd skate on the ice during winter and climb the cherry trees every spring. A smile tugged at her lips. Later in the year they'd sit in the trees and stuff their faces with those sweet berries until their bellies ached.

When he'd been admitted to Eton, she'd been there to share in his celebration. They'd written each other weekly, and when he'd been denied the woman he loved on account of the Marquess of Ottersburg not finding George good enough for his daughter, Wilhelmina had comforted her friend as best as she could. She was probably the only person in the world who knew he'd never fully recovered from the heartache he'd suffered. He'd only just turned eighteen when he'd made his intentions known. When Lady Katherine had become engaged to the Earl of Merriweather shortly after, George had been crushed.

Three months later, Wilhelmina's life had been turned upside down, and George, confident he would never again find the kind of love he'd harbored for Lady Katherine, had saved her. In hindsight, she shouldn't have let him do it. They'd both been too young to understand the ramifications of their decision to wed. Not that she regretted one moment of her marriage. She'd had her best friend by her side, and Cynthia had been awarded the legitimacy Wilhelmina so dearly wanted for her.

The carriage slowed and drew to a halt, offering Wilhelmina a welcome reprieve from her reminiscing, even as it forced her to face a different kind of torture. With a sigh, she gave her attention to Mr. Dale, who was already in the process of climbing out. He stepped onto the ground, then turned to meet her gaze with directness. His hand came into view as he raised it toward her.

"Allow me to help you alight." His voice was firm yet soft, completely devoid of judgment or displeasure though it did contain a hint of impatience.

Wilhelmina's heart gave an unsteady thump. She scooted along the bench toward the door. Leaning forward, she gripped the opening with one hand and placed the other in his. Strong fingers curled around hers, lending support as she climbed down. Her unsteady heartbeats leapt into a faster rhythm, and to her dismay, she struggled to catch her breath until he released her.

The effect was not dissimilar to the one he'd had on her two years earlier, but it was somehow more unexpected in light of all that had happened since. It also felt stronger – as if her body recognized what she'd been missing, and rejoiced over merely a touch.

"I'm going to inquire after our children." Mr. Dale hesitated briefly as if unsure as to whether or not he ought to say something more. Eventually he asked, "Are you hungry?"

They'd only been on the road for two hours and this was their first stop of many throughout the day.

"Not especially," Wilhelmina said, though she probably would be in a while. She considered Mr. Dale. "You?"

He shrugged in a manner suggesting he might be starving but refused to be the sole cause for delay. "I'll manage."

"We could purchase some bread, ham, and cheese to take along," Wilhelmina suggested once she'd wrestled the smile that threatened due to his grumpy tone back under control.

His features relaxed. "Excellent idea, Mrs. Lawson. I'll be back within a few minutes."

"Make sure to order something for your coachman as well."

Mr. Dale gave her an odd look. "Of course."

As soon as he'd gone inside the inn, Wilhelmina walked around the side of the building and made use of the necessary she found there. She washed her hands at the nearby pump and returned to the front. Mr. Dale arrived soon after with three separate bundles wrapped in cheesecloth. He handed one to the coachman.

"According to the innkeeper, our children stopped for a bite to eat here some five hours ago," Mr. Dale said while sending his coachman an expectant look.

"Seeing as they're on horseback, they'll be tough to catch," the coachman informed them. "It's not impossible though if we make the most of each day and the weather holds."

"Then let us be off," Mr. Dale said. He lent Wilhelmina his hand and helped her back into the carriage before climbing in behind her. The door slammed shut and the vehicle lurched into motion.

Once back on the road, Mr. Dale gave Wilhelmina one of the bundles. "Exactly what you suggested."

"Thank you." She accepted the offering and retrieved her reticule. "How much do I owe you?"

Surprise lit his eyes. "Nothing."

She reached inside the small bag and pulled out some coins. "As much as I appreciate your generosity, I must insist on paying my share."

"Why?"

"Because the last thing I want on top of everything else is for you to think I'm a leech."

He tilted his head as if in thought while studying her. The intensity of his gaze tempted her to avert her own. Instead she forced herself to stare back until he eventually said, "It's a paltry sum I would have been more than happy to cover, but if you insist, I'll not deprive you. A shilling will suffice."

She dropped the coin into his palm, avoiding further contact for the moment. He pocketed it and glanced at the parcel of food he'd placed beside him on the bench. Indecision caught his features. He huffed a breath and looked out the window.

Wilhelmina considered his strained expression. "You don't have to wait with your food on my account. If you're hungry, go ahead."

The edge of his mouth lifted as he glanced her way. "You won't think me rude?"

"Well…" When he frowned, she laughed. "I'm sure I could find a reason to do so, but it won't be for satisfying your appetite."

"Thank you, Mrs. Lawson." He pulled the parcel into his lap and unwrapped it. A roll of bread came into view along with some slices of ham and cheese. Mr.

Dale tore the roll in two and placed the ham and cheese between the halves, then took a bite.

A satisfied sigh filled the air, prompting Wilhelmina to chuckle. "My husband also…"

She stopped herself and bit her lip. She'd spoken in haste and now Mr. Dale was staring at her as if curious to know what she'd left unspoken. Intent on steering his mind away from her ruined marriage, she forced a smile. "How's the food?"

Mr. Dale raised his eyebrows. *I know you're deflecting,* he seemed to say. He nodded. "Tasty."

Wilhelmina leaned back and tried to think of a subject with which to distract her travel companion. Recalling his slightly scruffy appearance when they'd last met, she asked, "Why were you covered in dirt yesterday?"

He watched her while he chewed. Once he'd swallowed the bite he said, "One of my father's tenants is having a flood issue. I was helping him and his sons dig a canal of sorts in order to redirect the water from their farmland. Michael's decision to elope could not have come at a worse time. After I realized he was gone, I had to ask one of the grooms to manage the work on my behalf since I hadn't the time to waste on hiring a laborer."

"Hmm…"

"What?"

"Nothing." She shook her head.

He almost smiled. "Come now, Mrs. Lawson. You're not one to shy away from speaking your mind."

"I wasn't about to do any such thing." When he gave her a look of disbelief she said, "I merely wonder at your decision to work for a living and shovel dirt when I'm sure you don't have to. Most men in your position would welcome the leisure with which they could pass each day, yet you seem determined to struggle while making your son do the same."

He popped the last of his sandwich into his mouth and dusted the crumbs from his hands. After rolling the leftover cheesecloth into a ball, he tossed it onto the bench beside him. "I'm a firm believer in idleness being the enemy of the soul. People need to experience some degree of accomplishment in order to enjoy a sense of worth. This is what I'm attempting to teach Michael."

"I find it commendable and wise."

"Really?" He watched her as if she were an alien creature from another world.

"While other men of privilege will be dependent on their inheritances, your son will be self-reliant. No matter what life throws his way, he will always have the benefit of a useful education."

"Precisely." Mr. Dale stretched out his legs and crossed them at the ankles.

The pose accentuated the snug fit of his breeches and alerted Wilhelmina to the firm contours of his thighs. She sucked in a breath and dragged her gaze away from his legs only to find herself snared by the gleam in Mr. Dale's eyes. The blasted man knew she'd been admiring his physique.

Damn him.

"Now that you know the reason behind my scruffy appearance," he said while she fought the oncoming flush to her cheeks, "perhaps you'd care to share yours?"

She took a deep breath and willed the unpleasant self-awareness she suddenly experienced to subside. Eyeing him, she dared to ask, "Does this mean we've agreed to a temporary truce?"

He dipped his head in agreement. "If you like. I think we can both agree that our journey will hasten along with greater ease if we talk."

"Very well." She would not trust him completely, but she would allow herself to engage in a bit of companionable conversation. "Cynthia and I arrived in Renwick with our maid, Betsy, the day before yesterday to find the house in dire need of cleaning. Yesterday, I managed the animals with the aid of my caretakers while Betsy mopped all the floors and gave the kitchen a good scrub. Cynthia helped her until I asked her to go and purchase a few supplies."

"During which she happened to cross paths with Michael."

"Again, I'm sorry for that. I—"

"A truce, Mrs. Lawson. Remember?"

"Right. Well. The reason I looked as I did was because I'd been mucking out stalls and milking cows."

A frown creased his brow. "Could you not hire additional help?"

Deciding to avoid the subject of her tight budget, she said, "Much like you, Mr. Dale, I see nothing wrong with pitching in when there's work to be done."

He seemed to mull that over for a moment before he said, "Tell me about your family, Mrs. Lawson. If memory serves, you come from Cornwall?"

"Yes. I grew up in a smallish town by the name of Wadefield."

"And your parents?"

"My father was a soldier. He fought in the American War of Independence. During his time in America, he developed a taste for travel and exploration. So when he returned home he quickly left again for other parts of the world."

"Did you and your mother ever go with him?"

"No. He always went with his best friend. I think they were both restless after the war. Fitting back into everyday life was a challenge, or so my mother told me later. I was very young at the time." She took a deep breath before adding, "He died when I was ten. The ship he was on went down in a storm. No one survived."

"I'm sorry."

A nod conveyed her appreciation. "It was devastating. Even though he was largely absent from my childhood, he was still my father. I loved him."

Curiosity danced in his eyes. "What's your fondest memory of him?"

A smile tugged at her lips. "During his last visit he built a bonfire in our garden. I remember the three of us sitting around it and listening to him tell stories of all the marvelous places he'd seen. We stayed up until the early hours of the morning – until my eyes grew heavy and I fell asleep. When I woke later in the day, he was gone."

"My apologies if this is an impolite question to ask, but how could he afford to support you and your mother while being away as much as he was? I mean, a soldier's salary isn't much and after the war he'd have had to find some other work, surely."

"My mother was an heiress in her own right," Wilhelmina confessed. "Not that she was especially wealthy, but she had enough for us to enjoy a comfortable life and to sponsor Papa's adventures. When she passed, she left the remainder of her inheritance to me, her only child."

"And yet, you do not strike me as particularly well off."

Wilhelmina bristled. "Forgive me, Mr. Dale, but do you often make a habit of quizzing people you barely know about their financial situation?"

He started slightly. "I beg your pardon, Mrs. Lawson. How inconsiderate of me."

She crossed her arms. "Perhaps we can speak of something less personal. Like the weather?"

"Heaven forbid," he muttered. "I'd rather perish from boredom."

"Well, we can't have that," she told him in a lighter tone, "Considering my reputation, I'd likely be charged with your murder."

He grinned. "Do you honestly think so?"

She raised an eyebrow. "I am despised, Mr. Dale."

"Would this be the wrong time to remind you that you only have yourself to blame?"

When she didn't respond, he said nothing further. It was as if the mention of her disgrace had ruined the mood. A weight had once again lodged itself in Wilhelmina's breast. She had no desire to argue or give explanations in her defense. In fact, she very much feared she'd reveal too much of the truth if she did talk about her divorce. So she picked up her parcel of food, turned her gaze away from Mr. Dale, and focused on eating so she wouldn't have to speak.

It was six o'clock in the evening by the time they stopped for the night. James climbed out of the carriage and turned to offer Mrs. Lawson his hand. The lady had not said much of anything to him during the course of the last few hours. For the most part, she'd slept – or pretended to do so.

Of course it was all his fault. By reminding her of her wrongdoing, he'd prompted her to retreat. And he'd regretted it ever since because he'd actually enjoyed the conversation they'd shared up until that point. He'd found himself missing it during the dull stretch of time that had followed.

The touch of her hand sent a shock of awareness through him. Unprepared, he sucked in a breath and held it while she stepped down from the carriage. One booted foot came into view, above it a flash of ankle, before Mrs. Lawson's long skirt fell into place with a swish.

Strangely unsteady, James went to collect their bags from the boot. Clasping one in each hand, he led the way inside the inn while Mrs. Lawson followed.

"I'd like to book two rooms for the night along with a spot in the loft for my coachman," he told a large burly fellow who'd introduced himself as Mr. Oaks, the innkeeper.

Mr. Oaks stared at James before shifting his gaze to Mrs. Lawson. "Does your 'usband's snoring bother you or something?"

"He's not my husband," she informed the man in a clipped, no-nonsense manner. "He's my brother. And yes, his snoring does tend to keep me awake."

James glared at her while Mr. Oaks chuckled. "Right then. I'll give you numbers three and five."

James took the keys the innkeeper gave him. "Any chance you've seen a young couple come through here on horseback earlier?"

Mr. Oaks scratched his head. "Blonde woman and dark haired gent in their early twenties?"

"Yes," Mrs. Lawson said. She snapped her mouth shut when Mr. Oaks gave her a curious look.

"Aye," Mr. Oaks said, returning his attention to James. "I'd say they stopped for a change of horses 'round three."

Happy to know they were gaining on Michael and Cynthia to some degree, James nodded his appreciation. Hopefully, an early start in the morning would help them catch up. "I trust the rooms are that way?"

"Straight up the stairs and to your left," Mr. Oaks said.

"Thank you." James started turning away.

"And Madam?" Mr. Oaks said, his eyes once again fixed on Mrs. Lawson. "There's no *Mrs.* Oaks. In case you was wonderin'."

"I can assure you I was not," Mrs. Lawson replied.

"Pity," Mr. Oaks drawled. "It's not every day a woman as lovely as you stops by."

"If you don't mind," James told the impertinent innkeeper tersely, "my sister never said she wasn't married, merely that she's not married to me."

"In that case I do beg your pardon." Mr. Oaks smiled with humor in his eyes. "I'll leave you to go and get settled."

James waited for Mrs. Lawson to precede him, then sent Mr. Oaks one last scowl before following her up the stairs. They reached the landing and quickly located their rooms. Both were small but at least they looked clean.

James set her bag on the only chair her room offered. "Wait for me before going back downstairs. I don't trust Mr. Oaks not to try something with you."

She gave him a hard stare. "Neither do I."

James blinked. The certainty with which she spoke suggested she knew how brutal men could be from experience. He shook himself as the unpleasant thought of her having fought off such a man in the past invaded his mind.

Stepping back before he pressed her for answers, he said, "I'll knock on your door in ten minutes. Is that enough time for you to freshen up?"

"It's fine."

When she started opening her bag, James left and entered his own room. He shut the door and leaned against it with a hard sigh. There were traces of Mrs. Lawson's past in her expressions and the things she said. Earlier today, when she'd mentioned her husband, her face had lit up with fondness before she'd managed to school her features and change the subject. It didn't make any sense. If she'd loved Mr. Hewitt, as James was inclined to believe she might have, then why had she taken lovers?

Because Mr. Hewitt had failed to reciprocate her affection and had engaged in his own trysts?

James scrubbed his hand across his face and dropped his bag on the floor. The person Mrs. Lawson had been revealed to be two years earlier didn't square with the hardworking woman he'd just spent the day with. She'd been principled – had insisted on covering her share of the expenses for heaven's sake.

Straightening, James removed his jacket, waistcoat, and shirt. He filled the ceramic basin that stood on a table near the window, and wrung out a wash cloth. The cool water soothed the ache he'd sustained to his muscles by shoveling dirt. Sitting inside a carriage most of the day had only made him sorer.

He ran the cloth over the back of his neck, then over his chest and arms. An unexpected vision of Mrs. Lawson seeing to her own ablutions beyond the wall to his right sneaked into his head. Stomach tight, he glanced in the direction of her room and muttered a curse. He did not want to find her desirable any more than he wanted Mr. Oaks to do so. And yet, in spite of her representing everything he despised, he still wanted her in ways he knew were unseemly.

It couldn't be helped. His body obviously didn't agree with his brain where she was concerned. And damn it all but there was a niggling feeling that he'd somehow misjudged her. Or maybe he was just trying to make excuses so he could engage in more than conversation with her. Would she even allow him to make an advance? They weren't exactly on the best of terms, so there was a good chance she'd turn him away.

Considering the men who'd claimed to be her lovers and the lack of good looks they'd shared, he wasn't sure he'd survive a rejection from her.

And why the hell was he even letting himself wonder about such things?

They were travel companions. That was all.

James dropped his washcloth into the basin, dried quickly, and found a clean shirt for himself in his bag. Once dressed, he went to knock on Mrs. Lawson's door.

"One moment," she called from within.

James waited. He crossed his arms, uncrossed them again, and studied each plank of wood in the hallway until his veins itched with impatience. He prepared to knock on her door yet again when it suddenly opened, bringing them face to face.

Gone was the bonnet she'd worn since he'd picked her up in the morning, allowing him an uninhibited view of her glorious hair. He'd seen it before of course, and yet he could not seem to stop staring. Her beauty was simply divine, made more so on account of the blush now flooding her cheeks.

"Mr. Dale?"

James quickly offered his arm. "Allow me to escort you."

"That's really not necessary."

So she was still irritated with him. James had to admit he would have been as well, had their roles been reversed. Perhaps it was time for an apology. "I'm sorry about earlier, Mrs. Lawson. I promised a truce and yet I still managed to be accusatory. It would mean a great deal if you could forgive me."

She smiled and his heart sighed with relief. "Thank you, Mr. Dale. I actually enjoyed your company up until that point. It's just difficult for me to pretend a friendship with someone who finds me as lacking as you clearly do."

"You certainly know how to humble a man." He offered his arm once more. "Again, my sincerest apologies. It isn't my place to judge you."

"That doesn't mean you do not have an opinion." She took his arm and allowed him to lead her toward the stairs. "I know it's not a good one where I am concerned, but the nature of my marriage and the actions I chose to take within it don't have to make me a terrible person. Could I not simply be a woman looking to find a bit of happiness for myself?"

James guided her down the stairs while puzzling through her question. Was it possible his opinion of her might be tainted by his own experience with Clara? The world did not approve of wives taking lovers yet barely spared one thought to a husband doing the same. Was that really just? And what business was it of his anyway if Mrs. Lawson had been unfaithful to Mr. Hewitt?

All he knew was the disappointment and disgust he'd felt as soon as he'd been made aware of her actions. But again, maybe that was Clara's doing more than it was Mrs. Lawson's. He honestly wasn't sure anymore. What he did know was that Mrs. Lawson made him question the narrative he'd been fed about her. Which naturally increased his interest.

"Let's order some food and talk about something else," he suggested, not answering her question. "You can tell me about your hobbies."

CHAPTER NINE

S eated at a table in the inn's taproom, Wilhelmina sipped her beer and regarded the man opposite her. He wasn't her friend, no matter how much they tried to pretend otherwise. And yet, here they were, ready to pretend exactly that.

"Are you sure getting to know me better is wise?"

The force of his gaze quickened her pulse. "If the alternative is to pass the remainder of our journey as we did today, mostly in silence, then it is a risk I'm prepared to take."

"What if you start to like me?" The words were intended to tease in a self-deprecating way, to add some levity and ease the tension that always seemed to exist between them.

"Who's to say I don't already?"

Wilhelmina opened her mouth, ready to jump in with countless examples, until she saw he was smiling.

She blew out a breath and allowed a smile of her own. Mr. Dale was trying. He'd handed her an olive branch for the second time that day, and it would be ungrateful of her to decline it.

So she took another quick sip of her beer and considered the topic he had suggested. Hobbies. Not just pastime activities she enjoyed, but actual interests she devoted time to on a regular basis.

"I used to weave a lot. Before we moved to London, that is. The activity always relaxed me."

His eyes lit up. "What sort of things would you make?"

Just then a maid arrived with the food they'd ordered. She set their bowls filled with beef stew before them and went to take another order. Wilhelmina picked up her spoon and inhaled the fragrant smell of cooked meat, vegetables, and spiced broth.

"Any number of items." She took a bite of her food and savored the warming effect it had on her tummy. "My favorite was a set of rainbow-colored cotton towels. They're ridiculously bright, but I get so happy whenever I use them." She chuckled and ate some more, a little embarrassed by the confession. Having Mr. Dale's gaze fixed upon her didn't help. Her cheeks burned with the awareness and prompted her to hastily add, "I also made a couple of woolen blankets, some dish cloths, and even a shawl. The shawl was the hardest. I'm not sure I'll ever attempt one again unless it's plain and simple. But there was this intricate pattern I wanted to try. Took me forever and..."

Wilhelmina stopped herself. She was rambling on and now he'd probably think her batty on top of everything else. Splendid.

"Do you still have your loom?" he suddenly asked.

The note of interest in his voice took her by surprise. She stilled, spoon hovering over her soup, and raised her gaze to his. "I had two. Unfortunately, I was forced to give up the large floor model one because we couldn't make room for it in London, but I still have my tabletop loom, which is big enough for smaller projects. Hopefully, at some point, I'll reacquire a full-sized loom again. And some sheep."

He gave an unexpected laugh. "Sheep?"

"I think it would be wonderful if I could collect the wool myself from sheep I've raised, spin it into yarn, dye it, and weave it into practical items."

A thoughtful look entered his eyes. "Have you ever considered selling your work?"

Wilhelmina grinned. "It wouldn't be much of a hobby anymore if I started profiting from it. Would it? And besides, I'd have to become a lot more productive in order to make a business of it, which I'm just not sure I can. Selling eggs, milk, and baked goods would probably be simpler."

"Baked goods?"

Wilhelmina ducked her head to hide her self-awareness. She'd not meant to mention that, but whether because of nerves or some other reason, Mr. Dale had managed to get her to talk. She bit her lip before admitting, "I also enjoy making bread, pastries, and cakes."

He frowned at his soup as if the dish confounded him in some way, then returned his gaze to hers. Curiosity and something else - a far more subtle emotion she couldn't define - warmed his eyes. "It looks like there's more to you than meets the eye, Mrs. Lawson."

Wilhelmina felt her cheeks heat. She cleared her throat. "I believe the same can be said of most people, Mr. Dale. What about you? What are your hobbies?"

He took a few more bites of stew while she did the same. It was an easily recognizable stalling tactic - one she was guilty of using herself a few moments earlier. He pushed his bowl aside and drank some beer. The tankard thunked against the tabletop when he set it down. Brow knit, he crossed his arms and leaned back in his chair, eyeing her with a cautious sort of pensiveness. Clearly, he was trying to decide on how open to be.

Eventually he sighed and it seemed his shoulders relaxed. "Aside from enjoying the pleasure of a good book, I suppose I like to work with my hands."

"As you did yesterday when you assisted your father's tenant?"

"Not exactly. I'd say that was more of a duty and keenness to help than a hobby. But laying down paving stones at Clarington House in order to create a terrace for my parents, installing new windows at my townhouse in London, or re-plastering the upstairs are projects I have enjoyed."

"And here I was, imagining all you did all day was

pore over legal documents," Wilhelmina told him with a smirk.

He shrugged. "I'll admit I've not had as much time lately as I'd like for my own interests. Being forced to get out of Town and away from my desk was probably a good thing."

She couldn't help but laugh. "I'm sure you don't really believe that."

"I'll admit I'm not fond of my reason for choosing to take a sojourn in the country, but I do think I needed it. Your daughter's persistent interest in Michael was a welcome kick to the backside."

She pressed her lips together while smiling back at him. How easy it would have been for him to use her comment against her - to agree and blame her and Cynthia for giving him trouble. Instead he'd admitted to being grateful for the disruption to his work, even though he didn't approve of the circumstances. Only a man of true integrity would be so honest.

"So the countryside agrees with you then?"

He tilted his head as if in thought. "I'm only in London because the courts are there. If it were up to me though, I'd much rather live far away from the noise and all the busybodies. But I do enjoy arguing complex cases. Challenging my mind keeps it sharp."

"By contrast, I expect working on a house, whether it be your own or your parents', relaxes you."

"It does." He held her gaze and it was as if a deep sense of shared understanding passed between them. He liked laying paving stones much in the same way she enjoyed weaving or baking. Because it soothed the soul and offered a sense of accomplishment that could only come from creating something with one's own hands. He leaned forward and set his elbows on the table. "It also tempts me with all sorts of innovative ideas."

"Such as?"

He shook his head in an almost bashful sort of way before locking eyes with her once again. "You'll think I'm filling my head with impossible notions."

"Possibly," she agreed, "though you'll never know my true opinion unless you tell me what you have in mind."

"Hmm..." He paused for a moment before he said, "The Romans had intricate plumbing systems and underground sewage. John Harrington developed a flushing toilet for Queen Elizabeth - an idea Alexander Cummings expanded upon last century. Yet here we remain, without running water or flushing toilets in even the wealthiest homes. Only America is showing progress in this field. Are you aware that Philadelphia - an entire city - had a water delivery system installed more than a decade ago?"

"I did not." It wasn't really something Wilhelmina thought about, though she supposed such a system would be immensely practical. "I do believe a contraption capable of spraying water into a tub exists."

"You refer to the shower, which is of some interest, I suppose, although that just recycles water over and over again and requires the constant management of a pump. Personally, I'd rather avoid the trouble. But to have a steady flow of water brought upstairs to my bath, now that would be something else, Mrs. Lawson."

The twinkle in his eyes conveyed his passion for the subject. It was so infectious Wilhelmina felt herself caught up in the energy of it. Mesmerized, she could not look away from the man who sat across from her. He was her unexpected travel companion, the most unlikely partner in her quest to find her daughter. A foe turned temporary friend.

That would not go away. Once they caught up with their children, when her need for him and his obligation toward her ended, their truce would cease. She was certain of it, because of the righteous man he was.

But until then, she would allow herself to enjoy a brief reprieve from the solitary existence she could look forward to as a fallen woman.

"I suspect you already have an idea of how to make that happen," she mused, hoping he might elaborate on his plans.

A smile pulled at his lips, affording him with a youthful roguishness. The expression swept all remaining traces of seriousness from his face. "Of course, but maybe it would be best to wait with that until tomorrow's ride? Considering the hour and our early departure, I would suggest we retire for the evening."

"You're right." Wilhelmina withdrew the cost of her meal from her skirt pocket and placed it on the table. While Mr. Dale did raise an eyebrow, he didn't comment this time.

Instead he stood, added his own payment to hers, then offered his arm and escorted her upstairs to her bedchamber.

Releasing her when they reached her door, he took a step back. "Shout if you need anything, Mrs. Lawson."

His dark piercing gaze sent a curious thrill down her spine. She shivered slightly and hugged herself. "Thank you, Mr. Dale. I'll see you in the morning. Good night."

She entered her room and gently closed the door, leaving him there in the dimly lit hallway. Only when she'd turned the key did she hear him move away. A smile pulled at her lips as she leaned against the wall. He might not like what he thought she'd done, but he cared enough to protect her from the likes of Mr. Oaks. And that in itself made her heart swell with appreciation and fondness.

James wasn't sure what he was doing, but he was beginning to think he might be a terrible judge of character. Either that, or very confused. Hell, Mrs. Lawson was a baffling woman - a conundrum he couldn't quite seem to figure out. He watched her now as they continued their northbound journey. The food the inn had prepared for them was wrapped and stowed on the seat next to James. Much to his relief, Mr. Oaks had not caused any trouble, allowing James to avoid an unpleasant altercation.

The last thing he needed right now was having to defend a woman about whom he wasn't sure how he felt. Everything was hot and cold with her. Initially, at the Pennington ball he'd been drawn to her beauty and the joy she emanated. That same evening, he'd felt as though the princess he'd admired had turned into some hideous slug. Then came the hearings, next the difficult situation involving her daughter and Michael, and now...

If he were being totally honest, he'd really enjoyed her company yesterday. Especially their conversation during dinner. She'd shown a keen interest in his pursuits, which was rather nice for a change since neither his friends nor Michael enjoyed discussing plumbing at great length. But could he allow himself to view her as anything other than a villainous harridan - as the weaver and baker she had described? Would it not be unwise to do so?

He wasn't sure. Then again, when it came to Mrs. Lawson, James was starting to think there might be a lot of things he was no longer sure of. Like the villainous harridan part. Which posed a problem since this was the keystone to his opinion of her. Without it, everything he believed to be true about her fell apart.

"Did you sleep well?" he asked, deciding to pack away these complicated musings for now.

"Yes. And you?"

"Well enough."

A soft smile deepened the blue in her eyes. "I forgot

to ask about your friends yesterday. Mr. Grey and Mr. West, I believe? How are they doing?"

"They were both in good spirits when last I saw them." James hesitated briefly, unsure of how much to share about the personal details of his life. Deciding to welcome her thoughtfulness, he puffed out a breath and added, "We meet on the twenty-first of March every year to honor our friend, Mr. Richard Hughes, who died during the Battle of Aboukir."

"I'm sorry for your loss."

"As am I. Hughes left this world long before his time."

"Too many people do. Like my father and his friend. Or my son-in-law." A pained look overcame her. "Cynthia was made a widow a year and a half after her marriage."

James sympathized. "That must have been terribly hard on her."

"It was." She seemed to consider him for a moment before she said, "It must have been hard on you too when your wife passed away. Raising a child on your own cannot have been easy."

James held her gaze while the usual displeasure he experienced whenever he thought of Clara chilled his blood. It also served as a swift reminder of who Mrs. Lawson was and what she was capable of. As much as he liked her company and sought to see the best in her, she'd broken her vows and made a mockery of her marriage.

With this in mind, he told her evenly, "I managed."

She gave him a quizzical look, but refrained from prying further. Clearly she'd hoped he'd expand, but speaking of Clara was out of the question. It was time for them to move on.

"Last night I promised I'd tell you more of my indoor plumbing ideas. I'm happy to do so now if you are still interested."

Relief swept her features. "Absolutely."

Relaxing as much as he could in the wake of the tension she'd foisted upon him, he cleared his throat and began. "The Romans relied on gravity to move water through pipes. Archimedes, however, invented an ingenious method by which to push water upward using a screw - driven technique. However, I am more interested in the Savery pump which runs on steam. According to my research, mines have used such a device, though not too effectively since their depth makes it hard to maintain decent pressure. But for a house, I'd imagine it ought to be most effective."

"It would be useful if water no longer had to be hauled upstairs in jugs or buckets." Mrs. Lawson tapped her chin. "Would it be possible to heat it prior to delivery?"

"I wondered the same thing, so I'm actually working on trying to solve that problem. Some upper-class homes already have a copper connected to a hot water heating system. But these depend on thermo syphoning to circulate heat and won't deliver water as fast as I want."

"But if you combine this idea with the copper and add the pump you mentioned—"

"Then one should be able to bring hot water to an upstairs bedroom or, if space allows, to a separate bathing room. Of course, one would still need to find a way in which to adjust the temperature so the water isn't too hot, but I do believe that's a minor detail."

Mrs. Lawson stared at him in wonder, and then she said, "Last night you suggested I might think this idea impossible or even foolish. But the fact is, Mr. Dale, I think it's brilliant."

James sucked in an unsteady breath. He'd not realized how much her opinion mattered to him until then. His heart tripped over. Not even Michael, West, or Grey had been so supportive. To be sure, they'd patiently listened to his idea, but in the end they'd thought it complicated, too hard to implement, and near impossible to realize. Mrs. Lawson on the other hand marveled at his creativity. Whether achievable or not, she believed in him, and that alone made him want to pull her into his arms and kiss her.

Not that he'd ever be quite so bold, but the sudden enthusiasm pumping through his veins was as hard to ignore as the woman who presently watched him as though he could do whatever he set his mind to.

"Thank you, Mrs. Lawson."

A sweet pink hue colored her cheeks. "Perhaps you'll allow me to see your preparatory notes and sketches one day? Or better yet, the final result?"

"How do you know I have notes and sketches?"

Truly, the woman confounded him every day for different reasons.

"All inventors do. Do they not?"

His mouth fell open. He'd been many things in his life so far: a son, a brother, a soldier, a husband, a father, and a barrister. But he'd never been an inventor until Mrs. Lawson turned him into one with her blasé remark.

"They're in London, I'm afraid."

"Of course they are." She turned her gaze to the window, though not before he managed to catch a hint of sadness in her expression.

His words, the implication that there would never be another moment like this for them in the future, no shared discourse or exchange of ideas, no notes or sketches for him to show her, and no display of the final result, had hurt her. Because they both knew that once they reached Scotland, this partnership of sorts they'd acquired would end, and they'd each go their separate ways.

Oddly depressed by the notion, James eyed the food beside him. "Care for something to eat?"

She took a moment, perhaps to gather her composure, before she turned back to face him. Eyes brighter than he'd ever seen them, she dealt him a tremulous smile. "As a matter of fact, I would."

CHAPTER TEN

As they raced onward, lighter conversation helped pass the time. They spoke about books, their favorite spots in London, and places they'd like to visit. At some point, Wilhelmina's eyes grew heavy, and when she opened them again, she learned she'd slept for two hours.

"Are you certain I cannot persuade you to let me pay for our food and board tonight?" Mr. Dale asked when they'd agreed to stop for the night at the next inn they reached. It was nearing six o'clock. If they pressed on they would get caught on the road in the dark, subjecting themselves to the hazard of low visibility for the coachman or worse, to highwaymen. So as much as they wished to catch up with their children, they had little choice if they were to travel safely.

"Quite, Mr. Dale. I'd never permit myself to take advantage of any acquaintance in such a way."

He angled his head and studied her in a contemplative manner. "Surely these last two days make us more than mere acquaintances, Mrs. Lawson. Indeed, I would more readily call you my friend."

"As honored as I am to hear you say so, I fear you may be fooling us both by suggesting such a thing. For although we may have found a brief reprieve from our differences, you would not wish to be associated with me in public. After all, is that not the basis for this entire journey? To prevent a connection between us?"

"It is. But…"

"But?"

He narrowed his gaze upon her, causing her to shift with sudden discomfort. It was almost as though he saw past her façade to that which she tried to hide from the world. A shiver ran the length of her spine. She stiffened her shoulders and braced herself for what he might say.

"Having gotten to know you better, I find it increasingly hard to believe you are capable of being the unfaithful wife you've been portrayed as."

Fear crept through her until she could scarcely move. All she could do was sit there, frozen in place while holding his gaze. "I assure you, Mr. Dale, I am no saint. You heard the testimonies against me yourself. I saw you in court."

"Yes. I was there and I will admit my opinion of you was influenced by what I heard. As a barrister, it's in my nature to judge the evidence, and the evidence against you was certainly damning."

"So there you have it," she managed, though the words were not as exacting as she had hoped. "If you don't mind, I've rather enjoyed a reprieve from it all these past two days. If we could continue avoiding the subject until we find our children, I would be grateful."

"The thing is though," he said, still watching her in a manner that made her squirm, "I was married to the very kind of person you are supposed to be, so I know what cool indifference looks like now. I recognize selfish disregard for others and the sort of woman who only seeks to please herself. While I'll admit you seemed that way in court when all you had to do was sit and respond to occasional questions, you no longer do."

Worried the sacrifice she'd made would be for nothing and the legitimacy of George's new marriage threatened if Mr. Dale learned the truth, Wilhelmina steeled herself in preparation for battle. She leaned forward slightly and forced her mouth into a wicked smirk. "Would it help if I told you that when we met at the Pennington ball, I meant to proposition you?"

Mr. Dale's eyes flared, though not with the horrified shock she'd hoped for, but rather with interest. "Really?"

She swallowed. Since the moment they'd been introduced, she'd felt a magnetic pull to this man. He'd made her long for what she could not have. His anger and resentment toward her had not lessened the attraction. In a curious way, it had somehow turned it into a crackling ball of energy constantly on the brink of bursting.

"You're incredibly handsome," she added before including the part she hoped would remind him of his disgust for her. "More so than the rest of my lovers. The way I saw it, you would have been quite the conquest."

He leaned toward her, closing the distance between them farther. Wilhelmina's breath hitched as prickly awareness caressed her skin. His features were drawn in tight lines, but the darkness swirling within the depth of his gaze suggested he might not be averse to what she was saying. In truth, there was no anger to be found there, but rather impassioned desire.

"Then why, pray tell, have you made no advances toward me since we departed from Renwick?" He reached out before she was ready and placed his hand on her knee. Wilhelmina drew a shuddering breath and struggled to keep her cool while a shock of heat spread up her thigh. Mr. Dale stared at his hand for a moment before slowly curling his fingers into her flesh. He dragged his gaze back to hers and gave her a devilish smile. "You've had two full days in which to do so."

Good lord, she was a fool. In her effort to prove her point she'd maneuvered herself into dangerous territory. Reputed to be a woman of the world, a seducer of men who cared not for their hearts but only for how well she could use them, she ought to be able to spurn Mr. Dale's advance with some flip remark.

But as a woman who'd never experienced passion until she'd met him, who'd not known the meaning of having her senses stirred by a man until her body quivered with need, who'd no idea what it was like to engage in lovemaking with a partner who showed her respect and who cared for her pleasure as much as she cared for his, she'd no idea what to say.

And yet, she knew she had to act quickly if she was to make him believe she was every bit as bold and seductive as the woman she pretended to be. Driven by instinct, she placed her hand over his and closed the distance between them until their lips met. Before she could fully appreciate the ramifications of her actions, a strong arm swept around her and pulled her onto the opposite bench.

She gasped in response, allowing him to deepen the kiss in a way she would never have thought herself capable of enjoying. Only one other man had ever had his mouth on hers before, and it had been far from pleasant. His tongue had forced its way inside while frantic hands ripped at her bodice and hitched up her skirts. By contrast, this was exciting in a way she'd not believed possible until now. Somehow, in the fervent craving of this kiss and the heat of his touch, Mr. Dale managed to make her feel beautiful, wanted, and desired, rather than weak and used. Perhaps because she wanted him in equal measure? No, it was more than that. It was because she knew he would stop if she asked him to, and that made a world of difference.

His hands held her steady while the carriage raced onward, keeping pace with the beats of her heart. A satisfied groan rumbled through him, vibrating from his body straight into hers. She gripped his shoulders to steady herself against the storm he produced within her. This experience was unlike any she'd had before and far more wonderful than she would ever have thought it could be. Frankly, she did not want it to end. Instead, she wanted more.

"We probably shouldn't be doing this," Mr. Dale murmured while pressing her closer. His mouth roamed over her cheek before scorching a path down the side of her neck. "I'm sure it's a very bad idea, but I can't seem to stop."

She angled her head to welcome each kiss, then gasped when his teeth scraped her skin. The effect was like a thunderbolt to her nerves. Every part of her body hummed as her bodice drew taught across her breasts. "Then don't."

Instead of progressing, he leaned back, adding distance and leaving a chill in his stead. His hand rose to her cheek, his fingers gently stroking her there while his eyes held hers. "As much as I'd like to heed your command, we probably should."

Wilhelmina gazed at him in bewilderment. She wasn't used to this sort of thing and didn't quite understand what had happened or why he no longer wished to continue. "I'm not some innocent debutante, Mr. Dale. Quite the contrary."

"Nevertheless." He took her hand in his, pushed the glove back enough to expose her wrist, and then raised it to his lips for a reverent kiss.

Unsure of what it all meant, she shook her head and

withdrew to the opposite bench where she straightened her skirts and attempted to gather her frayed composure. "I do not comprehend you, Mr. Dale. Indeed, you confuse me beyond compare."

"No more than you confuse me, Mrs. Lawson. I assure you."

She knit her brow and glanced at him. Reclining against his corner, arms crossed and legs stretched out at an angle, he wore the expression of someone attempting to make a tough calculation. Deciding it might be best if she gave her attention elsewhere, she turned to the view of wide open Lincolnshire fields and meadows preceding the hillier landscape they'd find farther north.

James' mind and body were both in turmoil. He'd not intended to kiss her, but then again, he hadn't. Mrs. Lawson had been the initiator. *She* had kissed *him*, and in so doing, she'd unwittingly shown him her hand. Because one thing was now abundantly clear. Either her husband and her lovers had been deplorable tutors in the art of seduction, or she was as untried as a virgin.

Neither possibility made an ounce of sense. She was a mother after all, so even if she and her husband had grown estranged over the years, she had some experience. Even Clara had learned how to kiss well before she'd gone off to another man's bed. It didn't take extensive practice, but what he'd just enjoyed with Mrs.

Lawson suggested a confounding degree of ignorance on her part. Indeed, it was as if she'd never been kissed before.

Not that he minded this in the least. The possibility she wasn't nearly as worldly as she wanted people to think only increased his desire for her. It was also what caused him to stop. With everything else he'd learned about her in recent days taken into account, he knew he had to give serious thought to his assumptions before he made a mistake and treated her like the wanton he'd once believed her to be.

But if she wasn't guilty of multiple counts of adultery, why on earth had she not protested the charges? Why hadn't she tried to fight her husband's accusations? Could it be because she'd not thought she had a chance of winning?

No. She'd actively gone along with his claims and continued to do so even now. James was still trying to make sense of this when the carriage drew to a halt. He opened the door and stepped down, then offered Mrs. Lawson his hand to help her alight. It seemed unfathomable to him that a woman her age, who'd been married and given birth, would be as innocent as she appeared to be.

She did not meet his gaze as he handed her down, prompting him to make an attempt at expelling the awkwardness brewing between them. "I hope you will join me for dinner again this evening."

Accepting his arm, she gave a stiff nod. "Of course."

Relieved, James grabbed their bags and led her inside while his coachman saw to the horses. "We'll inquire after our children first, then see about booking rooms." Thankfully, the innkeeper at this establishment, a Mr. Sellers, was an older fellow who looked to be in his seventies. Best of all, he was married to a pleasant woman for whom he had nothing but smiles and warm glances. Not once did he show an indecent interest in his Mrs. Lawson.

James stopped himself and shook his head. She wasn't his. Not by a long shot.

"I wonder if you've seen a young couple come through here earlier today," James inquired of the innkeeper.

"The woman is blonde and roughly this tall," Wilhelmina said while holding her hand an inch above her own head.

"The man she's with has dark brown hair," James added. "They may have gone by the name of Dale."

"Hmm..." Mr. Sellers scratched his head. "I saw two young couples who fit that description. One spent the night and left this morning. The other stopped by around four, to swap out their 'orses. One pair came by buggy, the other was ridin' which was somethin' of a sight with the lady sittin' astride, but neither went by Dale."

"How about Lawson, Petersen, or Hewitt?" Mrs. Lawson asked.

"None of those names rings a bell. The couple who spent the night went by Ross, but I did over 'ear the other lady callin' the gent she was with Michael, if that's any 'elp."

"It is," James said. Apparently they'd assumed a false surname. "Thank you very much."

"We're still far behind them," Mrs. Lawson said as she climbed the stairs moments later with James close behind her. "I worry we'll never catch up."

"They did have a good head start," James told her, doing his best to ignore the alluring sway of her hips. He tightened his grip on the bags he carried. "They're also on horseback, which makes them faster, but if we set out early tomorrow we might be able to gain on them. Michael isn't a morning person. He's always enjoyed sleeping in."

"So has Cynthia."

"There's our solution then. If we rise at five we'll be ready to set out as soon as it starts getting light. Or is that too early for you?"

"I can be up by then," she assured him.

They'd reached their rooms and just like the previous evening, James carried Mrs. Lawson's bag into her chamber and set it on a chair. Whether because of her close proximity to him in this confined space or because their kiss was still fresh in his mind, James's gaze instinctively moved to the bed.

Disturbed by the wicked intentions she stirred in him, he quickly retreated to the door. "I'll knock when I'm ready to go back down. In ten to fifteen minutes?"

"All right."

James glanced at her and noted she avoided looking

directly at him. Clearly she wished to ignore the issue that hung between them like a thundercloud waiting to burst. He'd never been a coward, though, and he wasn't about to start being one now, so he cleared his throat. "About earlier. I—"

"Perhaps we should chalk it up to a momentary lapse in judgment on both our parts?"

He blinked. So she meant to go on as before, as if the spectacular kiss they'd shared had never happened. Well, he didn't suppose he could blame her, considering their odd relationship. Still, her rejection stung. More than he ever would have expected.

Irritated, James gave a curt nod. "If that's what you wish."

She started as if he'd just pushed her. Wide blue eyes stared back at him in dismay, until she managed to get a grip on whatever emotions she warred with. She crossed her arms. "It is."

"Fine."

"Fine."

James stared at her for a moment more before turning on his heels and walking away. A bit of cold water to his face would soothe the burning sensation he felt at the back of his neck. Damn Mrs. Lawson for making him want her and damn him for goading her into kissing him. He'd never be able to rid his mind of how good she felt in his arms or how sweet she tasted, how perfect she was because of the innocence she had revealed. And God help him if he didn't want more.

The worst part was when it came to her, he feared he'd always want more.

But she was right to deny them more intimacy. It wasn't as if they stood a chance in hell of sharing a future. Even the friendship they'd managed to forge through conversation and shared experiences these past two days would come to an end once their journey was over. It didn't really matter if she wasn't the heartless adulteress her husband had made her out. The world believed her to be this person, which pretty much meant that was who she was from now on. Guilty or not.

As such, James could not permit himself to get closer to her, not just for Michael's sake but for his own. At best, Mrs. Lawson would cause tongues to wag. At worst, she'd destroy his career. For who would want to hire a barrister willing to associate with someone of such ill repute?

"Damn!"

He freshened up with jerky movements and went to collect her. She accepted the arm he offered and together they made their way down to the dining room without saying a word. It was awkward and awful. James hated every second. He wanted things to go back to how they'd been before they'd kissed, but to do so he'd have to re-write the past. Impossible.

Thankfully a maid soon arrived to take their order, providing them with a brief reprieve from what could only be described as the most uncomfortable situation he'd ever had to endure.

"The lamb sounds good to me," he said.

"I'll have the pork," Mrs. Lawson said.

James glanced at her. "Beer or wine? We could share a jug of red, if you like?"

When she gave a swift nod he put in the order. The maid departed and they were once again left with little to say. James wracked his brain. It hadn't been this difficult before. He just had to think of a subject, that was all.

"My parents had a clock almost identical to the one right over there," she suddenly murmured with a sort of breathy sentimentality that would suggest her thoughts had strayed to the past. "It stood in our parlor." A soft chuckle accompanied a winsome smile. "My father inherited it from his parents."

James turned in the direction she was looking and spotted the piece she referred to. It was a beautifully crafted longcase clock. At a glance, it appeared to be made from oak and walnut.

"It's beautiful."

"Mmm. I'm not sure how many functions that one has. I'd need to inspect it more closely. But ours could do a lot more than tell the time." Her sparkling eyes met his and James's heart leapt. "Besides indicating the hours and minutes, it showed the date, the cycle of the moon, as well as the times of high tide at London Bridge. It was ingenious. I used to study it for hours, watching the hands and dials turn and click into place."

James grinned, prompting her to sharpen her gaze. "What?"

The maid returned just then with their wine. "The food will be along shortly," she said.

As soon as she'd walked away, James filled Mrs. Lawson's glass and then his own. "I just had this image of you as a little girl in short skirts and a pinafore, with long plaits on either side of your head, marveling over a clock."

She pursed her lips. "Just so you know, I rarely wore plaits. My hair was almost always down until I reached the age of sixteen and Mama insisted I start to pin it."

James's stomach clenched in response to a new and far more provocative image – of her hair spilling down her naked back, or better yet, strewn across his pillow. He shifted in his seat and desperately reached for his wine. "To wonderful memories."

With a grateful sort of smile that caused heat to swirl in the pit of his stomach, she raised her glass as well and drank. Their food arrived and they both dug in. Somehow, with the mention of the clock, the awkwardness from before had been replaced by conviviality. James no longer felt the need to fill the silence between them with inane conversation. He was comfortable simply sharing a meal at the same table as her.

A few sips of wine and bites of food later, he did decide to say something though. Whether unwise or not, he feared he'd never forgive himself if he weren't completely honest with her. "You should know that I don't regret kissing you." He waited for her to meet his gaze before admitting, "It's the best kiss I've ever had."

Her lips parted. Dismay filled her eyes. "You ended it though."

"Only because I worried where it might lead."

She shook her head as if with incomprehension. "Considering what you know of me, I confess I'm surprised. Most men in your position would have taken advantage, and while I must admit a part of me wishes you'd take more liberties, I appreciate your restraint and consideration."

It was James's turn to gape at her. She wished he'd take more liberties? By God he was a saint for not dragging her upstairs this second and showing her just how many liberties he'd like to take. He closed his eyes briefly and shook off his lustful notions before he dared look at her again.

Expelling a breath, he told her plainly, "You muddle my head, Mrs. Lawson."

"How so?" Somehow, she managed to sound genuinely puzzled.

James sat back in his chair, utterly stumped. "Because you wear the veneer of a harlot and yet underneath it all, you seem to be as chaste as a maiden."

"I've borne a child, Mr. Dale." A hint of annoyance clung to each word.

"You've also been married to a man who is both young and handsome. I am aware of all this and yet there's something about you that doesn't add up."

"I thought you said you liked the kiss – that it was the best you've ever had."

"Because it suggested you'd never been kissed

before. That I was your first. Except that cannot possibly be. I know it's ridiculous and yet I can't shake the feeling that you're not anywhere near as corrupt as you would have me believe. I just can't imagine why you'd want to misrepresent yourself like that and—"

"I'm not misrepresenting anything," she told him firmly. Leaning forward, she glared at him from across the table. Her eyes shone like shards of broken ice caught in the sun. Lowering her voice, she said, "If you like, I can show you. Shall we go back upstairs?"

Every last vestige of honorability crumbled in the face of what she offered. Here was his chance to have her. She was propositioning him and in spite of his conflicting thoughts about her, he did not have the will to resist. Not when he knew he'd always regret turning her down – would always wonder what he'd missed out on.

So he steadied himself, expelled a deep breath, and prepared to dive into a situation that would in all likelihood lead to disaster, when a familiar voice drew his attention. It was one of those moments in which he prayed he was mistaken, where reality seemed to slow to a near halt as blood rushed through his veins. He turned, hoping to find another man than the one he feared he would see.

Unfortunately, luck was not on his side.

~

Standing by the bedchamber window in the room of the inn where she and Michael had stopped for the night, Cynthia gazed out at the darkness beyond while trying to find her courage. They'd been on the road together for two days now and still she'd not managed to share the matter that pressed upon her with such force it seemed to squeeze the air from her lungs.

Talking wasn't easy while tearing along the North Road on horseback. They'd had stops but all had been made with a sense of haste and urgency that made it hard for her to confide the monumentally important detail she'd thus far omitted. Their meals and evenings spent together before retiring had offered the most appropriate opportunities. But when she tried to think of how to ease into the subject she had to address, her stomach flipped over while nervous jitters made her skin shiver, and then before she knew it her chance had passed.

Time for hesitation was swiftly running out, however. No matter the risk, she had to reveal the one thing she knew might ruin her chance of marrying Michael forever. And because she loved him, she had to give him the chance he deserved to make an informed decision – she had to protect him from the unhappiness that had destroyed Henry's love.

One thing was certain: she would not start her second marriage with a deception.

So she took a deep breath in preparation of his rejection, and turned with every intention of forcing the truth from her throat. Only to see that Michael was stretched out upon the bed, eyes closed, while his chest rose and fell with slow movements. A soft snore followed and Cynthia sighed in response before climbing onto the bed beside him and snuggling close to his side.

CHAPTER ELEVEN

P anic had driven Wilhelmina to make the most preposterous suggestion ever. She knew she played a dangerous game where Mr. Dale was concerned, but when he'd revealed his suspicions to her she'd determined to prove him wrong. Judging from the gleam in his eyes, he had every intention of taking her up on her scandalous offer.

Her heart pounded with trepidation, though not without some degree of excitement as well. Since the moment they'd met, the pull she experienced in his presence had been steadily growing. It didn't matter if he spoke to her in anger or showed resentment toward her. She still wanted him with a primitive sort of fierceness that scared the living daylight out of her whenever she stopped to think on the subject.

It was like a fated connection – the sort one could

not escape no matter how fast one tried to run in the opposite direction. And to actually lie with him...

If their kiss had been a fiery experience their coupling would surely incinerate her.

Voices from newly arrived guests sounded from somewhere off to her left. Mr. Dale's gaze shifted and then his expression darkened. Instinctively, Wilhelmina turned to discover the cause of his upset. And instantly froze as the blood in her veins turned to ice.

"Cloverfield." She barely got the word out.

"You're acquainted with him?" The lack of warmth to Mr. Dale's voice chilled her even further.

"No. I mean once... It was a long time ago and... Different." She shook her head. This man bore a striking resemblance to another she'd once known, yet it couldn't be him. He was much too young, so this must surely be his son.

"It doesn't sound as though you wish to cross paths with him any more than I do. So let's go. Before he or his friends see us."

Somehow, Wilhelmina managed to stand. Her head felt as though it was upside down, her legs too weak to carry her weight. Memories she'd long since buried rose to the surface and flooded her mind. She gripped the back of her chair even as her hand shook.

"Mrs. Lawson?"

She pressed her eyes shut, willing away the unpleasantness as it pressed in upon her with suffocating force. An arm swept around her, steadying her against a solid frame.

"It's all right," Mr. Dale murmured next to her ear. "Just lean on me."

She managed a nod and carefully opened her eyes, then took a step forward. Somehow, little by little, they moved toward the dining room exit. But before they managed to reach it, Cloverfield stepped into their path.

"Well, I'll be," the duke said with an arrogant snort. "If it isn't the infamous divorcée I've been hoping to meet. And you're with Mr. Dale, I see. How deliciously unexpected yet wonderfully useful since he can now see to the introductions."

Wilhelmina felt Mr. Dale's already tight muscles strain even further. "Mrs. Lawson. Allow me to present the Duke of Cloverfield. Your Grace, this is Mrs. Lawson."

Gleaming green eyes bore into hers. A smirk formed upon the duke's lips as he bowed. "A pleasure. I assure you."

"Likewise," she replied even though it was nothing of the sort. Handsome as sin, Cloverfield had to be ten years younger than she at least. But this was not the reason why he failed to make her pulse race. Rather, it had everything to do with the fact that the man reminded her of a venomous snake. Stiff and with a very distinct urge to flee, she held on tightly to Mr. Dale's arm.

"If you'll forgive me for prying," the duke went on in a blasé tone while dropping his gaze to the spot where Wilhelmina's hand latched onto Mr. Dale.

"What brings the two of you to these parts together?"

Wilhelmina sucked in a breath. It felt like her blood was struggling to squeeze its way through her veins. Also, she feared she might be violently ill at any moment due to the sickening memories swamping her brain. Cloverfield looked too much like his father. She needed to get away from him before she burst into tears, cast up her accounts, or started to scream. None of which would help her situation.

"I am escorting Mrs. Lawson," Mr. Dale said.

The duke grinned. "I can see that." His eyes darkened as all signs of humor vanished. "I wish to know why."

Apparently, he believed impertinence to be his right. Wilhelmina bristled. While it might be best to keep quiet and let Mr. Dale handle the situation, she decided to speak. "He's a longtime family friend."

Her intention had been to cement a solid relationship between herself and Mr. Dale in the hope the duke would back off and leave them in peace.

Instead, he responded with a low chuckle – the sort she imagined a murderer might be inclined to produce right before he slashed one's throat. Her skin pricked on account of the cool sweat sweeping her shoulders. She shivered in response.

"Is he really?" the duke asked. He leaned toward her, infusing every fiber of her being with extreme discomfort. "And how, pray tell, do you reward him for his loyalty, Mrs. Lawson?"

Mr. Dale drew her back a step, pushing her slightly behind him. "You insult us both with your implication." The duke did not look the least bit put off by Mr. Dale's accusation. He merely shrugged and shoved his hands into his pockets. "Very well. If you prefer me to speak frankly, then answer me this. Is Mrs. Lawson under your protection, Mr. Dale?"

"Yes."

Wilhelmina was too shocked to respond in any form whatsoever. Mr. Dale hadn't hesitated. He'd answered promptly and in so doing, had practically informed the man that she was his mistress.

Cloverfield's jaw tightened for a moment. He looked on the verge of launching a verbal attack. But then he took a deep breath, straightened, and offered them each a tight smile. "In that case, I do apologize. Considering your renown, Mrs. Lawson, I merely sought to discover if you were available to me or not."

"She is not," Mr. Dale reiterated.

"Quite." Wilhelmina did not care for the pensive look the duke gave her. As if sensing her wariness, he suddenly turned and swept his arm toward the table where the friends he'd arrived with were sitting. "Perhaps you'd care to join us. After all, it's not every day one has the chance to enjoy the company of a lady who has graced the front page of every paper in the land."

"Thank you," Wilhelmina said, "but I've had a long day and prefer to retire. Good evening, Your Grace."

While Cloverfield did not look pleased, he inclined his head and gave a short bow. "Perhaps we'll meet again in the coming days." When neither Wilhelmina nor Mr. Dale commented quickly enough, he explained, "My friends and I are bound for the new Earl of Brixton's estate in Carlisle."

Wilhelmina could only manage a tight nod. She did not hear what Mr. Dale said since she was too busy considering Carlisle's proximity to Gretna Greene where they themselves were headed. They'd have to stop twice more along the way, with a good chance of crossing paths with Cloverfield again.

"I despise that man," Mr. Dale muttered while escorting Wilhelmina upstairs a few moments later. "Sorry for overstepping, but I thought it best for him to believe we're involved."

"Well, you are protecting me, in a sense," she said in a hopeless attempt at levity. "My comment about your being a longtime friend was more of a lie than anything you said."

"You were wise to say what you did. I just hope it's enough." Mr. Dale drew her to a halt in front of her bedchamber door. "Cloverfield strikes me as the sort of man who likes getting his way, and he was very clear about wanting you."

Wilhelmina shuddered with vile displeasure. "The very idea disgusts me."

"So I gathered, based on your overall response to him. In spite of his crudeness, your reaction was stronger than what seemed normal. As such, I cannot help but wonder if this is truly the first time you've met him."

"It is."

Mr. Dale studied her face for a moment, then slowly nodded. "All right, Mrs. Lawson. I suggest you get some sleep. Given this turn of event, I'd like us to leave this place in the morning before Cloverfield rises. Lock your door and rest assured, I will protect you if necessary. Just give me a shout if you need anything."

The altercation with the duke had clearly made him forget about the proposition she'd made, for which she was grateful. It had been done on a whim, and now that they were at her door, she wasn't sure she was ready to follow through on her offer.

"Thank you, Mr. Dale." Without warning, he leaned in and pressed a tender kiss to her brow before retreating a step. Befuddled, Wilhelmina unlocked her door and entered her room. When she turned, she found him watching her with a new sort of look she couldn't quite read.

"Good night, Mrs. Lawson."

She echoed his words and closed the door, shutting out the one man she'd ever wanted to share her bed with. Unsure what her feelings for him were, unable to untangle her desire from the increasing fondness with which he filled her heart, she crossed the floor and started undressing.

Once her clothes were neatly folded and stacked on a chair, she slipped into bed. The glow from the dying flames in the grate provided the room with a cozy feel that eased Wilhelmina's troubled mind until she finally slept.

Only to be awakened later that night by the touch of a hand.

She did not want to leave her dream-like state where Mr. Dale kissed her with wild abandon. Shifting onto her back, she tried to hold on to the perfect press of his lips against hers and the glorious feel of his body settling against her own. Lord, how she wanted this. Except there was something about it that wasn't quite right. The fumes of alcohol on his breath didn't fit the man she'd gotten to know.

"You're just as willing as I expected," a low voice purred against the edge of her mouth. Wilhelmina gasped in horror, which only made Cloverfield chuckle. "I see you enjoy my touch."

His fingers dug into her thigh with bruising force but before she could scream, his mouth covered hers once more. She was fully awake now, fully aware of whom she was with, and it wasn't the man she wanted. Indeed, this was a nightmare she'd already lived through twenty-one years ago. Back then, she'd been too young, too terrified, and too weak to fight back. This time, however, would not be the same.

With every intention of stopping what Cloverfield planned, she started to struggle. Placing her hands against his chest she attempted to shove him away while trying to roll out from underneath him. It was to no avail. He simply grabbed her arms and, clasping her wrists in one hand, pushed them behind her head where he held them in place.

She kicked and wriggled and silently cried out against the assault on her mouth while he shoved his hand up under her nightgown. Desperate to stop him, she did the only remaining thing she could think of, and bit down hard on his tongue.

A howl of pain accompanied the taste of blood on her lips. She called out for Mr. Dale as loud as she could, barely making herself heard before the duke's palm connected with her cheek in a stinging blow that vibrated through her skull.

"Bitch," Cloverfield sputtered so harshly his spittle landed upon her face.

"Mr. Dale!"

Cloverfield's hands closed around her throat. "Make one more sound and I'll—"

The door crashed open to the sound of splintering wood. An angry growl followed and then the duke was hoisted away. Wilhelmina gulped down a series of breaths and grabbed at her bed sheets in order to cover herself while Mr. Dale pinned the duke against the opposite wall.

"You are no gentleman," Mr. Dale seethed, "but a predator underserving of his rank."

"And you, sir, are a liar," the duke responded. "If Mrs. Lawson were truly under your protection, you wouldn't be sleeping in separate rooms."

"How did you get in here?" When the duke didn't response, Mr. Dale shoved him harder against the wall. "Tell me."

"Anything can be had for the right price and nobody keeps a single copy of any key. There's always another," Cloverfield spat.

"I want to kill you," Mr. Dale said, his voice so low it sent chills through Wilhelmina's veins. There was no question he meant it.

"I doubt you'd want to hang for murder on my account," Cloverfield said. Somehow, in spite of having Mr. Dale's hands on his throat, he still managed to sound smug.

Silence hung like thick morning fog in the air, until Mr. Dale unclasped his hands and took a step back. He gestured toward the door where other people, alerted by the ruckus, were starting to gather. "Get out."

Cloverfield glared at Wilhelmina. "We're not done, you and I. Not after this."

"Is everything all right in here?" a man's voice asked from the hallway.

"It's fine," Cloverfield snapped on his way out the door.

"Looks like the lock's been broken," another voice Wilhelmina recognized as Mr. Sellers' said. "I'll have to charge you for that."

"Take it up with Mr. Dale," Cloverfield said. "I had the courtesy to use a key."

"Give me a moment," Mr. Dale told the innkeeper while Wilhelmina hugged her knees and did her best to fight back the tears that threatened.

It was to no avail. Now that the moment was over and she was allowed to reflect on what had transpired –

the attack she'd just been subjected to and where it would have led if Mr. Dale hadn't shown up—an almost violent response took over. She shook so badly she feared she would never find calm again. For the past two decades she'd run from the worst experience of her life. As she'd grown older, wiser, and stronger, she'd convinced herself she would never again be the victim.

Only to have the security of this belief torn to shreds in under five minutes.

"Mrs. Lawson?" Mr. Dale spoke with caution. "Are you hurt?"

To some degree, but not as much as she could have been. "No."

"You're certain?" When she gave a quick nod he said, "Good. I'm glad to hear it. Not just because I care for your well-being, but also because we ought to leave. Can you manage to dress?"

"Yes. But..." She stared at him. Even amid the dark shadows of night she could tell that his shirt was untucked from his breeches, his legs and feet bare, and his hair in wild disarray. "Can you stay while I do so? In case he comes back?"

He hesitated briefly. "Of course."

Wilhelmina breathed a sigh of relief. She and Mr. Dale might not have gotten off to the best start, but she now viewed him as her ally. Most importantly, she trusted him. She waited while he exchanged a few more words with the innkeeper, and then the door to her bedchamber closed.

He leaned against it, holding it shut. "I promise not

to look."

With a quivering, "Thank you," Wilhelmina got out of bed.

CHAPTER TWELVE

The rage James experienced on Mrs. Lawson's behalf was like a vicious beast with claws and fangs. He longed to set it free and let it taste blood – Cloverfield's blood. Instead, he kept his ire under control for her sake, no matter how much restraint that required. It was no easy feat when her cheek still glowed on account of Cloverfield's brutal slap, clearly visible despite the dim pre-dawn light. But after all she'd just been through, the last thing she needed was to witness a violent display of anger.

However, one thing was worth mentioning as they continued their onward journey. Just to be sure she didn't think him impervious to what had happened. "If I did not have the responsibility of being a father and a son, I would have seen that bastard into an early grave and taken my chances with the legal system."

Sitting diagonally opposite him, she'd positioned

herself in an awkward sort of way with her body turned slightly away from him so she faced the window more fully. This prevented him from seeing her face and thus from judging her emotional response to what he said. He believed her position was mostly to do with her wanting to hide her tears.

"I'm glad you didn't or I'd be to blame for that too." Each word was like a shard of anguish. "I'm sorry this happened, Mr. Dale. It's all my fault."

"What?" Fresh anger directed toward this misplaced belief of hers bubbled inside him. "How are you to blame for Cloverfield's despicable ill-treatment of you?"

"He wouldn't have behaved as he did if I were respectable. My reputation—"

"Does *not* give him or any other man the right to force himself on you, Mrs. Lawson." His attempt at keeping a level tone failed. Mrs. Lawson flinched in response and James muttered a curse. He scrubbed his hand across his jaw and huffed a breath. "No one deserves to be treated so crassly – to be abused in such a crude manner. I'm sorry if you are convinced you do."

She shook her head and he heard her gulp down a breath. "Forgive me, Mr. Dale, but it is not merely what happened to me but also what happened to Cynthia, to your son, and to you." She glanced at him over her shoulder through liquid blue eyes. "You had an altercation with a duke because of me, Cynthia cannot marry the man she loves, and your son can't marry her unless he's willing to risk his reputation. In spite of my best intentions, I have a destructive impact on other people's lives."

James couldn't quite argue that view. Even if he was starting to doubt she was guilty of being the adulteress she'd portrayed herself to be, the only thing that mattered was public opinion. And since the world believed she was guilty, she could be as innocent as new fallen snow and it wouldn't make an ounce of difference. She'd still cast a dark shadow over anyone she associated with.

Still, he wanted to understand her. The artless kiss they'd shared suggested she'd never been properly kissed, not even by her husband. Which was something that boggled James's mind. And then there was her reaction to Cloverfield. There had been a sort of terrified recognition, yet based on Cloverfield's response and on the lady's own assurance, they'd never met before.

Since the first issue was trickier to broach, James decided to address the second. "May I ask you a delicate question, Mrs. Lawson?"

She gave her eyes a hasty swipe and turned more fully toward him. "About what?"

James took a moment to ponder how to begin. It occurred to him he'd be best off doing so, not as the barrister who'd judged her, nor as the man who longed to kiss her again, but as her friend. With this in mind, he crossed to her bench so he sat beside her, and reached for her hand. When she didn't resist his touch, he wove their fingers together and gently inquired,

"You told me you were unacquainted with the duke. Is that true?"

She produced a strangled sort of sound at the back of her throat. "Yes."

"You are certain of this?"

"Of course."

"Then I can only assume you had a bad experience once with someone who looked a lot like him." When she attempted to pull her hand away, James held on and angled himself toward her. "Mrs. Lawson, I realize you and I had a bumpy start to our relationship, but I'd like for you to count me as your friend, so if there's anything else you want to share – some burden you'd like me to help you carry – I will keep your confidence."

"Thank you, Mr. Dale, but everything there is to know about me has already been revealed."

"I cannot believe that."

"You think I'm trying to deceive you somehow?"

He searched her outraged expression. It seemed genuine enough and yet James's instinct compelled him to doubt the story she and her husband had told the world. Yes, he thought she was trying to deceive him, but since admitting as much was unlikely to benefit either of them at this point, he shook his head. "No."

If she was determined to pull the wool over his eyes, then he saw no reason why he shouldn't do the same. As long as she thought he accepted her farce, the greater the chance she'd reveal more clues pointing toward the truth. So rather than ask further questions, he drew her against his side and offered the comfort he suspected she needed.

They sat like that, holding hands and with her head resting on his shoulder, until they reached the next posting inn.

"I'll buy some food for the journey and inquire after our children. Why don't you stretch your legs in the meantime? I shan't be long."

She caught his arm. "I'd rather come with you."

Noting the frightened look in her eyes, James nodded. "All right. We'll go inside together."

His heart swelled with protective fierceness when he saw her panic subside as relief took its place. Stepping down, James turned and offered his hand. She took it, clasping it in her own as though it contained all the strength she required to carry on. He hated seeing this woman who'd otherwise faced him with flint in her eyes look so afraid. But he was glad he was there to help and grateful to fate for making them travel together so he could guard her.

Pausing for a moment beside the carriage, James reached up and tucked a stray lock of hair beneath her bonnet, securing it behind her ear. He wasn't sure why he felt so compelled to touch her, but he liked that she did not flinch or retreat. Perhaps this was why he allowed his fingers to linger a fraction longer than necessary, or why he let them trace the edge of her jaw as he drew them away. Maybe recent events made him want to be closer to her, to show her he cared in a way he did not yet know how to express with words.

"Thank you, Mr. Dale."

He smiled at her upturned face. Her red-rimmed eyes contrasted against the paleness of her skin did not detract from her beauty. She was still the loveliest woman he'd ever seen, and if they'd still been inside the carriage, away from prying eyes, he believed he might have kissed her. Which would without doubt have been a mistake. After having one man press his advances on her, the last thing she probably wanted was for him to make a go of it too. Most importantly, he didn't want her to think she owed him or that his help and protection came with certain expectations on his behalf.

So he broke their eye contact, effectively letting the tension between them fizzle, and led her inside the inn. Fifteen minutes later, they were back on the road with a new team of horses, food to enjoy as they rode, and the knowledge that Michael and Cynthia were only a couple of hours ahead now on account of their having a later start. If the young couple decided to stop for luncheon, James and Mrs. Lawson had a real chance of catching up to them before they reached Gretna Greene.

As if reading his mind, Mrs. Lawson asked, "Are you still determined to stop them from marrying?"

After resuming their journey, James had reclaimed his seat beside her since this was where he felt most at ease. And since she did not complain about his proximity, he told himself she welcomed his nearness.

Chewing the bread and cheese he'd just taken a bite of, he gave her question serious consideration before he said, "I wish I didn't have to, but I must put my son's best interest first."

A brief hesitation followed before she said, "Surely if these past few days have taught us anything, it is that there may be consequences to trying to separate people who love each other."

She had him there. It was indeed a strong argument in favor of letting Michael have the woman he'd chosen, but as long as he doubted Mrs. Lawson was being completely honest with him about her situation, he dared not risk any permanent form of attachment to her. Not to mention that nothing would truly change as long as she remained the fallen woman she gave herself out to be. She'd still threaten Michael's reputation and the career James wanted for him.

Unless...

He studied her as she ate, observed the kindness in her eyes and the gentle curve of her friendly smile. "As you know, my reluctance to offer Michael and Cynthia my blessing has nothing to do with Cynthia. I'm sure she's a lovely woman, but if Michael marries her, he will form a close family relationship with you, and I fear this will have dire repercussions on his future."

A shadow fell over her face. "Just so you know, I intend to keep to myself from now on. Believe me, I have similar concerns. The last thing I want is for Cynthia to suffer because of me, which is why I've no intention of showing my face in London as long as she is living there."

"I fear your absence won't be enough."

"You don't believe people will forget my scandalous divorce in a year or two?"

"To be sure, they might stop thinking about it. Certainly, something else will likely grab their attention and push your divorce into the background. But your daughter will always carry the burden of your actions in much the same way as an illegitimate child would."

Her gasp was sharp and full of indignation. "I beg to differ, Mr. Dale."

Deciding to strategize as a barrister would, he chose his next words carefully. "Unfortunately, I see only one way in which your daughter's happiness might be secured."

"And how is that?"

"There's no guarantee, mind you."

"Nevertheless, I'd like to hear your idea."

He pretended to give the matter some serious thought. If he was right about Mrs. Lawson lying to everyone with regard to her marriage, then surely she'd give up doing so if it meant saving her child from unhappiness.

Cautiously, so as not to remind her of his suspicions about her, he told her, "Society has painted you as Jezebel. But suppose you were to prove you're not that person. Perhaps then you could be forgiven, welcomed back even, and see your daughter happily wed to the man she loves."

~

Wilhelmina stared at Mr. Dale. Her heart fluttered in an anxious sort of way. Not so much because of the awful encounter she'd had with Cloverfield – she'd more or less recovered from that – but because she couldn't seem to figure out the man with whom she travelled. Did he still think her sexually inexperienced in spite of her trying to play the seductress?

She wasn't sure. But in her experience, limited though it was, men lost all control when they were in a state of want, yet Mr. Dale had made no further advances in spite of her brazen proposition. Unless it all came down to him not wanting to form a closer attachment with a woman he did not respect – not even for a fleeting moment of passion.

Which was fine with her. Really. It wasn't as if she'd actually wanted him to accept her invitation to bed her. All it had been was a necessary ploy to convince him. And to this end, she believed she'd succeeded based on the hunger she'd noted in his expression. So then how exactly did he imagine this idea of his would work?

"I don't see how such a thing would be possible, Mr. Dale. I am who I am. Statements were made against me during the course of nearly two years. My lovers came forward and identified me as the woman who sought them out for pleasure"—Mr. Dale winced at this—"repeatedly, I might add. All of this while I said nothing in my defense."

"Why didn't you, by the way?"

Wilhelmina hesitated briefly while holding his sharp eagle-eyed gaze. Nothing seemed to escape this man.

She had to be cautious. "Because there was nothing to say. My husband caught me in the act."

"Hmm…"

She did not like the skeptical sound he made. But if she persisted in trying to persuade him, she feared she might appear less credible. So she shrugged and attempted an air of indifference. "Think what you will, Mr. Dale. The point is I cannot help my daughter as you suggest since no one would ever believe me now. Not with my reputation determined in a court of law and before Parliament. All it would do is stir up the past, creating more scandal, and branding me a liar on top of everything else. So no, Mr. Dale, my insisting I'm innocent after the fact – after making no attempt at doing so before – will not clear my name or help my daughter. And even if it did, would it really make any difference to you?"

"Of course it would."

Wilhelmina gave a snort in disagreement. "Your moral compass is exact, Mr. Dale. It does not wobble about, uncertain of which direction to point. You defend the innocent by arguing the truth."

"Your point, Mrs. Lawson?"

"Supposing we lived in a world where everyone would believe me if I came out and said it had all been one big mistake, that I was in fact a faithful wife who never did anything wrong, how could that possibly alter your stance? Knowing it isn't true, that I am still the adulteress I've been accused of being, how then could you allow your son to marry my daughter? How could you accept me as your son's mother-in-law any more than you do now?"

He knit his brows until deep grooves puckered his skin. "Are you trying to dissuade me from supporting the match now after spending the last few weeks attempting to do the opposite?"

"No. I..." Wilhelmina wasn't sure what she was trying to accomplish with her argument. She knew she'd had a goal in mind when she'd begun, but somehow she'd wandered off track somewhere and no longer knew where she was headed. "Sorry. I suppose I misjudged you."

"In what way?"

"I never would have believed you to be the sort of person who cared more for public opinion than for the truth." And there it was, the point she'd been trying to make without really being aware. It represented his strength of character, which was something she'd always admired about him although it had put them at odds with each other. He'd witnessed nearly every moment of her downfall and had spared her no mercy in his judgment, regardless of the pleasant discourse they'd shared at the Pennington ball. Mr. Dale had looked at the facts she and George had presented, and had based his opinion of her entirely on that. But if he suddenly started forgiving what she'd supposedly done just because she convinced everyone they'd been wrong, her respect for Mr. Dale would crumble.

"You mistake my meaning if that is what you think I would do." His eyes darkened while boring into hers.

"The truth is everything, Mrs. Lawson. It is the very foundation upon which I've built my career. Furthermore, it is what defines me as a man of integrity."

"Then…" As relieved as she was to hear him say this with such conviction, his words made his previous statement all the more confusing.

"Forget I said anything." Mr. Dale leaned back and crossed his arms. "It was a fanciful notion – an argument for the purpose of ethical contemplation. Nothing more."

"Oh." She felt oddly deflated and silly now. "I had no idea you dabbled in philosophy."

A wry smile lifted the edge of his lips. "On occasion. Forgive me, but I probably should have preceded my idea with, imagine if…"

She chuckled. "Yes. That would have helped. I'm sorry I took you so seriously."

"No matter, Mrs. Lawson." His smile broadened. "How about we play a game in order to pass the time?"

"All right. What do you have in mind?"

"When we first met, you surprised me by knowing where Aboukir is, so I'm thinking we ought to test our geographical knowledge." He gave her a pensive look. "We'll take turns naming the countries of the world in alphabetical order."

"Is this where I should warn you that geography is a favorite subject of mine?"

"Absolutely not, Mrs. Lawson. Why spoil the fun?"

As it turned out, Mr. Dale was a formidable match for Wilhelmina's knowledge although she could have kicked herself for forgetting Burma. With one point against her she grinned at him with smug satisfaction when they got to the M's and he insisted they had depleted all the names.

"Are you certain?" she asked.

"Of course I am." He listed all the countries they'd already mentioned. "There aren't any more."

"What about"—she paused for effect while he raised an eyebrow in question—"Moldavia?"

"Damn." The expletive was spoken with a laugh. "Forgive me, Mrs. Lawson."

"It's quite all right. I cursed too when you mentioned Burma."

"No you didn't."

She gave him a teasing smile. "Just because you didn't hear me doesn't mean I didn't. Shall we continue?"

He grinned at her with open abandon. How easy it was to forget the difference of opinion and the deception wedged between them when they were having fun. Eventually, it would drive them apart once more, but for now Wilhelmina took pleasure in the joy she found in Mr. Dale's company. He was a good and decent and altogether wonderful man. Handsome as sin as well, not to mention charming, protective, and caring. A pity she couldn't have more than this with him, but the die had been cast before they'd even met. She'd had a family – a husband and a daughter – and even though it hadn't been perfect, they'd all loved each other. Now, with George gone and Cynthia ready to move on from her grief, Wilhelmina's future promised solitude.

"Can't you think of any more?" Mr. Dale asked once they got to the S's. "There are at least two."

They'd stopped again for a change of horses, during which they'd learned that the distance between them and their children was rapidly closing. They were only one hour apart now and while Wilhelmina grew increasingly anxious at the thought of putting an end to her daughter's plan, she looked forward to seeing her soon.

"Are you sure?" She couldn't think of another country beginning with S.

He gave her a resolute nod. "Would you like a hint?"

"Absolutely not."

"Very well then."

She tapped her chin with her index finger while eyeing him. "Singapore is a British colony, so that doesn't count."

"I am aware," he murmured.

"And the Principality of Serbia is only semi-independent. The Ottomans still have a presence there, so that doesn't count either."

"Quite right." Mr. Dale tilted his head in contemplation. "I suppose you studied a globe when you weren't otherwise occupied with the workings of your parents' longcase clock?"

"The vastness of the world, the difference in climate, geography, and people found throughout, has always intrigued me."

He studied her. "Sounds like you might want to travel one day. As your father did?"

"As much as I missed him while he was away, I cannot deny that his stories instilled in me a thirst to know more. Not that I'm likely to go anywhere." The expense alone was enough to put an end to any such notion.

"Why not?"

Since Wilhelmina had no desire to bring up her financial straits, she said, "Adventures are meant to be shared, Mr. Dale. My father had his best friend for company whereas I have no one."

"What about Cynthia?"

"I don't believe she has any interest in learning what's outside of England," Wilhelmina said with a wistful chuckle. "Besides, her life is here. With her husband gone and no children to speak of, she ought to set her mind to starting a family while she's still young."

"It looks like she shares your belief," Mr. Dale said. He frowned but didn't apologize for reminding her that Cynthia was in fact trying to get herself married. Instead he fell into silence, allowing Wilhelmina to continue wracking her brain.

"I give up," she told him after a good fifteen minutes. "I've gone over all the countries again and I just can't think of any others."

"You're certain?"

"Quite."

A sly smile slid into place, softening the hard edge of his jaw. With two and a half days' worth of stubble affording him with a rough appearance and the cravat he'd hastily tied in place that morning when they'd fled the inn, he looked devilishly handsome. A funny sort of liquid heat swirled in her stomach.

"I see," he said, dragging her attention away from the strange desire she suddenly had to run her fingertips over his cheek. "Perhaps that's because there aren't any more."

"What?"

"We covered all the countries beginning with S."

"But you told me—"

"I lied." Mischief played in his eyes, bringing out their warmer tones.

"How awful of you," she chided with sporting levity in her voice. Reaching out, she gave him a playful swat, in response to which he chuckled.

"Forgive me, Mrs. Lawson, but I could not ignore the chance to tease you." A thoughtful expression brought his features back under control. He gazed at her as if in wonder and Wilhelmina's pulse leapt in response. "I'll never regret making you smile."

Unsure of what to say in response, Wilhelmina could only sit there. She was trapped by his gaze and acutely reminded of what his lips felt like against her own. When she'd kissed him last, it had been impulsive – the means by which to win an argument. Now, it was something else entirely, perhaps a need to be close to someone she felt a genuine connection with, a desire to blot out all lingering remnants of her encounter with Cloverfield, or simply the deep attraction she'd harbored for Mr. Dale since the moment they'd met now reaching its zenith.

"Mrs. Lawson." Her name suggested a shared awareness on his part. He leaned toward her.

She sucked in a breath, and was suddenly in his arms. Not because she'd moved or because he had, but because the entire conveyance jolted and tossed her straight off the bench.

Strong hands held her steady while concerned eyes searched her face. The moment they'd just enjoyed was not only lost but pulled further out of reach when the carriage jerked to a jarring halt and the coachman could be heard cursing.

"Are you all right?" Mr. Dale asked Wilhelmina. When she answered in the affirmative, he eased her back onto the bench. "You're certain?"

"Yes. You should probably go and see what has happened."

With a nod he left, only to return moments later. "One of the horses has sprung a shoe, which leaves us in a bit of a bind, seeing as it will start getting dark in another hour or so."

"Can we not walk to the nearest inn?"

"My coachman reckons that's at least ten miles away, which is much too far."

"What do we do then?"

"Well..." Mr. Dale gave her the sort of look that suggested she wouldn't like his idea one bit. "With Cloverfield on our heels, I'm unwilling to leave your side. And with nightfall ahead, we're going to need to seek shelter somewhere off the road so we can avoid him in case he comes looking for us. Now, there are a couple of houses in the distance – a mile away or so. I would suggest we head toward them. If we're lucky, the owner can help with the horse as well."

"And if we're unlucky?"

Mr. Dale gave her a tight smile. "Let's be optimistic, shall we?"

CHAPTER THIRTEEN

I t was slow going getting to the first house James had spotted. With one horse limping along and the other forced to pull harder, it took at least twice as long as it would have done at a regular pace.

Eventually when they did arrive, James saw that the first house wasn't nearly as large as it looked from a distance – more of a cottage really.

Nevertheless, he went to knock on the door.

"Yes?" inquired the older man who answered. About a head shorter than James, he was slim of build with large bushy eyebrows resting above a pair of inquisitive eyes.

"Excuse me for bothering you," James said, "but one of my horses' shoes has sprung and with the next inn quite a ways off, I'm hoping you'll let us make use of your home while my coachman tends to the horse."

"Aye, but considering the late hour, I reckon you'll want to stay until morning unless you mean to travel by dark." The man peered past James. "We can put up your coachman, but you and your wife will have to stay with the Mitchells. Give me a second. I'll be right back."

The door closed, leaving James alone for a moment. He briefly considered correcting the man's misconception regarding Mrs. Lawson. She'd probably prefer it if they continued pretending they were brother and sister. But setting them up for the night would be simpler if they were able to share a bed. The very idea of such a thing occurring was enough for him to keep his mouth shut on the subject when the old man returned.

"I've told the missus to offer your wife some tea while I help you and your coachman with the horses." The old man shoved his arms into his jacket while striding toward the carriage. "Once they've been taken care of, we'll take you up to the Mitchells."

"Thank you, sir."

"Name's Walker."

James glanced at the older man. "Pleased to meet you, Mr. Walker. I'm Mr. Dale, and this here is my coachman, Green. If you'll excuse me a moment, I'll just have a word with my wife."

Funny how easily that particular word slipped off his tongue. James strode after Mrs. Lawson, who'd wandered a bit farther up the road.

"It looks like we're in luck," he said when he reached her.

She turned toward him, the glow from the late afternoon sun affording her with an ethereal look that nearly took his breath away. Shading her eyes, she glanced toward the carriage where Mr. Walker and Green were presently unfastening the horses. "It's kind of him to help."

"There is one catch though," James confessed. When she directed her gaze to his he said, "Mr. Walker assumed you're my wife and since I'd rather not complicate matters, I didn't correct him."

Mrs. Lawson stared at him for a moment as what this implied sank in. Her eyes widened a fraction. "Why wouldn't you tell him what we've told everyone else thus far?"

"Because I don't think it would make any difference."

"Of course it would. One implies a familiar bond that could allow for separate rooms if such a possibility exists, whereas husbands and wives are expected to share the same bed."

"Given the number of lovers you claim to have had," James told her in a low voice while stepping so close to her he could see the rapid beat of her pulse at her neck, "I don't see why spending one night with me should be an issue. I promise to keep my hands to myself if that's your concern."

Spinning away, he went to assist the two other men. He knew he was being unreasonable. After her recent altercation with Cloverfield, it made sense she'd want to sleep alone – that she'd not want to risk another man making advances. It made even more sense if she was not as experienced as she claimed. And yet, the panic he'd seen in her eyes when she'd realized they'd have to share a room and possibly even a bed irked him. Maybe because he knew she had nothing to fear from him, and the fact that she might presume she did put him in the same box as Cloverfield.

But there was something besides the anger this possibility stirred in him. There was also the jealously he'd harbored toward every man who'd claimed to have had her in the past. No matter how much James had resented her these last two years for being unfaithful to her husband, he'd secretly wished he'd met her sooner so he could have been among her lovers.

But if she'd not been as wanton as she pretended, maybe there weren't any lovers at all and she was just nervous. In which case he was a fool for getting wound up over her reluctance to sleep by his side. Even though he would have thought their friendship had advanced to the point where it ought not be a big deal, provided they both kept their clothes on. After all, lovers or not, she had been married, so it wasn't as if she'd never shared her bed before. Apparently, she just didn't want to share it with him, which bothered him more than he cared for. Most likely because he'd been certain she shared his attraction.

Muttering a curse, James snatched the healthy horse's harness from Green and followed Mr. Walker to the back of the house. The coachman soon caught up, leading the lame horse along at a much slower pace.

"I've not got too much to offer in terms of a stable," Mr. Walker said with a hint of apology, "but it'll have to do."

Grateful the man had some shelter to offer the horses, even though it was just a fenced-in structure consisting of six wooden posts and a roof, James gave his thanks. At least there was fresh hay and water. He guided the horse he was leading into the spot directly beside Mr. Walker's cart horse. A donkey standing a little further along brayed.

"Right then," Green said. "Let's see about changing this shoe."

Almost one hour later, with twilight settling in around them, James wiped his brow and patted the horse's flank. Mr. Walker had not had the strength to hold the horse's leg steady while Green worked, so James had done so instead.

"Will he be all right by tomorrow?" James asked.

"If we keep a leisurely pace he'll get us to the next inn," Green assured him. "We'll switch him out there."

"Let's have a quick bite to eat then," James suggested. He turned to Mr. Walker. "If it's not too much imposition?"

"Not at all," Mr. Walker said. "My wife's stew is divine and now that she knows you're here there'll be more than plenty to go around."

Thankful for the hospitality, James washed his hands at the pump and dried them off on a linen towel Mr. Walker handed to him. He and Green then followed the man inside where Mrs. Lawson was in the process of setting the table in the Walkers' small parlor. A stool placed at one corner, most likely brought in from the kitchen, provided additional seating.

"The food's almost ready," Mrs. Lawson said as soon as she noted their presence. Her cheeks were flushed and her voice slightly breathless, as if she'd been rushing about for a while. James stepped further into the room and watched while she arranged the napkins and silverware. He noticed that she avoided looking directly at him. Instead, she smiled at Mr. Walker. "Thank you so much for inviting us into your home and for your help with the horses."

"Ah, think nothing of it," Mr. Walker said with a grin. "I'll just see if my wife needs help."

"Please allow me," Mrs. Lawson said. "I've been sitting all day so I'm happy to move about a bit while you rest."

Mr. Walker's eyebrows lifted, but he did not argue. As soon as she was gone from the room though, he turned to James. "Spirited thing, isn't she? I can see why you married her."

James glanced at his coachman and, noting the look of surprise on his face, gave him a quelling look while saying, "She certainly keeps me on my toes."

"The best of them will do that," Mr. Walker said. He located a bottle of some sort and filled three glasses which he distributed among them. "My Marjorie challenges me every day. Not a boring second to be had with her, I tell you. Not even after fifty years."

"I'll drink to that," James said as he raised his glass. The brandy was stronger than any he'd had before, most likely because it was of the home made variety. He and Green both winced, prompting Mr. Walker to laugh.

"This stuff will put some hair on your chests," Mr. Walker claimed as the women returned. Each carried a pot. "Isn't that so, my dear?"

"Yours is certainly full of it," the older woman who followed Mrs. Lawson announced. She was as wide as her husband was slim with an upward curve of her mouth and a twinkle of merriment in her eyes. "I could sheer him like a sheep and earn a fat penny to boot at the wig makers."

Mr. Walker hooted in response. "What did I tell you, lads? Allow me to introduce you to the sharpest tongue north of London. Mr. Dale and Mr. Green, behold the love of my life, Mrs. Walker."

The lady in question blushed in response to her husband's affectionate words and even managed a bashful giggle. James grinned and instinctively glanced at Mrs. Lawson who swiftly averted her gaze from his the moment their eyes met. So she'd been watching him had she? Perhaps she wasn't as opposed to spending the night with him as she'd suggested. Maybe she was just worried that doing so might lead them both down a dangerous path.

Regrettably, he had no intention of letting that happen. Not because he didn't want to, but because he feared a dalliance with her would no longer be as meaningless as it once would have. Because when it came to lovemaking, there was a world of difference between a quick tup with a woman who spread her legs with careless abandon and one who only pretended to do so. If he was right about Mrs. Lawson, walking away from her afterward would not be an easy matter. As such, he had to be certain that he was prepared to pay the price and face the ramifications. And since he wasn't, he knew he'd do well to keep his hands to himself.

"I mentioned your arrival to the Mitchells while you worked on the horse," Mrs. Walker said while they ate. "Thought they might appreciate a bit of fair warning. They'll be ready to receive you as soon as we're done with our meal."

"Thank you." James took another bite of his food. "It's a wonderful stew."

Mrs. Walker beamed with pleasure. "My mother, bless her soul, taught me how to cook. She insisted it was a skill that would always pay off."

"I'm certainly grateful for it," Mr. Walker said.

"My wife is quite a keen baker," James said while letting his gaze rest on Mrs. Lawson. An unexpected sense of pride filled him as he spoke, which was curious since he'd never even tasted anything she had made. Perhaps he just liked that she found joy in such a domestic skill. It warmed his heart to think of her in a kitchen, pouring her love into a cake or a loaf of bread, the aroma filling the air and the flour staining her cheeks while she worked.

"My daughter is especially fond of my scones," she said.

"Oh?" Mrs. Walker straightened. "You have a daughter?"

"And a son," James said without thinking.

Mrs. Lawson's spoon struck the side of her dish with a clang.

Green coughed and reached for his wine. "Sorry. Went down the wrong way."

"Then you are truly blessed," Mr. Walker said, seemingly unaware of the effect James's comment had wrought on Mrs. Lawson and his coachman. "We've only one child but he has given us three lovely grandchildren to dote on, though we don't see them nearly as often as we'd like. They live a half day's ride from here near Hawick."

"The mills there provide more profitable work than what can be found in these parts," Mrs. Walker explained.

The conversation lingered on production for a while before moving on to what life in London was like. The Walkers were enthusiastic listeners with a genuine interest in learning more about what the wider world had to offer.

"The air's not as fresh there as it is here though," James said when the Walkers marveled at his description of Vauxhall Garden and gas lighting.

"It's also very crowded," Mrs. Lawson added while

looking directly at James. "I personally prefer the simplicity of country living."

What was she saying? That they belonged in two separate worlds? Or was she simply reminding him that he would eventually return to the City while she would remain in Renwick? He'd no idea, but he realized in that moment that he longed to find a middle ground – a way in which to avoid the rift destined to come between them as soon as their journey ended.

It was madness for him to think that way, but these last few days together had forged a bond he did not want to give up on. Rather, he wanted more. But how?

"There are a couple of extra blankets in the bottom drawer over there in case it gets too cold for you," Mrs. Mitchell told Wilhelmina later after showing her up to the room she'd made available. "There's not enough space for a proper wash stand, but the bowl on top of the dresser is filled with water. You'll find some soap in the tin right next to it. The wash cloths and towels beside it are all clean."

Standing immediately inside the tiny room where she and Mr. Dale would be staying, Wilhelmina did her best to hide her panic. The bed, which she'd learned belonged to the Mitchells' eldest daughter, Amanda, had been pushed up against the wall to allow enough space to open the door and pass to the dresser. Intended for two very slim people at best, it wasn't nearly as wide as Wilhelmina had hoped. For a married couple, however, it should not pose a problem.

She smiled tightly. "Thank you. My husband and I are tremendously grateful to you for your hospitality and to your daughters for agreeing to share a room for the night."

"We're happy to have you," Mrs. Mitchell said. "Our lives here can get pretty monotonous, so it's nice with a bit of change. Do you get thirsty at night? I can prepare a jug of water and a couple of glasses for you if you like."

"I'd appreciate that."

"Oh, and there's a clean chamber pot under the bed, should you need it."

Mrs. Mitchell left Wilhelmina with those words hanging heavily in the air. Heaven above, she'd not even started to consider what she would do if she needed to empty her bladder during the night.

Swallowing, Wilhelmina moved to the bed and sat. Mr. Dale's bag stood next to hers at the foot end. He'd brought them up when Mrs. Mitchell offered to show the room, but had since gone to find Mr. Mitchell in the hope the man had a shaving blade he could borrow.

Stiffly seated, Wilhelmina clasped her hands and bit her lip. She'd never shared a bed with anyone in her life. During their unconventional marriage, she and George had always slept apart. Although they had made one attempt to be intimate on their wedding night, they'd had to call it quits because of how wrong and awkward it felt. Neither had made an effort afterward and he'd eventually sated his needs with other women.

Unsure of what to do, Wilhelmina's mind was still in turmoil when Mr. Dale stepped through the door. He brought the jug and glasses Mrs. Mitchell had promised with him, along with a small wooden box. "Help me, will you?"

Wilhelmina stood and relieved him of the jug and glasses, which she placed on top of the only bedside table the room had to offer. She glanced at the box he was now in the process of opening. "I gather you found what you needed?"

"Yes. I always travel with my own set but in my haste to depart Clarington House, I forgot to pack it." He grinned as he stroked one hand over his jaw. "I'm not used to having a beard."

"It doesn't look bad," Wilhelmina told him, although she had preferred it yesterday when it was shorter.

He angled his head while studying her. "Would you rather I leave it?"

The fact he was asking her made her already jittery stomach turn over. She held herself as rigidly upright as she was able. "Honestly, Mr. Dale. I'm not sure why my opinion should matter."

"Hmm…"

There it was again, that sound he made when he seemed to have a lot to say yet chose to keep all thoughts to himself. She huffed a breath in frustration and went to busy herself with her bag. Perhaps then she'd forget how small the room was or that she would soon be lying down beside him on the narrow bed.

An unbidden thrill of excitement swept through her on that notion, even as she did her best to ignore it. If the kiss had taught her anything, it was that she was out of her depth where Mr. Dale was concerned. Considering what he'd told her last night before Cloverfield's arrival, she feared she'd not been as skilled in the art of kissing as she should have been if she'd had as many lovers as she claimed.

For now, she believed her proposition had made him unsure of his suspicions about her, but if things progressed between them, there'd be no doubt in his mind at all. He'd call her on her deception and while she didn't know how he'd react to the truth, she could not take any chances.

The sound of something landing upon the bed made her turn. Apparently Mr. Dale had shucked his jacket. She stared at the garment and blinked when his waistcoat landed on top of it. Her gaze darted toward him, and then to the door behind him. When had he closed it? She'd not heard the click.

Mouth dry, she watched from her crouched position by her bag as he stood, slightly turned away from her, fiddling with his cravat. Was he truly getting undressed with her right there?

Of course he was, she chastised herself. How else was he meant to shave or get ready for bed? She shook her head and gave him her back lest he see the hot flush she could feel in her cheeks. Her fingers curled 'round her nightgown. It wasn't the most scandalous garment in the world. The linen was densely woven and would protect her modesty while she slept. But how on earth was she meant to put it on without him seeing her in a state of undress? She almost laughed. If anything would convince him of her lacking experience it would be prudish and shy behavior.

Biting her lip, she considered her options. Perhaps she could make an excuse, tell him her nightgown had gotten torn during the incident with Cloverfield, and sleep fully clothed? It wouldn't be comfortable, but at least it would save her from having to strip in front of a man whose hands she longed to feel on her skin.

"I can't get this bloody knot undone." Mr. Dale muttered another curse followed by an apology and an irritated sigh. "Can you please lend a hand?"

Jolted out of her contemplations, Wilhelmina flinched. She glanced at him over her shoulder. "What?"

He tugged on his cravat. "I think I pulled the wrong end and made the knot tighter."

"And you want me to try and get it off?" Lord, she sounded daft.

"That is the idea," he said with a frown that suggested he might be worried she'd hit her head. "Hence my reason for inquiring after your help."

"Right. Of course." She stood and closed the distance between them, which only required taking a couple of steps. Reaching up, she focused all her attention on the knot in question, not on the enticing scent of sandalwood filling her nose or the fact that she feared her heart might run off without her if it raced any faster. Her jaw set, her fingers loosed one part, wove a strip of white cotton through, then tugged here and pulled there until the entire cravat came free. She saw Mr. Dale's throat work and heard his hard intake of breath as she stared at his neck.

She'd felt this tension before, in the carriage when he'd placed his hand on her thigh and held her gaze with his own. The kiss that followed had been inevitable – just as inevitable as it was now. Only now, in this room, there was no telling where it might lead.

Wilhelmina stepped back. Away from danger. "There you go."

"Thank you, Mrs. Lawson." She gave a swift nod and started to turn away when he said, "I hate to trouble you with this, but I worry I'll nick myself with the blade unless you shave me."

She stilled. "I beg your pardon?"

He sighed. "At home I have two large mirrors set up. When I'm at Clarington House, my father's valet helps out. But here there's only one small mirror." He indicated the one that hung on the wall. "It's barely big enough for me to see my entire head."

His disgruntled tone made her lips twitch. "Are you saying you're big headed?"

"I would never admit to any such thing," he told her lightly. "Seriously though, you had a husband for what, twenty years? I reckon you must have some experience with a blade, unless a servant did the task."

"We only had a maid of all works, so you're quite

correct in your assumption, Mr. Dale. I do know how to shave a man." She'd done so for George most mornings before breakfasting. Until the last year of their marriage when he'd spent every night with Fiona and she'd accomplished the deed. For Wilhelmina, it had always been one of those chores she'd enjoyed helping her friend with. She'd chatted away while he sat and listened to whatever thoughts struck her fancy. Later, he would do most of the talking, relating the news of the day to her while reading the paper. It had been habitual, but this did not make her oblivious to the intimacy of the task.

She stared at the box Mr. Dale held toward her as if it threatened to burn her fingers. Carefully, she reached out and took it. There was really no way around this unless she planned to explain her reluctance to touch his face, which she did not.

Wilhelmina willed her hands not to tremble and gestured toward the bed. "Have a seat."

He did as she asked while she set the box on the nightstand. "I'll need to lather your face first."

"Of course."

She went to locate the soap. How on earth did he manage to act as if all of this was perfectly normal? Wilhelmina had no idea. Her nerves were jumping about and Mr. Dale looked completely at ease. Damn him. With a shake of her head she opened the tin box beside the wash bowl and was instantly overcome by the fragrance of roses. An unexpected chuckle rippled through her at the thought of covering Mr. Dale's face with such a feminine scent.

"What's so amusing?" he asked.

"Nothing." She soaked one of the washcloths, wrung it, and gathered the soap.

When she turned to face him, every bit of amusement she'd just experienced vanished, as if swept away on a breeze. For there he sat, shirtless of all things, patiently waiting for her to proceed.

CHAPTER FOURTEEN

I t wasn't easy, feigning indifference while Mrs. Lawson stared at him. For a second, he worried he'd pushed her too far. But he never shaved while fully clothed since water and soap invariably dripped. Plus, he'd thought it a great excuse to gauge her response. Wide-eyed and with her lips slightly parted, she seemed visibly shocked by his state of undress. Yet another hint she wasn't as worldly as she tried to appear.

There was something else in her gaze, however – a flicker of interest and, dare he hope, appreciation. James's stomach clenched. He could scarcely wait for her to touch him, the anticipation of the moment when they would come skin to skin tightening every muscle. So he held his breath and watched her approach, his gaze never leaving her as she laid out a towel on the bed and placed the soap on top.

Her palm settled firmly against the back of his head

to hold him steady, and James nearly growled with pleasure. Tamping down the response with all his might lest he scare her off, he stayed completely silent while she wet his jaw.

She dropped the washcloth on the towel she'd placed beside him on the bed, picked up the soap, and slowly massaged it between her fingers. God help him but he found the simple task seductive. Or maybe it was just the scent of roses that fogged his brain. One thing he did know, and that was that he had to keep his hands to himself at all cost or she'd be straddling his lap in a heartbeat.

Christ. Perhaps the shave had been a bad idea?

He could have managed it on his own if he'd taken extra care, but he'd wanted to bond with Mrs. Lawson in a way he'd never bonded with anyone else. For some peculiar reason, he wanted more from her – a shared experience intended to bring them closer. Not even Clara had been this intimate with him. She'd been his wife and they'd shared the same bed until he'd learned of her unfaithfulness, but she'd always thought the task of shaving him to be beneath her.

Mrs. Lawson's fingers began working over his cheeks, forcing her nearer as she leaned in. Her leg pressed up against his, prompting him to grab the edge of the bed and hold on tight while need spiked through him. Perhaps it was because he was starting to see her for who she truly was that he wanted to craft this pointless memory with her. Initially, she'd been alluring, exactly the sort of woman he would have chased after if she'd been available. But then she'd become the villainess, the very antithesis of what he wanted. Until fate had thrown them together and forced him to see.

He wasn't sure why she'd chosen to go along with her husband's claims or why she continued insisting she was a fallen woman, but with each new experience James shared with her, it became increasingly clear to him that she'd never taken a lover in her life. Hell, even sharing a room with him for the evening had put her on edge.

He took a deep breath and breathed in her scent, not of rich perfume but rather of honey and lemons. His heart answered with a hard thump. More homely woman than crafty temptress, she was exactly what he'd always wanted, and it pained him to think she'd ruined their chance of being together for any reason. But at least there could be this.

"Hold still," she murmured, her breath teasing over his skin right before the edge of the blade scraped his jaw.

James tried not to shudder as her fingers raked through his hair at the back of his head to adjust his angle. It wasn't easy. Least of all with her bending at the waist in a manner that brought her breasts down to his eye level. He told himself not to look, but hell, he was only a man. He'd be a fool to squander the chance he'd been given to admire her lovely attributes this closely. So he boldly committed the shape and size of her curved perfection to memory while secretly hoping he'd one day see her completely bared to his gaze.

Arousal gripped him on that thought. He closed his eyes, did his best to bank the sensation while praying she would not notice his inappropriate response. But God help him, she sparked a craving inside him unlike any he'd ever known. And it had been an eternity since he'd last lain with a woman. He didn't care for brothels and had only made one attempt at having a mistress years ago after learning of Clara's deception. In spite of it all, bedding a woman who wasn't his wife had just made him feel more wretched.

And then she'd died and... Well, there had been a widow once while Michael was still away at university. But it had been a passing affair and James hadn't been with anyone since.

Mrs. Lawson wiped the blade clean on the wash cloth and adjusted her position, bringing her around to his other side. "I trust you'll tell me if I hurt you, Mr. Dale?"

He made a gruff sound in answer. It was all he could manage at this point.

"It's been a while since I've done this so my skill may not be what it once was." She chatted away with a nervous lilt to her voice. The blade scraped James's cheek. "And with the dim light from the oil lamp it's not so easy to see. I hope you won't have random tufts of hair showing tomorrow."

He was about to form a response when she tilted his head back and went to work on his neck. She angled herself to one side as if attempting to get at him from the front. Eventually she moved so she stood directly before him. Her knees bumped his as she tried to reach him, and James instinctively parted his legs, allowing her to step between them.

It wasn't clear to him whether or not she noticed the lack of resistance she suddenly found or the reason for it. Perhaps she was too caught up in her task to realize what he'd done, or that she'd moved in closer – so closer she'd sit on his thigh if she sank a bit lower.

"I have to say," she whispered while she worked, "I'm surprised you were willing to trust me with this."

"Why wouldn't I?" he asked, still gripping the bed sheets so he'd not grab her.

"Because it allows me to hold a knife to your throat?"

He could hear the smile in her voice and felt an answering chuckle roll through him. "My coachman would not help you find your daughter if you were to harm me, Mrs. Lawson."

"No, but given your low opinion of me, it still makes me wonder."

Without thinking, James reached up and grabbed her wrist. She stilled on a gasp and James eased his hold though he did not let go. "My opinion of you is rapidly changing. I'm starting to think you're a much better person than I ever thought."

She swallowed. A broken laugh rushed past her lips. "Why, Mr. Dale, if you're not careful, you might start to like me a little."

He already liked her a lot, but since he wasn't sure

saying as much would be wise, he just allowed a wry smile and told her, "God forbid."

She grinned in response, easing much of the tension that had been between them since they'd been alone in the room. James relaxed and she finished the shave, completing it by wiping his face clean with the washcloth before patting it dry with the towel.

"There." She stood back, adding distance and leaving him with an odd sense of loss. Using the washcloth, she cleaned the blade and returned it to its box before tidying up the rest of the items.

"I've a question for you," James said. He stood and waited until she faced him before he asked, "Would you mind if I removed my breeches?"

She blinked in rapid succession. "Um…"

"It'll be more comfortable for me that way. Of course I'll leave my smalls on, but if you prefer I can—"

"It's fine."

She spun away from him and made all sorts of quick movements with her hands. James grinned as he pulled off one boot. Even in the dim evening glow from the oil lamp, her blush burned bright red. Mrs. Lawson was no more a scandalous harlot than he was Chinese.

Immensely pleased by this certainty, James pulled off his second boot and discarded his hose while she continued to busy herself with something or other. Aware of her discomfort, James tried to think of something to take her mind off the fact that she would soon be climbing into bed with him.

"Have you ever visited Vauxhall?" He wasn't sure

where the question had sprung from, except he could clearly see her there, gazing up at the night sky while colorful fireworks burst overhead. Pushing down the bedcovers, he settled himself on the narrow mattress.

"Once. When George and I first moved to London with Cynthia, we went there one evening."

James frowned. Perhaps his question had not been the best. He'd no desire to speak of her husband right now. "Not to rush you or anything, but it is getting late and we should try to make an early start. Any chance you might begin preparing for bed?"

As if the very idea of doing so came as a shock, Mrs. Lawson's gaze roamed around the small room. "Right. Of course."

James flung one arm over his eyes and pretended he paid no attention to her, though that wasn't true at all. His every sense was on high alert, his ears tracking each move she made as she started to get herself ready. He heard her open her bag and riffle through some of her things. Fabric rustled and then...nothing.

"Promise you won't look?" she said after what seemed like endless silence.

"My eyes are tired, Mrs. Lawson, and I just want to sleep. So yes, I promise I will not look."

Another moment of silence followed – clearly a hesitation on her part – before a series of rushed movements followed. Without peeking, James followed the sound of her taking off her shoes and setting them aside. Next, her dress swooshed as it landed upon the floor. It sighed as she picked it up and hung it upon a hook. A brief pause followed before he heard the ties of her stays give way. Then the smack of the boned material as it landed somewhere, most likely on top of her bag.

James held every muscle in check while forcing himself not to look. Familiar with women's clothing, he knew she only wore her shift now. She'd have to remove that too if she wanted to put on her nightgown.

Tension coiled through him at the prospect of her getting naked. But then he heard her footsteps approach. The mattress dipped and all remaining light was snuffed out as she turned down the oil lamp completely.

Unless he'd missed something, she had decided to sleep in her shift instead of her nightgown. Most likely because she'd not wished to risk a state of complete undress, if only for a second. But this meant she'd be far more scantily dressed than otherwise. For although James was not acquainted with Mrs. Lawson's underthings, he knew shifts were shorter than nightgowns, made of finer linen, and tended to have shorter sleeves.

And given the narrow width of the bed, avoiding contact would be impossible.

"Are you all right?" he asked once she'd stretched out beside him and pulled up the covers. His shoulder and hip were both pushed into the wall and since he could not feel her, she had to be lying on the very edge of the bed.

"Yes."

"If you want more space you can come a bit closer."

"I'm fine."

Deciding not to argue, James clamped his mouth shut and told himself to go to sleep. He wanted to get an early start in the morning since progress would be slow until they managed to switch out the injured horse. And with every second they dallied, Michael and Cynthia moved closer to their goal.

A disgruntled sigh caught his attention. Mrs. Lawson shifted, pulling the blanket they shared as she turned. She still didn't touch him, which meant her knees were probably hanging over the side of the bed. James yawned and tried not to worry about her wellbeing. If she said she was fine, then who was he to insist she wasn't?

But when she continued to wriggle about in a futile attempt to get comfortable, James decided he had to do something for both their sakes. Either that or suffer a sleepless night.

"Mrs. Lawson?"

"Yes?"

"I'd like to suggest something without frightening you."

A pause, and then, "What?"

"If both of us sleep on our sides and without any distance between us, we'd have more space."

"I...ah...that probably wouldn't...I mean that's completely—"

"Mrs. Lawson. I'd never attack you as Cloverfield did. You know that don't you?"

"I do." Her lack of hesitation with regard to this response pleased him.

"I'm not trying to coax you into doing something you don't want to do either. All I'm suggesting is that we might benefit from applying a bit of practicality." When she didn't respond he gently asked, "Do you trust me?"

It seemed like forever before she answered. "Yes, Mr. Dale. I trust you completely."

James's heart tripled in size as a surge of warmth swept through him. "Good." He rolled onto his side and scooted backward, as far up against the wall as he could manage. "Come toward me then."

She did as he asked, proving to him that she valued his word. He'd stick to it. But since he wasn't a saint, he failed to avoid scandalous thoughts as the length of her body connected with his. Christ, it would be easy to run his hand over her thigh, to hike up her shift and pull down his smalls...

The very idea caused an ache in his groin. He backed up a little to give her more space – to avoid any inappropriate contact. She sighed with contentment and he briefly paused. A smile caught his lips as he casually wound his arm over her waist, hugging her to him. She didn't protest but rather reached for his hand. As she held it, her breaths grew deeper, steadier, until James knew she slept.

A deep sense of rightness pushed through his veins, calming his spirit and sending him after her into oblivion.

~

"There's something I need to tell you," Cynthia said. Lying in bed, she stared up through the darkness while holding Michael's hand. Another day had gone by without her coming any closer to confiding in him. It was past time for that to change.

He rolled onto his side, propped himself on his elbow and dipped his head until their lips met. She welcomed the sweet caress, lost herself in it for a brief moment, but when his hand stole up her thigh, she placed her palm against his chest and pushed him back.

"This is important, Michael. Please listen."

He took a deep breath and expelled it, then flopped back onto his pillow. "Go on."

Cynthia worried her lip, struggling once more to find the right way to begin – to ease into a subject she knew might ruin the bliss they presently shared. Eventually, she chose to simply spit it out. "I can't have children."

A dreadful silence followed during which her heart leapt along with unsteady beats.

"How do you know?"

The whispered words meant he'd heard her and understood the consequence. There was no escaping the issue any longer, and in spite of the dread she'd felt over Michael knowing, it also brought a welcome relief.

"Henry and I tried to conceive." Michael winced at that, no doubt because he did not enjoy thinking of her with another man. "But it never happened."

"That doesn't mean anything," he said, his voice defiant. Rising back up onto his forearm, he gazed down at her through the darkness. "It can take time."

She desperately hoped he would not be able to see the tears that gathered at the corners of her eyes. "I'm sorry, Michael, but the doctors have confirmed it. I am…" She took a deep breath, afraid her voice might crack with emotion, yet somehow she managed to force out the necessary word. "Barren."

The mattress shifted as Michael moved into a sitting position. He still held her hand, but his lack of words were telling. Eventually he asked, "Why didn't you mention this sooner?"

"Because I fell in love with you and feared you'd react as Henry did. With anger. We had a terrible quarrel about it the day he died. I'm sure he wouldn't have driven so recklessly if we hadn't. Which means his death could very well be—"

"It wasn't your fault. The only person to blame for what happened was Henry and a damned unfortunate crack in his curricle's wheel." Leaning forward, he placed a soothing kiss on her brow.

"I knew I had to tell you this eventually – before we married. I just…I wanted to hold on to what we have for as long as I was able. Please, Michael. Forgive me."

Her voice shook with the pain of knowing what would surely follow.

"There's nothing to forgive. You're not to blame for this and while I could be frustrated with you for not telling me sooner, I would not wish to take back the last few days we've spent together." Michael cleared his throat. "Being an only child, however, having children is important to me. I won't pretend otherwise, but you not being able to have them doesn't change how I feel about you. It doesn't diminish my love, but it does give me cause to stop and think. As hard as it is for me to say this, I cannot marry you tomorrow or the day after that. I need more time in which to be sure I can make such a sacrifice. I'm sorry."

So was she, but at least he hadn't extinguished all hope.

CHAPTER FIFTEEN

When Wilhelmina woke, the first thing she became aware of was the weight of a leg pressing into her thigh. An arm, loosely wrapped around her waist, served as an added reminder of the man who slept beside her. His breath stirred the nape of her neck with each exhalation he made, instilling in her a comfortable sense of security.

Her eyes fluttered open, bringing his hand into view. Neatly trimmed nails without a hint of dirt beneath showed no evidence of the hard work Mr. Dale enjoyed to do. A thin white line contrasted against darker skin, tempted her with a curious urge to stroke her thumb across the scar traversing his knuckles in order to feel its raised texture.

She resisted and let herself savor whatever remained of this moment. Soon they would have to rise and be on their way. The brief pretense of being married would come to an end, denying them the intimacy they'd been allowed to enjoy while tucked away in this room. It defied social norms, yet Wilhelmina had no regrets. As worried as she'd been at first about spending the night with Mr. Dale, the experience had been wonderful. And he'd not even tried to kiss her.

Instead, she'd shaved him.

The memory prompted a smile. An added tendril of warmth curled through her stomach. If this was what happily married couples had every night, she envied them with every fiber of her being, though she'd always stand by the choices she'd made. They were the right ones, even if they did deny her the peaceful calm of being held by Mr. Dale forever.

Her heart thudded slightly harder as it occurred to her she'd developed a fondness for him. One that hadn't been there before they'd set off on this journey together. Until then, there had been respect and attraction. Now, after getting to know him better, she feared parting ways with him once they accomplished their goal would leave her feeling hollow inside. His company had become important. He'd faced down a duke for her without second thought, and managed to make her feel cherished even though he was meant to despise her.

And then there was the kiss.

Lord help her but she longed to experience that again. But if there had ever been a chance to do so, it had been last night, and neither of them had taken it. Which was probably for the best since it could only lead to heartache. She squeezed her eyes shut and bit back a curse. How could she have been so foolish as to let herself fall for a man who'd never want her?

Yet it occurred to her that this was precisely what had happened. It explained the pleasure she found from simply being close to him, from the joy she'd found in shaving him, and from the anticipation of spending more time in his company as they continued their onward journey. He impressed her with his principles, his innovative ideas, and his willingness to grab a shovel and help his father's tenants dig a canal. He frustrated her like nobody else with his stubborn refusal to let their children be happy together, but he also made her laugh until she forgot all the troubles she faced.

And since he denied Cynthia and Michael his blessing because of the very principle Wilhelmina respected, she couldn't really fault him for it. After all, his perspective was based on what he knew and as such, it made perfect sense, even if it wasn't in Cynthia's or Michael's favor. Furthermore, he had tried to theorize a situation in which a union between Cynthia and Michael was possible, even though his suggestion was an impossible option.

With a sigh, she lifted his arm and pulled her legs out from underneath his. A low murmur rumbled through him. He shifted and Wilhelmina stood.

"What time is it?" he asked with a sleepy yawn.

"Five, I should think, judging from the dim light." She glanced at him while padding across the floor to the wash basin. Last night, it had made perfect sense to sleep in her shift. Now, with a muted glow beginning to seep past the edges of the curtains, it would offer him a far more daring glimpse of her body than if she'd worn her nightgown.

To her surprise, she wasn't as shy about that as she'd been before. Somehow, being confined to close quarters with him, having him discard his own clothes as if it were perfectly normal, and sharing a bed, had helped her pack away some of her inhibitions.

Or maybe her courage was simply bolstered by the fact that his eyes remained closed.

She shook her head on that thought and began washing her face.

"We need to depart soon," Mr. Dale said. "If we're lucky, Michael and Cynthia will be at the next inn, still sound asleep. Provided they take their time to rise and eat breakfast, we might be able to catch them before they set out on the final leg of their journey."

"And if we're unlucky?" Wilhelmina washed under her arms and across the back of her neck, then dried herself. She twisted her hair into a knot and pinned it. "Hmm?"

When Mr. Dale still didn't answer, she turned. And instantly froze in response to the dark intensity of his gaze. Eyes wide open, the unashamed man lounged with one arm behind his head while boldly staring at her in a way that caused every nerve to draw tight with awareness. Tiny shivers dance across Wilhelmina's shoulders. Her mouth grew dry. She could not recall what they'd just been discussing. All she could do was stand there while he looked his fill.

"Do you have any idea how much I want you," he murmured, and instantly blinked as if surprised to hear the words spoken. "I know I shouldn't. It's inappropriate of me to even admit it, but God help me if it's not true. You're stunning, Mrs. Lawson. I can't get the kiss we shared out of my mind and..." He scrubbed one hand across his face. "Sorry. Forget I said anything."

Wilhelmina could scarcely breathe. Forget he'd said anything? He had to be mad. His words would undoubtedly stay with her forever, bringing regret and heartache since that was all they could ever be – words. To act on them would be reckless, no matter how much she longed to forget who they were for a while and just...

A sudden need to move overcame her. She snatched up her stays and started putting them on, desperate to focus her mind on something besides the man who'd just claimed to want her. Heaven above, she wanted him too. The longing to give herself up to the passion she sensed they could find with each other burned through her, leaving a smoldering path in its wake. Her fingers worked the laces of her front-closing stays, pulling them tight with jerky movements.

He promised her something with his words – the chance to have what she'd never had before, what she knew she would never have again once they went their separate ways. Mind reeling, she grabbed her gown, tossed it over her head, and pushed her arms through the sleeves.

Mr. Dale was up now as well. Still dressed in only his smalls, he moved toward the washbowl, pushing past her.

His arm brushed hers and Wilhelmina turned. Her hand reached out before she could think, staying his progress. This idea of hers – not really an idea at all but more of an instinct – would probably be a mistake. But after giving up all of her own dreams in order to constantly do what was right, where was the harm in letting herself enjoy a brief slice of happiness?

Mr. Dale stilled beneath her splayed fingers. She curled them more firmly around his arm and felt his muscles flex in response. Her gaze swept over his torso, across the hardened planes wrought from physical work and activity. Smooth skin rising and dipping in ridges and valleys lured her gaze lower, to the dark trail of hair right under his naval. She brought her other hand to his abdomen and slid it upward while committing each spot her fingertips touched to memory.

Pulse racing, she raised her gaze to his and instantly sucked in a breath on account of the hunger she found there. He watched her much as she imagined a cat on the prowl might consider its prey. Refusing to let it deter her, she held it. Even though she had little clue about what she was doing, she hoped he'd understand she not only shared his interest, but welcomed it.

"Mrs. Lawson..." The low timbre of his voice teased her senses, drawing her nearer.

"You may call me Mina, if you like."

A hiss of breath left him and then his mouth was on hers, plundering her with wild abandon as if he were starved. Teeth grazed her skin and he answered her gasp with a growl. An arm came around her, clasping her to him, and Wilhelmina was lost – lost to a pleasure she'd only known once before in her life, when he'd kissed her in the carriage. Before that, she'd pushed all thoughts of ever engaging in lovemaking from her mind. Bad experience was after all a wretched thing to deal with.

But now, here with him, she felt no fear or apprehension. Perhaps because there was mutual consent, and because she knew he would never insist on more than what she was willing to give.

His hands shifted lower. She wound her arms around his neck and arched against him while kissing him back with equal fervor, tasting him as he tasted her. It was decadent, completely indecent, and utterly wonderful all at once.

"Mina." Her name, roughly whispered against her cheek, held a scandalous promise. "We ought to get going."

"I know," she agreed, even as she raked her fingers through his hair and kissed him again.

He turned with her in his arms, stepped back a little, and lowered himself to the edge of the bed while bringing her with him. She had no choice but to bend her legs and place her knees on either side of his legs as he drew her to him. Her gown rode upward, and then her body connected with his, and it was as if stars sparked behind her eyes.

Yet it wasn't enough.

Compelled by instinct, she moved, and was met by delicious sensation. Her breath hitched in response to the pleasure and as she gazed into his dark eyes, she knew he felt it too. Embracing the moment she leaned back a little, pushed down her bodice, and started undoing the stays she'd just tied a few minutes prior.

"Please." It was all she could manage to say as they fell from her shoulders.

Mr. Dale dipped his gaze, and then he ran one finger along the edge of her shift's neckline, toward the ribbon holding it closed in the front. "I've dreamt about this since the moment we met."

Before she could voice a response he'd undone the bow and pulled down her garment, baring her to his gaze. His eyes flared and then his mouth was upon her, worshiping her in a new and glorious way. She gripped his shoulders and sighed with pleasure while gently moving against him. With a keen awareness of what she desired, he lifted up just enough to shove down his smalls. Returning his mouth to hers, he kissed her again while guiding her into the right position and bringing her back down on top of him.

The invasion that followed caused her to tense. She braced herself and took a deep breath while praying Mr. Dale had not noticed how truly inept she was with this sort of thing.

"Are you all right?" he asked, dismissing any such

hope.

She forced a smile. "Fine."

Leaning back a little, he searched her face. "If you've changed your mind just—"

"No. I, um...I'm just not used to doing it like this."

He gave her a funny look. "You're certain?"

His determination to make sure she was all right and that she was willing stood in such contrast to the only other experience she'd had, it almost made her weep.

"Yes." She needed this more than she'd known – needed him to replace her ugly memories with one of beauty. So she placed her palm against his cheek and kissed him.

"Try to relax then," he murmured against her lips.

She did as he instructed and allowed him to give her what she required – the illusion of being wanted and cared for in ways she knew she never would be. Clinging to him, she turned to him for guidance and let him set the pace.

"You're perfect," he murmured while pressing his cheek to hers. "Better than I imagined."

Wanting to be as bold as he, she chose to return the sentiment. "So are you."

Heat flashed in his eyes right before he brought his mouth back to hers. Passion travelled the length of her spine, prompting a gasp right before the sensation peaked and she shattered.

A swift movement followed and then a satisfied growl filled her ears as he came undone in her arms.

CHAPTER SIXTEEN

He had to be out of his bloody mind, James decided as he and Mrs. Lawson – Mina – set off once more. After thanking the Mitchells for their hospitality over a quick cup of tea and a slice of bread, they'd gone to find James's coachman.

Propped against one corner of the carriage, diagonally across from Mina, James studied her profile as she gazed out the window. What the hell had he been thinking to claim her in such a rushed manner, like some common whore he could toss aside after? He must have taken leave of his senses. Thank God he'd at least had the presence of mind to withdraw at the very last moment.

He'd wanted to form a closer bond, but this was really taking the idea a step too far. Not that he hadn't considered bedding her. Of course he had. Multiple times. But given his rising suspicions about her, he'd decided it would be unwise to press for anything more than a temporary friendship.

Too late for that now. They were officially more than travel companions, more than partners with a common goal, and a hell of a lot more than friends. And if she'd meant to keep him in the dark about herself forever, she'd failed spectacularly, because his eyes were now wide open. He saw her for exactly who she was – a woman who'd never taken a lover in her life.

Which begged the question: what the hell was going on?

Determined to get to the heart of it, he took a deep breath and braced himself for the subject he meant to address. "Mina?"

She turned away from the window and faced him, her cheeks flushing the moment their eyes met. "Yes?"

"I do not wish to cause you discomfort or embarrassment, but I'd like to discuss what occurred between us this morning."

"Must we?" Apprehension shadowed her words. "It doesn't change anything."

Was she truly that naïve? "On the contrary, it changes everything. First and foremost, the way I see you."

She clenched her jaw and dropped her gaze. Her posture stiffened. "I don't know why it would when all we did was act on our mutual attraction. Aside from that, I am still the adulteress who shamed her husband. This is what I do, Mr. Dale, and while I'll admit I liked it better with you than with anyone else, you do not owe me anything, if that's where this is going."

Disappointment slashed through him. "Why do you persist in lying to me?"

Her gaze snapped back to his. "What do you mean?"

"If I were to hazard a guess, you've only been with one man prior to me – your husband – and not very often, I'll wager."

"Mr. Dale, I—"

"You cannot fool me any longer, Mina. I know what it means to have an experienced lover, and you don't fit the description." She turned away from him again, forcing her gaze back to the view. "I'm sorry. That's not a criticism. In fact, I'm immensely glad to know you're not the person I believed you to be for the past two years. I just wish you would be honest with me."

"Why?"

"Because I like to think of you as a friend and as such I want to advise you as best as I can, but doing so isn't easy unless you confide in me."

She was quiet for a moment before she slowly said, "Thank you. I appreciate the offer, but opening up to you won't do any good. In fact, the best thing you can do for me is to keep on pretending I am exactly who I say I am."

He crossed his arms and glared at her. Why was she being so stubborn? A possibility struck – one he did not care for in the least, but at this point it was the only thing that made sense. "He's blackmailing you somehow. Isn't he?"

She frowned. Her gaze shifted back to his once more. "Who?"

"Your husband. He clearly wanted to end the marriage, perhaps because of his wish to re-marry, only he had to get rid of you first."

"Mr. Dale, I—"

He cut her off with a frustrated sigh. "If I am to call you, Mina, then you must call me James in return."

She stared back at him for a long moment before she finally nodded. "Very well. James."

A wave of pleasure rolled through him. He felt a smile tug at his lips. "Now, I have to say your husband seemed like a likeable man when I met him, and I sympathized with him during the hearings, but I'm also familiar enough with scoundrels putting on a good show for the courts to know people aren't always what they seem. So if he has something on you, perhaps I can help."

He made the suggestion even though his theory didn't square with the fondness she'd shown while speaking of Mr. Hewitt.

"How?" A genuine hint of curiosity sharpened her eyes. "Suppose you're right and I am being blackmailed. How would you change public opinion and save my reputation?"

"I'd start by making a case, which would lead to an investigation. Blackmail is a serious offense. As is perjury."

"Of which he and I would be equally guilty."

She had him there. Even if she'd been forced into it,

surely she could have sought help at some point. Unless she'd been too afraid.

The possibility of any person threatening her, of possibly causing her harm, made James sick to his stomach. Yet he had to ask, "Did your husband strike you, Mina. Is that why you fear him?"

Surprise widened her eyes before fierce intensity took over. "My husband would never lay a hand on anyone. He is the best man I have ever had the honor of knowing and as such he deserves more than I was able to give."

"I don't understand."

"Stop trying to."

The tortured look in her eyes before she shuttered all emotion was enough to crack his heart wide open. He wanted to cross to her and pull her into his arms, comfort her and bolster her spirits until she righted herself once more. He wanted to know the secrets she kept and help her find a way out of a situation she clearly didn't deserve. But how?

What could he possibly offer her? Marriage was out of the question and if he suggested she be his mistress, he reckoned she'd tell him to bugger off. He almost smiled at that. Mina was strong and independently minded. She had a property to return to once they were done chasing after their reckless children. And he had his life in London.

An unpleasant feeling presented itself as he thought of their parting ways. Even though Clarington House was close to where she lived, he'd have no reason to see her unless he came with a proposition. And yet, the idea of not having her in his life was like knowing the sun would never rise again. He wanted her, but more than that, he clamored for her in a way that made his soul weep at the prospect of losing her forever.

Because...

James sucked in a breath and held it. He studied her as she sat there, proud and unyielding – determined to win at whatever game it was they were playing. Her love for her daughter was undeniable, her fortitude in the face of adversity indisputable. She stood up to him when he judged her in anger, figured out how to go on when most other women would crumble, she took every insult flung her way, protected a husband who'd clearly wronged her, and worked alongside her servants.

She was a gem of a woman if ever there was one, and while he hated the secrets she kept, he knew they would never threaten the high regard he had for her. Because whatever the truth was, it couldn't be worse than the lie she'd already told. If anything, he sensed the truth would destroy the very foundation upon which her divorce was built. And she clearly didn't want that.

James didn't either. He wanted her to be free he just...wished she would trust him more than she did. It actually shocked him how much he longed for her to lean on him. Maybe if he shared a bit more of himself she would do so?

"I happily bought the story you and your husband sold, perhaps because it was easy for me to relate to him." He waited for her to glance his way. Once he knew he had her attention he said, "My wife was unfaithful. She was every bit the person you tried to portray, so I hated you for putting your husband through the pain I'd had to endure."

"I'm sorry. I didn't know."

"Apparently she was unhappy." He still couldn't keep the bitterness from his voice after all these years. "The lifestyle I chose for myself did not live up to her high expectations."

"Did she not realize you wanted to have a career?"

"Of course she did, but she thought she could change my mind. She believed she could convince me to buy a grander house and get my father to issue a large allowance."

Mrs. Lawson snorted. "Then she was a fool."

"No more than I since I was sure she'd gradually gain an appreciation from knowing I earned every penny we spent." He shook his head. "Truth is I was young and blind. But my eyes were opened the day I returned home to fetch some papers I had forgotten and found her in bed with another man."

"Oh no." Genuine sympathy filled Mina's eyes.

"We managed to muddle through for Michael's sake, but our marriage was in tatters after that. And then she caught influenza one winter and died."

"James..." Mina crossed to his bench and clasped his hand. Her palm settled gently against his cheek. Stormy blue eyes snared his, holding him captive for a brief moment before she leaned in and kissed him. Unlike the previous kisses they'd shared, this was a gentle caress intended to soothe. It eased the anger that still reared its head whenever he thought of Clara, and made him feel cherished.

He'd not expected that, nor was he prepared for how good it felt. But the fact was he'd loved Clara, only to realize she didn't spare his feelings much thought. His wife had broken his heart, crushed it as if it were made of glass, and stomped all over the miserable remains. Since her, he'd had only superficial encounters with women.

Until Mina Lawson came along and turned his world upside down.

Grateful to her for the comfort she offered, he kissed her back, ever conscious of the fact that he tightened the bond between them by doing so. James couldn't muster the strength to care. Not when the feel of her lips on his own was like tonic. He needed her more than he dared to admit.

"I'm sorry your wife was so beastly," she said, her forehead propped against his. "You deserve so much better."

"I think you do too." When she started moving away, he wound one arm around her and held her in place. "Whatever your troubles, I'm here if you need me."

A smile of acknowledgement captured her lips as the carriage drew to a stop. James looked out. They'd arrived at the coaching inn. "I'm going to inquire after Michael and Cynthia while the coachman switches the horses. Would you like to join me or do you prefer to wait here?"

"I'll take every chance I get to stretch my legs," Mina said.

James helped her down and issued instructions to the coachman, then started escorting her into the inn. Before they reached the door though, it swung open. A handsome, perfectly clad gentleman stepped outside. His eyes glinted mercilessly as they settled upon James and Mina. A sneer tugged at his lips.

"Speak of the devil," Cloverfield drawled while striding toward them. His friends, the Earl of Everton, Viscount Rockburn's youngest son, and two others who'd now spilled from the inn as well, stood at his back. Each wore an arrogant look of contempt.

James felt Mina's hand grip him harder. He straightened his back and raised his chin. "Gentlemen, please step aside."

"Not until you agree to grant me what I desire," Cloverfield said.

"If it's Mrs. Lawson you speak of," James said while drawing Mina closer, "you'll not have her if I have anything to say on the matter."

"Everything in due course." Cloverfield's smirk warned James that what he said next would not be pleasant. "First, I'll have satisfaction. Once you're dead, I'll have the lady as well."

∾

Ice seeped into Wilhelmina's veins. Her stomach contracted, not so much in response to what Cloverfield meant to do to her but rather at the idea of James getting hurt. The duke merely grinned while his vile friends snickered, their eyes filled with diabolical humor.

"Duels are illegal," James said with a calmness she did not share. "So is murder and rape, last I checked."

"Details," Cloverfield murmured. He leaned forward, bringing his face within one inch of James's – so close, Wilhelmina had no trouble seeing the tight pull of resentment curling his lips. "You humiliated me, Mr. Dale, and denied me what I wanted. I'll not stand for that. Not from an untitled nobody such as yourself. So name your weapon, *sir.*"

Wilhelmina closed her eyes and held her breath while clinging to James for all she was worth. Cloverfield's father had spoken similarly to her once, and it had not ended well. Bile rose in her throat and her heart began trembling with fearful unease.

"I'll do no such thing," James said.

"Then you shall be branded a coward. Make no mistake, Mr. Dale, I will destroy you one way or the other."

"My reputation is unflappable," James gritted.

Cloverfield straightened with a snort. His gleaming eyes slid across Wilhelmina until she felt soiled. "Are you certain it won't suffer once the world learns you've sided with the most shameful woman in England?

Against a duke, I might add. If you were just using her, that would be one thing, but you're not. Are you?"

James glared back at the duke. "My relationship with Mrs. Lawson is none of your affair."

"In fact," Cloverfield continued, "I think the two of you have a partnership of some sort, and that alone will be enough to discredit you."

"You're wrong," James said.

"Am I?" Cloverfield's gaze slithered over her once again. "Last I checked, the two of you weren't even sleeping in the same room."

James's hand moved with lightning speed. His hand curled around the duke's snowy cravat, crumpling the fabric. "I remember your intrusion upon her privacy all too well. Touch her again and I'll have your head."

Wilhelmina's skin tightened as every nerve drew to attention. She gave Cloverfield's friends a wary glance. All hints of amusement had vanished from their faces. Instead they looked ready to pounce.

"Dangerous words," Cloverfield said, "coming from a man who refuses to fight."

"I never said I wouldn't fight you," James said as he let the duke go. "Just because I won't pick a weapon doesn't mean I shan't take pleasure in planting you a facer."

Cloverfield tilted his head and grinned with eerie delight. "Fists it is then."

"James." Wilhelmina turned toward the man she wanted to share her secrets with but couldn't. "Don't do this."

The corners of his eyes creased with compassion. "I've not much choice. Cloverfield won't relent until we've had it out with each other once and for all."

"There's no guarantee he won't spread false rumors about you anyway," she said. "The man has no honor. And what then? You'll be hurt and your reputation ruined. At least if you walk away—"

"I'll do no such thing, Mina." He held her gaze with fierce determination. "We'll need witnesses though, so go inside and see if you can gather a few willing men while I discuss terms with the duke."

"James, I—"

"Go."

Wilhelmina's heart sank. Was he truly so afraid for his reputation – so worried about what people would think if they thought he'd stood up for her – he was willing to put himself in danger? She backed away, adding distance between them. It had been so easy for her to pretend they were getting along while they were alone. She'd basked in his kisses and savored the close bond they'd shared while making love just a couple of hours ago.

But that wasn't real. *This* was.

James was willing to fight a duke in order to stop him from feeding suggestions to the public. He could have said he was helping her with a private matter, which was true. But no. He didn't want anyone knowing he'd travelled with someone so shameful.

She turned for the door just as it opened. Wilhelmina stared at the blonde woman who blocked her path and at the man directly behind her. "Cynthia."

"Mama?" Cynthia's lips parted in surprise.

Michael looked equally shocked as he stared past Wilhelmina. "Papa?"

A shudder raked Wilhelmina's spine when Clover-field laughed. "Well, isn't this a delightful turn of events? Your travelling together is finally starting to make a great deal of sense."

"If I win, you'll keep this to yourself," James growled. He suddenly stood at Wilhelmina's shoulder, facing their children. "What the hell were the two of you thinking?"

Cynthia and Michael both frowned, but Michael spoke first. "I thought I made that clear in the note I left you."

James muttered a curse. "We'll discuss this later. For now, I've a more pressing matter to see to. Mina, the witnesses, if you will."

Wilhelmina bristled but chose not to argue.

Cynthia's eyes widened while Michael stared at his father as if he barely recognized him. "Mina?"

Wilhelmina pushed past him and Cynthia. "I'll explain later. After your father has finished fighting the Duke of Cloverfield."

"Mama," Cynthia said, trailing Wilhelmina as she entered the inn. "I can't believe you followed us here."

"Are you mad?" Wilhelmina asked, rounding on her. "You are my daughter. Michael is Mr. Dale's son. Of course we were going to follow you and make sure you were both all right."

"That may be your reason, but we both know it isn't his. Mr. Dale just wants to stop us from getting married."

Wilhelmina sighed. "Yes. He does. But only because he's concerned for his son's future. He worries he won't have the promising career he deserves with me as his mother-in-law."

"That's nonsense, Mama."

"No it isn't, Cynthia. He actually has a valid point, however infuriating it may be."

"Well." Cynthia firmed her lips. "Then he'll be pleased to know that the wedding is off."

"What?"

Cynthia answered with a weak smile. "It appears we may have been too hasty with regard to getting married. We'd actually just decided to return to Renwick when you showed up."

"Oh." Wilhelmina allowed the weight of Cynthia's words to settle. James would be pleased, but the special time they'd shared these past few days was now officially over. There would be no more chances to spend the night in each other's arms, no more stolen kisses or private exchanges in the carriage. "What happened?"

"I cannot give him the children he wants," Cynthia muttered.

Wilhelmina stared at her daughter in disbelief. "I beg your pardon?"

"I was ashamed to mention it to him, and afraid I'd

lose him if I did. But the closer we got to Scotland, the worse my guilt became and the more I realized how wrong it was to keep such a thing from him."

"Oh, Cynthia." Wilhelmina drew her daughter into her arms and held her. "But are you certain?"

"Yes, Mama. Without a doubt."

Wilhelmina sighed. "You did the right thing then, my darling. I'm proud of you."

"It doesn't make it hurt any less," Cynthia confessed.

"I know." Heavy hearted, Wilhelmina gave her daughter a comforting squeeze before she released her. "We'll discuss this in greater depth later. For now, let's help Mr. Dale with securing those witnesses he asked us to find."

It had been years – decades – since James had engaged in a brawl, but he'd stayed in decent shape and was fairly sure he'd beat the duke because of this. The younger man circled him, fists raised, while a dozen people looked on. Both men had removed their jackets. James had even rolled up his sleeves. Cloverfield sneered and suddenly struck. James blocked the blow with his forearm, stepped back, and waited for the duke to charge him again. As much as he loathed the man, James had no interest in hurting him unless he had to.

Cloverfield's fist shot forward once more and connected with James's shoulder. A dull ache pulsed through him as he staggered back, but the strength of the blow revealed the duke's weakness. He was the sort of young fool who thought he was better than everyone else, but the punch he'd just delivered belonged to a man of leisure – the sort who pranced about at Gentleman Jackson's for show without knowing what it truly meant to fight with one's fists.

As if encouraged by his ability to push James around, Cloverfield grinned, pulled his fist back, and prepared to punch James again. This time, James ducked to one side, made a swift turn, and struck the duke squarely in the chest. Cloverfield's eyes bulged in surprise, his mouth going wide as the air was forced from his lungs. His knees gave way and his hand reached out, gripping James for support.

"Are you done yet?" James spoke next to Cloverfield's ear.

Fury lit his opponent's eyes, growing in strength as he regained his balance and straightened his spine. "Go to hell."

Cloverfield stepped back, panting for breath while snarling at James like a rabid dog. He rolled his shoulders and flexed his fingers, bounced a few times on the balls of his feet, and finally struck out again. His fist connected with James's mouth. Wilhelmina cried out and James swiftly blocked the sound to stop the distraction. This last blow was stronger. James was sure he tasted blood. When the next strike came, pushing Cloverfield's fist into James's cheek, he decided he'd had enough. It was time to stop being nice and to give the young pup exactly what he deserved.

SOPHIE BARNES

With this in mind, James drew his fist back and pushed it forward once more as hard as he could. Knuckles connected with cartilage to produce a satisfying crunch. Blood spurted and Cloverfield grunted as he lost his balance. His hand caught James who followed him down. They landed in a sprawl of frantically moving limbs. An elbow connected with James's forehead – damn, but that would surely bruise. Cloverfield shoved and James withdrew, only to lunge at him once again.

This was the bastard who would have raped Mina if he hadn't been stopped. He deserved the thrashing James gave him – had instigated the whole damn thing – and now that James had enjoyed the pleasure of wiping his arrogant smirk from his face, he lost all restraint. He beat him for the bastard he was, for the misplaced sense of entitlement that put others in danger, and for lacking the honor his title ought to demand.

Until hands caught him and dragged him away.

"That's enough," Michael said while James panted for breath.

"We'll get you for this," Everton spat while hauling Cloverfield to his feet.

"He challenged me," James said since the fact was worth remembering.

"Nevertheless," another pompous young dandy said while helping the bruised and bloodied duke inside the inn. "You'll live to regret this,"

James huffed a breath and swiped his palm across

his jaw. His lip felt swollen, his knuckles raw, and there was a very uncomfortable pain in his knee from when he'd landed on the ground. "I'm too bloody old for this nonsense."

"Come," Wilhelmina said. She took him by the arm and placed one hand at his back to nudge him forward. "We ought to get you inside as well so we can tend to those wounds."

"Not with him in there," James protested.

She flattened her mouth and gave him a don't-be-so-impossible look. "You've a nasty cut on your lip that needs cleaning. The same can be said for those knuckles. So let's go. We'll find a spot at the opposite side of the taproom from where that prick is sitting."

An involuntary grin pulled at James's mouth. He winced and cut a look at Wilhelmina. "Prick eh?"

"No sense in pretending he's anything less."

She did have a point, and as such, James very much feared the duke would find a way to retaliate, if for no other reason than to assert his superiority.

CHAPTER SEVENTEEN

Wilhelmina was immensely relieved when she found the taproom devoid of Cloverfield and his cohorts. They must have returned upstairs to the rooms they'd spent the night in.

"I'll ask for a bowl of warm water and a washcloth," Cynthia said.

"And I'll make sure you receive a tall glass of brandy," Michael added.

He disappeared after Cynthia, leaving Wilhelmina and James to find a table. They agreed on one that stood in a corner. She pulled out a chair and sat while he did the same, selecting the chair directly beside hers. Their knees bumped together as he twisted toward her.

"Mina..." He sought her hand beneath the table. Warm and sturdy fingers clasped hers. A troubled look dulled his eyes beneath the deep grooves of a frown. "Is it foolish of me to wish we hadn't found them just yet?"

She shook her head. "No."

His thumb stroked over her knuckles. "I wanted another night with you."

Heat stole into her cheeks. She glanced toward the back of the taproom where their children presently chatted with one of the barmen. "We knew our alliance would be brief from the very beginning."

"That doesn't mean I'm ready for it to end."

His whispered words, wrought with desperation, forced her gaze back to his. Her heart ached on account of the loss she knew she would soon be forced to endure. "It has to though, and it will. Especially since they've decided not to marry after all." When his frown deepened she said, "They were planning to return to Renwick when we showed up. We can travel back together of course, but…"

"It won't be the same," he muttered and closed his eyes as if in pain.

Wilhelmina wasn't sure she understood him. He'd gotten what he wanted. His son would not be marrying Cynthia. There would be no shameful family connection to ruin his or Michael's reputation. And while they might have given in to desire, she doubted it had affected him as deeply as it affected her. How could it when he'd been with other women before?

She would never regret giving herself to him as brazenly as she had. He'd given her a beautiful gift by replacing the awful experience she'd once endured with one that filled her heart with warmth. It had, as it turned out, been her only chance, and she'd hold on to that shared moment for the rest of her life.

"Days, weeks, and months will pass," she told him without quite managing to keep her voice as strong or steady as she'd hoped. "You will return to London, go back to work, and this will gradually become a distant memory."

He stared at her as if she were mad, but rather than argue he said, "Please tell me the truth."

She knew what he asked of her. He'd already figured out more than she had intended about her, but to tell him more could prove disastrous. Thankfully, she was saved from having to answer him by Cynthia, who placed a bowl on the table. Wilhelmina hastily withdrew her hand from James's and took the washcloth her daughter held toward her.

"Are you going to tell me what happened between you and Mr. Dale?" Cynthia asked Wilhelmina later once they'd left the inn and were heading south.

Mother and daughter shared the carriage while the men rode outside, increasing the strain on Wilhelmina's heart. She missed James already and was half-tempted to glance out the window in order to make sure he was still there. "I don't know what you mean."

Cynthia raised both eyebrows. "He addressed you by the shortened form of your Christian name, which I've only ever heard George do."

Wilhelmina sighed. "We agreed to a truce."

"I...see." There was a brief moment of silence before Cynthia asked, "Have you kissed him?"

"Cynthia!"

"Well, it is a fair question considering how he was looking at you."

Perplexed, Wilhelmina frowned. "And how would that be?"

"Like this." Cynthia tilted her chin a little and matched the expression of a puppy in desperate need of affection.

Wilhelmina rolled her eyes. "Don't be absurd."

"And you regarded him in much the same way, which is quite a departure from the unhappy faces you used to wear in each other's company."

The thoughtfulness with which Cynthia spoke put Wilhelmina on edge. She had no wish to discuss this – had no desire whatsoever to be reminded of how happy she had been while travelling north with no one but James for company. "You've clearly taken leave of your senses."

"Do you love him?"

"What?" The question came so abruptly it felt like a punch to the stomach. Wilhelmina gaped at her daughter. Inquisitive eyes stared back in expectation. "I...I...I..."

Cynthia chuckled. "I gather that's a yes then?"

Wilhelmina was not about to admit any such thing. "Let's talk about something else, like you and Michael, and all the trouble you've caused."

"Have you told Mr. Dale the truth?" Cynthia persisted, ignoring her completely.

Wilhelmina crossed her arms and looked out the

window. Clouds blocked the sun, casting dark shadows across the landscape to match her mood. "No."

"Perhaps you should."

"Why? So he can despise me for the right reason instead?" When Cynthia looked unconvinced Wilhelmina said, "He knows I'm not the adulteress I claimed to be, but he has given me no reason to think he won't resent me if he learns how far I have gone to deceive everyone. Mr. Dale is on the law's side, and I bent that law to my will until it broke. However good my intentions may have been, George and I got away with something we shouldn't have because we lied. What if people find out? What if the consequence of our true actions makes everything worse? I could go to prison, Cynthia. The divorce could be reversed and George's marriage to Fiona annulled, the children they have, made illegitimate. I'll not risk that."

"Surely that's not possible," Cynthia said.

"Perhaps not, but what if it is?" Wilhelmina shook her head. She and James hadn't stood a chance of finding happiness together. In light of his recent deductions, it was probably good they'd been denied more time alone.

"Michael knows."

A shiver stole across Wilhelmina's shoulders. "I beg your pardon?"

"I didn't want to enter into my marriage with a lie, so I confided everything in him."

"Oh God."

"Don't worry, Mama. I swore him to secrecy, but

maybe you can take comfort in his reaction. He actually applauded you for your selflessness and begged me to let him tell his father. He's certain the truth will alter Mr. Dale's opinion of you for the better."

"I cannot risk it," Wilhelmina said. "And you had no right to betray my trust."

"I'm sorry, Mama."

Wilhelmina dug her nails into her palms and fought the urge to scream. The secret she'd carefully guarded for more than two years had been shared with someone she barely knew. Control had been removed from her grasp and the realization made her feel like she was spinning. "We were wrong to confide in you."

A pained look stole into Cynthia's eyes. "Don't say that, Mama."

"You're too young – too naïve to appreciate the repercussions of your actions."

"I'm sorry, but Michael can be trusted. I assure you."

Wilhelmina closed her eyes for a second. "You cannot assure me of any such thing."

"Mama..."

"We will return to Renwick. Once there we'll arrange for you to go back to London. The sooner you re-enter Society, the quicker you'll find a husband. That will be your goal from now on – to marry and get yourself settled as fast as possible, before the decisions George and I made destroy whatever remaining chance you have of securing a happy future."

~

As much as James wished he was inside the carriage with Mina, he was glad to be able to race alongside it. The exertion did him good. It cleared his head and brought the last few days with her into focus. His heart pounded with each heavy hoofbeat, drumming a rhythm that spurred him onward. He glanced across at Michael whose stark expression suggested his thoughts were elsewhere. Tightening his hold on the reins, James returned his own to the woman who'd not only charmed him, but captured his heart.

The fact she would rather end things between them – walk away from him forever – than take a chance on being honest, angered him in the most unexpected way. Before, when he'd thought she was just like Clara, he'd loathed her. Now that he knew she was anything but, he wanted to try and find a way for them to nurture their relationship rather than see it destroyed. He'd no idea how to do such a thing without getting targeted by the gossips and bringing scandal to his name, but maybe if they worked together they could figure it out.

She didn't want that though. In fact, she had every intention of keeping him in the dark and in so doing, of forcing distance where there had been closeness that very morning.

He cursed her stubbornness and the loyalty she seemed to have for a man who'd since taken off to God knew where. James had not seen Mr. Hewitt's name in the papers since the divorce was announced, whereas Mina's kept popping up. Apparently there was an interest in knowing what a treacherous woman got up to and how many times she'd been cut in public. Mr. Hewitt, however, was allowed to move on with his life with no concern for the damage done to Mina. James hated him more with each passing second.

A village came into view and James slowed his horse to a trot. Michael did the same, and together they followed the carriage's progress through the narrow main street.

"I trust your opinion of Mrs. Lawson has changed since last we spoke," Michael said while they rode. When his horse shook its head and snorted, Michael leaned forward to stroke its neck. "The two of you seem surprisingly amicable with each other."

James swung his gaze toward his son. "What makes you say that?"

"Maybe the fact that you called her Mina? A bit familiar, wouldn't you say, seeing as you have claimed her to be the most awful woman in existence besides Mama."

"I'll admit she's not as bad as I initially believed," James said with a shrug. He'd barely gotten used to liking her more than what was wise and was not about to share the struggle he now faced with his son of all people.

"No. She's not," Michael said with a hint of sugges- tiveness. "In fact, she's probably the best person there is."

James raised an eyebrow. "Why would you think that?"

Michael's lips twisted. He seemed to consider how

to respond. "Cynthia told me everything, but she swore me to secrecy, so I cannot share what you don't already know."

How bloody perfect.

"Not very helpful," James muttered.

"I know, and I'm sorry, but you can trust me when I tell you that you have seriously misjudged Mrs. Lawson."

"I know that much already. She's not the cavorting wife she and her husband gave her out to be, but I cannot for the life of me figure out why she would willingly go along with a scheme that was destined to make her suffer." James met Michael's gaze. "Her refusal to tell me irritates me to no end."

"Because you care for her?"

James expelled a heavy sigh and allowed a nod to reveal the contents of his heart. "More than I ever thought possible."

"Then you must fight for her, Papa."

"How?" The magnitude of what Michael suggested, what he himself had considered, was daunting. "Even if there's a different reality hiding behind her façade, it won't make any difference with her reputation torn to shreds. It's unsalvageable, which prevents me from having any kind of respectable relationship with her. Hell, she's not even fit to be my mistress – not that I would suggest such a thing, mind you – but it does indicate how bad the situation is."

"It seems to me you've given up trying to win her before you've begun."

"What would you have me do, Michael?" It was odd asking his son for advice on such a personal matter, but it also felt good. Especially since it seemed like forever since they'd last bonded over something.

"Figure out what's more important to you, a life with Mrs. Lawson by your side or your reputation. If you cannot have both, then ask yourself which would enrich your life more? Which one would you regret losing the most? And before you answer, bear in mind that you don't have to live in London and you don't have to work for a living, which allows you the freedom to give that life up for her if you choose." When James kept silent, Michael asked, "Have you assured her you would stand by her regardless of what the truth may be?"

James frowned. "How can I make such a promise without knowing what the truth is?"

"Honestly, Papa," Michael said as if he were the parent and James the child, "for a man of your intelligence, you can be extraordinarily thickheaded at times."

Surprised by the set-down, James couldn't help but smile a little. "Have a little respect, will you?"

Michael rolled his eyes. "It's no wonder she hasn't confided in you. How can she when she can't be sure she can trust you?'

James blinked. "Of course she can trust me." When Michael gave him a skeptical look he hastened to add, "While I cannot say how I'll feel about the information, I would never betray her confidence."

"Does she know that?"

"I..." James stared at the carriage as it rolled along. He'd begged her to tell him what she was hiding, but he'd never said he wouldn't use the information against her. He'd just assumed she'd know he wouldn't.

"Look," Michael said, "you've made a name for yourself because of your strict adherence to the law. Men respect you for this. I admire you for it. But it also poses the greatest threat to the life you could have with Mrs. Lawson, because it's going to require you to keep a very open mind."

"And yet," James said, "based on everything you've learned, you believe her to be the finest person there is."

"Without a doubt." Michael seemed to reflect on what to say next. "She's incredibly brave, Papa, loyal to a fault, and more selfless than any other person I've ever met. Indeed, if I were in your position and felt what you clearly feel toward her, I would risk everything to be with her. Because she deserves to be happy more than you could ever imagine."

James considered this as they plodded toward the edge of the village. The leather from his saddle squeaked as his thighs pressed against it. He glanced at Michael. "Why didn't things work out between you and Cynthia?"

A shadow fell across Michael's brow. He shrugged one shoulder as if intending to show indifference, but failed. His turbulent thoughts were written all over his face. "She confided something in me last night."

"Besides the facts regarding her mother?"

Michael nodded. "I want to have children one day and as it turns out, Cynthia can't."

Aware of the difficult blow this must be to his son, James could think of nothing to say besides, "I'm sorry."

Michael slanted a disbelieving look in his direction. "You wanted me to break things off with her."

"For good reason, Michael. But that doesn't mean I relished coming between you and the woman you love or that I'm glad to know she can't have children."

"We wouldn't be here if it weren't for your disapproval." He expelled a heavy sigh. "I love her, and as such, there's a good chance I'll still choose to go against your wishes and marry her. But this new information requires a great deal of contemplation. Going through with a hasty marriage would have been rash in light of it."

Michael's words stayed with James as they left the village and pushed their horses into a gallop. His son had been willing to ignore social mores and risk being ostracized in order to be with the woman he wanted. He still might. Initially, James had believed him to be naïve, foolish, juvenile. But what if he was wrong? What if there was wisdom to be found in Michael's view of what was important?

Michael had loved his mother, but he'd not been ignorant of her flaws. He'd experienced first-hand the destructive effect a marriage could have if it were entered into for the wrong reasons. Perhaps then finding true love, no matter the hardship it promised, mattered more to him than making a respectable match for the sake of necessity, of risking a permanent union with the wrong woman. And his decision to give the new situation he found himself in some careful consideration before rushing into marriage conveyed an element of maturity James hadn't credited him with.

By the time they arrived at the same posting inn where they'd first met Cloverfield, it was late afternoon. James leapt from his saddle, stirring up a plume of dirt from the ground, tossed his horse's reins to a groom, and strode toward the carriage in which Wilhelmina and Cynthia sat. His heart pounded as he opened the door and peered inside, more so when he locked eyes with the woman who made him question some of his most firmly held beliefs. Never in his life had he second-guessed himself more than he'd done after making her acquaintance. All because he lacked the information he needed in order to judge her fairly.

Obviously, the only way for him to make any headway at all and figure out whether she might be worth every risk he feared to his own reputation was for him to uncover her secrets. With this in mind, he moved to one side and offered his hand. Cynthia stepped down first, thanked him for the assistance, and went to speak with Michael.

With his stomach coiled in a tight knot, James held his breath and waited for Wilhelmina to appear. Her gloved hand settled over his so carefully it seemed she feared he might scorch her. The half boots she wore peeked out from beneath the hem of her lilac gown when she placed her foot on the step, allowing a flash of delectable stocking-clad ankle to burn its way into his brain. A lovely shade of pink stole up her neck and into her cheeks as her fingers curled more securely around his hand.

James's heart beat so fast it began tripping over.

Too affected to speak, he guided her onto the ground. She raised her gaze to his in a shy sort of way that reminded him of a young girl fresh out of the school room. A warm sensation spread through his chest on that thought, for it wasn't entirely misplaced. Whatever it was she was hiding, Mina might as well be a debutante waiting to make her debut. She was almost that innocent.

"Thank you, Mr. Dale."

He dipped his head. "What happened to James?"

She bit her lip and looked askance, perhaps attempting to locate her daughter. "We probably ought to return to propriety and—"

"We're friends, you and I. There's nothing improper about you calling me James. Will you still allow me to call you Mina?" God, he hoped so.

A rapid pulse beat at the side of her neck. She seemed to consider, then gave a swift nod. "Yes."

A smile caught his lips. Lord, how he wanted to kiss her. Later, perhaps? He bent his arm at the elbow and offered it to her. "Let's go inside and see to our rooms. Once we've gotten settled, we can go for a stroll."

Wariness settled deep in her eyes, but she didn't protest his idea, for which he was grateful. Half an hour later, he knocked on the door to the room

Wilhelmina and Cynthia shared. The object of his desire answered.

"Ready?" he asked.

She glanced at her daughter who sat on the bed with something in her lap. "Cynthia?"

"You go ahead," Cynthia said. "I want to finish my mending."

"We can wait for you," Wilhelmina said.

"No need. I'll take a walk with Michael if I feel like a bit of fresh air once I'm done."

Wilhelmina's eyes widened enough to convey her uncertainty with this plan. "Alone?"

Cynthia glanced up then and stared at her mother. "I'm a widow, Mama. I don't need a chaperone."

"I...um...of course you don't. I just..." She gave James a hesitant look.

Cynthia sighed. "Go, Mama. Stretch your legs with Mr. Dale. I'll see you when you return."

"All right." Wilhelmina frowned. "I'll just fetch my shawl."

The door closed in James's face. When it opened once more, Wilhelmina looked far more composed than she had a few moments earlier. It was almost as if she'd put on her armor. He glanced at the shawl – a lovely deep purple one with an intricate lilac pattern running through it, to complement her gown. "Is that the one you wove?"

She turned to him in surprise, as if she'd expected him to forget this hobby of hers. "Yes."

"It's pretty." He reached out and stroked the fabric between his fingers. "Soft too."

"I mixed cotton and wool to reduce the coarseness."

Not knowing what else to say on the matter, he offered his arm. "Shall we?"

She placed her hand in the crook of his elbow and let him escort her. They descended the stairs to the inn's entryway and continued outside. The sun had dipped lower, affording a magical glow to the landscape. James breathed in the countryside air and drew Wilhelmina toward a path next to the inn. It led to a copse of trees and a narrow river.

They walked in silence until they reached the embankment where reeds and tall grass prevented them from getting too close to the flowing water.

"Do you fish?" Wilhelmina asked in a curious sort of way that suggested she'd tried to imagine him doing exactly that.

"On occasion. My father used to take me out on the lake behind our property when I was a boy. This would be an excellent spot for it, I should think."

"George loved to fish," she said, her voice soft with sentimentality, as though she were lost in the past. "He taught me after our fathers died. Helped get me through it."

Unpleasant emotion filled him. It bothered him to think of her with her husband, huddled together as children, marveling over each catch they made.

As children...

James stared at the water and watched it ripple.

She'd mentioned losing her father when she was ten. *Our fathers.* Mr. Lawson had travelled with a friend, but the identity of that friend had seemed irrelevant until now. "You and your husband grew up together. You lost your fathers at the same time."

The disaster would have bound them together in ways few people could comprehend. Hell, not even James could grasp the close ties she would feel to the only person who'd shared her grief in equal measure.

Choosing to follow Michael's advice, James quietly told her, "If you confide in me, I swear on my life I'll never tell another soul or use the information against you."

She hesitated, so long he feared she wouldn't respond. When she finally did, her voice was softened by reminiscence. "I love him, James. I'll always do so."

Her words shook him. This wasn't what he'd hoped to hear, and he hated the jealousy crashing through him because of it. He took a shuddering breath and tried to stay calm – to not speak in pain lest he hurt her. But it was hard. Her heart belonged to another, to a man who did not want her and this knowledge broke him.

He winced and closed his eyes for a moment, tried to concentrate on the ground beneath his feet and the gentle breeze tickling his face. Life was unbelievably unfair. Because against his better judgment, he'd fallen for her. And he'd been prepared to reconsider the ingrained beliefs he lived by so they could be together. Only she loved George. How bloody perfect.

"I owe him so much," she added.

"Because he taught you to fish?' James snapped, forgetting himself completely. Anger and heartache collided until he knew he was being unreasonable. But he couldn't seem to stop himself. "You don't owe him a damn thing, Mina. He used you in the worst possible way and left your life in shambles. Why the hell can't you see that?"

"James, I—"

"Your husband ought to be drawn and quartered for what he did to your reputation. So help me God, I'd strangle him myself if he were here."

"You're wrong about him. George is a good person."

Furious with himself for losing his grip, with George for convincing her to play along with the scheme he'd concocted to get himself out of the marriage, and with her for still caring about the bastard, James leaned into her with clenched jaws. "Stop. Defending him."

Her eyes widened. She gave a quick shake of her head. "You've got it all wrong."

"Have I?" Even though it felt like the bond they shared was unraveling, or possibly because of it, he needed to touch her. His hands settled heavily against her shoulders, holding her steady. "Then where is he now?"

She took a sharp breath and blinked back the tears he could see welling in her blue eyes. "In America."

The man had well and truly abandoned her then. So much for the friendship she kept insisting upon. "Alone?"

"No." When he didn't budge or speak, she finally admitted, "George has remarried."

Her confession and what it implied slammed into James with unrelenting force. Everything began making sense. She loved him and so she'd thrown herself on the proverbial pyre in order to save him from a marriage he'd clearly regretted. They'd been childhood friends, bound together by tragedy. They'd probably been fated to wed, but they'd been young and it hadn't worked out as they'd hoped. So when George found someone else, a plan had been forged.

Unable to bear it, James crushed Wilhelmina to him and pressed his mouth to hers in a fierce kiss intended to blot out the last few minutes. He wanted to forget this conversation forever – the fact that she loved a man who not only didn't deserve her, but who had cast her aside. It made him feel raw and helpless, for he stood no chance of making the scoundrel pay. Unless James followed him all the way to the God damn ends of the earth.

Bloody hell!

He tore himself away from her with a frustrated growl. Her breaths came just as harshly as his. As much as it hurt, he made himself step away and add distance, to ignore the imploring look in her still-damp eyes. "I'm sorry."

"For what?"

Unable to find the right words – unwilling to try – he turned away and started back toward the inn without her. He'd been prepared to risk his career for her, to cut ties with anyone who'd not accept her, to live in seclusion if that was what was required for them to be together. He'd been one step away from considering marriage. Until she'd pledged herself to the husband who didn't want her – who'd never wanted her, based on how little she knew about kissing and making love. She'd wasted her youth on that man and would keep on wasting her life. James set his jaw and continued to walk. He refused to stay and watch.

CHAPTER EIGHTEEN

Wilhelmina couldn't move. When James had offered assurance, she'd wanted to explain herself – to let him into her confidence so he'd understand her situation. But she'd muddled her words, started in the wrong place, and made things worse.

He'd drawn his own conclusions, had painted George as the villain and her as a fool. And when she'd tried to correct him, he'd no longer wanted to listen.

As shattered as she felt watching the man she loved walk away in anger, she knew it was probably for the best. Considering his values, the weight he placed on proper conduct, integrity, and respectability, she could never be more to him than a brief affair. Wilhelmina had to be mad to suppose he would ever consider a lasting attachment with her.

Expelling a heavy sigh, she started back toward the inn. She'd known life would be challenging for her after the divorce. The wretchedness she experienced now was as unsurprising as the regret that caused her heart to limp along with sluggish beats. Happily ever afters belonged to other people. She and James never stood a chance, because what it eventually came down to was that she'd been a married woman when they met. Only George's death would have let her remarry while retaining her reputation.

She shuddered and chastised herself for allowing such a thought to surface. Even though she might never see him again, he was her dearest friend. She loved him and could not imagine a world without him in it.

"Did you and Mr. Dale quarrel?" Cynthia asked that evening when she came to meet Wilhelmina in the private supper room she had procured.

"Why do you ask?"

"Because you're in here while he's made himself comfortable in the taproom."

Wilhelmina gestured for Cynthia to have a seat, then poured her a glass of red wine before taking a sip of her own. "I took your advice and tried to tell him the truth, but it came out all wrong and now he thinks I'm in love with George."

Cynthia gasped and covered her mouth with her hand. Eyes dancing, she stared at Wilhelmina who promptly frowned. "It's not funny."

Cynthia shook her head, then nodded before choking out, "It is a little funny. In a *Comedy of Errors* sort of way."

"I suppose," Wilhelmina agreed with some reluctance. She gave her daughter a weak smile. "We're quite a pair, aren't we?"

"You ought to correct his mistake," Cynthia said. A serving maid arrived just then, allowing a brief reprieve in conversation while mother and daughter placed their orders.

"What would be the point?" Wilhelmina asked once the maid was gone.

Cynthia's eyes widened. "The point, Mama, is for him to know how you truly feel. Even though Michael disapproved of me not telling him my secret sooner, and in spite of the fact that he's chosen to break things off, he knows I love him just as I know he loves me."

"And doesn't that make it harder, knowing you love each other but that you cannot be together unless he's willing to give up on being a father?" When Cynthia didn't respond, Wilhelmina said, "I fell in love with Mr. Dale and I believe he fell for me too, but it will be easier for him to walk away and move on if he believes my heart belongs to another. Especially since he'll never choose me anyway."

"You don't know that, Mama."

"I do."

"But, Mama, if you care for him, surely—"

"Let's not discuss this further," Wilhelmina said. She was exhausted by all the powerful emotions she'd experienced since that morning, from passion, to love, to hate, and pain. "It's pointless to ponder that which will never be. Instead, I would suggest we set our minds to getting you back into London society. If you can find a good man who's a widower with children in need of a mother, perhaps you can still build a happy life for yourself."

Cynthia didn't look the least bit convinced, but Wilhelmina was certain this would pass. Cynthia's heart was raw at the moment, but once she accepted reality and set her mind to finding a more appropriate match, Wilhelmina believed she would move on. Of course, her connection to Wilhelmina might remain an obstacle, though Wilhelmina was sure this too would change with time, provided she stayed away from London.

"Have Mrs. Lawson and her daughter not come down yet?" Michael asked when he plopped down into a chair at James's table.

"They're in that supper room over there," James said, raising his gaze from the paper on which he wrote just long enough to jut his chin at the back of the taproom.

"And yet you're here," Michael said. He seemed to hesitate before asking, "Should we not join them?"

"No." James went back to his writing.

"Seems a bit rude of us not to," Michael murmured. "Did you and Mrs. Lawson have a row or something?"

James raised his gaze to Michael's. "Turns out, she's in love with her husband."

Michael frowned. "She said that?"

"Yes."

"Hmm..."

"Hmm?"

A thoughtful expression slid into place on Michael's face. "I think you may have misunderstood her."

"Indeed?" James leaned forward in his seat and perched his elbows on the table. "She said she loves him, Michael. What is there to misunderstand?"

"The nuance, I suppose. I mean, she might love him without being *in* love with him. There's a difference, you know."

James stared at his son for a long hard moment. He wasn't wrong, and yet... "If you know something that might be helpful, by all means tell me."

"I can't."

"Right. Because you're sworn to secrecy."

"Exactly."

Pushing out a deep breath, James reached for the tankard of beer he'd ordered earlier and took several gulps. "Well, I'm tired of trying to figure it out. Point is she made no claim of caring for me in a way that would ever compel me to fight for her. If she had, things might be different, but I don't have the patience for playing games or unraveling truths I'm not meant to find. Instead, I'll focus on more pressing issues, like the threat Cloverfield will continue to pose unless we find a way to stop him."

"You believe he'll attempt to strike back?"

"It would be naïve of me not to given the fact that he's an arrogant duke intent on having his way and that I've now humiliated him in public."

Concern stretched across Michael's brow. "When do you expect him to act?"

"I don't know. If he continues toward the house party he was headed for when our paths crossed, it could be weeks before he's back in London."

"At which point he may have come up with a crafty plan," Michael muttered.

James nodded. "Hence my attempt to work on my own defense. I'm preparing an outline of the events that took place while they're clear in my mind. Furthermore, I've secured written statements from a couple of people who witnessed the fight between myself and Cloverfield. My next step is to ask the innkeeper here to provide a similar account of Cloverfield's brutal assault on Mrs. Lawson during our stay here the day before yesterday."

"He attacked her?"

"While she slept, if you can believe it."

"Christ!" Michael looked just as horrified as James had felt at the time – how he still felt when he thought of Mrs. Lawson's cries for help, the fear in her eyes, and what would have happened had James not managed to save her. "That poor woman. What she has been forced to endure at that family's hands is insupportable. Heaven help me, but I wish you'd have beaten him until he choked on his own damn blood."

James stared at Michael. "That's uncharacteristically callous of you." Michael clenched his jaw and returned James's stare with a hard one of his own. "You're usually more forgiving than I. Tell me, what did you mean with *what she's had to endure at that family's hands?* "

"Nothing," Michael gritted. He gestured for a maid and ordered a beer along with a couple of plates of food when she answered his summons. "Forget I said anything."

That was about as unlikely to happen as him forgetting Mina existed. Her face had gone pale when she'd first seen Cloverfield in this very taproom. Recognition had filled her eyes with a wild sort of panic. So he'd known she must have crossed paths with him before, yet they'd both pretended to meet for the very first time.

Weary of the secrecy and the lies, James pinched the bridge of his nose and muttered a curse. Moving on from Mina would not be as simple as he'd have liked. Even though she clearly kept a great many truths about herself stowed away beneath her façade, he could not change how he felt, which meant he could not stop from caring or worrying over all the things she refused to share with him.

She doesn't love you, he reminded himself for the hundredth time since their conversation.

More importantly, she did not seem to want his help.

Perhaps then, the only thing to do was walk away and leave her be. If she came to him later, he'd be there for her. At least then it would be on her terms and not because he'd pushed her for more than she was ready to give.

The rest of the journey back to Renwick was uneventful and dreary. By the time the carriage pulled to a halt outside Wilhelmina's cottage, she was more than eager to put as much distance between herself and the last five days' experience as possible. Without waiting for Mr. Dale or his son to come and offer assistance, she flung the carriage door open, hitched up her skirts, and leapt to the ground unaided.

"Mina," James said. He'd dismounted and hastened to help her collect her bag from the boot. He arrived just in time to watch her retrieve the item – too late for him to do it for her. A scowl darkened his gaze.

"Thank you for helping me bring my daughter home safely," she said. "I owe you a debt of gratitude, Mr. Dale."

"You owe me nothing," he told her fiercely. "I was more than happy to assist."

"Nevertheless, I'm much obliged." She stepped back while Michael helped Cynthia collect her things. The pair exchanged a few discreet words in parting while Wilhelmina and James stood in awkward silence. Desperate for a reprieve from his glower, she averted her gaze, though this did nothing to ease the awareness of having his eyes fixed upon her with piercing intensity.

Eventually, Cynthia joined her and Michael remounted his horse. Wilhelmina raised her chin and gave her attention back to James. "Good day, Mr. Dale."

He said nothing as she turned away and started toward the garden gate. Forcing herself to stay strong, to not look back at him with longing, she stayed her course until she reached the front door of her cottage. Only then did she turn, just in time to catch the back of him as he galloped away. Michael, who remained, touched the brim of his hat before chasing after his father. The carriage lurched into motion immediately after and followed the two men to Clarington House.

When Wilhelmina opened the front door she was immediately met by Betsy who rushed toward her, skidded to a halt, and managed an awkward curtsy. "I thought I heard something that sounded like a carriage. Oh, it's good to have you home again, Mrs. Lawson, and with Mrs. Petersen too, I see."

"Thank you, Betsy." Wilhelmina removed her bonnet and handed it to the maid while Cynthia set hers on a narrow entryway table. She began removing her gloves. "I don't suppose you have a pot of tea ready?"

"No, but I can make one," Betsy said while tying the bonnet ribbons in a bow so she could hang it from a peg on the wall. "It won't take long."

"Did you and the Wilkins get along all right while we were away?" Wilhelmina asked once she and Cynthia were seated at the kitchen table. Betsy filled the kettle with water and hung it over the fire.

"Oh yes," Betsy said. She picked a tin off a shelf and began scooping tea leaves into a strainer. "They've been taking care of the animals, milking the cows, and collecting eggs. Allowed me the time I needed to do some more cleaning. This morning I laundered the parlor curtains. They're hanging to dry out back."

"Thank you, Betsy. You're a gem," Wilhelmina told her. The maid smiled, glanced at Cynthia inquisitively, but refrained from asking questions, for which Wilhelmina was grateful. She knew the maid would wonder what happened, but it wasn't something Wilhelmina cared to discuss with a servant. Instead she told her daughter, "I think you ought to prepare your return to London as soon as possible. The Season there is well underway and I have to get to work here so I can secure an income. The funds I have from the sale of the house will not last forever."

"What are you planning?" Cynthia asked while Betsy offered them each a biscuit.

Wilhelmina took one and bit into its buttery crispness. "We've a dozen pigs, so I'm thinking of selling the fattest ones to the Renwick butcher along with some chickens. The milk from the cows might be welcomed by one of the dairy shops."

"Why not sell to people directly?" Cynthia asked. "In doing so you would avoid giving part of your profit away to a middleman."

Cynthia had considered this herself, but...

"I was thinking of the convenience for the shopper. I'm not sure the average person would be willing to come all the way out here for their purchase."

"They might if you make it worth their while," Betsy chimed in. She frowned when both Wilhelmina and

Cynthia looked at her. "Sorry. I shouldn't have said anything."

"It's all right," Wilhelmina said. "Please, elaborate."

Betsy pressed her lips together for a second before saying, "If your pricing is good, people might be willing to make the trip as long as they know they're saving some coin. And you should be able to have a competitive price, seeing as you don't have to pay for a shop in town."

"I suppose," Wilhelmina agreed while Betsy set a cup and saucer before her. The maid took the kettle off the fire and filled the teapot. A rich aroma filled the air as the tea leaves soaked. "But if they buy their meat from me they'd have to see to the butchering themselves and I'm not sure they'd be willing or able."

"Maybe the pigs and the chickens should go to the butcher then," Cynthia said, "but there are other items you could sell yourself. Like baked goods. You make the best breads and cakes I've ever had, Mama. It's a shame not to share that talent with the world."

Wilhelmina smiled at the compliment. "I do love to bake, so I suppose there's some sense in trying to make a living from it."

"Exactly so," Cynthia said. "And with the fruit trees and vegetable patches you've got, you can make jams and preserves as well. Honestly, the possibilities are endless. Plus, I think the townsfolk will find some charm in buying these items directly from their source."

Betsy filled the cups and Wilhelmina picked hers up. She blew on the steaming liquid, then took a tentative sip. What Cynthia proposed would not make her rich, but it would probably be enough for her to get by on. Plus, she'd be doing something she liked. Best of all, it would keep her mind off a certain gentleman she preferred not to think of.

Only it seemed the gentleman in question was determined to keep her mind sharply focused on him, she realized a week later when a cart pulled up in front of her cottage. With Cynthia gone to London three days before, she was in the process of making a list of supplies she'd have to purchase for her new business when a series of thuds caught her attention. A knock at the door soon followed and one minute later, Betsy arrived in the parlor.

"There's a delivery for you, Mrs. Lawson."

Surprised, Wilhelmina set her writing utensils aside. "What sort of delivery?"

Betsy looked uncertain. "I think it might be best if you come and see for yourself."

Wilhelmina followed her maid outside. She blinked in confusion while gaping at the large item propped against the side of her cottage. Granted, it was in pieces. It had to be in order to fit through the door. But it was…it was…

"That's a loom," Wilhelmina blurted while pointing her finger at the most gorgeous piece of craftsmanship she'd ever witnessed.

"Aye. 'Tis that," said one of the two men who'd brought it.

Wilhelmina turned to him. He scratched the back of

his head and squinted through the noonday sun. When he said nothing more, she asked, "Where did it come from?"

She could have kicked herself for the foolish question since there was but one logical answer.

"Mr. Dale told us to bring it over. Said you'd like it."

Baffled, Wilhelmina kept staring at him until he frowned and began looking slightly unsure of himself. She shook her head in an effort to clear it. "Of course I do. Thank you."

"So where should we put it?"

"In the parlor I suppose. Just give me a moment. Betsy, please help me prepare a good spot for it."

"I wager it'll take up half the room," Betsy said once they'd chosen to clear a spot near the window so Wilhelmina would have enough light while she worked.

"I'm sure you're correct. It really ought to have its own room, but since that's impossible, we'll have to make do. Grab the other end of the sofa would you? We'll put it up against that wall."

Ten minutes later the loom was brought in and one hour after that, it had been fully assembled. The men who'd delivered it left and Wilhelmina allowed herself to fully appreciate what she'd been given. Words could not describe how she felt. James knew she loved to weave. He also knew she'd had to give up her big loom when she'd moved to London. And even though they'd not parted on the best of terms, he'd still purchased a replacement for her. It was beyond thoughtful and most deserving of her thanks.

Until that very moment she'd not realized how grateful she'd be for the chance to see him again. Perhaps he wanted the same and hoped his gift would provide an excuse? A letter would be sufficient, but maybe he would invite her for tea if she stopped by Clarington House. Perhaps then, the two of them might make amends. So much more could be said in person than through writing. Given the lengths he'd gone to on her behalf, he deserved nothing less than for her to call on him directly.

Eager to be on her way before she overthought her decision and changed her mind, Wilhelmina told Betsy where she was going, then grabbed her bonnet and spencer and set off across the fields.

Forty-five minutes later, Wilhelmina strode up the graveled path leading to the grand estate. Her heart drummed a fast rhythm, partly due to exertion but mostly because of excitement. Now that she was here, she could scarcely wait to see James again, to thank him for the gift but also to set things straight between them. He deserved a proper explanation from her and she'd failed to provide that. Instead, she'd let him believe she loved someone else, and although this might make things easier in the long run, it wasn't right.

Steeling herself for his response to her arrival, she took a deep breath and gave the knocker three resounding raps. It took a while for the butler to arrive.

He stared back at Wilhelmina with a perfectly schooled demeanor. "Yes?"

"I wish to see Mr. Dale. Mr. James Dale, that is,"

Wilhelmina hastily added when it occurred to her that James, his father, and Michael, could all be referred to as such.

"Mr. James Dale is no longer in residence. May I ask who's calling?"

"Oh. Yes of course. Mrs. Lawson." Honestly, she sounded like a nitwit and would not blame the butler for saying as much before shutting the door in her face.

Instead, he stepped back and opened the door even wider. "Do come in."

"But I thought...that is to say...if Mr. James Dale isn't here then—"

"I do believe his parents would like to meet you, Mrs. Lawson."

Oh God.

Disheartened by the thought of receiving a set down from two people who probably wouldn't be welcoming of her, Wilhelmina hesitated. She considered the butler who quietly waited for her to make up her mind. He hadn't treated her with condescension. So maybe there was a chance the master and mistress of the house would not do so either.

She took a step forward. "Thank you."

The butler dipped his head in acknowledgement. He closed the door and led her into an adjacent parlor, beautifully decorated in ivory tones accented by sage green. Without breaking his stride, the butler continued toward a pair of gaping French doors and led Wilhelmina out to a shaded terrace surrounded by perennials in various stages of bloom. The uneven flagstone paving lent a rustically romantic atmosphere to the oasis.

A round wrought iron table stood in the center of the space. Seated at it were an elderly couple with carefully guarded expressions, though neither looked hostile or the least bit unwelcoming.

"Mrs. Lawson," the butler said with a gesture in Wilhelmina's general direction. "I thought you might like a word with her before I let her run off."

"Certainly," James's father, Mr. Dale, said. He stood. "Would you like to take tea with us, Mrs. Lawson?"

Too dazed to speak, Wilhelmina nodded, then promptly managed a faint, "Yes," and, "thank you."

"If you could please bring another cup and saucer, Warren," Mr. Dale said.

"I'll see to it right away," Warren said and quickly disappeared inside.

"Please have a seat, Mrs. Lawson," Mr. Dale said. He swept his hand toward the chair he intended for Wilhelmina to occupy.

She thanked him and followed his suggestion since it gave her something to do besides standing about feeling awkward and unsure of herself. This day was not turning out as she'd expected when she woke that morning.

"I understand your son has returned to London," Wilhelmina said when silence ensued.

"Yes, and not a moment too soon," Mrs. Dale said, surprising Wilhelmina with her frankness. "As lovely as it was to have him visit, his brooding manner grew tiresome. Brought a dull mood to every corner of the house."

"I'm sorry," Wilhelmina murmured.

"And so you should be," Mrs. Dale said, though not unkindly. "According to what we were able to draw from our grandson, you are behind James's gloomy mood."

Wilhelmina clasped her hands tightly in her lap. She thanked the maid who brought a cup and saucer for her, then thanked her hostess for pouring tea. Back straight and shoulders stiff, she fought the urge to run from what could turn into a very difficult conversation, but she wanted to know what had been said about her. "What exactly did your grandson tell you?"

"Not much of anything really," Mr. Dale said with one raised brow. "Hopefully you can enlighten us."

"What I can say is that Michael was very conflicted." Mrs. Dale took a sip of her tea. Wilhelmina followed suit. "As I understand, he had in his possession the information required to end his father's turmoil, but he'd made a promise to your daughter and did not wish to betray her trust."

"So he stayed silent?" Wilhelmina was grateful. If anyone ought to divulge the truth it was she.

"Look," Mr. Dale said, his manner grave. "I don't know what happened between you and James during your journey, but I can tell you he came back a changed man. For three whole days he did nothing but help my tenants make various repairs. Whenever we saw him, he hardly spoke one word – kept himself hidden away in his bedchamber for the most part. And then he left."

"I've only seen him like that once before," Mrs. Dale said. She was studying Wilhelmina with an unnerving degree of shrewdness. "When he realized his wife didn't love him."

Wilhelmina sucked in a breath. "What are you saying?"

Mr. and Mrs. Dale shared a look and then Mr. Dale said, "Michael may not have revealed your secrets, but he told us enough to make one thing clear. James fell in love with you, Mrs. Lawson, and you did not return the sentiment."

"What?" Wilhelmina stared at the older couple while trying to make sense of what they'd just told her. A forceful surge of joy grabbed her heart and quickened its beats. "He gave no indication."

"Didn't he?" Mrs. Dale asked, her voice soft and gentle.

Wilhelmina shook her head, but she knew she was being dishonest. James's response to what she'd said had certainly revealed deep emotion on his part. He'd been angry with her, but it never occurred to her until this moment that she might have hurt him. She'd been so caught up in her own heartache, she'd not thought of his. Because she'd believed he wouldn't want her, no matter what. But what if he'd changed? What if he'd been willing to toss everything he believed in aside for her? He'd given her a loom for heaven's sake. Surely that was a declaration of deep devotion if ever there was one.

"I'm such a fool," she muttered. "But I was scared of how he'd react to the things I would say. I feared he would think less of me once he realized what had happened and the choices I made in the years since. I've ruined lives and all I wanted was to try and fix it."

"Then you should tell him that," Mr. Dale said. "Otherwise you're just denying him the ability to make an informed decision and to choose his own path."

"You're right. Of course you are." Wilhelmina took another few sips of her tea. "But it's a bit late now that he's gone to London."

"You could follow him," Mrs. Dale suggested with a twinkle in her eyes.

Mr. Dale smirked as he glanced at his wife. "Ever the romantic, my dear."

"I wish I could," Wilhelmina said, "but with the Season in progress and my daughter attempting to make a new match for herself, I'd like to keep my distance lest I ruin her chances with my reputation. Which leads me to wonder why you would want a woman like me to pursue an attachment with your son. Surely you'd wish to avoid a scandal."

"Naturally," Mr. Dale said. "But if a bit of scandal is the price we must pay for our son's happiness, then so be it. He deserves to love and to be loved in return. We'll weather whatever storm comes our way."

"Besides, we don't really go out into Society much

these days, so I hardly think it will have an effect on us,"
Mrs. Dale said.

"It could have dire consequences on your son and
grandson," Wilhelmina warned.

"Perhaps," Mr. Dale agreed, "but Michael was willing
to take that chance for your daughter. Correct? And I
believe James will do so for you if you return his
affection."

Wilhelmina shook her head. "He loves his work. I'd
never forgive myself if he had to sacrifice that for me."

"I thought we already established that he must be
given the choice," Mr. Dale said. "Having you or anyone
else determine what's best for him would be wrong."

"True," Wilhelmina agreed. And wasn't that why
she'd come here in the first place? Besides thanking
James for his generous gift in person, she'd hoped for a
chance to dispel this idea of her being in love with
George. A point which only mattered because she was
in love with James and couldn't stand having him think
she was lost to him. Because she wanted more – hoped
for more – even though she knew obtaining it would be
hard.

But so what?

She'd fought to save her reputation, fought to save
her daughter's, and fought to ensure George's happiness. Should she not then fight for the man she loved
instead of just giving up?

"I can't go to London right now. The chance of
ruining Cynthia's prospects is too great. I shan't risk it.
But once the Season is over in a month or so, I'll make

the journey." Hopefully by then she'd also have gotten her business started. As long as Betsy and the Wilkinses pitched in, she ought to be able to manage a few days' absence.

"At least write to him then," Mrs. Dale urged.

Wilhelmina nodded. "I will."

She thanked the couple for their hospitality and started her homeward journey. They'd offered her the use of their carriage but Wilhelmina preferred to walk. Being out in the open provided her thoughts with the extra room they required, and by the time she returned home, she'd figured out what she would say in her letter.

For now, she would thank Mr. Dale for the loom, tell him she missed seeing him at Clarington House when she stopped by for a visit, and convey her hope of meeting him soon. As for the rest, she'd rather say it in person.

Satisfied, she penned the letter and dispatched it the following morning. While in town, she purchased all the ingredients she would need to start baking and even took out an advert in the local paper so Renwick's inhabitants would know where to get milk, fresh eggs, and bread for less than what the local shops offered.

"I'm thinking I'll make five plain loaves for tomorrow," Wilhelmina told Betsy when she returned, "some buns and biscuits, along with a couple of cakes. We'll have to adjust once we know how well it sells."

"It might be a bit of a struggle the first few days," Betsy said, "but once a couple of people try your goods and they tell their friends how fantastic they are, I wager you'll have customers banging down the door."

As it turned out, seven people showed up the next day. One only wanted eggs and milk, but Wilhelmina still sold all her bread along with every biscuit and cake she'd made. So she baked twice as much for the day after that and was pleased when even more people stopped by.

A busy week followed, during which Wilhelmina barely slept one wink, and then the response from James arrived.

Dear Mrs. Lawson,

Not Wilhelmina or Mina, Wilhelmina noted.

It pleases me to know you are well and that the loom will be useful to you.

I hope you can forgive me for not saying goodbye. To be honest, it was easier not to.

With respect,

Mr. James Dale

Wilhelmina reread the note a dozen times, searching for a hidden endearment that didn't exist. Although he had acknowledged finding it hard to part ways. If his parents were correct in their assumptions, this was due to his feelings for her. Feelings he did not believe she reciprocated.

Nothing could be further from the truth, but telling him that would have to wait a while yet. Folding the letter, she placed it in her apron pocket and went to start on a fresh batch of biscuits. As pleased as she was by her success, there was a definite snag to it, for she'd no idea now when she'd manage to go to London and speak with James. First, she needed to find a routine that worked – one which Betsy would be able to follow during her absence.

As of right now, Wilhelmina still struggled with figuring out how many items to make and when to start making them. She'd quickly discovered that there was a difference between baking one or two loaves of bread and baking twenty. Each dough had to rise but she could only fit four in the oven at the same time. Scheduling became imperative, especially since she was starting to feel like she worked every minute of every day without pause. Plus, she had to teach Betsy how to make everything exactly the same way she did, which meant she had to allow for time to let the maid practice.

The process demanded dedication, and Wilhelmina still didn't feel she was ready to hand over all responsibility for her new business to Betsy and the Wilkinses by the time the next letter arrived two weeks later. But when she opened it and learned what had happened, she knew she'd have no choice.

She sucked in a breath. It felt like a prickly rash was spreading across her skin as she read Cynthia's words. Her heart tumbled over as sickening disquiet swirled in her stomach.

Cloverfield was back in London, and he was not only telling the world that Wilhelmina was Mr. Dale's whore, but that Mr. Dale was the man behind Wilhelmina's divorce and that all her other lovers had simply been used to conceal his involvement.

It was beyond the pale. Lies perpetuated by a high ranking peer – a man who deserved to be scorned for his lack of honor. Wilhelmina knew she ought not be surprised for his father had been no better, but she had hoped it would not come to this and that James would not be made to suffer on her account.

Wilhelmina swallowed and set the letter aside with trembling hands. There wasn't a choice any longer. She absolutely could not allow James to face this alone. All she could do was hope her going to London would not have an adverse effect on Cynthia, and that Betsy would somehow manage to keep things afloat in Renwick during her absence.

CHAPTER NINETEEN

J ames knocked back the last of his brandy and set
the empty glass on top of the newspaper that had
been lying on his desk for the past week. The
headline still mocked him – *Another one of Mrs. Lawson's
lovers revealed* – but he got some satisfaction from all
the ring stains he'd left on the paper since he'd started
using it as a coaster.

Damn Cloverfield.

When James first learned of the lies the bastard had
spewed to *The Mayfair Chronicle*, he'd been ready to
march on over to Cloverfield House and knock the
sod's block off. Thank God Michael had managed to
talk him out of it, though the quarrel that ensued had
not been helpful. Now Michael was gone – off to spend
some time away from his grouchy father. James knew it
was probably for the best. Michael had a new job he
needed to concentrate on, but James still missed him.

He missed *her*.

Huffing a breath, he scrubbed his palm across his jaw and felt the bristles. It was past time for a shave and a bath, not to mention a change of clothes. He could probably do with a haircut too, but he just couldn't seem to make the effort.

Wearily, he glanced at the papers and files comprising the brief he'd accepted after returning to Town. It pertained to the theft of some silverware from Sir Walter Bannon's household, for which the house-keeper had been arrested. A solicitor friend of James's had brought the case to him after James had mentioned a keen desire to bury himself in work.

Since Cloverfield's statement however, Sir Bannon had requested a new barrister. James was supposed to return the files he'd been given no later than this after-noon. Which was just as well really. Reading statements and compiling evidence against a woman whose guilt would be hard to prove held little appeal. He'd much rather spend his energy on an entirely different project.

A knock at the front door caught his attention. He muttered a curse and thought of telling Atkins not to answer. But it was too late. Voices already sounded and then Atkins entered his study. "Mr. Grier and Mr. West are here to see you, sir. Should I show them in?"

James gave his butler a weary nod. Not because he felt like the company but because he knew his friends would not let up until they'd seen him. Best get it over with then. "Please do."

"Are you aware you've got pipes strewn about your

hallway?" Grayson asked once he and Colin had finished greeting James.

"They're not strewn about," James said. "They're neatly stacked."

Colin frowned while giving James an uncomfortable head to toe perusal. "You look like a heathen."

"I've not been out in a while," James said. He'd not really thought much of his rolled up shirt sleeves, the lack of cravat, or the fact that he wore no shoes, until this very moment. "Thought I might as well be comfortable."

Colin snorted and went to pour himself a brandy. He offered one to Grayson as well, who refused. "The scandal surrounding you and Mrs. Lawson will pass, old chap. These things always do."

"What prompted Cloverfield to make such an outrageous statement anyway?" Colin asked. "I mean, we both know how much you loathe the woman, so the duke must truly have it in for you if he's prepared to make such incredulous claims."

James snatched up his glass and went to refill it. He took a fortifying sip and savored the burn as the spicy liquid slid down his throat. "I do not loathe her. In fact, it will likely shock you to know that I've…"

"What?" Grayson asked when James hesitated.

How to answer without implying more than what was proper? James shifted his gaze from one friend to the other. "Mrs. Lawson's daughter eloped with Michael while I was off visiting Clarington House. We tracked them down together, during which she and I became…friends."

Silence. Thick and suffocating. And then, "You tupped her, didn't you?"

"Damnit, Grayson," James growled.

"I wouldn't blame you," Colin said. He held up his hands and backed up a step. "She's definitely the tupping sort, but—"

"Say one more thing against her and I'll strike that grin off your face," James growled.

"Oh God," Grayson groaned. He added a dramatic sigh and eye-roll. "He's in love."

"Huh." Colin tilted his head and studied James as if he were some rare artifact that defied the laws of nature. "Well, I suppose that explains all those pipes in the hallway. From what I hear, people do the strangest things when they fancy themselves in love."

"I don't fancy myself being anything," James said. He took a deep breath and expelled it. "Truth is, I completely misjudged her and now…" He shook his head.

"Now what?" Colin pressed.

"Shush. Let him speak," Grayson said.

James sank into a nearby chair and considered his friends – men he'd known most of his life. He'd fought by their side, shared the death of a brother-in-arms with them, bared his soul to them during his troubles with Clara. No one knew or understood him better than they did, not even Michael. "I'm smitten with her.

Completely enamored. Ironically, she's still emotionally attached to Mr. Hewitt."

"You're certain of this?" Grayson asked with clear disbelief.

"She told me she loves him," James said and promptly took another sip of his brandy to wash down the bitter taste those words left in his mouth. He knew there was a distinction between loving someone and being in love with them, as Michael had put it, though it hardly mattered which sentiment she harbored for Mr. Hewitt when she'd not shown James either emotion.

"Odd, in light of the lengths he went to in order to rid himself of her," Colin murmured. He frowned. "One would think a woman would hate a man for airing her personal indiscretions in public."

"I agree," James said, "but Mrs. Lawson had nothing but praise for the man."

"Maybe there's more to the story than meets the eye," Grayson suggested.

"I'm sure there is," James said. "In fact, I'm certain she and her husband lied in order to get the divorce he wanted. Which proves her devotion to him."

"And where is Mr. Hewitt now?" Colin asked. "Do you know?"

James shrugged. "In America with his new wife, from what I gather."

"Blimey." Grayson stared at James. "If his reason for getting divorced was so he could marry another woman and Mrs. Lawson helped him with this, she ought to be respected."

"Though it does seem to prove your belief," Colin said, "about her loving him."

"Colin," Grayson hissed.

"What? We all know it's the only thing that makes sense," Colin said.

"He's right," Grayson said when no one else uttered another word. "No woman would willingly ruin her reputation and risk being permanently ostracized for any reason, unless it was a selfless act of love."

James had concluded the same, which was part of the reason why he was in such a bitter mood lately. He wanted Mina in his life, but he could not bear the thought of being her second choice. Figuring out how to have a relationship with her now after what they'd shared was difficult. Hence the loom. In her thank you letter she'd sounded happy with the gift, but had offered no other hints pertaining to her thoughts about him. Did she even think of him as often as he thought of her? Or had she moved on?

"Sorry," Colin said, "but we're your friends. It's our job to tell you the harsh truth, no matter how unappealing it may be."

"And I value that," James said. "Truly I do."

"What happened with Michael and Mrs. Lawson's daughter?" Grayson asked after a brief pause in conversation. "I trust you found them before they married?"

"Indeed we did." James eyed his friends. "Turns out the daughter's unable to have children. When she mentioned it to Michael, he realized he needed to give the whole marriage idea more thought. So they were actually of a mind to return to London when Mrs. Lawson and I caught up with them."

"Blimey," Colin muttered.

"I second that sentiment." Grayson leaned forward in his seat. Lines puckered his brow. "I trust Michael plans to move on? Forget Mrs. Lawson's daughter and make a more suitable match?"

James took a deep breath and expelled it. "Actually, he's of a mind to go ahead with the wedding. When he and I last discussed it, he said he'd rather have the bird in his hand than the two in the bush. I..." He gave his head a weary shake. The fact that Michael was willing to give up on children for this woman proved that he loved her more than James had ever imagined. So who the hell was he to stand in the way of their joyous union? From now on, he'd do what he could to offer the support he ought to have given right from the start.

Lord, he'd been wrong about so many things of late – so bloody righteous and unyielding.

"It's no wonder you look as you do," Grayson said. "Considering what you've had to deal with of late, I'm shocked you're not ten sheets to the wind as well."

"Perhaps the cure would be to get you cleaned up a bit and out of this house." Colin saluted his friends with his glass. "We could go to Mivart's for supper and then on to Vauxhall Gardens for a bit of distraction."

"I don't know," James hedged. He really didn't feel

like going anywhere, or like making the effort required to get himself ready. "Maybe tomorrow?"

"I'll be heading back to my estate tomorrow morning," Grayson said. "I am...reluctant to remain absent for longer."

The way he said that gave James pause. He considered his friend and his sudden reluctance to meet his gaze. "Why is that?"

"Because..." Grayson shrugged.

When he added nothing further, Colin sighed and rolled his eyes. "Apparently he misses the governess."

Grayson raised an eyebrow. "No more than you miss Mrs. Leighton, I'll wager."

"How intriguing," James said with a chuckle. "Do tell me more."

Grayson sighed. "Suffice it to say I came back to London in order to think. I can't do that at Sutton Hall with Olivia turning my head every time she glances my way."

"Olivia, is it?" James murmured with a wry grin.

"Don't you start as well," Grayson warned. "It's bad enough that *he* won't shut up about it. Honestly, I don't know what I was thinking when I confided my dilemma in him."

"I've already told you to marry the chit," Colin said.

"Hence my intention to set off tomorrow," Grayson said.

"You mean to propose?" James asked.

"Maybe." Grayson seemed to mull something over,

then added, "For starters I plan on figuring out how she really feels about me."

"And how do you intend to do that?" James asked, hoping his friend might provide the answer he himself sought.

Grayson met James's gaze. "By asking her, of course."

Of course.

How stupidly simple. James wondered why he hadn't thought to take this approach. No doubt because he'd been too caught up in his own emotional turmoil to think straight.

Well, perhaps it was time he began doing so. He was forty-five years old, for God's sake – well beyond the age where it made sense for him to wonder what the woman he fancied thought about him. If he really wanted to know, then he should just ask her and be done with it.

Wilhelmina stepped down from the carriage she'd taken to The Swan with Two Heads, collected her bag, and started walking. It would take her a good half hour to reach Cynthia's house and while she had considered hiring a hackney, she'd decided she could do with the exercise after sitting for several consecutive hours.

With her head held high and her bag gripped firmly in one hand, she made her way to Oxford Street before dusk started to settle. The crowded street, packed with carriages, horses, and wagons at this hour, was noisy. Merchants who lived west of the City were heading home while gentlemen tried to get to their clubs.

Up ahead, a couple of ladies approaching halted their progress. They stared at Wilhelmina, exchanged a few words with each other, and promptly crossed to the other side of the street, weaving their way through oncoming traffic as they went. She shook her head and tried not to let their reaction sting, but it was hard not to when they'd rather risk getting trampled by an oncoming carriage than having to cross paths with her.

She reached the corner of Berner's Street and turned right. Three streets later she arrived at the front door of Petersen House. Glancing both ways before she approached, Wilhelmina made sure no one saw who had come to call on the widow who resided here and, noting that the coast was clear, quickly went to knock.

Cynthia's maid of all works, Mrs. Rubins, answered Wilhelmina's call. Her eyes widened the moment she saw who it was. "Oh, thank goodness you're here, Mrs. Lawson. Please come in."

Wilhelmina frowned on account of the maid's agitation. She stepped into the foyer and began removing her gloves. "Is everything all right?"

"I wish I could say it were, but I have to confess I'm mighty worried about the mistress. She's been horribly ill for more than a week now – can't seem to keep anything down."

Concern rippled across Wilhelmina's shoulders.

Cynthia hadn't mentioned feeling unwell when she'd written. "I trust she's upstairs in bed then?"

"Aye, that she is. I'll show you up right away."

"No need to trouble yourself with that." Wilhelmina drew off her bonnet, hung it on a peg, and patted her hair. "If you're able, I'd rather you make a pot of ginger tea."

"All right, ma'am. I'll see to it straight away."

Wilhelmina thanked her and started up the stairs. She'd visited here many times in the months following Cynthia and Henry's wedding. The last time she'd come had been the day after Henry's funeral. She'd stayed away for the solemn occasion itself since she'd already started making headlines and had no wish to make life harder for her daughter or Henry's family.

Just like then, she was on her way to her daughter's bedchamber now to see how she was faring. She found the door she sought with ease and gave it a gentle knock.

"Come in."

Wilhelmina pushed the door open and peered inside the dimly lit room. Her gaze swept to the bed where Cynthia lay, propped against a pile of pillows. A book was in her lap. She shifted her head and glanced at Wilhelmina. "Mama?"

"Mrs. Rubins tells me you're feeling poorly." Wilhelmina stepped into the room, closed the door, and approached the bed. She reached for Cynthia's hand.

"What on earth are you doing here?" Cynthia asked, not addressing Wilhelmina's comment.

Wilhelmina perched on the edge of the bed. The mattress dipped beneath her. "Did you honestly think I would stay away after learning of Cloverfield's outrageous actions against Mr. Dale? I needed to make sure you are all right. That he is as well." She placed one palm on Cynthia's forehead. "You don't have a fever."

"I know," Cynthia groaned.

"What are your symptoms?"

"My stomach is queasy. The mere thought of food makes me feel like I'm about to be sick."

"Could you have caught this ailment from someone you've socialized with?"

Cynthia gave a weak laugh. "I do not think so."

"Then it must be something you've eaten. For it to trouble you more than a week though is highly unusual."

"Mama." Cynthia licked her lips and gave the glass of water on her nightstand a longing look. Her features contorted. She took a shuddering breath and seemed to relax. "I'm fairly certain I know what's wrong."

"Oh?" Wilhelmina handed the glass of water to Cynthia so she could drink.

Cynthia did so. A weak smile followed. "Apparently the impossible has happened."

"You're…" Wilhelmina tried to control the mixture of joy and concern her daughter's insinuation stirred in her breast. "When did you last have your courses?"

"Nearly two months ago. Before you and I left for Renwick."

A rush of air left Wilhelmina. "Then you are expecting."

Tears sprang to Cynthia's eyes. She nodded. "It would appear so, though how on earth this can be I do not know. Henry and I tried to conceive. We visited three separate doctors. I was subjected to the most intrusive examinations, Mama, only to be told that I was to blame."

"My poor darling." Wilhelmina stroked Cynthia's hair with gentle movements intended to soothe.

Cynthia jerked away and gasped for air. "Sorry. It's your fragrance."

Wilhelmina pulled back. "I'd like to give those doctors you saw a piece of my mind."

Cynthia snorted. "It would be interesting to show up on their doorstep once my belly grows bigger and ask them how this might have happened."

"They'll probably chalk it up to a miracle," Wilhelmina told her dryly. She sobered. "Obviously the issue was with Henry, not you. I'm thinking they treated you ill because they did not want to offend him."

"I have to tell Michael, but I'm scared his father will try to interfere again. Especially after your falling out with him. He might prevent us from marrying out of spite and then—"

"Mr. Dale isn't like that, Cynthia. He's a reasonable man who's trying to do what's best for his son."

"Exactly!"

"He would never deny his grandchild the chance to

have a father." Wilhelmina was certain of this. "I'd stake all my worldly goods on it. But he has to be warned before you or Michael makes another drastic decision."

A humorless laugh escaped Cynthia. "I'm in no position to run away any more, Mama."

"Perhaps not, but I wouldn't put other things past you, like having a clandestine wedding right here in this room. And that would be wrong. Mr. Dale deserves to be included in this. He has the right to oppose, but also to help as I believe he would. So..." Wilhelmina took a fortifying breath. "I shall speak with him."

"Mama..."

"It's the correct thing to do, Cynthia. No more secrets."

"Then you are prepared to tell him everything?"

Wilhelmina nodded. A strange sense of calm embraced her. "I am."

A knock distracted Wilhelmina from her thoughts of facing James. Mrs. Rubins entered with a tray. "I've got the ginger tea – made certain it's not too hot."

A cup was poured upon which Wilhelmina helped Cynthia drink. It was slow going. Cynthia recoiled from the tea to begin with, but Wilhelmina persisted. She knew her daughter needed the liquid. She'd need sustenance too, which was something Wilhelmina intended to set her mind to later.

"If you don't mind," Cynthia said once she'd finished the tea, "I think I'd like to rest now." She looked at Mrs. Rubins who'd lingered near the door throughout, ready to help in any way she could. "Would you please prepare a room for my mother?"

"Aye. I'll see to it straight way, Mrs. Petersen."

"I shouldn't stay here," Wilhelmina told Cynthia "It isn't good for your reputation."

Cynthia met her gaze with a serious look. "I think there are more important things than my reputation right now. Besides, it's not as if I'm going to try and entice anyone other than Michael into marriage."

Wilhelmina nodded. "See you in the morning then?"

"Yes, Mama." Cynthia yawned. "Sleep well."

Wilhelmina gave Cynthia's hand a squeeze. She glanced at the clock on the dresser which showed it was almost eight o'clock, and followed Mrs. Rubins out into the hallway.

"Maybe I should prepare some food for you before I start fixing your room," Mrs. Rubins suggested as they descended the stairs together. "You must be awfully hungry."

Wilhelmina was rather, but there was a matter of greater importance she ought to attend to before she relaxed for the night. "Please prepare a plate and leave if for me in the dining room. I'll eat when I return."

"You're going back out?"

"Yes. After what my daughter has told me just now, there's someone I have to speak with." She knew she could wait until morning, but the truth was she doubted she'd get much sleep until she'd confronted James. "I'll be back in a couple of hours."

Donning her gloves and her bonnet, Wilhelmina

stepped out into the dim evening light and started along the pavement at a brisk pace. It took no more than fifteen minutes for her to arrive at James's front door where she gave the knocker a few firm raps.

"May I help you?" asked the butler who answered her call.

"I would like to speak with Mr. Dale."

The butler frowned but refrained from commenting on the late hour. "I'm afraid he is out."

Wilhelmina's stomach dropped as the wind went out of her sails. A deflated feeling of disappointment assailed her but since she was here, she'd not be deterred. So she raised her chin. "Then I am happy to wait."

The butler seemed to consider his options. He'd know who she was from her previous visit. Eventually, he stepped aside to grant her entrance. "You'd better come in then before someone sees you."

Glad to have her bad reputation work to her advantage for once, Wilhelmina swept inside the townhouse where she came to a sudden halt. Piles of long metal pipes were stacked up against the stairs. She blinked. "What's that for?"

"It's not my place to discuss the goings on in this house with visitors," the butler said. He held the parlor door open for her.

"Mr. Dale is creating a plumbing system, isn't he?"

"I wouldn't know."

"Of course you would since I'm not sure how he'd go about it without your doing so." She entered the parlor and turned to face the butler. "Has he built the pump yet?"

The edge of the butler's mouth twitched. "Possibly. Shall I fetch some tea for you to enjoy while you wait?"

"Thank you," Wilhelmina told him with a bright smile. "That would be welcome."

He gave a stiff nod and departed. She surveyed the room. It looked no different than when she'd last been here, but now that she knew James better, it seemed more feminine than before. Exaggeratedly so and completely at odds with his personality. Perhaps a memorial to his wife? If that were the case she doubted it was for James's sake. More likely, he'd left the space untouched so Michael could keep a connection with his mother. Another thoughtful and utterly selfless gesture, considering how much the woman had hurt James with her philandering.

Wilhelmina sighed and lowered herself to a sofa dressed in pink silk. Porcelain figurines littered every available surface – a nightmare for any maid tasked with dusting.

The tea arrived along with a plate filled with biscuits and a selection of cucumber sandwiches.

"Should you be hungry," the butler said before he retreated once more.

Wilhelmina filled her cup and took a sip. Perfect. She ate one sandwich followed by another and turned to the mantelpiece clock. It was nearing nine thirty and while she wanted to wait forever in order to see James, she couldn't. It wasn't proper and—

It sounded as if the front door opened. She heard the butler speak and then...James's voice reached her. A fluttery feeling caught hold of her stomach and travelled toward her heart. She set her teacup aside, smoothed out her skirts, and tried to stop from fidgeting. Holding her breath, she waited. She felt like a rabbit caught in a hunter's sight, unsure of whether to stay still and hope he'd not see her, or run and hide.

The parlor door opened and there he was, as handsome as she remembered if not more so. He stared at her and she stared at him.

"Mina." Her name, so softly spoken and without a hint of anger, unlocked her reserve.

She stood, or jolted upright more like, and stepped toward him. "I came to tell you..."

Oh God, where to begin? It suddenly seemed like there was so much for her to say, regarding her past, her feelings for him, and Cynthia's pregnancy.

When all he did was raise an eyebrow and wait, she blurted the one thing that filled her heart to overflowing. "I love you."

CHAPTER TWENTY

J ames stared at Mina. He'd had his fair share of
wine tonight and wasn't sure if his ears deceived
him or if he'd heard her correctly. When Atkins
had mentioned her presence, elation rushed through
him even though wariness quickly followed as he'd
wondered why she'd come. And then he'd seen her and
it had been as if they'd never quarreled at all. His only
thought was of crossing the distance between them and
pulling her into his arms. Until she'd spoken, freezing
him with her words.

His heart pounded against his ribs in painful
desperation. He needed to be certain he'd not misheard
her. "What did you say?"

She took another step toward him. "I love you,
James, and I'm sorry if I hurt you or made you angry,
but I'm not good with explanations so I made a hash of
it when I tried to tell you before."

"Tell me what?" he somehow managed to ask while resisting the urge to stride forward and kiss her.

"Everything," she whispered. "It's just that there's so much to say I scarcely know where to begin."

He swallowed and forced himself to admit the reason why he'd been angry with her. "You told me you love Mr. Hewitt."

"Because I do. I always will, James, but not in the way I love you."

Lord help him but her words undid his finely held control. He wasn't sure he understood her, though he desperately wanted to. But for now, in this moment, knowing she returned his affection, he did not care.

So he closed the remaining distance between them and pulled her into his arms. "My love for you torments me, Mina. I need you by my side, across the breakfast table from me, in my bed and... Lord help me how I've missed you."

His mouth met hers with endless regret and yearning. Intent on not holding back, he kissed her with all that he was, with the pain of each second they'd spent apart, and with a renewed spark of hope. He held her close and breathed her in while moving his lips over hers. The familiar fragrance of citrus and honey infused his senses, filling him with the vibrancy of her essence. Her fingers raked through his hair, scraping his scalp and bringing him closer until the kiss deepened.

James wound his arms tighter around her, securing her against him so he could feel her heartbeats drumming in time with his own. She tasted exquisite – like happiness bursting above the world in a bright display of sparkling color. And she loved him. Lord help him how he'd longed to win her affection, to have her trust him with her heart, and welcome his love in return.

He turned with her and lowered himself to the sofa behind him while drawing her onto his lap. A sigh of pleasure escaped her and James was lost to the mindless hunger that had relentlessly built inside him with each passing day they'd spent apart. No other woman had ever affected him so. Not even Clara. Only Mina wielded such power and while he was with her, the world could burn for all he cared.

For now, he just needed to love her. Even if it was awkward on the sofa in the parlor, and neither had the patience to divest of their clothes, it was as perfect as getting caught in a downpour on a hot day. With her skirts hitched up and his placket undone, she welcomed him with fervor, and laughed against his mouth when his movements nearly sent them both tumbling onto the floor. His hand gripped her thigh, his fingers curling against her flesh in order to hold her securely in place.

"I love you," he told her fiercely while gazing down into her ocean blue eyes.

Her lips parted on an ardent sigh that nearly sent him over the edge. "I love you too."

Dipping his head, he crushed her mouth with his while worshiping her with his body. How foolish he'd been to think he could ever forget her. His heart raced faster as passion careened through his veins. This was the woman he wanted to spend the rest of his life with. She was his – would always be his – and as she found her release, he let himself soar as well, content in the knowledge that the bond they now shared was strong enough to withstand anything.

Weightless, with every limb reduced to jelly, Wilhelmina savored the weight of James's body. He would probably feel obliged to move soon, but for now, she welcomed the feel of him. His body surrounded hers, still filled hers, while the musky scent of their lovemaking served as the sweetest reminder of what had transpired moments earlier.

She'd not come here for this, but as soon as he'd kissed her, making love had become as inevitable as a sunrise. Her fingers trailed loosely through his hair. A smile pulled at her lips. "You must think me an absolute wanton, letting you have me like this on your parlor sofa of all places."

A chuckle resonated from deep within him, vibrating through her. He raised his head and met her gaze. Wolfish intent darkened his eyes while a wicked grin played upon his lips. "My dearest, Mina. I plan to have you a great many other ways in the future."

His comment reminded her that there was so much she needed to say. "You cannot promise me that until I've shared all my secrets with you."

He didn't look convinced, but her words did prompt

him to withdraw from her. Offering a smile, he pulled her skirts back down and set about putting himself to rights. Once done, he stood and crossed to the sideboard. She felt his absence immediately, but knew it could not be helped.

"Would you care for a drink?"

"Please."

He filled two glasses and, taking a seat beside her on the sofa, handed one to her. She sipped the brandy and relished the burn. "This isn't easy."

"Would it help if I were to tell you that I won't walk away from you, no matter what?"

She turned to him sharply. "You cannot assure me of that until you know all there is."

Holding her gaze, he set his glass aside, then wrapped one arm around her shoulders and drew her against him. She leaned into his strength as he kissed the top of her head. "You're wrong. Trust me, Mina. Nothing you can say will make me leave you now."

A shuddering breath trembled against her breast as she exhaled and relaxed against him. She'd still been concerned he might do so, she realized, until he'd offered assurance.

Bolstered by his words, she began her confession. "When I was eighteen years old, the former Duke of Cloverfield and his wife attended a house party at Viscount Mayweather's estate, which is located near my childhood home – on the outskirts of Wadefield. As part of the festivities, they had a garden party one afternoon. Mama and I were invited to attend, so we did. It was a great honor, you see, as well as an opportunity for me to associate with a class of people I probably wouldn't have met otherwise. As my mother put it, there was little chance of my going to London for a Season, seeing as we had no London residence or relations able to put us up. So we had to make the most of every chance presented to us.

"Mama hoped I would win the heart of some upper-class gentleman. Instead I gained the wrong sort of attention."

"How do you mean?" His whispered words were spoken with a slow sort of wariness that suggested he dreaded the answer.

Wilhelmina clasped his hand and closed her eyes. "A few days after the party, Mama received a letter, inviting me to visit with the Duchess of Cloverfield for a private tea. The lady claimed to have taken a liking to me and wanted to see if I might make a suitable match for a nephew of hers who was looking to marry."

"That would have been quite the coup." His thumb stroked carefully over her knuckles.

"Indeed," Wilhelmina agreed, determined to force the rest past the knot in her throat. "Mama and I were honored and terribly excited by the thought of my having caught a duchess's notice. We didn't think twice about my joining her for the tea she'd suggested." She swallowed convulsively as the memories flooded back. Her eyes squeezed tight with the instinct to block it all out as shame curled around her heart to produce a terrible ache.

"Did the duchess deceive you?" James asked, his words soft and steady.

She shook her head. "No. She wasn't the one who summoned me. The duke was."

Everything stilled. Not even James's breath could be heard. "What?"

"I was shown into a small parlor at the back of the house where I waited nearly half an hour before the duke came to join me." She recalled the gleam in his eyes, the satisfaction of knowing he could have anything he wanted. "He apologized for his wife's absence and then he locked the door."

"Good God." Simmering fury encased each word as his hold on her tightened.

"He was very matter of fact about the whole thing." In spite of every effort to keep her emotions under control, her voice shook as she spoke. "He said he'd be gentle as long as I did as he asked. That if I didn't – if I screamed or tried to run – he'd ruin not only my repu-tation but my mother's too. He threatened to destroy us."

James's breaths were slow and steady, but there was a raspy sound, indicative of his growing rage. "The bastard used his title against you in the worst way possible. I swear if he wasn't dead already, I'd murder him myself."

"I've never told anyone this, not even George." She fought the tears that threatened. "I was too ashamed to let him know."

She was suddenly pushed into an upright position

and turned. James clasped her upper arms firmly and held her in place. "Look at me, Mina."

Raising her chin, she met the intensity of his gaze and instantly felt herself break in response to the violent tempest she found there. Tears spilled from between her lashes and dampened her cheeks. A sob worked its way up her throat. "I'm so sorry."

"You have nothing to be ashamed or sorry for," he told her fiercely.

She wanted to believe him and yet she'd always blamed herself for being too trusting, too naïve, or simply too stupid. "I should have run, I should have fought him off, but I was scared."

"For good reason, Mina. You were barely more than a child." He wrapped his arms around her and hugged her to him while she cried, whispering words of endearment until her anguish lessened. "Forgive me for asking, but is Cynthia by any chance—"

"Yes." Wilhelmina nodded against James's chest. "George was my friend. When he learned of my situation he begged me to tell him who'd caused it so he could seek vengeance, but I refused."

He hugged her closer. "You didn't want him to challenge a duke."

"I couldn't risk the consequence." She sat back and wiped at her eyes while James tucked a few strands of hair behind her ears. Without saying anything, he offered her a handkerchief so she could blow her nose. "When George offered to save me from being branded a whore and the child I carried from being labeled a bastard, I accepted. As wrong as it was to trap him, to deny him the chance of falling in love and having the family he deserved, I married him."

"He came to your rescue," James murmured while stroking one hand over her hair.

"Which is why I had to come to his when the woman he loved became pregnant." Feeling drained, she blew out a heavy breath. "How could I force illegitimacy on his child when he'd ensured that mine would not bear that burden?"

James shook his head. Then, without a word, he leaned in and kissed her – a slow caress that brought fresh tears to her eyes. Resting his forehead against hers he said, "You are the most remarkable woman I know, Mina. Who else would have given up their position as you did in order to help a friend? No one could have acted more selflessly than you or with more integrity."

She blinked away tears while letting his words of support sink in. "You should know that George and I never consummated our wedding. We were like brother and sister, James, so hopping into bed together seemed wrong. And after my only experience in that area, I wasn't eager to welcome any man's touch again until I met you."

He hugged her to him. "I only wish the scoundrel who hurt you were still alive so I could kill him for what he did."

A humorless laugh echoed through her. "There's still his son to contend with. Lord help me if he doesn't need to be put in his place as much as his father."

James took a deep breath and sat back. "I agree. The thrashing I gave him clearly wasn't enough. Beyond wanting to make an example of him, I'd like him to give you a public apology too."

As grateful as she was to him for wanting to champion her, she was keenly aware that there was more to be said. She braced herself for the next piece of information she had to impart. "Before we start climbing that hill, there's something else you should know."

"Tell me," he said when she hesitated.

She took a deep breath and tried to relax in spite of her growing concern. Although she was confident James would support Michael and Cynthia getting married now, his initial reaction toward them forming an attachment gave Wilhelmina pause. It had after all been the source of her disagreement with him, and the prospect of stirring that up again made her wary. Knowing she had little choice if she were to do the right thing, she took a deep breath and dived in head first. "Cynthia is carrying Michael's child."

"I..." James stared at Wilhelmina. "I didn't think she could...I mean...how?"

"In the usual manner, I suspect." She frowned and bit her lip while studying him. She wanted him to be pleased but he still looked too shocked for her to tell if he might be.

He blinked and seemed to focus on her. "Michael will be overjoyed by this news."

"And you?" She held her breath in anxious anticipation of what he might say.

"I have had a great deal of time to reevaluate how I feel." He wove their fingers together, and she sighed, releasing some of the tension. "It was wrong of me to deny my son the chance he had to marry for love. Truth is I let my own bad experience interfere with my judgment."

"James, you were only trying to do what was best for him – to protect him and guide him."

"Yes, but in the end the choice should have been his. He and Cynthia are both of age. They're old enough to make their own decisions without me ruining everything just because I had a grudge against you."

"Your reasoning wasn't entirely wrong, James. Michael will still risk his reputation if I become his mother-in-law." Concern filled her even as she longed for him to disregard his own. "Are you certain you can accept that?"

"If it's what he wants." He raised her hand to his lips for a kiss, then suddenly laughed. "I imagine the scandal will be much worse when you and I also marry, because then he'll in effect be wed to his sister."

Wilhelmina's mouth fell open. Too afraid to utter one word in case he'd spoken in haste and the comment carried no weight, she stared at James until she suddenly thought to ask, "Would such a thing even be legal?"

"They're not blood relations and neither are we. And in case you're wondering, that was not an official proposal." He drew her closer and kissed her until she was breathless. Smiling against her lips he told her, "I can do better than that, and I plan to. For now, however, I think we have a few things to sort out."

"I need to get back to Cynthia. The pregnancy is making her poorly so although she was sleeping when I left, I'd like to make sure I'm there when she wakes."

"Understood." He got up, pulled her to her feet, and gave her another quick kiss. "I'll notify Michael. Perhaps the two of us can stop by Cynthia's home tomorrow?"

"I think that would be lovely."

"And then, once we've made sure they're on their way to the altar, we'll deal with Cloverfield."

Wilhelmina groaned. "I'd nearly forgotten him."

James's expression hardened. "I certainly haven't, and I don't intend to do so either until he has been thoroughly punished for his slight against you."

Appreciating James's need to defend her, Wilhelmina chose not to argue, for although she was wary of crossing a duke more than necessary, she knew James needed this victory. Especially after what she'd just told him.

Nervous trepidation sent Michael's heart racing before he and his father arrived at Cynthia's home. The news he'd received this morning was joyous indeed, but he almost wished he'd not been informed until after he'd asked Cynthia to marry him. Now he feared she'd think he was only doing so out of obligation. He worried she might reject him.

Mrs. Lawson led the way upstairs and toward her daughter's bedchamber door. Michael's stomach shifted, making him slightly queasy as he waited for her to announce his arrival.

"Please," Mrs. Lawson said. She gestured for him to follow her into the room.

Taking a deep steadying breath, Michael advanced, instinctively searching the dimmed space until he met Cynthia's gaze. A smile lit up her face the moment his gaze met hers, banishing all concern.

"I'll wait downstairs with your father," Mrs. Lawson said. She closed the door as she slipped from the room.

"You came," Cynthia said. Her eyes shone brighter than usual.

"Of course I did," Michael said. He crossed to the bed and bent to kiss her brow. Straightening, he took her hand and perched himself on the edge of her mattress. "I even brought roses, but your mother warned the scent might upset you, so I left them down-stairs in the parlor."

Cynthia's features tightened at the mention of the flowers, revealing a hint of the malaise her mother had mentioned. It made him aware of her pallor and exhaustion, both of which made him long to take better care of her.

"Forgive me, but I am not at my best right now."

"No need for apologies, Cynthia. If anything it is I who should ask your forgiveness for taking so long to make my decision." He gave her hand a gentle squeeze. "As pleased as I am to know you're expecting, I need you to know that I'd already made up my mind and planned to marry you no matter what."

"Even if I couldn't have children?"

"Yes, my love." When tears spilled from her eyes, his own blurred in response. He drew a tremulous breath in an effort to fight the growing ache in his throat. "You are my world, Cynthia. To go through life without you would be untenable. And besides, no one can know what the future holds, but I do know what I have in you, and that is a partner more perfect than any other."

Emotion caused the words to crack. Cynthia's palm settled softly against his cheek in a tender caress that made his heart swell with affection.

"Marriage is a huge decision," she whispered, "so I would never begrudge your need to think it through carefully, Michael. But it does ease my mind, knowing you based your decision on more than duty. Please know that you and the child I carry are everything to me. I love you beyond compare."

"May I kiss you, or will that make you feel worse?"

She gave a small smile. "I'd like to try. Just briefly, at least."

Taking care not to stifle the air around her too much, he leaned in and pressed his mouth to hers with the utmost of care.

~

James paced Cynthia's parlor trying to figure out what to do next. He'd not slept a wink since seeing Wilhelmina safely back here last night. Too many thoughts crowded his mind, each one screaming for his attention.

"Would you not rather come sit with me for a bit?" Wilhelmina asked from her position on the sofa. She'd been watching his movements while sipping her tea. His fourth cup of coffee that morning remained untouched on the table. "I believe Cynthia's rather fond of that carpet you're wearing a hole in."

He stopped, scrubbed one hand across his unshaved jaw, and glanced at the mantelpiece clock. "It's nearly an hour since Michael and I arrived and you took him up to see Cynthia. He ought to have joined us by now."

"And I'm sure he will at any moment."

"It shouldn't take this long to propose. Unless of course..." He caught his breath and stared at Wilhelmina. "What if she has refused him?"

"I'm sure she wouldn't do that."

"But what if she has? What if she has decided he doesn't love her enough or...or..." He caught Wilhelmina pressing her lips together as if to stifle a laugh. "What?"

She chuckled and lifted one shoulder. "It's just that you were so set against their making a match before. It's rather endearing watching you get so riled up at the prospect of their no longer wishing to do so."

Her comment shook him. "But they must. If she is

going to have my grandchild, I'll damn well drag them both to the church myself if need be."

"And I'm sure they'd be thrilled," Wilhelmina said. She stood and moved toward him. Her arms came around his neck while a smile, so full of affection it soothed the tempest within, lit up her eyes. "It will not come to that though."

He wanted to believe her, but what other explanation could there be for the delay? "How can you be so sure?"

"Because they love each other. And because Cynthia is my daughter. As such she understands how far a mother must go in order to protect her child. She would never give birth out of wedlock, James."

"You're certain?"

"As certain as I am that you are the man with whom I intend to spend the rest of my life."

His heart jolted. "Mina…"

"Just a piece of assurance," she said right before she pressed her mouth to his for a sweet and gentle kiss.

"Sorry to intrude," Michael said, forcing an end to the lovely embrace. He stood in the doorway. "I just thought you should know that Cynthia and I intend to marry as soon as possible. If you could help me obtain a special license, Papa, I'd be grateful."

James grinned as he crossed to his son. He shook his hand, then pulled him in for a tight embrace. Stepping back, James met Michael's gaze. "Nothing would please me more."

"Considering how sick Cynthia feels at the

moment," Michael said, "we've decided to have the wedding here. Provided the two of you will serve as our witnesses?"

"We'd be delighted." James looked at Wilhelmina who nodded her agreement. "Once we have the special license, we'll find ourselves a clergyman."

"Shall we be off then?" Michael asked.

"Give me a moment," James said. Michael bid Wilhelmina adieu and retreated to the foyer. James reached for her hand and gave it a squeeze. "Happy?"

"Very much so. And you?"

"I finally feel as though the world is starting to spin the right way again." When she grinned, he caught her mouth in a deep kiss intended to serve as a promise. He would return with the special license, their children would marry, and then he and Wilhelmina would see to their own happily ever after.

This, unfortunately, would involve dealing with Cloverfield. God help him but there was not enough light in this world to banish the fury he felt when he thought of what the duke's father had done and what the duke himself had planned. It was contemptible. If anyone ever deserved to be drawn and quartered, it was they.

Suppressing the shudder that threatened to jar him at the awareness of how Wilhelmina had suffered – of all she'd been through – and how he himself had treated her later, with utter disdain, he did his best to convey only love as he took his leave. And as he did so, he reminded himself that if it had not been for that long ago atrocity against her, Cynthia wouldn't exist. Neither would the child she now carried.

There was beauty in the fact that they did, even if accepting the deed that had brought them into the world would never be possible.

Knowing about it would without doubt haunt him for the rest of his days, James realized while he and Michael made their way to Doctors' Commons to find the Archbishop. He loved Wilhelmina and hated the fact that she had been tricked into an abusive situation from which she'd had no escape. He'd never get over it, even if he would fight to keep his anger at bay for her sake.

Instead, he would dedicate the rest of his life to undoing the pain and heartache she'd suffered by loving her for all he was worth. To this end, he would pledge himself to her forever, a decision which prompted him to ask the driver to stop by Pennington House on the way.

"I hope you don't mind," James told Michael. "It's just a small detour. Shouldn't take long."

"Does this by any chance have something to do with you winning Mrs. Lawson's hand?" Michael asked wryly.

"As a matter of fact, it has everything to do with it." Pennington House was where they had met. It was where Wilhelmina's reputation had been torn to pieces. It seemed like the most fitting place to try and restore it, however much he was able.

"Then by all means," Michael murmured, "carry on."

They pulled to a halt outside the white stone edifice fifteen minutes later. James peered at it through the carriage window.

"Well?" Michael prompted.

"There's a good chance I'll be turned away," James said. "After that piece in the paper, my own reputation has suffered."

"Well, you won't know unless you try."

"Very true." James took a deep breath, opened the door, and stepped down onto the pavement. "I'll be back as soon as I can."

Leaving Michael to wait in the carriage, James climbed the front steps of Pennington House and approached the front door. He ignored the uncomfortable clenching of muscle in his stomach and reached for the heavy brass knocker.

The butler answered his call with a stiff expression and a pair of arched brows. "Yes?"

"Mr. Dale to see Viscount Pennington." James handed the butler his card and was promptly shown into a grandiose parlor not entirely dissimilar to the one at Clarington House. Feeling at home here wouldn't be hard provided he managed to get his nerves under control.

"Wait here please," the butler said. "I'll see if the master's at home."

James answered with a tight smile. He crossed to the window and glanced out at the street where the hackney he and Michael had hired still sat. Thankfully his son's life had gotten sorted. If all went well, his own would too.

"What an unexpected surprise," a dry voice remarked.

James turned, a little surprised to see Pennington approaching. Deep down, he'd expected the viscount to turn him away. The fact that he hadn't boded well. James stepped toward him and shook his outstretched hand. "I apologize for the intrusion, my lord."

"Not at all." Pennington gestured toward a chair and waited for James to sit before following suit. "Would you care for some tea or coffee? Something stronger, perhaps?"

"No thank you. I cannot stay long."

"Then let us proceed." Pennington leaned back in his seat. "To what do I owe this pleasure?"

"I trust you've read the Duke of Cloverfield's claims against me?"

"Indeed. Rather damning, unless you're a sensible person who knows how to spot a lie." Pennington frowned while James tried to come to terms with his statement and what it implied. "Can't believe *The Mayfair Chronicle* printed such tripe since they've always struck me as a respectable paper."

"So you don't believe Mrs. Lawson and I have been lovers for years or that I was the man behind her divorce?"

"No." When James merely stared at him in dismay Pennington added, "The Hewitts were good friends of ours. Gave us an insight into their situation."

Another statement that prompted the wheels and cogs in James's brain to turn. "Did you already know of their plans on the night of the ball?"

Pennington studied James with an inscrutable expression. "Why are you here, Mr. Dale?"

Deciding a frank approach might be best, he said, "To ask for your help in turning public opinion in Mrs. Lawson's favor. If such a thing can even be done."

"And why, if I may ask, would you wish to do that?" Pennington asked. "Last I heard, you shared that public opinion."

"A lot has changed since then." James met the viscount's gaze boldly. "I've gotten to know her better. Properly, that is, and…"

"And?" Pennington watched him with an undeniable degree of interest.

"I want to ask for her hand in marriage." When surprise widened Pennington's eyes James hastily added, "But before I do so, I'd like to make an effort to restore her reputation as much as possible. And set the world straight with regard to Cloverfield's lies."

"Well then…" Pennington gave James a slow smile. "To answer your earlier question, my wife and I were both aware of Mrs. Lawson's plan to help Mr. Hewitt gain a divorce. It's the reason we hosted the ball in the first place, so they would have the stage they required for their performance."

James took a moment to absorb this new information. "They had to make certain people believed the accusations he would make against her in order to break up their marriage."

"Quite."

Once again, the sacrifice she'd made for her friend astounded James. He held Pennington's gaze with sharp intent. "Would another such ball be possible?"

"As it happens, we actually have one planned for the twenty-third."

"That's in ten days. A little sooner than I'd hoped, but I suppose it could work." When Pennington tilted his head in question, James asked, "Would you allow me to use your event for a public announcement decrying Cloverfield's statements and to make a proposal?"

"I'd have to speak with my wife first, but I'm sure she can be persuaded. I'll send word tomorrow, if that's all right?"

Satisfied with the result of his meeting with Pennington, James thanked the viscount and took his leave.

"Did you meet with success?" Michael asked as they continued toward Doctors' Commons together.

"Time will tell," James said, "but I am more hopeful now than ever before that everything will turn out just as it should."

"Good. I'm glad to hear it." The steel spring suspension squeaked as they turned a corner. "You deserve to be happy, Papa."

"So do you."

"Is that why you've now agreed to give us your blessing?"

James considered the question. It was easy to just say yes, but that wasn't as honest as he'd like to be. "A series of things have caused me to do so, like the fact that I've been made aware of Mrs. Lawson's true character, which happens to be so admirable I still can't quite fathom it. And then I got to know her daughter better as well, and when I realized she's going to have your child, the only thing that made sense was for you to marry her.

"Of course I want your happiness, but that's why I chose to deny you in the first place, Michael, because I thought I knew best. I was horribly wrong though, and I fear I caused you a great deal of grief because of it."

"You acted out of love and I understood that, even if I didn't agree." Michael gave a wry smile. "Hence the elopement."

"I'm going to do my best to make sure your reputation doesn't suffer when you and Mrs. Petersen marry, but if life in London becomes too difficult for the two of you, I'm sure a smaller town like Renwick could use a skilled solicitor."

"About that..." When James raised an eyebrow, Michael confessed, "The law was always your passion, your dream. Personally, I'd rather do something else."

"Like what?" James asked, a little unnerved by the fact that his son might have spent several years receiving an education he didn't want.

"When we were at Clarington House, Grandpapa said he'd be happy to teach me how to run the estate since you never showed much interest."

"It's not that I wasn't interested, but I must confess the law held greater appeal." James considered Michael's comment. "Would you enjoy that, do you think?"

"I believe I might, though I cannot be certain until I try."

James studied him carefully. "You do realize I'm the heir and that nothing will change that?"

"I do."

"So you would in effect be acting like a steward, of sorts."

"Seeing as I am *your* heir," Michael said with a smile, "I would consider it time well invested in our family's future."

"It would certainly be a great help to your grandpapa," James admitted "As for me, I'd be able to keep on working, provided my career can still be saved."

"And if it can't?"

"Either way, I'll figure things out with Mina." Whichever decision he made, it would affect her too, so he had to make certain he had her approval.

The carriage drew to a halt outside Doctors' Commons and both men alit. Half an hour later, they had the special license. An hour after that, they'd made arrangements with the priest at St. James's Church and agreed that he would stop by Cynthia's home the next afternoon to officiate the wedding between her and Michael.

"Would you allow me to have another word with your daughter before we go?" Michael asked

Wilhelmina once he and James had provided her with an update a short while later.

"Of course," Wilhelmina said. "I'm sure Mrs. Rubins would be happy to show you up."

"Thank you, Mrs. Lawson."

"Please call me Mina," Wilhelmina said.

Michael agreed to do so from now on and followed the maid up the stairs.

CHAPTER TWENTY-ONE

Wilhelmina reached for James's hand and drew him into the parlor. "I'm ever so grateful to you for helping secure the special license and making sure the priest can come by as soon as tomorrow."

He wove his fingers between hers and smiled with so much warmth it filled her heart to overflowing. "Think nothing of it, Mina."

"But I do. Considering how opposed you initially were to their marrying, your change in stance deserves my sincerest thanks."

"A great deal has changed since you and I first met. And I wager much will continue to change in the coming weeks, not only for Michael and Cynthia but for the two of us as well. Which prompts me to ask you a pertinent question."

"Yes?"

"If your reputation were restored, would you want

to remain in London, or would you rather return to Renwick?"

"That depends," she said after careful consideration.

"On what?"

Noting the keen expectancy in his eyes, she took courage and said, "On whether you and I are married or not."

"I've already told you I plan to propose."

Her heart beat faster. "Then I suppose I'd choose London since this is where you'd need to live in order to be near the courts."

"Mina, after everything you have sacrificed in your life, for your daughter and for Mr. Hewitt and his new wife, I think it would wreck me if I believed you were giving up more for me." He drew her into his arms and held her tight. "I want your happiness, Mina."

"And I want yours."

His chest rose and fell against her breasts. Drawing back, he gazed into her eyes with such overwhelming affection it stole her breath. And then he kissed her, slowly and lovingly, as if determined to make her believe he would always be by her side from now on, no matter what.

"My career has suffered because of Cloverfield, and I'm not sure it will survive the damage he's caused. But maybe that's not a bad thing." His expression grew pensive. "What would you think of the two of us moving into your cottage in Renwick?"

His suggestion rendered her speechless for a moment. Since realizing she and he would form a more permanent attachment – that he intended to offer marriage – she'd been contemplating what to do with her cottage and had decided last night that she'd probably have to sell it. Which of course meant giving up on her new business. But if James wished to live there then...

"After you left for London, I started baking again."

His eyes widened with interest. "You did?"

She nodded. "Turns out the townsfolk love my bread and my cakes. I sold out nearly every day."

"You were selling your goods?" He gazed at her in wonder. "Out of necessity or because you enjoy it?"

"Both, if I'm to be honest." When he raised one eyebrow in question she said, "The bank froze my accounts on the basis of needing to figure out whether or not I owed George money. The funds currently at my disposal came from the sale of my London townhouse, which was thankfully in my name alone since George had the forethought to transfer the deed. But that money won't last forever, so I decided to find a way in which to earn more."

"And who is running this business of yours now while you are away?"

"I left Betsy in charge."

He shook his head. "Why on earth didn't you mention all of this before?"

She shrugged. Perhaps her reasoning had been silly. "For one thing it seemed unimportant compared with everything else we had to discuss. And for another, I know how much you value your work, and

I had no wish for you to even consider giving that up for me."

"Mina, you have to stop putting yourself second and feeling guilty when you don't. If we are to make our relationship work then I need to know you will voice your own hopes and dreams, even if they oppose my own. Somehow, no matter what, we'll find a way to compromise. But imagine how I would feel if I learned that my happiness came at the expense of yours? If the situation were reversed, would you enjoy knowing I gave up everything for you without you having a chance to do the same?"

"Of course not."

"Then promise me you will tell me what you want so we can build a life we can both enjoy."

"You're right," she said. "I'm sorry, James."

"There's no need for that. I just want you to think of me as your partner and your equal, rather than someone you constantly have to please." He pressed another kiss to her lips. "Agreed?"

"As long as you promise to finish the running water project you've started at your house."

He laughed. "You saw the pipes, did you?"

A smile tugged at her lips. "They were hard to miss."

"Very well then," he said. "We'll support each other and make sure we each fulfill our dreams."

The pleasure his words instilled in her was indescribable. While George had been her dearest friend and had always listened to her and offered advice, he'd never really understood her desire to bake when they had a capable servant to do the job. He'd also reasoned that her idea to open a bakery wouldn't help their family's social standing. When she'd tried to equate it with his furniture company, she'd been met with a look of incomprehension.

And because of the guilt she'd harbored over him getting stuck in a marriage with her, she'd dropped the subject because she'd believed she had no right to argue.

But James got it. Moreover, he encouraged her to assert herself and fight for more than a tolerable existence. It was a gratifying experience – one that made her reflect on just how much she and George had given up when they'd chosen to marry each other. Luckily, they'd both been given a second chance to find happiness with the right people.

This thought remained at the front of Wilhelmina's mind as she watched her daughter speak her vows the following afternoon. While Henry had been good for Cynthia, Michael's personality seemed to be more in tune with hers. Seeing the love that shone in their eyes as the priest pronounced them husband and wife was far more freeing than Wilhelmina had expected, and when she bid the newly married couple farewell later on and left the house together with James, it felt like a boulder had been removed from her breast.

"Are you absolutely certain you want me to come home with you?" she asked as soon as he'd helped her into a hired hackney and claimed the seat across from her. "If people find out they'll—"

"What?" James clasped her hand in his larger one. "Cloverfield already has the world thinking you are my mistress. If you ask me, we might as well use that claim to our advantage."

She felt the tightness of her own frown. "But I'm not your mistress, James, and I have no wish to be."

"It's only temporary, Mina." He angled himself toward her so their knees touched. His expression was suddenly marred by severity. "I have a plan, or at least I am working on one. If all goes well, Cloverfield's lies will be brought to light and you shall be understood rather than shunned. Now, I cannot promise you that your reputation will be restored to its fullest, but I do believe my efforts will lead to acceptance by many of those who have thought ill of you."

Panic gripped her. "James, if you tell anyone George's accusations against me were false then—"

"That's not my intention at all."

Her lips parted with surprise. She searched his face. "Then how?"

He placed his arm around her and drew her closer. "Do you trust me?"

"Yes." In the time she'd known him, he'd always been frank with her. He'd helped her in spite of their differences, because it had been the correct thing to do. No one was more honorable than he or more deserving of her good faith.

"Then let me do what I can in order to help you." He kissed the top of her head. "Rest assured, Mina, I'll marry you regardless, but first I'd like to see if it can be achieved with the approval we both deserve."

Unable to deny how wonderful it would be if their union were to be celebrated rather than reviled, Mina settled herself against James's sturdy frame and savored his warmth. She would not argue any further about the indecency of going home with him, or of their living in sin for a while. Instead, she'd enjoy every moment she was allowed with the man she loved.

An unexpected invitation arrived two days later during breakfast. James picked the crisply folded parchment off the silver salver Atkins brought and tore the crimson seal. He glanced at Wilhelmina, who sat adjacent to him, sipping her tea. Their eyes met and a wave of heat crashed through him.

These past two days with her had cemented his certainty. Never in his life had he loved a woman as much as he loved her. She was everything to him, a delightful companion who made him laugh with abandon when she teased and prompted him to reflect on more serious issues when she voiced her opinions on political matters. She was also his greatest supporter. The pump he'd installed in the kitchen and the sketches depicting his plans for the water pipes had impressed her so greatly, he might as well have discovered the fountain of youth.

Pleased to know he would soon be able to offer for

her in a grandiose gesture of great affection, he said, "The Penningtons have invited us to their ball next Friday."

Her eyes widened and her teacup rattled against its saucer as she set it aside. "May I see that, please?"

He handed her the invitation and watched while she read. "This note at the bottom wishes you luck." She returned her gaze to his with curiosity.

"Indeed."

A startled half grin, half snort, escaped her, then she slapped him over his hand with the invitation. "You're still not going to tell me what you're up to. Are you?"

He smirked and picked up his coffee. "Not a chance."

"Well, then."

Much to James's delight, no more was said on the matter, which allowed him a moment to mentally strategize. The coming week would be ridiculously busy. Flyers would have to be printed, an engagement ring purchased, and...

"You'll need a gown," he said. Good God, how long would that take to make?

"I suspect I shall. None of the dresses I brought with me are suited to a Society ball." She batted her lashes at him. "How do you suppose we handle that problem in only one week at the height of the Season?"

A cool sweat broke out at the nape of his neck. "I'm not sure, but as long as money isn't an issue, I'm certain we can find a seamstress willing to work overtime."

As it turned out, doing so was easier said than done. Every modiste's shop they visited the following afternoon was already overbooked. Apparently, having a ball gown made at short notice was harder than getting the printer James had met with that morning to deliver one hundred flyers within a week.

"This is hopeless," Wilhelmina said when they left the sixth dress shop. Having other customers turn their backs on them didn't help. "Perhaps it's time for us to accept defeat, James."

"Absolutely not." No one had been wronged more than Wilhelmina. Society would never know the extent of her plight, but since *he* did, he'd be damned if he'd let her go down without a fight. Hell, he would give his plan its best shot and if that didn't work, only then would he retreat from the battle he waged on her behalf. He turned to her with a fresh idea. "You bake and weave, you milk cows and pitch in to help your servants. Any chance you also know how to fashion a ball gown?"

Wilhelmina blinked. "I made a couple of day dresses once, but a ball gown is far more complicated, James. There's beading, fancy ruffles, tucks, and pleats."

"The alternative would be to borrow a gown from Cynthia," he suggested.

"She's more petite than I am." A deep shade of pink rose to her cheeks. "I'd need a much larger bodice."

James grinned. "Nothing wrong with that. I certainly shan't complain."

She knit her brow. "I'm honestly not sure I'm up to the challenge."

He raised an eyebrow. "Says the woman who's risen to all her previous challenges."

"But a ball gown, James? If it doesn't fit right I'll be humiliated."

"Oh, it will fit to perfection, Wilhelmina. Even if I have to pin it in place myself."

A startled laugh left her. "You cannot be serious."

"Perfectly so, my love." He turned her about and steered her back to the shop they'd recently left. Fifteen minutes later, they'd purchased muslin for a new petticoat, a four inch wide gold ribbon, and ten yards of scarlet silk. For as James had informed Wilhelmina when she protested the color, he wanted her to stand out like a ruby among all the boring diamonds.

"I have to get started on this right away if I'm to be ready in time," she informed him when they returned home. "Would it be all right for me to make use of the dining room table?"

"This is as much your home now as it is mine," he said and helped Atkins carry her purchases into what would be known as Wilhelmina's work space for the next week. He told the butler, "We'll take our next meals in the parlor without any fuss."

"Very good, sir." Atkins, to his credit, left without any hint of thinking the change in circumstance odd.

"I'll use one of my day dresses to make a pattern," Wilhelmina said. She was already in the process of unpacking the sewing equipment and pattern paper she'd bought.

"An excellent idea." James stepped up behind her and

placed his palm against her lower back. When she stilled, he leaned in and dropped a kiss on her cheek. "In the meantime, I'll get to work on the plumbing."

"Oh." She turned to him in a rush, placing herself in his arms. "What a wonderful idea. I wish you luck and look forward to seeing your progress."

Unable to resist, he dipped his head and captured her lips with his in a sweet caress that turned increasingly hungry. As much as he regretted it, he eventually forced his mouth away from hers. A rough laugh rippled through him. "I should probably go if you want to get started on your gown today."

She gazed at him with longing. "You know I'd rather keep kissing you, but if you want me to be ready by Friday, I don't have much choice."

"I know." He stepped back and took a deep breath. "Call me if you need help."

"You too," she said, prompting him to smile with adoration as he strode from the room.

The day of the ball snuck up on Wilhelmina faster than she'd expected. She'd barely left the dining room during the last week except to eat and sleep, which she accomplished quickly and in brief increments. And although she missed spending more time with James, she was able to follow his movements around the house thanks to the noise he made. The banging and clanging along with the heavy tread on the stairs gave her some sense of what he was up to.

She pulled her needle and thread through the stitch line she'd marked with white thread, attaching the last capped sleeve to the bodice. A quick glance at the clock alerted her to the time. It was nearly midday and she still had to hem the entire thing.

A knock on the door preceded James's arrival. He was coming to check on her for the second time that morning. And he brought with him a plate filled with sandwiches. "How are you faring?"

"I'm not done yet."

"Then let me help you save some time." He pulled up a chair and held one sandwich up to her mouth. "Eat."

She grinned and took a large bite of bread, ham, and cheese. A groan of pleasure escaped her as her stomach cheered in response to the offering. "Thank you."

"You're welcome." He kept the sandwich steady for her so she could keep eating while she worked. "I'm sure I could figure out how to use a needle and thread. It looks more tedious than hard."

"Don't you have enough on your hands?" She took another bite and tied off the thread.

"Not any more. I'm finished."

Her gaze snapped to his. "Truly?"

A grin lit up his eyes. He nodded. "Truly."

"And it works?"

"Yes, Mina. It works."

"That's marvelous news, James." She thrust her gown from her lap and flung her arms around his neck, nearly making a mess of the last bit of sandwich he held. He barely managed to set it aside before she hugged him to her, holding him tightly and simply loving him with all her might. "I want to see it right away. May I?"

"I've a better idea." He leaned back a little. "How about I help you finish your gown first? Once it's done, we'll prepare a hot bath so you can see the new system at work while taking some time to relax and enjoy it."

As impatient as she was to see it now, she appreciated his suggestion and prepared a needle and thread for him. A swift lesson in hemming followed, during which he paid close attention. "If you start there with small stiches and sew to your right, I'll begin here and sew to the left. Once we meet, we'll be finished."

They worked in companionable silence and completed the hem within a couple of hours. Wilhelmina breathed a sigh of relief and rubbed her temples. "We did it."

"With three hours to spare before we have to start getting ready. That's plenty of time for that bath I promised." James stood, placed Wilhelmina's gown carefully on the table, and reached for her hand. "Come on."

She got to her feet and followed him out of the room. Excitement bubbled inside her as he led her downstairs to the kitchen, past Mrs. Dunkley, who was making a pâté, and toward the copper. A metal pipe protruding from the side of the traditional looking water heater had been connected to a large metal cylinder while another pipe sticking out through the top disappeared into the ceiling.

"The water in the copper is hot," James explained. "If we switch this valve here, then the steam driven engine will push water up that pipe and out through an upstairs tap, filling the tub. I've added a speaking tube over here so the person operating the pump will know when to stop."

"How ingenious," Wilhelmina murmured. She studied the tube with the flexible end piece and glanced at James. "May I try it?"

"Of course." He asked Tabitha, the maid, to go upstairs and monitor the bath.

"Ready, sir," came her voice moments later.

Wilhelmina laughed. "Oh, this is brilliant, James. *You* are brilliant."

He smiled and gestured toward the pump. "Would you like to do the honors?"

"I would love to." She nearly bounced on her feet in excitement. "Should I just…"

"Here." He handed her a crocheted pot holder. "So you don't burn yourself."

Wilhelmina took the square piece of cloth, reached for the valve, and gave it a push. She glanced at James. A moment passed, and then she heard Tabitha speak from upstairs. "There's hot water, sir. It's got a steady flow to it."

"That will come and go as the pressure inside the engine eases," James answered through the speaking tube. "Let me know when the water flow weakens so we can close the valve and allow the pressure to build once more."

The maid did as asked and by the time she announced that the tub had been filled, Wilhelmina had lost track of the number of times the valve had been opened and closed. In between, they had to wait for the water to boil again in the engine.

Wilhelmina studied the device. "Is this like the Savery pump you mentioned during our travels?"

"This is a much simpler design. It lacks the mechanical automation of the Savery pump, which is also a great deal bigger. And although my design no longer requires hauling heavy buckets of water up two flights of stairs, it is still a time-consuming process," James said. He offered his arm and began escorting her up to what had once been a small sitting room between two bedchambers. He now referred to it as the bathing room, much to Wilhelmina's delight. "A great deal of work still remains."

"Like hiding the pipes and patching up your broken ceilings?" Wilhelmina asked with a touch of mischief.

James grinned. "One thing at a time, my love."

Together they entered the bathing room where a thick steam fogged the air. Wilhelmina crossed to the tub and carefully tested the water. "It's really hot."

"It should cool to the perfect temperature by the time you're ready to step into it." James came up behind her, wound his arms around her middle, and pressed a kiss to the nape of her neck. "Allow me to assist."

Working swiftly, he undid the row of buttons at the

back of her dress and pushed the garment down so she could step out of it. Her stays and chemise were removed next and finally her stockings. Turning her in his arms, James kissed her while pressing her naked body to his. As scandalous as it was, it was also incredibly right. After living with him for the past week, she no longer shied away from him seeing her like this, even though she knew her body was not that of a young woman in her prime.

With James, however, she'd never felt more beautiful.

"You're so incredibly stunning," he murmured as he released her. The heat of his gaze proved he meant every word. He offered his hand and helped her into the tub. "I look forward to showing you off this evening."

"And I look forward to being seen on your arm." She sank into the water and sighed in response to its soothing effect. "This is what heaven must feel like. You truly are a genius."

He chuckled. "I'll leave you to relax for a bit while I see to a few things I need to prepare for the ball."

She nodded and waved him off with a satisfied sigh.

When he returned later, he wore a navy blue brocade banyan. "Are you ready to get out or would you like some more time?"

"I'm ready. The water is still warm if you'd like to use it."

"I plan to," he said and collected a towel. Holding it up, he waited for her to stand, then wrapped it around her and helped her out of the tub. Without second thought, he took off the banyan and tossed it onto a nearby chair.

Wilhelmina's heart clenched in response to the intimacy of the moment. She'd not even realized how much she'd longed for this, for a man with whom she could comfortably share every part of herself without feeling guilt or shame. Someone who loved her as he did.

"I want this to last forever," she whispered while watching the perfect pull of muscles and tendons as he climbed into the tub.

"It will," he murmured. "We just have to get through tonight."

Wilhelmina hoped he was right. He'd said he would marry her and had even discussed with her what their future together would look like. But what if something went wrong? What if Cloverfield showed up and made things worse? The duke was a rash young man without scruples, who'd already proven he hated to lose. If he wanted further revenge against her and James, there was no telling what he might do. Or how his actions would influence them.

CHAPTER TWENTY-TWO

Dressed in his best evening black, James led Wilhelmina up the front steps of Pennington House and into the foyer. A footman standing at attention checked their invitation and offered to help them with their outerwear garments. As previously agreed with the viscount, James and Wilhelmina had arrived late, allowing them the grand entrance James wanted. The flyers he'd ordered had been delivered that morning and would, he hoped, be ready for distribution at his command.

"Are you ready?" he asked Wilhelmina once the footman had collected her cloak.

She answered with a tremulous smile. "No."

He leaned in and kissed her, not caring if anyone happened to see. "We're in this together, my love. I'm right by your side."

A small nod assured him of her trust. She'd placed

her faith in him in spite of her apprehensions. He understood. She would be stepping out into Society for the first time in over two years with every risk of facing censure. It had to be terrifying, but Wilhelmina was nothing if not brave. And James both admired and loved her for that.

He offered his arm and, when she took it, led her through the white marbled hallway. "You look incredible, Mina. Have I mentioned that yet?"

"Only a dozen times," she said with a hint of laughter.

"If your baking attempts fall through, you can always make a career as a seamstress. Mark my word, there's no woman in there who won't wish they had your gown."

"Truth be told, I'm rather pleased with the results myself."

"And so you should be."

They reached the entrance to the ballroom where the butler stood, ready to announce their arrival. James's stomach tightened. He squeezed Wilhelmina's hand, and prayed he wasn't about to make a colossal mistake by challenging Cloverfield's statement in public.

"Mr. James Dale and Mrs. Lawson," the Pennington butler declared, his voice unnaturally loud.

James tried not to flinch. The music accompanying the country dance currently underway kept playing, but from his vantage point, James saw that the dancers were no longer keeping time with the rhythm. They, like everyone else in the room, had turned to stare. Whispers began. They sped round the room like hounds giving chase to a rabbit. And then the music droned to a halt.

"I hate this," Wilhelmina murmured.

James heartily agreed although the response they received was nothing less than what he'd expected. He searched the crowd and finally relaxed a little when he spotted Pennington. The viscount was making his way toward them with his wife on his arm. James leaned a little closer to Wilhelmina. "Take heart, my love. Everything will be all right."

"Welcome, Mr. Dale," Pennington said as soon as he and the viscountess reached them. "We're delighted to have you and Mrs. Lawson join us this evening."

If Pennington was aware of the shocked expressions this statement led to, he showed no indication. "Perhaps you would—"

"What the hell is this?" an angry voice asked.

"Oh God," Wilhelmina muttered.

James had no need to look for the man who'd just spoken to know it was Cloverfield. He spotted the duke within the next second as he too marched forward, the crowd parting on either side of him as if he were Moses. "Surely these people have not been invited."

Anger hardened Pennington's eyes even as he smiled and turned to address the duke. "On the contrary, I issued the invitation myself."

Cloverfield's face turned a dangerous shade of red. "I never expected such despicable inconsideration from you, my lord. How dare you force upstanding members of Society to associate with such disgraced individuals?"

"As it happens," Pennington said, his voice clearly audible in the hushed silence now filling the room, "I believe they have something important to share."

Cloverfield sent James a look of disgust. "I doubt there's anyone here who wishes to hear it."

"I would like to," Pennington's brother-in-law, the Earl of Ashburn said.

"As would I," echoed Michael, who'd also been invited along with Cynthia. He raised a glass of champagne in salute.

James glanced at Pennington. The viscount merely gestured toward him. "Now would be an excellent time for you to say your piece, Mr. Dale."

Right.

James steeled himself and sent the duke a glare which he promptly returned.

"I recently lost a client due to a lie that was printed about me in *The Mayfair Chronicle*," James began. He cleared his throat and took a deep breath, ignored the duke's protest and kept on talking. "It was claimed that my acquaintance with Mrs. Lawson preceded her divorce and that I was in fact the one to set it in motion because she and I were lovers. This, I can assure you, ladies and gentlemen, is utter nonsense, fabricated by the Duke of Cloverfield for the purpose of tainting my reputation."

"I would never be dishonest about such matters,"

Cloverfield snapped. "Your charge against me is outrageous."

"What is outrageous, Your Grace, is what you are able to get away with due to your position. You think you can do as you please without consequence, do you? Then by all means, let us put that theory to a test." He met Pennington's gaze and gave a swift nod. The viscount immediately called on his footmen to bring out the flyers.

"I'll not have you spreading falsehoods about me, Dale," Cloverfield fumed. He turned to the crowd as guests began reading the flyers the footmen gave them. "Don't listen to him, do you hear. That man is not to be trusted!"

"What's happening?" Wilhelmina asked.

"Something I hope will prove what sort of man Cloverfield is." He glanced at her, noted the concerned look in her eyes. "I have no evidence to contradict his claim about the two of us, but I can offer proof of his violent behavior and brutal attack against you."

She clutched his forearm. "James..."

"Don't worry." He held her close. "The witness testimonies I have chosen refer to his cruel intentions rather than to the extent of his actions. There's nothing for you to be ashamed of, Mina, though the same cannot be said about him."

"Is this true?" someone asked.

"Of course not," Cloverfield blustered. His friends, the same men who had accompanied him on his trip, came to offer support.

"Mrs. Lawson agreed to an assignation with Clover-field," Everton said. "When Mr. Dale found out, he attacked him for it."

Wilhelmina gasped. "That's not true."

Before James could respond, the Earl of Bearfort, an older gentleman roughly twenty years James's senior, spoke up. "Not according to what these witnesses have reported. In fact, if I were to draw a conclusion based on this, when Cloverfield didn't get what he wanted, he went in pursuit of Mr. Dale and Mrs. Lawson with every intention of asserting himself through force. Not exactly the honorable actions one might expect from a peer, certainly not from a duke. Then again, your father wasn't much better, so I'm hardly surprised."

James gaped at Bearfort. Had he truly just spoken against two dukes and questioned their conduct in public? It was unheard of.

"I'll see you at dawn for that," Cloverfield shouted as he redirected his anger at Bearfort.

"Violence isn't the answer to everything," the Marquess of Stratton said. "Have some pride, Clover-field. And for God's sake, stop acting like a St. Giles thug."

"If what these witnesses claim," said a lady whom James now recognized as the Dowager Duchess of Gilford, "you treated Mrs. Lawson appallingly."

"She's a whore," Cloverfield thundered. "And as such she ought to have thanked me for taking an interest."

∼

Wilhelmina sucked in a breath. As did everyone else, it seemed. Wide eyes and slack-jawed expressions answered Cloverfield's statement. Silence reigned, as if everyone needed a moment to process the words that had just been spoken. The muscles in James's arm flexed beneath her gloved hand. Clearly he wanted to act, to bury his fist in Cloverfield's face.

But rather than give in to such temptation, he spoke between clenched teeth. "Mrs. Lawson is the most incredible woman I've ever had the honor of knowing. Unfortunately, she ended up in an unhappy marriage at a young age."

For a moment, Wilhelmina worried James might reveal the truth, only to chastise herself for even considering something like that. She trusted him and knew he would protect her secrets. Somehow, he'd find a way to argue her case without betraying her. He was an excellent barrister after all. Convincing people of what he believed in was his forte.

"It's not an unfamiliar situation," James continued. "I'm sure there are many who wish they could escape the man or woman they pledged themselves to. Few have the means or the courage to do so, however. For this, Mr. Hewitt must be commended. He strove to find a way out of his marriage, which unfortunately required him to disparage Mrs. Lawson. But..." James paused. He glanced at Mina, offered her an encouraging smile, "were her actions against her husband truly contemptible? According to statements made in court, Mr. Hewitt had several mistresses during the course of his marriage. Why then should Mrs. Lawson be criticized for the affairs she may or may not have had? Does the fact she's a woman deny her the right to happiness? Or are we a hypocritical lot who allow men leniency while placing all blame on the fairer sex?

"My point, ladies and gentlemen, is that Mr. Hewitt wanted to end his marriage so he could enter into a new one. Mrs. Lawson was equally happy to part ways with him, but unlike him, she was made to suffer. Now ask yourselves if that is just.

"I can only speak for myself," James added, "and while I'll admit to being her greatest critic when I first heard her husband's accusations, I have since reconsidered my position. You see, my opinion of her was rooted in my own past experiences – a situation which could not truly be compared with hers since it was entirely different. And so, with this in mind, I ask again if anyone here can truly say she deserves to receive the cut.

"Given the fact that the duke attacked her, then threatened to kill me so he could take her against her will, perhaps it is he who ought to receive such treatment?"

Wilhelmina snapped to attention. Had James just suggested the *ton* give a duke the cut direct in a show of support for a woman who'd fallen from grace? It was unprecedented. And yet, Pennington and his wife didn't hesitate for a moment. They both turned their backs on Cloverfield, as did the couples standing beside them. Other guests started following suit and when the

Dowager Duchess of Gilford and her sons did the same, everyone else turned away as well.

It was like watching a drop of oil repel water. Little by little, Cloverfield stood by himself. Not even his friends remained by his side.

"Damn you all to hell," the duke sputtered. Fists clenched and with a furious glint in his eyes, he strode toward James and Wilhelmina, who remained in front of the exit. He paused before them, his lip curling with malice. "I should have killed you while I had the chance."

Pushing Wilhelmina slightly behind him, James faced the duke. "Careful, Your Grace, lest you get yourself arrested for conspiracy to commit murder." When Cloverfield answered with a snarl, James added, "If any harm ever befalls me or my family, you may rest assured that you shall be the first man apprehended for questioning."

"Bloody bastard," Cloverfield snapped. His shoulder knocked against James's as he pushed past him, shoving him sideways into Wilhelmina.

James caught his balance and steadied her. "Are you all right?"

"Yes. I think so."

A smile lit up his eyes. "Good, because this isn't over yet." Addressing the crowd, he said, "As I mentioned, Mrs. Lawson is the most remarkable woman I've ever had the honor of knowing. I love her with all that I am, and if that means having to give up my good name and reputation, then so be it, for there is no length I would not go to in order to call her mine."

He reached inside his jacket pocket and retrieved a small velvet box before lowering himself to one knee. Wilhelmina's hand flew to her mouth as she realized his intent. Her knees began to tremble and tears sprang to her eyes. The foolish man was going to offer for her right here, before the very people who'd struck her from their lives. He was pledging his allegiance, defending her honor with his love and devotion, and showing her that there was nothing more important to him than her.

"Please, Mina." He opened the box and removed the ring, a lovely gold band with a gorgeous ruby to match her gown. Holding it between his fingers he reached for her hand. "Allow me to walk by your side and bask in your beauty. Let me be your companion, your confidante, and your protector. Marry me, Mina, so I may love you as you deserve to be loved every day for the rest of our lives."

She couldn't speak for the emotion clogging her throat. All she could do was breathe and even that seemed a struggle.

"Well, girl?" the Dowager Duchess of Gilford shouted. "Answer the poor man."

A nod was all Wilhelmina could manage, and the moment she gave it, the very second James had her agreement, he placed the ring on her finger, leapt to his feet, and swept her into his arms.

Cheers erupted along with applause and although

Mina knew most of those who were present would never truly approve of her nor welcome her into their midst, she appreciated the support they were willing to show in this moment.

"I can't believe you had witness statements printed," she said when James was done kissing her and she'd composed herself enough to gather her thoughts in the wake of all that had happened.

James grinned. "I'm a barrister, Mina. Being pre-emptive and making sure there's evidence to back up any eventual claims is part of my job."

She still couldn't quite come to grips with the magnitude of it all. "I'm so impressed by what you accomplished this evening. It surpasses all my expectations."

His palm settled gently against her cheek. "I will always fight for you, Mina. No matter the odds against me."

"Please tell me you plan on getting another special license."

"If I'm to be perfectly honest," he said with a mischievous gleam in his eyes, "I've already got it. So we can marry tomorrow, if it pleases my lady."

"Oh indeed, that would please her greatly, James." Upon which Wilhelmina kissed him for the sake of sealing the deal though also, if *she* were being perfectly honest, for the joy she found in simply loving him.

EPILOGUE

Renwick, seven years later.

"Why don't you let me help Betsy with this so you can go and get ready?" James asked.

Wilhelmina wiped her hands on her apron and glanced at where her husband stood, casually observing her from the doorway while she bustled about the kitchen. Dressed in preparation for their excursion, he leaned against the opening.

"We're almost done," Wilhelmina assured him. She finished restocking a tin with that day's unsold biscuits and handed it to Betsy for storage. Addressing the maid, she said, "If you could please prepare three more honey cakes for tomorrow?"

"Yes, Mrs. Dale."

Wilhelmina turned and instinctively gasped upon finding her nose a mere inch from her husband's chest.

Somehow the rascal had managed to sneak up behind her. His arm stole around her waist, steadying her while a couple of fingers brushed over her cheek. He chuckled, the sound a warm reassuring rumble of masculine affection. "You've got flour here. There's some in your hair too."

"Perhaps I should go wash my face." She sighed when he pressed her closer and kissed her forehead. His scent, so familiar now after all of these years, filled her with memories of long countryside walks, picnics under the oak tree in the garden, the laughter they shared while tossing snowballs after each other in winter, cozy evenings in front of the fire, and all the everyday moments in between. She smiled at him, at his dear face, and her heart tripped as it always did when he focused all his attention on her. "Do the twins look presentable?"

"They do." He dipped his head and kissed her with thorough abandon, forcing her to grip his shoulders for added support. Breaking the kiss, he leaned back ever so slightly and offered a roguish smile. "Now be off with you, my love, or we'll never be on our way."

Wilhelmina slipped from James's embrace with a grin, removed her apron, and hurried upstairs to prepare herself for their visit to Clarington House. His sisters had come for a week-long stay with their husbands and children, so Wilhelmina and James had agreed to remain at the estate overnight so they could enjoy their company to the fullest. The day after tomorrow, the sisters would be coming to see James and Wilhelmina's home, the bakery she'd created, and the bathing room James had constructed. Unlike the one at their London residence, this one also had a cold water pipe which functioned using a simple hand pump.

She used this now to fill the ceramic wash basin so she could splash cool water on her face.

It seemed like a lifetime since the Pennington ball when James had proposed. In the days that followed, an open letter of apology had appeared on *The Mayfair Chronicle's* front page.

Almost immediately after, James began receiving requests for legal representation from numerous high-ranking individuals. Apparently, his public defense of Mina served as the best advertisement he could have wished for and with Cloverfield's words against him dismissed, James was once again a sought after barrister.

But to Mina's surprise, James turned every case down. Instead he suggested a simpler life for them both in Renwick.

"I no longer want to bury myself in work," he'd explained when she'd questioned his decision. "I'll consult on cases from time to time and offer advice, but from now on my focus will be on family— on my parents, Michael and Cynthia, you and the children I hope we'll have. I don't want to miss another moment."

And so they lived in the cottage she had once purchased. It had taken nearly a year for her funds to be made available to her. James made numerous attempts to get involved from a legal standpoint, but it wasn't until an official declaration from George arrived that the court agreed to unfreeze her account. Not that she'd still required the money after marrying James whose wealth surpassed the realm of what she was used to. But she liked the independence – especially with regard to her business. So her own personal funds had since been used to build an additional kitchen and shop, the account reserved exclusively for her income and expenses.

With time, she and James had settled into a pleasant way of life that allowed for family gatherings and those invaluable moments they craved with each other. They only visited London now when a need for change struck their fancy, and to attend the yearly Pennington ball to which they always received an invitation.

Thankfully Cloverfield remained absent from their lives. As far as Mina knew, the duke lived in seclusion, away from London Society. And since no parent wanted a man of his low moral standing to wed their daughter, he was still unmarried, despite his impressive title.

Selecting one of the brightly striped towels she'd woven, Wilhelmina peered at herself in the mirror above her wash basin and wiped away the flour smudges. Time had deepened the creases next to her eyes, marking her as a woman well past her prime. She reached up and stroked her fingertips over each groove. They grew more pronounced as she smiled at herself in the mirror – an inevitable response whenever she thought of her good fortune.

"Mama," her daughter, Annabel, squealed as she burst into the room with her brother, Oliver, on her heels. "There's a man and a woman downstairs."

"It's true," Oliver said. "They've got children with them. Papa said to tell you."

Wilhelmina hung up her towel and glanced at the twins. Eager blue eyes stared back at her from beneath light blonde hair, so soft and fine it reminded her of sunbeams cresting the hill to the east in the morning. She'd been blessed with them eight months after her marriage, only shortly after Cynthia had delivered her daughter, Edith. Some thought it odd that Wilhelmina and James's youngest children were the same age as their grandchild, but Wilhelmina thought it a gift and knew James felt the same way.

"Do you know anything else about these unexpected visitors?" Wilhelmina asked as she picked out her purple shawl and draped it over her shoulders. Finally, she collected her bonnet and a pair of beige kid gloves James had given her one year for Christmas.

Annabel frowned. "No."

Oliver shook his head. "Sorry, Mama."

Wilhelmina smiled at her lovely imps and drew them both into her arms. "That's quite all right. They're probably customers." Though it did seem slightly odd for James to ask the children to fetch her if that were the case. He knew she was getting ready to leave and that they ought to be off as soon as possible. He also knew Betsy was perfectly able to make a sale without Wilhelmina's help.

Curious, Wilhelmina exited her bedchamber with Annabel and Oliver right behind her, and started down the stairs. Before she reached the foyer though, she froze in response to the sound of a man's voice coming from the direction of the parlor. Not James's voice, but one that was almost equally familiar to her.

Wilhelmina's throat tightened. It couldn't be. She and George wrote each other often. Surely he would have mentioned coming to England if he'd had plans to do so.

"Mama?" Annabel queried as if sensing something wasn't quite right. Her small hand caught Wilhelmina's.

"Everything's fine," Wilhelmina gasped even as tears sprang to her eyes. By the time she entered the parlor on shaky legs and located George, her longtime friend was barely more than a blur. Gulping down her emotions, she crossed to where he stood and flung her arms around his neck in a fierce embrace.

"I told you she'd be thrilled to see you again," James said with a laugh while George hugged her to him.

When Wilhelmina withdrew and had a chance to wipe away the tears, she saw that she wasn't the only one overcome by George's unexpected arrival. His eyes were moist as well though a huge grin filled his face. "It's good to see you too, Mina."

She glanced to his side and spotted Fiona who stood beside a boy who appeared to be some years older than the twins, and two younger girls. Although Fiona smiled, the children looked wary.

"Forgive me," Wilhelmina said, aware of how inappropriate her greeting must seem. She moved toward Fiona and caught her hand. "Welcome back."

"We're sorry to come unannounced like this," Fiona said, "but George insisted on surprising you. However, it does look like we've come at an awkward time. From what I gather, you're on your way out."

"To engage in a family gathering at my parents' estate," James said. "It's not far from here, so I would suggest you join us. There's plenty of space and there will be other children there besides our own for yours to play with."

"Oh yes," Wilhelmina said. She gave George a pleading look before regarding Fiona once more. Her hand squeezed hers. "Do say you'll come."

"We'd be delighted to," Fiona said, upon which she and Wilhelmina introduced their respective children to each other.

"Will you be staying long?" Wilhelmina asked George when they prepared to set off for Clarington House a short while later. The children were already chasing each other around the front garden while James loaded the last of their things into the carriage.

"For a month or so. I had some business in London regarding the shop I'm planning to set up there."

He'd mentioned it to her in his last letter. With the growth of the new furniture manufacturing company he had begun in the Michigan Territory, he was now looking to export his goods. "I'm so glad you brought your family with you," Wilhelmina said. She peered into his chestnut colored eyes and grinned. "And I am beyond happy to have you here."

"Likewise, Mina." He smiled at her warmly. "You've no idea how much it eases my mind to see how well you've done for yourself with my own eyes. It's different than reading about it."

"You've done well too," Wilhelmina murmured as she tracked his children's movements. Laughter filled the air.

"Thanks to you," he said. "I'll never forget what you did for me."

Her gaze caught his. "It's no more than what you did for me."

"Come on, you lot," James called. "Time to go."

Wilhelmina sent him a wave of acknowledgement and proceeded to round up her children while George and Fiona herded theirs toward the carriage they'd hired for their journey. Wilhelmina followed Annabel and Oliver through the garden gate. James lifted them up into the conveyance and turned to offer her his hand.

She clasped it gently and met his gaze with an overflowing abundance of love. Without the need for words, she leaned in and kissed him, pouring every joy they'd shared through the years into the sweet caress. Somehow, against all odds, she'd found her happily ever after. It was here, on the outskirts of Renwick, in a modest cottage with James.

Thank you so much for taking the time to read *Mr. Dale and The Divorcée*, the first book in my **Brazen Beauties** series. If you enjoyed this story, you'll also enjoy **The Crawfords** in which three independent minded women, shunned by Society, find love and happiness. The first book in this series, *No Ordinary Duke*, is FREE if you sign up for my newsletter! Head on over to www.sophiebarnes.com and get your complimentary copy today.

Or, if you haven't read my **Diamonds In The Rough** series, you might consider *A Most Unlikely Duke* where bare-knuckle boxer, Raphe Matthews, unexpectedly inherits a duke's title. Figuring out how to navigate Society won't be easy, but receiving advice from the lady next door may just be worth it.

You can find out more about my new releases, backlist deals and giveaways by signing up for my newsletter here: www.sophiebarnes.com

Follow me on Facebook for even more updates and join Sophie Barnes' Historical Romance Group for fun book related posts, games, discussions, and giveaways.

Once again, I thank you for your interest in my books. Please take a moment to leave a review since this can help other readers discover stories they'll love. And please continue reading for an excerpt from *Mr. Grier and The Governess.*

Get a sneak peek of the sequel!

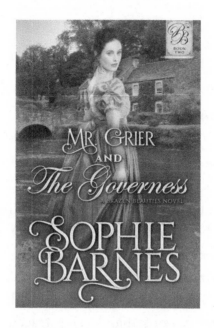

CHAPTER ONE

Somerset, 1820

Numbed by the cold, by the final loss that now gave her freedom, and the guilt this awareness stirred in her breast, Olivia Poole stared at the headstone before her. A frosty March drizzle dampened her black cloak. The smell of wet leaves and dirt teased her nose. Extending one hand, she traced the names adorning the uneven granite, the last one freshly carved.

Jonathan Mathis Poole.

A tear or two would be expected – a welcome relief even – but she had no more to shed. She'd spilled them all when death had reached out for her beloved sister, Agnes, thirteen years earlier. Her mother had died two years later, and now Olivia stood in the churchyard again, bidding her final farewell to her father, the vicar.

Most men rushed to marry off their daughters to reduce the financial burden on the rest of the family. But Papa had been different. Instead of considering daughters a disadvantage, he'd used them to plan for the future. A vicar was after all installed for life. Retirement wasn't an option unless he had the means to hire a curate who could assist him with his duties. And since Papa's parish was poor and his salary meager, he'd worried about the cost, which would be paid out of his own pocket.

Hands balled at her sides, Olivia swallowed that thought and stared at the ground. Flowers, already drooping, adorned the newly dug grave. Did she miss him? No. A twinge of renewed guilt pierced her heart as she read his name. Distant, devout, and unforgiving, Jonathan Poole had been a hard man to love. But there was one thing for which Olivia would always thank him, and that was his insistence that she receive a broad education.

As much as she'd loathed the strictness with which each lesson had been delivered, she was grateful now for the knowledge he had imparted to her. His reason for teaching her Latin, German, and French, for ensuring she was mathematically skilled, no longer mattered. For although she was now five and thirty, unmarried and without prospects, he had, in his effort to save the cost of hiring a curate, given her the tools with which to make something of herself.

Intent on making the fresh start she not only needed but knew she deserved, Olivia picked up her travelling bag and turned away from the past. With steady footfalls she followed the wet gravel path out onto the street. It was time for her to live, not only for her own sake, but for Agnes's too.

She gripped her bag as she approached the inn, hastening her steps when she spotted the coach. Water dripped from the brim of her bonnet, and in her hurry she stepped into a puddle. The icy water seeped inside one of her half–boots and soaked her wool stocking.

"Drat."

Setting her jaw she ignored the discomfort. Just a few more strides and she'd reach the coach. Her hand dove into her pocket, retrieving the ticket she'd purchased the previous day.

"Will you be passing through Varney?" she asked a man who was in the process of loading bags. She wanted to verify that she had the right coach. Having never left Treadmire before and with only a few funds at her disposal, she'd no desire to end up in the wrong part of the country.

He shoved a trunk into the boot, then peered at her from beneath the wide brim of his hat while raindrops slid over his shoulders, glossing the capes on his greatcoat. "Aye."

"And you're one of the coachmen?" Just to be sure she'd approached the right person.

"That I am."

Olivia took a step forward and held out her ticket, the paper sagging between her wet fingers. "Will you be able to drop me off at Sutton Hall?"

He nodded and glanced at her bag. "I can pack that in with the rest if ye like. Or ye can keep it in yer lap."

Olivia paused to consider. Her stomach twisted at

the idea of letting her only belongings out of her sight. "I'll keep it in my lap."

"Suit yerself." The man pulled the brim of his hat a bit lower and strode to the front of the coach where he placed one foot on the step. "Ye'd best get in if ye want to come with us."

Propelled by a mixture of dread and excitement, Olivia pulled the door open. Four passengers, crammed inside the confined space, greeted her with varying degrees of curiosity. Recognizing the Brennants and Mr. Marsh, all parishioners, Olivia offered a smile in the hope they'd be willing to make some room.

"You can squeeze in next to me," Mrs. Brennant offered after a moment. She was a robust woman, roughly twenty years Olivia's senior. Her husband, a broad–shouldered fellow, flattened his mouth but said nothing. Olivia was grateful, for although Mr. Marsh and the younger man who occupied the bench across from the Brennants were slimmer, Olivia would much prefer sitting next to another woman.

"Thank you." Olivia climbed inside, squeezed herself into the tiny slot of a space she'd been allocated, bag in lap, and barely managed to shut the door before the conveyance rocked into motion.

"Where are you off to, Miss Poole?" Mrs. Brennant inquired while Olivia clasped her chilled hands to her mouth, attempting to breathe warm air onto them.

"To Varney," Olivia told her.

"Varney?" Mr. Marsh frowned. "What's in Varney?"

"Opportunity," Olivia said, realizing belatedly that

she'd rather not share her dire circumstances with the Treadmire townsfolk. She sighed in response to the unspoken expectation that she elaborate further. "I plan to seek a position advertised in the paper."

"But..." Mrs. Brennant's voice faltered. She shifted her shoulder, pressing Olivia into the side of the coach as it rounded a corner and picked up speed.

Water droplets on the glass hampered Olivia's vision when she glanced toward the river where she and Agnes had learned to swim. Her heart gave a squeeze as the coach clattered across the bridge.

"Your father was a vicar," Mrs. Brennant added. "A gentleman, by all accounts."

Torn away from the view at those words, Olivia clutched her bag more fiercely. These people, save the stranger of course, had been at the service. They'd offered their condolences and had welcomed Papa's replacement who'd arrived last week. But even though the Pooles had been a part of Treadmire for well over thirty years, they'd mostly kept to themselves. Neither the Brennants nor Mr. Marsh could know what life had been like behind the vicarage doors.

Olivia swallowed. "Social rank doesn't always constitute wealth, Mrs. Brennant."

"No, I don't suppose it does."

Thankfully, nothing more was said on the matter. Olivia returned her attention to the dismal view of naked trees and barren fields in the hope of avoiding more uncomfortable questions. Much to her relief, the

Brennants seemed to accept her disinclination to chat and chose to engage Mr. Mathis instead.

The carriage bounced along the country road, taking Olivia farther away from the only place she'd ever known. Her eyes slid shut as exhaustion took over. There had been so much to do since Papa's death she'd not had time to rest until now. Not when she'd had a funeral to organize and a future to worry about. The incumbent, a curate from a neighboring parish who'd already been appointed when her father's health worsened, had given her one week to vacate the premises. With no relations left, she'd had no choice but to make her own way in the world.

So she'd set her mind to finding a position. Given her education, she'd hoped to become a teacher or governess, but such required references and acquiring that would take time. Right now, her most pressing concern was gaining an income. Once this was done, she could take her time looking for better employment. So she was prepared to accept a lower position, and since the only options advertised in the local paper had been for charwoman, laundress, and housemaid, it hadn't been hard to decide which to aim for.

A hand gripped her arm, gently shaking, and Olivia's eyes flew open.

"Miss Poole?" Mrs. Brennant's voice called her to attention.

Olivia blinked. Mr. Brennant was sitting opposite now where the stranger had been before. The young man had probably alighted while she'd been sleeping.

She straightened as she realized the carriage was no longer moving. "Yes?"

"This must be your stop," Mrs. Brennant informed her. "The rest of us are continuing onward."

Olivia leaned forward and peered through the rain–streaked window. A large building, wedged between the sky and the ground, sat in the distance with sprawling expanses of nothingness stretching to either side. She opened the door and called to the coachmen. "Is this Sutton Hall?"

"It is. Time to get off or ye'll have to find yer own way back from the village."

She scrambled forward, bag in hand, and clambered from the coach, out into the dismal weather. The muddied road was slick, forcing her to brace herself against the carriage door before she lost her footing.

"Go on," yelled one of the coachmen. "Ye've kept us from our schedule long enough."

Olivia bid a hasty farewell to the Brennants and Mr. Mathis, then shut the door and stepped away from the coach. The snap of a whip preceded the rattle of carriage wheels as the horses were forced into motion.

Clutching her bag with frigid fingers, Olivia turned toward the imposing edifice looming at the end of a long, tree–lined driveway. Built from grey stone, it appeared to be three stories tall, large enough to encompass all of Treadmire.

She sucked in a breath. "Good lord."

Sutton Hall surpassed Olivia's wildest expectations. It also reawakened the nervous flutter she'd felt in her stomach that morning when she'd climbed into the coach. But a thrill of excitement also assailed her as she began walking, eager to get out of the rain.

The words her sister had spoken when she knew her end was near reminded Olivia of her purpose.

"Promise me, Livy. You must live the life I shall be denied."

"It will not come to that," she had insisted. Olivia's throat tightened with the memory. The sun had warmed the air that day, offering Agnes a pleasant reprieve from her constant struggle to breathe. So they'd taken a blanket outside for a picnic beneath the old cherry tree in the garden.

"You have the list," Agnes had said, her head in Olivia's lap. "Promise me you will find the means to escape this place, so you can have all of these great experiences."

"I have a better plan," Olivia said, brushing stray locks from her sister's cheek, "and that is for you to have them yourself."

A smile had pulled at Agnes's lips – so vibrant it embedded itself into Olivia's memory forever. "On days like today I feel as though such a thing might be possible, but if it isn't and I must go, then it will be up to you."

Unwilling to disappoint her sister, Olivia had sworn to do as she asked. One month later, shaking with sorrow, she'd dressed Agnes for burial. That day, so achingly beautiful despite its bleakness, had marked her mother's denial of God while prompting her father to cling more firmly to his faith. For Olivia's part, she no longer knew what she believed, except that life was unfair.

A wind swept over her shoulders and Olivia quickened her pace. The rain had turned to sleet and it blew in her face, the icy chill seeping into her bones as she pressed onward. Frozen fingers curled around the handle of her traveling bag while one soaked foot slid back and forth inside her boot with every step she took.

Determined, Olivia plodded through the worsening weather until she reached the end of the driveway. Pausing briefly to catch her breath, she swiped the rain from her eyes and stared at her destination. A pair of square columns guarded the massive front door while an endless number of windows, each at least as tall as she, left her dazed. The tax on those alone was inconceivable.

A spark of hope ignited within her and she forgot her discomfort for a moment. This was what she needed – the means by which to earn her way and get one step closer to keeping her promise to Agnes.

Intent on getting out of the rain and on with her new life, Olivia tightened her grip on her bag and recommenced walking. The front entrance wasn't for her. She needed to find the one meant for servants.

With heavy feet scraping the gravel, she staggered toward the side of the building and rounded a corner. There it was, not too far – a stairwell leading down toward the basement entrance. Relief poured through her, her goal just a few more paces away. And then she was finally descending the stairs to an area where a pump stood with several buckets stacked nearby. A wide window offered a glimpse of Sutton Hall's kitchen, a space that looked to be ten times larger than the kitchen at the vicarage.

Olivia sucked in a breath and approached a green door. Hesitant, yet eager to get indoors, she raised her hand and knocked.

A young man with a white footman's wig perched on his head answered her call. He wore a stunning black jacket adorned with gold braiding, breeches to match, and a very costly looking brocade waistcoat. His eyes widened and his lips parted, and then he promptly stepped to one side and ushered her in with such speed Olivia nearly stumbled right into his arms.

The door swung shut behind her. "I…"

He didn't wait for her to say anything more before he grabbed her by the arm and pulled her inside. The door closed and before she could utter another word, she was being steered into the kitchen and over to the heavenly warmth from a wide iron range where a plump woman was in the process of pouring something into a pot.

The woman's eyes widened the moment she spotted Olivia. "Who's your new friend, Roger?"

"I've no idea, Mrs. Bradley," said the footman, "but she can certainly do with some drying off."

"No doubt about that." Mrs. Bradley eyed the puddle beginning to form at Olivia's feet and clucked her tongue. "Poor thing. You look as though you were dragged from the river. Do you have a name, dear?"

"O…Olivia Poole."

"I don't suppose you're willing to tell us what's brought you all the way here on a day like today?"

"A…" Goodness, she could not keep her teeth from chattering. "An…ad…advertisement."

"Well, I'd advise you to have a seat over there by the fire." Mrs. Bradley gestured toward a chair. "Warm yourself and…would you like a hot cup of tea?"

Olivia almost fell to her knees in gratitude. She nodded. "Pl…please."

"Nancy," Mrs. Bradley instructed, "bring me a brick for the oven, would you?"

A young girl with frizzy blonde hair leapt into action. Mrs. Bradley spun away and began bustling about while Roger guided Olivia to a chair. Tremors swept through her body as she set her bag on the floor. With trembling fingers she struggled to undo the soggy bow tied beneath her chin and finally managed to remove her bonnet, which she set aside on the corner of a nearby work table. She took off her cloak next and hung it across another chair's back so it could dry.

After taking her seat, she stuck out her hands and breathed a sigh of relief as the warmth from the fire soothed away the chill in her fingers.

"I hope you do…don't mind," Olivia said, indicating her discarded garments.

"Of course not," said Roger

Mrs. Bradley handed Olivia a steaming cup of tea.

"We're just glad you found your way here before you caught your death out there in that dreadful weather."

Moved by the woman's geniality, Olivia had to gulp down a breath to stop tears from welling. Unaccustomed as she was to words of kindness and with bone–weary tiredness wearing her down, Mrs. Bradley's words threatened to break her for the first time in over a decade.

"Tha...thank you."

"You're most welcome." Mrs. Bradley shifted her gaze to Roger. "We probably ought to inform Mrs. Hodgins of Miss Poole's arrival and of the state she's in."

"I'll see to it right away."

Roger strode off just as Nancy arrived with the brick. "Let's get those wet boots off then."

Olivia gaped at her. "I can't possibly."

"You can and you must," Mrs. Bradley's voice was firm. "The stockings too, I'll wager."

"But—"

"Don't risk your health just because you're too shy to show us your toes. Besides, taking ill will only give us more work." Mrs. Bradley smiled and glanced toward Olivia's bag. "I trust you've some dry clothes in there."

Olivia nodded and took a hasty sip of her tea. Truth be told, the idea of drying her feet and getting them warm was much too tempting for her to offer much resistance. She set her cup aside and searched her bag for a fresh pair of stockings. As soon as she found them, she removed her boots, her wet stockings too.

She quickly put on the dry ones and then the brick was pushed under her feet.

Ahh. Heaven.

Her relief, however, was short lived, evaporating as soon as Roger returned with a mild–faced woman who wasted no time introducing herself as Mrs. Hodgins, the housekeeper.

Oh dear.

Trailing water through the kitchen and keeping the servants from their work while they tended to her was not the sort of first impression Olivia had wanted to make on the woman in charge of hiring her. "I apologize for the inconvenience I've caused."

"Can you walk?" Mrs. Hodgins asked.

Could she walk? Olivia blinked. Did she truly look so wretched?

"Yes."

Mrs. Hodgins glanced at Olivia's feet, then at the sopping wet stockings she'd hung to dry on a chair. Her eyebrows rose and Olivia slumped, certain her chance of employment had been extinguished.

But to her dismay, Mrs. Hodgins quietly asked. "Do you have a dry pair of shoes?"

Olivia swallowed. "I've a pair of slippers."

"Put them on and come with me." She waited while Olivia readied herself, then guided her out of the kitchen, along a hallway, and into a small room containing a desk and two chairs. "Please have a seat and tell me why you've come."

Olivia stared at her. "To seek the position you advertised in the paper. The opening was for a house-maid and... Please tell me it's still available and I haven't come here for nothing?"

Sympathy stole into Mrs. Hodgins's eyes, causing Olivia's spirit to plummet. "I'm sorry, Miss Poole. That advertisement was posted more than a week ago."

Olivia drew a ragged breath, the tears she'd managed to keep at bay until now finally spilling onto her cheeks. She'd come all this way, had spent a whole ten shillings on the coach fare, and could think of nowhere else to go. The helplessness she experienced as this awareness sank in was absolutely terrifying.

Hands clutched together, she held herself upright by sheer force of will as she asked the only question pressing upon her mind at the moment. "What on earth am I to do now?"

Order your copy today!

AUTHOR'S NOTE

Dear Reader,

Few historical romances feature divorce, which isn't surprising considering how unlikely and near impossible it was to accomplish prior to the 20th Century. Also, considering the rules involved, either the husband or the wife would have to be written as awful people. Unless of course they chose to help each other out of the trap they were both caught up in...

This idea intrigued me. It felt fresh and different and like a challenge - something I always welcome when writing. I liked having George and Wilhelmina pull the wool over everyone's eyes, which also helped with her characterization. She became an incredibly brave individual willing to sacrifice her reputation for a dear friend.

Meanwhile, the whole situation forces James to

question his beliefs while constantly being at odds with Mina. Both must come to terms with their pasts while learning to trust and love again. A feat they can only truly accomplish through absolute honesty.

I hope you enjoyed their story and look forward to sharing more adventures with you in the future.

SOPHIE

ACKNOWLEDGMENTS

I would like to thank the Killion Group for their incredible help with the editing and cover design for this book.

And to my friends and family, thank you for your constant support and for believing in me. I would be lost without you!

ABOUT THE AUTHOR

USA TODAY bestselling author, Sophie Barnes, has spent her youth traveling with her parents to wonderful places around the world. She's lived in five different countries, on three different continents, has studied design in Paris and New York, and speaks Danish, English, French, Spanish, and Romanian with varying degrees of fluency. But most impressive of all - she's been married to the same man three times, in three different countries and in three different dresses.

While living in Africa, Sophie turned to her lifelong passion - writing.

When she's not busy dreaming up her next romance novel, Sophie enjoys spending time with her family, swimming, cooking, gardening, watching romantic comedies and, of course, reading. She currently lives on the East Coast.

You can contact her through her website at
www.sophiebarnes.com
And please consider leaving a review for this book.
Every review is greatly appreciated!